AMBER CASSIDY

First Touch

First edition

ISBN: 979-8-9890036-2-4

This book was professionally typeset on Reedsy.
Find out more at reedsy.com

Contents

Preface   vi
Chapter One   1
Chapter Two   8
Chapter Three   14
Chapter Four   21
Chapter Five   30
Chapter Six   37
Chapter Seven   46
Chapter Eight   54
Chapter Nine   61
Chapter Ten   68
Chapter Eleven   77
Chapter Twelve   86
Chapter Thirteen   91
Chapter Fourteen   99
Chapter Fifteen   107
Chapter Sixteen   115
Chapter Seventeen   123
Chapter Eighteen   129
Chapter Nineteen   135
Chapter Twenty   142
Chapter Twenty-One   148
Chapter Twenty-Two   155
Chapter Twenty-Three   162

Chapter Twenty-Four	169
Chapter Twenty-Five	174
Chapter Twenty-Six	182
Chapter Twenty-Seven	190
Chapter Twenty-Eight	199
Chapter Twenty-Nine	206
Chapter Thirty	213
Chapter Thirty-One	219
Chapter Thirty-Two	226
Chapter Thirty-Three	231
Chapter Thirty Four	239
Chapter Thirty-Five	245
Chapter Thirty-Six	253
Chapter Thirty-Seven	259
Chapter Thirty-Eight	266
Chapter Thirty-Nine	272
Chapter Forty	278
Chapter Forty-One	286
Chapter Forty-Two	293
Chapter Forty-Three	300
Chapter Forty-Four	307
Chapter Forty-Five	316
Chapter Forty-Six	323
Chapter Forty-Seven	331
Chapter Forty-Eight	341
Chapter Forty-Nine	350
Chapter Fifty	357
Chapter Fifty-One	366
Epilogue	371
The End	376
About the Author	377

Preface

My romance novels are written with a happily ever after in mind but have dark topics intertwined. This story is about finding love and overcoming fears while navigating the obstacles of life.

This novel is intended for adults. It contains explicit sexual content, and mentions of sexual assault, domestic violence, and physical violence.

Meet Jesse and Thea, I hope you enjoy!

Chapter One

Thea

"*Rapunzel, Rapunzel. Let down your long hair!*" My deepened voice shouts to the top of the "tower," my pinkie finger and thumb wiggling enthusiastically inside the gnome puppet. It's a haggard representation of a prince, but the library only has so many options for story time, and it's up to me to challenge the imagination.

With my left hand resting on the top of my head, pretending my upper half is the tower from the story, I wiggle my fingers to gain the attention of the children sitting in front of me.

"*Oh, my prince, my prince!*" The squeaky princess voice earns a few giggles from my little crowd.

"The prince has just arrived from a long journey. Should Rapunzel let her hair down for him?" I ask my eager audience in my normal voice, ad-libbing the story because I don't have the book in front of me.

"Yes! Yes! Yes!" The children shout before covering their mouths and snickering. They know to keep their voices down, but they also know I wouldn't truly scold them for being excited.

I flip my long blonde hair over my shoulder, letting the

braid that I wore specifically for today hang down past my chest. "Okay, here he goes."

With an exaggerated display, my gnome prince climbs the strands of my braid until he makes it to the top of my head. My hands embrace, letting my puppets hug, while some of the children giggle and others gag, unimpressed with the love story that I'm telling.

"Rapunzel, I sent your mother far far away. You won't be trapped in this tower ever again!" The gnome prince professes.

"Thank you, my prince. You've saved me!" Rapunzel squeaks. My hands fall back down to my lap with fatigue. Holding Rapunzel over my head for so long made my shoulder tingle.

"They lived happily ever after." I finish with a seated bow, folding at my waist over my bent knees, while the kiddos clap from the big rug in front of me that resembles a map.

The average age in the story time group is four years old, so they don't mind a simplified fairy tail. They also don't care if I mess up any details in the stories I tell. They simply enjoy being here, making fun of my silly expressions, and giggling at my demonstrations.

"Miss Thea?" Junie asks from her seat on the floor, her red pigtails swaying from the intensity of her raised hand bouncing in the air.

"Yes, Junie," I answer, though I'm sure I know what she's about to ask.

"Can we have one more story? Please, please!" She pleads, and all the other seven kids take note, pretending to beg. Their little voices in unison make me laugh.

"No more stories today. I'm sorry you guys. Our time is up and your grown-ups are waiting." The kids turn and twist in their crisscross applesauce positions on the rug trying to get a peak at their parents who are lingering on the edges of the library, kindly giving us space.

Sometimes the children get pulled into the world I've created for them, forgetting where they are temporarily. I take it as a sign that I'm doing a good job.

Once they get a sight of their loved ones, they're jumping up from their spots and taking off, but not before telling me thank you. Some even take an extra second to hug me.

"Next story time is on Tuesday. 3 o'clock!" I announce to their retreating forms, knowing that most of them will most likely be here, rain or shine.

That's what I like about New Hope. In the two years that I've been here, the small town has embraced me and made me fall in love with its charms. My college was in a beach town and you'd hardly ever see a familiar face. It's different here.

I've been around the same families since I started, the locals know my name, and my coworkers are my friends. Although, none of them are my age. It's cozy and the interactions are warm and familiar.

I gather my story time props, storing them away for next time, silently reflecting on my story about Rapunzel. Maybe I chose it because I know what it feels like to be locked in a tower. Figuratively trapped away in solitude with my future just out of reach. Desperately hoping my circumstances will change even though they seem to be set in stone… If only it was as easy as a prince saving me from myself.

Sighing, I shake those thoughts as I join Latisha at the front island. It's the checkout counter for all intents and purposes, but we call it the island because it sits precariously in the center between the adult and children's sides of the library.

It forms a perfect circle and also gives us a nice view out the windows into the courtyard.

I love this library. I love this town. I love my coworkers. Everything is perfect. Aside from the one void in my life that is out of my control. A void that I've spent years trying to overcome. Years of crying and feeling sorry for myself.

I've promised myself that I'd try to accept that I might be broken forever. It's easier than getting my hopes up for a different outcome. The reality is that we don't all get our fairy tale ending like Rapunzel.

"Hey Miss la la land," Latisha snags my attention by whispering over my shoulder. She, more than almost anyone, knows how far I get into my head. At the young age of 53, she has become like a second mom to me. She welcomed me into her library with open arms. I say *her* library because she's the one who put her blood, sweat, and tears into making it as extraordinary as it is.

She applied for grants and donations until her fingers went numb, would sleep on it, and then start again the next day. Her determination got us the updates in the building, the courtyard, and our fancy island with our new computers.

She was also responsible for creating my position and tells me often that she wants me to take over running things once she retires. I always remind her that it will be at least twenty more years before she's ready to give it up.

"Snap out of it, sister."

"I'm sorry. What?" I give her my attention, pulling my oversized cardigan tighter around my body. This building stays cold but at the same time, I don't mind guarding myself with the extra-knit barrier.

"Our newest eye candy is back," she whispers to me, not

managing to hide her amused chuckle. Although I know exactly who she's referring to, I glance anyway, needing a small peak.

As suspected, the new mystery man in town is strolling through the far doors of the library. Just as he has the past two weeks, he walks up and down a few aisles before grabbing a book and sitting at one of our open tables. Just as I have the past two weeks, I slyly watch him the whole time.

It's pathetic.

I've already memorized the way his jeans hug his muscular thighs, and how his arms look in the Henley he's usually wearing. I know exactly how his dark blonde strands start curling at the ends, hanging just past his ears. Some days he wears a weathered baseball cap, but today he's not. I have an unobstructed view of his chiseled face that I do not need.

I don't need to look at him to know that his nose is slightly crooked as if it's been broken, or that his facial hair is barely uneven. It's as if he's kept it longer around his mouth at times and trimmed the rest, but has recently let it grow out.

I do have to imagine what color his eyes are. From where I hide in my little island across the library, I can't see his eyes. Whether he's wearing a ball cap or not, his eyes are always shadowed. I don't think I would be able to see them clearly unless I was standing right in front of him, and that is *not* going to happen.

He's never borrowed a book. He reads at his table and then puts it exactly where it belongs back on the shelf. I've checked. I've been a little more than curious about what he likes to read from the non-fiction section.

At 4:25 he'll walk into the meeting room exactly five minutes before the support group starts, every time. It's been the same routine each Tuesday and Thursday. My shift ends at five o'clock on these days, so I never get to see him leave.

I'm a certifiable stalker, but I wouldn't tell anyone that. Not even Latisha.

"Who?" I finally respond, playing dumb as if I haven't already been caught staring at him.

"You know who." She rolls her eyes at me, not letting me off the hook. "You should go ask him on a date!" She suggests, excitedly. I cringe.

"You know that I can't do that." I exhale my defeat. She knows that I have *problems* with men, but she doesn't know the extent of it. My problem is a burden and I make sure to leave everyone in the dark for their own sake.

"Sweetie, you never know unless you try. Besides, you deserve love no matter what," she sympathizes.

"A man like that would never settle for what I have to offer. Which is practically nothing." I wrap my cardigan tighter around myself like a shield. The drab gray material hides the bright yellow sunflowers all over my dress. Yellow is cheery and happy. I wear it almost every day for the kids, but nothing makes me feel more dull and lifeless than talking about my problems.

"You have so much to offer. Never sell yourself short," she scolds. I've heard it before, and I'm sure she'll make me hear it again. All I can offer is a small smile and nod, effectively closing the topic. A patron walks up to her side of the counter, saving me from any further conversation about the new library man candy.

However, it doesn't stop me from stealing one more glance in his direction. Nor does it stop me from noticing that he hasn't turned a single page of his book in the five minutes he's been staring at it.

Chapter Two

Jesse

"Look. It's the little orphan. What are you doing out here all alone? Little orphan." Jeremiah shoves my shoulder like he's done hundreds of times since I've been in this horrible group home.

I ignore him like usual, not bothering to mention that he's here just like me. No parents to be found for either of us, but I'm the one he calls a little orphan.

I stand up from the broken-down porch steps that lead into the backdoor of the two-story home, intending to find a new location to sulk.

Before I can escape, Jeremiah grabs me by my collar and tosses me down the steps into the grass. It's not the first time he's tried to rough me up. He's a bad kid who takes all of his problems out on the world.

At 12 years old, I've had enough problems of my own without dealing with this bully.

"Leave me alone, Jeremiah," I say through gritted teeth.

I don't like to fight. I've seen my fair share in my life. I'd been beaten by my daddy plenty of times before him and my momma died. I could take it, but I hated seeing him hurt her.

I swore to my momma that I'd never be a mean man. She'd just smile with her sad eyes, telling me she knew it. She'd always tell me she believed me because I had a good heart. But, now she's dead and I'm all alone. My heart doesn't feel good. It feels broken, every day.

"What are you going to do? Go cry to your mommy? That's right. You don't have one!" He shouts in my direction, spewing spit as he does.

Him mentioning my momma is all it takes. I launch up from the grass and tackle Jeremiah at his waist, knocking him back. Before he can regain himself, I throw punch after punch, determined to shut him up for good.

"Don't ever talk about my momma!" I yell in his face as I continue punching him until my arms get tired. "I hate you! I hate you!"

* * *

A child's laughter snaps me out of my daydream, or rather, my nightmare. I glance subtly around the library to make sure no one is looking in my direction, confirming that things are just as they were before I zoned out.

My hands press the book closed, only making it through page two. It doesn't matter. Reading it was only a ruse. Which is good since I can't stop my mind from wandering to things that I'd rather forget.

My watch vibrates, signaling it's time to make my way into the group room for 'Coffee with Veterans.' After placing my book back on its designated shelf, I stroll into the meeting with as much steel in my spine as I can. I don't want to look eager to be here.

There are only five others in the room as I make my way to my seat. The plastic blue desk chair sits in a circle of about fifteen, though they're never all filled.

Dennis, the moderator of the group, rolls in the cart with the coffee pot and Styrofoam cups just as two more guys enter the room from the outside door. It makes me nervous that this room is accessible from two points, but I do my best not to flinch every time someone pushes through the door unexpectedly.

"All right boys." Dennis claps his hands. "Go ahead and get ya some joe then we'll get started."

Continuing to do my best to blend in, I pour a cup of shitty coffee and I'll make sure to finish every drop even though I know it sits like a rock in my gut.

A young guy sneaks in from the outside door just as I'm sitting back down. With his shoulders slumped and his hood up, he gives the impression of someone who is hiding. Only I know that he actually is in hiding. Curtis Debaugh. 21 years old. Currently AWOL from the United States Army. *My target.*

"Thank you all for coming today, I'm glad to see each one of you. And I am glad for those of you who have returned again and again," Dennis interrupts my thoughts to start the meeting.

He's a nice old man. Retired from the Navy. His pot belly threatens to bust the buttons on every shirt he wears but he's so welcoming that I almost feel guilty being here under false pretenses.

The truth is that I am not a veteran. I am active duty

military, currently as a Special Investigator. I've been in this gig for about nine months, but this is only my third investigation.

It's odd. I was used to completing missions within a couple of days and always on foreign soil. The change of pace and location has been an adjustment.

I'm not strapped down with a vest and my firearms, I'm not surrounded by my team, I'm just pretending to be a regular dude.

The undercover unit they pegged me for is a hard unit to fill. Most guys can't commit to the time it takes to complete an investigation. It doesn't bother me though. Probably because I have nothing to look forward to. No family to go home to. No ties.

When my best friend quit the Army last year it shocked the hell out of me. I understood why he did it, but it threw me for a loop nonetheless. Staying in our old Special Forces unit without him put a bad feeling in my gut. I was worried that going back into the field without my battle buddy would mean the end of the road for me.

Everyone has each other's backs, but he and I were different. We started as a pair in Special Ops school and it only seemed right to quit when he quit, but the military is all I have. One day, I hope to be white-haired and retired like Dennis, running support groups for fun.

"Who would like to share first?" Dennis claps his hands together, signaling the beginning of our introductions and reason for being here. As usual, the older man to his right begins, Frankie is his name. I tune him out, not needing to pay attention. I've heard his story before.

Instead, I eyeball Curtis. He's still receded into himself,

hardly lifting his head enough to make it look like he's awake. I know he's troubled. Hell, he's still a kid. Unfortunately, he's made bad choices, and that's why I'm here.

The Special Investigators handling his AWOL case found him pretty quickly. The kid grew up about thirty minutes outside of New Hope. So, it's no surprise he'd end up back here eventually. The problem was with what they found while investigating him.

Curtis has been corresponding with domestic extremist groups online. Not only did he leave the military without permission, he's now become an adversary of the United States government.

My job is to find out how deep his involvement goes and anything else I can about the extremist group that he seems to be linked to within this area. Whether they are legitimate or if they have any plans to cause harm to others.

"Jay, you're up," Dennis states, gesturing to me. Jay is my undercover name. Not very creative, but close enough to my actual name that it's hard to fuck up.

"I'm Jay. I'm here because I am struggling to adjust back to civilian life after being injured in combat." I have been injured in combat, it's not a complete lie. My training made it clear to always stick to as close to the truth as possible.

"I feel like the Army just shipped me back home and left me to suffer by myself. So, I'm here." I finish my introduction with as little flourish as possible, remaining stoic and pissed off to the outside eye.

My plan is to use my disgruntlement to lure Curtis into trusting me. From the way he's studying me as I peer around the room, I think it might be working.

"Alright, folks. Let's talk about it." Dennis advances into the meeting offering advice and services to look into for support. He really is a great guy. When this is all over, I'd love to have a genuine conversation with him as myself, Jesse. Not as Jay.

One week later...

"Hey, man. I'm going to the bar with a couple of buddies tonight. Would you want to come?" Curtis asks after our meeting concludes. I try not to let my satisfaction show that my plan is working. "I mean if you don't want to, it's cool. Just thought I'd ask since we've both been coming to this dumb meeting for a while now."

He's nervous. He's young. Desperately seeking friendship or comradery from anyone.

"Yeah, man. That'd be cool." I give him my phone number and tell him to text me the details.

Step one of my plan is a success. Form a relationship with the target -*Check*.

Chapter Three

Thea

I look over my ironed straight hair one last time before flipping off the bathroom light switch, trying to ignore the stranger in the mirror. My round, gold-wire-framed glasses are already tucked away in my vanity, replaced by contacts.

My eyelids are shadowed and lined. My lips have a sheen of lipstick that feels foreign. My usual daily routine involves concealer and mascara, anything more than that seems unnecessary for a day in the library.

It didn't used to be this way. During undergrad, I loved getting dressed up on weekends, and doing my hair and makeup in excess. But, that was before. Before it made me uncomfortable to draw attention to myself unnecessarily. Before my innocence was ripped away from me.

I bound down the creaking wooden stairs in my house, effectively dislodging the negative memories from my brain. At least for the moment.

My Victorian-era-inspired home, built more than one hundred years ago, has its disheveled quirks, but I love it. I've kept the original floors and gold light fixtures and darkened the walls to give it an old Gothic feel. I thrifted my furniture to make it feel authentic, and because it's what I could afford.

I've spent the last year renovating small sections at a time as my paychecks allowed. I was doing well maintaining my finances, not wanting to go into debt from all the projects, until this last one.

My usual contractor was booked for a six-month job, and instead of waiting for him, I decided to hire someone else to update the main floor bathroom. As I stand here using the full-length mirror on the back of the door, I can tell there has been almost zero progress made. The sink is sitting on the floor and the toilet isn't connected to anything.

The new "contractor" is already two weeks past his estimation date and giving me the runaround. He's asked for more money twice already, and like a rookie, I paid him more.

The latest issue was that my plumbing wasn't up to code and he'd need to replace pipes. I should've gotten a second opinion, but I was nervous it would make him quit the whole project on me. Now I'm regretting that.

I don't know what to do to resolve the issue with my contractor, but I do know that I am getting behind on bills and I need cash quickly. Which brings me to my unusual (for me) outfit. Light brown cowboy boots, frayed jean shorts, and a black tank top with five embroidered suns right below the top seam. My uniform.

Against Latisha's advice, I decided to pick up a couple of shifts at Sunny's Bar downtown. The owner goes by Sunny, hence the golden thread stretching across my chest currently. He's also a grandparent of one of the kids I read to and offered to let me work for him two nights a week to get tips. I've never technically been a bartender, but I worked for a catering service throughout college and was stuck filling drink orders on understaffed nights. Rowdy wedding guests aren't all that different from rowdy bar guests on most occasions.

I step around the porcelain sink on my way out of the bathroom, hoping I can get through this reno and I'll put a hold on all other projects until my normal guy is available. He's never given me any issues, cut costs where he can to help me out, and always kind of reminded me of my dad before he passed.

Kyle is the complete opposite, young, inefficient, and always gives me the creeps. In his defense, most men give me the creeps. Luckily, he's usually only here while I'm at work and I can avoid most interactions.

By the time I get downtown and into the swing of my bar duties, my thoughts of my ridiculous outfit and frustration with Kyle are quickly replaced with drink orders and keeping customers' tabs straight.

The bar isn't super wild, but it's a hometown joint and stays busy because it's the only one. There's a small stage for musicians and a few tables scattered throughout. No dance floor, but there are two pool tables and two dart boards that keep customers occupied.

Tonight is a jukebox night, Sunny only brings live music in on Fridays and Saturdays. Picking up a Thursday shift after working at the library makes for a long day, but this gig is only temporary. I can handle it.

I'm bouncing from one side to the other behind the bar keeping up with drink orders, when a man squeezes in between two of the regulars occupying the bar stools.

"Hey little lady, I've got a big one for ya." He raises his eyebrows in my direction to enunciate his attempt at a lewd joke. As if his wrinkled shirt and the stale odor of cigarette smoke wouldn't be enough of a reason to be put off.

Luckily, I've become an expert at ignoring things like that, so I continue without acknowledging his "joke."

"What can I get for you?" I ask with a straight face. He looks unimpressed that I didn't even give him a fake laugh, but leans against the bar anyway to place his order.

The good thing about this job is that despite being put on display for far too many eyes, I hold the power in my position. No one wants to piss off the bartender.

"I need four tall Buds and four shots of Jäger. Actually, make it five shots." He raises his hand, flexing his fingers to clarify as if that small change of his request would be too advanced for me.

"Where's your table? I can bring them over once I get clean glasses. My bar-back is running ragged." I don't mention that my bar-back is Sunny, who is just old and slow.

"Over there." The guy indicates over his shoulder to the corner where one of our tables sits out of the way of the main bar area. "Thanks, honey." He taps the bar top with his knuckle and throws his credit card down to start a tab, winking at me before he turns to leave. Ick.

Almost five minutes later, my skin is still crawling from the interaction as I make my way to his table, walking slower than I probably need to because I'm not super confident that I won't drop my tray. I'm used to carrying stacks of books, but not over my shoulder like this.

"Sorry guys, I tried to get these over to you as fast as I could," I apologize as I sit the tray down on the table, pretending not to care that I'm no longer behind the safety of the bar. It's for the tips. I need the tips.

17

I distribute the glasses onto the tabletop before my audience. Their eyes on me are making the back of my neck sweat and I haven't even looked up from my tray yet.

There is an aura put off when people are staring. My brain has learned to pick up on the clues and I'm hyper-aware when it feels like I'm being watched closely.

As predicted, when I look up all of their focus is on me and my face heats instinctively. I don't like being the center of attention, especially male attention. It's my worst nightmare.

My gaze flicks between them because they're not saying anything and their staring is making the bar's music sound hollow in my ears. All of my other senses are pushed aside as the awkward air becomes stifling.

When I lock on the face directly across from me, my eyes bulge. Holy crap. I quickly remove the tray from the table in an attempt to hide my reaction.

That familiar handsome face from the library was the last thing I had expected. Why is he here? Why tonight of all nights? I only work two nights a week… This is a bad coincidence.

I nod my head in dismissal to no one in particular, trying my best to make a clean break back to the bar. I need to get away from them and I need to get away from the man that stars in my thoughts already.

Unfortunately, the one who started the tab speaks up. "Well hold on, sugar. This shot's for you."

Dang it.

I turn back to their table, forcing myself not to look at the hottest man I've ever seen, instead looking at the man who spoke. He's pointing to a shot glass, intending to give it to me. "I'm sorry, I don't drink," I admit reluctantly.

"What?!" A chorus of reactions rings out, giving me the exact reaction I have encountered from other customers since starting here. Aside from the library man, he's been silent the whole time.

I can't help it, I glance in his direction, not able to stem the urge to punish myself. He's looking at me, curiously, but intimidatingly so. His gaze is sharp and intense.

"I know. A bartender who doesn't drink." I shrug with faux humor, giving the same response I always do. "Sunny gave me a chance anyway."

I need to leave and walk away, but I can't stop looking at library guy. It feels like a tease to be this close, but still so far. *Look at what you will never have.* My brain chastises me.

The dim lighting in this corner barely allows me any more details of his face than I'd get across the room at the library, but I can't stop staring.

Though, I am surprised by his choice of friends. He seems a lot more put together than the other three, not that it's my place to judge. Nor do I know him well enough to form an opinion.

"I bought it for you. Take the shot, anyway." The original guy chimes in again, but harsher, breaking my spell with library man. The guy on the other side of me scoots the glass over until it's in front of me. I can sense the entrapment like a cloud of impending doom.

"Um. No, thank you," I force out because I'm already overwhelmed. "I can take it off your tab." I'm trying my best to avoid the confrontation happening but my chest warms, the skin there undoubtedly getting red with my discomfort.

I pick the shot glass up, intending to take it back to the bar when a large hand plucks it out of mine. It was barely there,

19

a feather-light touch, but his fingers brushed mine, making my stomach flip.

"No worries." Library guy downs the dark liquid quickly, ending the issue of the wasted shot, and effectively putting all the attention on himself.

"What the fuck?" The third guy from the group exclaims, disappointed that their little game ended. As if harassing the bartender is their main source of entertainment.

Library guy shrugs. "I didn't want it to go to waste." He takes his time, arranging their now empty shot glasses in front of me before looking at me pointedly. "All yours, Sunshine." His eyes burn into mine, holding my gaze until I forget to breathe.

I'm going to faint. I am going to pass out right in this spot. I've experienced it enough to know the lightheadedness I'm experiencing is usually a precursor to my fainting spells, but this is different.

I can't do anything but snatch the glasses up and practically run away. God, I am so embarrassed.

I am so out of touch with men that I can't even handle an attractive one speaking to me. Yet, he touched me. Just a breeze of a touch, but I was okay.

Maybe, I'm not so broken after all?

Chapter Four

Jesse

Who the fuck is that? My mind is reeling trying to recall her. Fuck. This isn't good.

I can't risk blowing my cover because I can't place how I know this girl. I've probably just seen her around town. It's a small town, with plenty of chances to bump into the same people.

What if that's not the case though?

One slip-up connecting me to my real identity could blow this whole investigation. She's gorgeous. I would remember seeing her before...

"She was pretty hot, huh?" Curtis leans towards me, snickering on a hiccup. Unbelievable that someone so immature is of legal age to drink.

"Yeah. She was." I drink my beer, not wanting to continue discussing the hot blonde bartender who just threw my whole fucking night into a tailspin.

I swear there was something in her eyes when she looked at me, but I can't be sure. Something that made my gut tighten and stole my breath for a moment. Was it recognition or something else?

Either way, when her discomfort with my table-mates became apparent, I couldn't help but step in. The rosiness of her cheeks had an uncanny ability to force my hand.

I'm not supposed to be playing the good guy tonight, these guys are not the crowd for that. If I don't watch myself, I'm going to screw this up early on.

"Curtis tells me you're a vet," Derrick states, putting a pause on my internal panic.

"Yeah. I am. Army." I keep my answer short and simple. Don't get caught up in any lies. That's my mantra.

"They screw you over like they did us?" He downs his beer quickly and then belches, leaning back in his chair smugly. I have to fight to keep the disgust off my face.

"Yeah. You could say that." I finish mine off too, trying to keep pace. From what I've heard and seen so far, these guys might be part of the group that Curtis was communicating with. I need to stay in their circle as long as I can until it leads me somewhere.

"Well fuck 'em," he grunts. Derrick is older, maybe 45 or 50. He gives the impression that he's the leader of this little group that's at my table, though I can't imagine he's been very successful at leading much of anything in his life. He reeks of pot and cigarettes, and he pulled up to the bar tonight in a van that most would classify as concerning. Especially if it was parked outside of a school.

"I'll drink to that." Mitch finishes his beer, leaving Curtis the only one still nursing his. He probably doesn't like the taste, though he'd never admit it.

"I'll get another round." Derrick moves to stand, but I stop him, jumping up before he does.

"I'll go, you got the last one."

Making my way up to the bar, I'm careful to remain out of Sunshine's line of sight. It's easy to do, her blonde hair is like a beacon with the lights above the liquor shining on it all the way down to her waist.

I need a closer look at her. I want to see her eyes when she sees me again. I need to know if it was recognition in her gaze or if I imagined it.

Just as I approach, a man stands to leave, vacating one of the bar stools. I slide into the spot right as she turns back to grab his receipt slip.

"What can I…" She stutters to a stop when she sees that it's me sitting in front of her.

Her eyes widened just a fraction, but I saw it. Recognition.

"Get you? What can I get you?" She finishes, stammering over her words.

Even in the harsh bar lighting, I watch her cheeks pinken. The sensation in my gut comes back.

"I wanted to apologize for earlier. The guys I'm with are…" I'm not sure how to finish my sentence. Idiots? Cavemen?

"Your friends?" She asks. It's a simple question, but I hate to even pretend to be associated with them. Especially not in front of this beautiful woman.

I can't stop staring at her tan skin. Her chest and arms look sun-kissed against her black top.

Everything about her is appealing but not necessarily familiar. Maybe I haven't seen her before and my mind is only playing tricks on me because I find her so attractive.

"No. They're not my friends. Not really." I feel the need to clarify. To explain that I'm only associating with them because I have to would put me at risk, so I bite my tongue.

"Okay… Well. Did you want another drink?" She steps

back a few steps, reaching for a basket of glasses that the old man just brought out, giving me the chance to see her tan legs made of all-toned muscle.

"Yeah. Four more beers, please. No more shots." I offer her a small smile, intending to charm her a bit to get her defenses down.

Instead of taking the bait and smiling back, she looks startled. Not the usual reaction I get, but maybe I'm losing my touch.

It has been a while since I've seen anyone because I've been so focused on work. Doesn't matter, I'm not here to flirt. I need to secure my cover.

"Can I ask you something?" I drop the act and get to the point of being up here.

"Uh. Sure," she responds while she fills the glasses. I study her as she does, looking for clues, but I'm drawn to her features for selfish reasons instead.

Slender arms, dainty hands. Her nails are short, not painted. Seems unusual since her face is all done up with makeup. Even a female-dense man can tell when a woman is high maintenance.

Her look and her personality don't seem to match. A dolled-up bartender who can barely make eye contact with her customers is abnormal.

"Have we met before?" I watch her closely after I ask.

She stays focused on the last glass she is filling but the tinge on her cheeks deepens.

"No. We've never met." She tops off the last draft, arranging all four in front of me before finally looking up. Her long lashes frame her eyes in a way that pulls me in.

"Your eyes..." I blurt out before I mean to. My impulse

control is always something I've had trouble with. That's why they liked me on my Special Ops teams, I'd never hesitate to take the shot or volunteer for the short straw task. I didn't have anything to lose.

"What about my eyes?" She sounds more worried than any woman should. Her cheeks redden even more and a sick part of me loves that she can't hide her reactions.

"They're such a bright blue, almost silver," I utter like a complete idiot as if she doesn't know her own eye color. They shine while she looks at me across the bar top. "It's um... It's pretty," I add, my usual confidence flies out the window the longer she stares at me. Her eyebrows crinkle like she isn't sure what to do with what I'm saying.

Something about her eyes is nagging at my skull. They're beautiful, but that's not it. It's something deeper.

"It's probably the lighting, but thank you," she whispers. If I wasn't already looking at her I would've missed her words, but I'm staring hard. I'm transfixed by the way she's blushing at a simple compliment.

Before I do something stupid like keep flirting with her when I'm in the middle of an undercover op, I grab the beers in front of me and turn to leave. My head is already running a loop of our conversation. Pretty? Really? I'm way off my game.

"Wait." Her soft voice stops me in my tracks, forcing me to turn back toward her. I falter when I see how she's leaned across the bar top. I wasn't expecting her to be so much closer than before.

Her hands are braced against her workstation, silently beckoning me toward her. If possible, she looks even better than half a second ago.

I take a step closer, but as I do, she steps back, once again putting the entirety of the bar between us.

"Green. Your eyes are green." She smiles brightly after she says it, stunning me. It's as if she just won the biggest prize that only she knows about.

I don't know what I did to deserve that, but I'm glad to be a witness. She turns back to her other customers at the bar, leaving me dumbfounded, and staring at her backside for a few seconds longer than necessary. I only realize it once my fingers start to cramp from holding all four beer glasses.

Who is this girl?

* * *

The next couple of days are spent debriefing my handler, the investigator assigned primarily to me to coordinate information and to oversee my safety during these undercover operations.

Along with debriefing is all the documentation. I have to make a physical report after each encounter with my targets. When I see Curtis multiple days a week, or multiple times a day, it makes for a stack of paperwork.

I don't mention the girl from the bar, whom I can't stop referring to as Sunshine in my head, even though I should've been transparent about my concerns. Something about her makes me want to keep her out of this. There's an innocence about her that should steer clear of "Jay" and this investigation.

However, I'd be lying if I said I didn't want to see that smile again. I haven't been able to stop thinking about her or the way her cheeks blushed when I spoke to her.

My phone rings, thankfully giving me a reason to stop typing on my current report, and interrupting my thoughts about my mystery girl.

"Don't tell me that your senses are so good that you somehow knew I was in your area?" I ask as soon as I pick up, seeing "Wolfe" on the screen.

"You're nearby and you haven't fucking called me yet?" Nathan acts hurt, even though we both know he doesn't let things like that bother him.

"I'm on an assignment, but I was going to get a hold of you as soon as I have some downtime. Plus, I've got to get over there and hug my girl," I tease him, knowing how stupid protective he is of his fiance, Callie.

"My girl," he corrects, and I just grin to myself knowing how well I know him. "You get one hug when you arrive and one when you leave. That's all."

This time I laugh out loud. "Okay, deal."

There's a healthy pause, making me wonder what's going on that he felt the need to call. He's a pretty stone-cold guy, doesn't let much affect him. As I've been doing this undercover assignment, I've channeled Nathan's grumpy demeanor to give off my "I hate the world" vibe and it's worked like a charm.

"I decided to re-enlist," he says, surprising me. I selfishly hoped he would, I wanted my partner back, but I'd never told him as much. I never wanted him to feel swayed because of my lonely ass.

"Wow. That's great, man." I know how bad his mental health got toward the end of his last year, and I know how much Callie helped him after he met her. I'm thankful that he has someone like her in his life, he deserves it. Hell, I always joke that she's too good for him, but I'm honestly just jealous that he found someone.

I've always been missing that connection with someone. I don't know if it's because I grew up without a family and I never learned the basic skills to form a relationship, or if the risk of losing someone else never seemed worth it. After the hand I've been dealt it seems useless to try.

I learned a long time ago that hoping for anyone to come in and change your life was wasteful thinking. Foster families were hard to come by. An adoptive family was even more unheard of.

If they did place me somewhere, it was always temporary and almost always worse than the group home I was usually in. So, I stopped getting my hopes up. I stopped wishing for my circumstances to change. I waited until I was old enough to walk into the army recruiting office and made the first decision in my life that was totally mine.

The army became my home, my life's plan. For some, it might seem small, but it was the better alternative for me when I saw most of the other teenagers in the group home go from one prison to another when they turned 18.

"I talked to someone at the local base and they're looking to fill a few spots in their Criminal Investigation Division. I'm not interested in the undercover work, I don't want to leave Callie for days or weeks on end, but they said they need guys in all capacities with our security clearance.

"I mentioned that I knew a guy who needed to get the hell out of Texas and they said you could transfer here, permanently. As long as you don't mind the possibility of working with me again," he adds the last part for good measure, knowing I wouldn't fucking mind.

He knows how much I hate the Texas heat. I've been complaining about it for years. He also knows how alone I am now that he lives here in North Carolina.

"I'll think about it, man. Thanks for looking out for me." I can't gather the energy to throw a friendly jab at him like I normally would. I'm too glad that he's the one person in my life that I can count on to stick around.

I pace the floor of my subpar motel room. The New Hope Inn was the only accommodation available in this town, making me feel even less at home than I would almost anywhere else. Plain white bedding, beige walls, tan curtains. It's not terrible, but I understand why they have such a hard time keeping people undercover. Living out of a bag sucks. The monotony sucks.

We end our phone call with a promise to get together as soon as we can. The small spark of joy that my friend's call gave me starts to fizzle as soon as I return to my hard-as-a-rock desk chair, my laptop that looks like a fucking cinder block, and the cold microwave meal that I've left untouched.

I tip my head back, peering through the gap in the curtains to look at the sky. After a few seconds, the clouds separate, sending a stream of light into the room. It's not even close, but it reminds me of the moment I saw Sunshine smile.

Chapter Five

Thea

I can do this. I'm a grown woman. I can make this phone call. I take a deep breath, blowing all the air back out of my mouth before I hit the call button. As soon as he answers I dive into my carefully thought-out spiel.

"Hi, Kyle. It's Thea. I was calling to let you know that I can no longer afford your services. Thank you for your hard work, but I will not be going forward with my bathroom renovations at this time. If I have any future projects, I will consider reaching back out." A total lie, but it felt necessary to add some cushion to my figurative breakup with my contractor. Not that I should even call him that when he's terrible at his job.

"But, the job's not done." He huffs.

"Um. I know, but I can't afford to pay you anymore. So you'll have to stop working, and I'll need my house key back." I squeeze my eyes shut and hold my breath prepping for his reaction. God, why can't I just avoid all confrontations for the rest of my life?

The line clicks dead. Okay… Not what I expected. Now what?

I store my phone away in one of the drawers inside the island, ignoring my problems for the moment.

"Did you do it?" Latisha asks as she joins me behind the counter. She urged me to make my call here while I was at work to lean on her for emotional support if I needed to. I can't decide if it worked or not.

"Um, yeah. Kind of," I tell her as I shake my hair out from the scrunchy I had it in, letting all my hair fall down my back.

"Kind of?" She asks for clarification, giving me the 'mom' look.

"I told him he was fired, but then he hung up on me." I use the sleeve of my sweater to clean my glasses, avoiding her eyes.

"You just let me know if he gives you any more trouble. I'll handle it," she tells me. I have no doubt either, she's very protective of me and all of her workers here. I wish I had just an ounce of her confidence.

"Thanks, Latisha. You know I love you." I blow her a kiss as I leave the counter to set up for story time, leaving my real-world problems behind.

It isn't long after I get my curtain backdrop set up that the kids start rolling in. They each take turns excitedly hugging me as if they didn't just see me last week. I can't help but to reciprocate their infectiousness.

Children are so inherently kind and gentle. They have their moments when their little bodies have big reactions, but luckily we've never had any big issues. The parents are usually ready to step in if it becomes too much.

"Okay, everyone find your spot on the carpet. Plant your butts! Crisscross applesauce so you all have room!" I whisper-shout, giving them my excited energy but maintaining a respectful library volume.

"Who can tell me what is behind me?" I ask, pointing over my shoulder to my backdrop.

"A farm! A pig! Grass! A big red barn!" They all take turns answering, each one pointing out something different.

"Yes. Exactly right. Any guesses for what I'll be reading today?" I keep my book tucked behind my back so they can't peek, shrugging my shoulders as they take turns guessing.

"Charlotte's Web!" I finally concede, showing them the cover of the book. They all clap, even though I'm sure they have no idea what it's about. Another thing I love about children is their ability to be happy about everything.

I spend the hour putting on an excellent display of reading the story, acting out the actions, as well as identifying and sounding out all of the animal noises as we come across them. Ending our time together letting the kids tell me about all the animals they've seen in the wild. Cadderpillers, uhskeetas (mosquitos), and wild squirrels (not to be mistaken for the pet squirrel that Junior's cousin has) were my favorite contributions.

I'm still laughing to myself as I put my props away and return to my computer station. I don't know how I got so lucky to get paid to do this job and to listen to these silly kids on a biweekly basis.

I look to Latisha, planning to fill her in on story time since she usually asks when I notice her eyes are big and round under her red jeweled glasses. She pings her gaze off to the side and then back to me quickly, trying to direct my attention.

My good mood deflates instantly as I see Kyle stalking toward me. Oh no.

"Hi, Kyle." I can't hide the tremor in my voice. I hate confrontation! Even as a little girl, before my life went to shit, I couldn't stand being scolded. I was a teacher's pet, a people pleaser. The thought of someone being angry with me causes deep emotional turmoil and being talked down to or yelled at has always resulted in tears.

"You can't fire me. I need the money," he barks the words at me. He's not yelling yet, but his voice is way too loud for comfort in the near-silent library.

"I'm sorry. I can't afford it. I'm sorry." I keep apologizing as if I'm the problem and not him, hoping this conversation doesn't escalate.

"You don't care that you're screwing me over?" He almost shouts this time and I can tell we're being watched. My skin is already on fire and I know my face is red.

"Please, let's talk about this outside." I motion him toward the courtyard where the sound will be muffled from the rest of the library. I'm not brave enough to go out the front doors and out of sight of Latisha's watchful eye. She'll let me handle this by myself because I prefer it that way, but I know she'd have no problem stepping in if necessary.

He storms in front of me, launching the glass door open that leads to the courtyard. I have to catch it before it slams shut, doing my best to lessen this dramatic display he's putting on.

"I need the money!" He launches right back into his argument, completely disregarding that I have no more money to give him.

"Kyle. I am so sorry if you feel like you're losing out on money, but the bathroom has taken too long. I can't afford to let you keep working, and I can't afford more materials," I tell him truthfully.

"Oh. So I'm the problem? I'm too slow and you don't like how I'm doing things?" He spews, taking my words out of proportion. He's angry, his face is twisted and he keeps shoving his hands in and out of his pockets, pacing back and forth.

"Please, Kyle. I just need my key. Then you never have to talk to me again. Please." I barely manage to get the words out, my whole body is shaking. I can't handle stressful situations like a normal person, my adrenaline is running rampant.

Despite the heat of this courtyard at the end of summer in the south, I hug myself, clutching my sweater around my torso as if it will protect me from this situation.

"Here's your damn key." He throws, no, absolutely beams it in my direction, barely missing me. All I can do is flinch as it hits the glass and clatters to the ground behind me.

"Get. The fuck. Out of here." A dangerously deep voice growls from the other side of the courtyard. My gaze whips to the door that leads to the Adult Literature section and it's as if time freezes.

Standing there with all the authority of someone who isn't afraid of anything, is the man that won't escape my thoughts. Library man. Bar man.

His frame fills the doorway, the corded muscles of his forearm bulging as he grips the door in his hand. His hat is low on his head, making his eyes appear darker than I now know them to be. If his stare was directed toward me I'd be terrified, but it's not. The full force of his disapproval is directed at Kyle.

Kyle, who is looking back at him menacingly, debating on whether he wants to keep arguing. After a few tense seconds, he ultimately decides it's not worth it. It's obvious that he would lose any type of fight against this opponent.

"Man. Whatever." He spits on the concrete a few feet from me before taking a step to leave.

"This way. Don't take a step in her direction." My green-eyed savior demands, holding his door open wider, forcing Kyle to walk right past him. "Don't come back either," he orders.

We both watch him stomp through the library and exit through the double doors with a hard shove. I'm having a hard time reminding myself to breathe.

The two of us are alone in the courtyard now, but I'm still in too much shock to find any words to say. I'm hugging myself where I stand while he stays where he is by the door, not moving any closer.

The light breeze from the opening above the courtyard flutters my yellow floral skirt. The tiny white flowers micro-printed all over it are one of my favorite patterns. Now I'm afraid I won't be able to put it on without thinking of this moment.

"Are you okay?" His voice is completely calm compared to how it sounded a few moments ago, gentle even, sending a whisper of a chill down my spine.

Still, all I can manage to do is nod my head, unable to look at him. Never mind the fact that I've been publicly humiliated, I'm also not ready for him to realize I'm the girl from the bar. It would make this situation much more embarrassing.

"I'm sorry that he yelled at you. No man should ever treat a woman like that," he adds. His sympathy makes my bottom lip quiver. I'm not used to receiving any type of empathy from men.

Most won't give me the time of day once I don't humor

their advances. They catch wind of my problems and scoff at me or accuse me of lying. Or worse, they try to push my boundaries. I've never received an apology from one man on behalf of another.

I can't speak though, afraid I'll cry. He probably thinks I'm broken. Oh well, it's the truth.

"Listen. I'll go. Just... Don't let that punk take your sunshine," he pleads sincerely.

My head snaps up at his use of that last word. *Sunshine*. That's what he called me at the bar. He gives me a small wink and spins on his heels, leaving me staring after him.

Chapter Six

Jesse

E*arlier that day...*
If I'm stuck in this room any longer, I'll lose my mind.

Before I even consider what I'm doing, I'm out the door and down the street. The motel is right off the main drag through town, so I take my time walking past all the shops and admiring the small town.

This job has been as slow-paced as this place. I haven't made enough progress on infiltrating the extremist group and it's driving me crazy. The cabin fever that I'm experiencing being trapped in a single-bed motel room with only a tiny 24-inch TV to occupy me leaves too much room for my thoughts to wander.

How can I do my job properly when the majority of it feels like a waiting game? I complained to my handler that it seems like I'm sitting on my ass doing nothing. He assured me that it was normal for undercover work, 80% of the job is gathering intel and doing paperwork. Adjusting to that practice is worse than watching paint dry.

A little boy, probably about eight years old, comes barreling out of the diner almost colliding with me as I pass by. His mother is hot on his heels, apologizing profusely on his behalf. I smile and assure her, no harm no foul, as they take off across the street.

I find myself staring after them.

I never got to experience life with my mom at eight years old. She was gone by then. How different would my life be if I had even a few more years with her?

On their own accord, my feet keep walking while I drown in the memories I do have.

* * *

Jesse- Six years old

"Momma, momma! Can I have some cake now?" I ask through her bedroom door. Today's my birthday and I have a whole cake just for me. Momma put some of my plastic dinosaurs on top and made fake grass with some green sprinkles. It's the coolest cake in the whole world.

"Go ahead, baby. We'll be out soon." She doesn't open the door because she's in there getting a "talkin' to" from my daddy. I don't know what she did, but he's been yelling forever already. It's probably making her sad. It makes me sad when he yells at me. Sometimes I cry, but I try not to let Daddy see. If he sees, then he hits me. Hopefully, Momma doesn't cry.

I climb onto the kitchen chair, making sure the cake is sitting right in front of me on the table. My fork digs into the green sprinkles but then I remember that Momma never got a chance to light my candles. That's okay, we can do it later. She said I could eat my cake now.

Something shatters down the hall and Daddy's voice is louder now. It's always like this on the days he doesn't get home til morning. Momma says he's working all night and that's why he gets home when I'm eating breakfast. I don't know why it makes him so angry.

When I hear her start crying, I know what comes next, so I put my fork down before I take my bite. I don't want to eat the best birthday cake in the whole world while Momma is getting hit on.

I crawl under the table and lay on the floor. The tablecloth doesn't stop the noises I hear, but it makes me feel safe. I close my eyes and pretend I'm in a cool fort like my army guys. I bet they'd know what to do to help me and my momma.

* * *

Despite being lost in my mind, my meandering deposited me right outside the doors of the New Hope Public Library. It's a Tuesday, I had plans to come here anyway but I'm a little ahead of schedule since I left the Inn so early.

Fuck it. I'll go in and try to actually read a book today. Maybe if I get lost in someone else's story, I'll stop remembering mine.

The crisp air conditioning greets me as I walk through the two sets of double doors, a nice change from the humidity outside. Unlike the other days since I usually drive, I'm walking in through the street entrance and not the parking lot. The building isn't huge, but it means I have to walk past all the other sections to get to my usual table that's closer to the support group room.

A bout of laughter draws my attention to the vibrant Children's Literature section. The carpets and bookshelves are all themed and colorful, much more exciting than the Adult's side. Another chorus of giggles rings out and I can't help but step closer. Something about seeing kids be carefree and happy heals something deep inside of me that's shattered.

Being distracted by the children is short-lived because the prettiest smile that I've ever seen stops me dead in my tracks. The breath escapes my lungs and everything in me recalibrates upon seeing her. The man I was ten seconds ago is a different man than the one standing here right now, recognizing that beautiful smile.

Front and center, atop a stool, is a version of the girl from the bar that I never would have expected. Her hair isn't pin-straight at all, it's full of thick waves and curls.

She looked beautiful the other night, but the heavy makeup wasn't doing her any favors compared to what I'm seeing now. If anything, it hid her. Even today, behind her delicate glasses, I can tell she looks fresh and authentic. Her natural beauty is radiant.

She looks at home here, not at that damn bar. She's animating excitedly to the kids in front of her and it makes my heart ache in a way that I'd only feel comfortable addressing with a doctor. Or a therapist.

Another smile breaks out across her face and I feel myself mirroring it. My thoughts nearly jump from my brain and out of my mouth. *Gotcha, Sunshine.*

Having a hard time tearing my eyes away, I watch for a few

more minutes. I want her to see me, but at the same time, I don't. Not yet, anyway.

I want to be closer. I want to stand in front of her without anything between us and see the look in her eyes when she sees me. I want to watch the pink stain her cheeks. It's all I've been able to think about.

To avoid disturbing her in her element, I drag myself away and over to my usual table. Now that I know where the recognition came from, I'm wondering how I didn't notice her before… She's stunning. Her whole being lights up when she smiles.

How could I be so unaware when I've been coming here for weeks? Why didn't she say anything when she recognized me?

The egotistical side of my brain feels burned to think she might not have actually recognized me at all. I didn't recognize her, but in my defense, she went through an entire wardrobe and personality shift from her day-to-night job.

Dammit. I came in here to read, not obsess over the girl with blonde hair and icy blue eyes. The one that parts the clouds when she smiles.

Something exciting needs to happen with this job so I can get my head out of my ass. I open up a book, but only get through the first page before the words start blurring together and I realize I'm not absorbing anything. Taking a second to rub my eyes and some sense into my brain, I stare at the page again, trying to take it in.

It doesn't work. After a few moments, my focus goes hazy. My eyes are lasered in on the brown table top, my thoughts are moving a mile a minute on their own trajectory until I'm back in the desert with my Special Ops team.

The sand is thick in the air. The dust covering every surface is deep in my lungs. This op escalated quickly and now we're sitting ducks. Despite the chaos around me, my pulse is steady and even. It's hard to rattle me when I have nothing to lose. I'm more concerned about my team.

I strain my neck to get eyes on anyone else.

Nathan's shouting at me from behind the cover of a Humvee about five yards away.

It's too loud, shots are being fired from every side and an explosion has already left my ears ringing. His mouth keeps moving and I'm trying to decipher the words.

He shouts again, but I can only make out the last word. "... money."

"Money?"

What? Why would he say that?

"You don't care that you're screwing me over?" The heightened volume snaps me out of my thousand-yard stare.

The words carried over from the other side of the library, loud enough to rouse me from my flashback and to pique concern.

I shake my head to clear it, confirming that what I'm experiencing is happening in real time and not in my mind.

Others around me are taking notice as well, craning their heads to see what the drama is. On instinct, I'm up, casually walking back toward the center of the library, needing to get my sights on what's going down.

A young guy, probably Curtis' age, is standing in front of the counter with his hands balled into fists on his hips, clearly agitated. It's a library, what the hell does he have to be mad about?

I walk until I can get a clear view of everything, but I keep my distance. I don't need to be involved, I just need to make sure I'm aware if something is wrong. When things turn ugly, I prefer to know all the details. The number of kids prancing about, where each person is in relation to the exits, and who else might be helpful if danger arises. Some of it is natural instinct, and some of it is military training that's ingrained in me.

None of it matters as soon as I see what's happening and who the dude is yelling at. *My* girl. The one I can't stop thinking about.

As I absorb what I'm seeing, I watch her motion him out the doors into the courtyard. Fuck, Sunshine. Don't put yourself alone with a man who's yelling at you.

The other librarian, an older black woman with bright red glasses that match her bright red sweater, is looking on worriedly. She must sense my presence, because she cuts a look in my direction, maintaining eye contact with me for an entire breath before turning back to the courtyard.

I don't know what it was about that look, or maybe I'm just looking for permission to intervene anywhere I can get it, but it felt like a signal.

I glance one more time at Ms. Red as I make my way closer to the courtyard from my side of the library, and I swear she nods her head in approval.

Another older gentleman using one of the computers looks on worriedly into the courtyard as I pass him. We make eye contact and he gives me a slight nod as well. No one in this building has any interest in seeing this woman be terrorized, especially me, but it doesn't mean I have a right to disrupt my cover by getting involved.

As I reach the glass door that leads into the courtyard, I hear the fucker yell and watch him launch something in Sunshine's direction, narrowly avoiding hitting her. I shove the door open without another thought.

"Get. The fuck. Out of here," I demand through gritted teeth.

It takes everything in me to stay calm, not to storm up to him and drag him out by his collar. That would cause a scene and I can't afford to draw unnecessary attention to myself during an undercover mission, but I can't not help her.

If eyes could kill, he would be stabbing me to death right now. I can see the crazy in them.

"Man. Whatever." He goes to leave and I get a feeling akin to panic skating down my spine at the thought of him walking past her and grabbing her. Hurting her.

"This way. Don't take a step in her direction," I redirect him to walk past me, and like an obedient puppy, he does exactly as ordered. "Don't come back either," I threaten through a locked jaw, still fighting the urge to manhandle him.

What I want to add is *"Don't look at her, don't breathe in her direction, if you see her on the street, go the other way."* Instead, I let him leave, turning my attention back to the object of my sudden protectiveness once he's gone.

She's withdrawn into herself. The vibrant girl I saw before is shaking like a leaf, clutching her baggy sweater like her life depends on it.

"Are you okay?" I use the calmest voice I can muster for her benefit, afraid I'll spook her if I attempt to speak in my normal tone.

She doesn't answer me, keeping her eyes glued to the ground, but she nods. I've seen that body language before. It's almost the only memory I have left of my mom or rather the shell of a mother she was toward the end.

My body is thrumming with energy, urging me to go to her, but I know that would be a mistake. The last thing she needs is another man coming into her bubble and the last thing I want is to be perceived as another threat.

"I'm sorry that he yelled at you. No man should ever treat a woman like that." I mean it wholeheartedly. I can't stand to see men use their power to abuse women. Even if I didn't come from a violent home, I'd have the common sense to never use anger against a woman.

Especially one so small and full of light, and wearing a yellow skirt that looks exactly how she should feel. Bright, lively, not lifeless like she is right now.

She still hasn't spoken and I'm afraid I'm making her uncomfortable by being here so I say the only thing I can think of.

"Listen. I'll go. Just... Don't let that punk take your sunshine."

She snaps her head up, shocked.

Yeah, Sunshine. I gotcha.

Chapter Seven

Thea

I motion through my end-of-shift tasks in a haze, taking twice as long to complete what I need to. My mind is reeling, replaying what happened with Kyle and the guy that keeps popping up in my life when I least expect him to. I wish I knew his name.

I need to at least thank him for stepping in when things were escalating out in the courtyard. He had no reason to help me, but he did anyway.

By the time I'm walking out to my car, the normally quiet parking lot is filled with voices. I check over my shoulder to see that the support group is letting out. The members are exiting through the side entrance that goes into that room. I quicken my pace, not quite ready to run into my hero once again. I'm still too humiliated by what he witnessed.

I'm fumbling with my keys, trying to unlock my doors when I hear footsteps approaching me. "Hey." The now recognizable voice soothes my nerves, yet startles me in a way that makes me yearn to hear it again.

"Hi." I turn to look at him, wrapping my sweater tighter around myself despite the heat. If I'm lucky, maybe I'll melt into the pavement from my embarrassment.

"I wanted to check again and make sure you're okay." His eyes are filled with nothing but genuine concern. No judgment, no mockery of how I acted earlier.

He removes his baseball hat to wipe his forehead with the back of his hand before righting it and I watch with ample fascination.

My gaze is drawn to the hair curled slightly below his ears and I have the strongest urge to touch it. My fingers burrow deeper into my sweater instead.

"I'm okay. Really. I was startled earlier, but I'm fine," I lie.

"It's not any of my business, but was that guy an ex-boyfriend or something?" He asks, taking a small step closer to me as if to be discreet.

I sense his curiosity and maybe a little judgment mixed in at the prospect of me dating Kyle because clearly, he wasn't a winner. Even though his proximity isn't threatening, I shuffle back a step toward my car anyway, needing the safety of the gap between us. If I'm not mistaken, he notices.

"Uh no. Kyle's just someone I hired to work on something at my house. He wasn't doing a good job and I tried to let him down easy, but... You saw how that went." I shrug but he continues looking at me curiously, with his brow slightly furrowed.

Even though I owe this man nothing, I feel the need to explain myself. "Thank you for stepping in earlier. I appreciate your help. And, for taking that shot at the bar the other night," I might as well get it all out in the open. "I don't handle confrontation very well... Men make me uncomfortable." I bite my bottom lip, scolding myself for not keeping that last thought to myself.

Instead of looking at me with any type of disdain for not being able to handle myself, a slow smile appears. A lopsided grin that makes my stomach do a little somersault. His teeth are perfectly straight and he has dimples underneath his scruffily stubbled cheeks.

I could die. The butterflies in my stomach are going to burst out of me if he keeps looking at me like that.

"It's probably a good thing you work with kids then," he teases, taking a small step back and further away from me. "You're slightly taller, so you can take them if they act up."

"Only slightly?" I ask, relieved at the shift in conversation. "I have at least a foot on most of them." I can't help but giggle, feeling a lot lighter now that I know he's trying to make me feel better. He doesn't laugh with me, but rather studies me, quirking his head subtly as if amused.

"Why did you lie?" He asks suddenly, sobering me.

"About what?"

"I asked you the other night if we knew each other."

"We don't know each other," I clarify.

"But, you did recognize me?"

I consider lying for a millisecond, but there is no point. "Yes."

His sharp intake of breath at my answer makes his nostrils flare slightly, but he just nods his head. He stares at me for a second, slowly letting the grin overtake his face again.

There's a calm confidence that he carries and it's spell-binding. The energy between us feels charged suddenly, but instead of exciting me, I retreat into my shell. It makes me too hopeful that he might like me and I can't think like that.

"I'm sorry, I need to head home. Thank you again for -well everything." I add in that last part because I do genuinely appreciate him not making me feel inadequate for how I handled the situation he witnessed today and for being kind to me at the bar.

"I don't mean to worry you, but do you want me to follow you home?" He asks, taking me off guard.

"What? Why?" I can't hide the confusion in my voice or the panic at his suggestion.

"You said that Kyle guy was working on your house. If there's any chance he might be waiting for you to get home..." He trails off, but it still takes another second for my brain to catch up to what he's saying. "I'd feel better making sure you get home safe."

He tucks his hands into his jeans pockets casually, but the way he's looking at me from under the brim of his hat oozes worry.

"I didn't even think about that," I tell him truthfully. "But... Am I supposed to just show you where I live? I don't even know your name."

It seems silly at this point to be worried about stranger danger when he's not given me any reason to be afraid of him, but that's what past trauma does to a person. Gives them trust issues.

He laughs, cocking his head to the side. "You're right. I'm sorry."

Now would be the time he should tell me his name, but he doesn't. Instead, he's looking at me intently, hesitating.

"My name is Je-" Someone from the other side of the parking lot shouts, cutting him off.

"Hey, Jay! There you are, man!" A young guy comes walking towards us, but instead of acknowledging him right away, Jay? I assume, squeezes his eyes shut and blows a deep breath out through his mouth.

"I'm sorry. Give me one second. I'll be right back." He turns to his friend, grabbing him by the shoulder and spinning him back toward the way he came before he can reach me. The young guy looks over his shoulder, trying to get a peek at me, but Jay tugs him along making him look forward.

I'm not sure what to do, so I get in my car and blast the a/c. I think about leaving, I don't really have a reason to stay, but the thought of going home and running into Kyle again keeps my hand off the gear shift. Would he show back up to my house?

Why didn't I consider that possibility?

Of course, this is happening to me. Another reason that I'm going to spend the rest of my life fearing men. I rub my face under my glasses, feeling exhausted from the day. Feeling exhausted from this life. I didn't ask for the bad things that have happened to me, yet I'm stuck dealing with the consequences forever.

A tap on my window makes me jump out of my skin, nearly biting my tongue to keep from screaming.

Get out of your head, Thea. It's only Jay.

I crack my window, willing my pulse to ease, but it doesn't. Not with him so close.

"I'm sorry, I didn't mean to scare you." His hands are raised in surrender, his apology genuine.

"It's okay. I'm a little jumpy after the day I've had." And the life I've had, but I don't add that part.

"I forgot that I walked here today, but I can still make sure you get home okay. Want me to ride with you?" That question startles me and I can only imagine what my face looks like because he jumps back in before I can respond.

"It's okay if you say no, but at least take my number and text me when you're home safe." He holds out a small yellow paper with his number on it, a *-J,* at the bottom.

"You carry around post-its with your number on them?" I ask, skeptically.

He laughs again, not at all put off by my question. "I wrote it down earlier. I was going to give it to your coworker after my meeting in case you guys had any problems with that guy again. I didn't know I'd run into you out here."

Wow. Of course, I would never have assumed that. Now I feel like a jerk.

I carefully take the paper with his number but need another minute to work out whether I should let him in my car or not. He seems safe. He goes to a support group for veterans, which means he's probably ex-military. That could be a good sign, but he's still a man. A man much bigger than me.

Except, he's given me no indication that he's anything but sincere and genuinely concerned about my safety...

"How will you get home if I drive?" I ask, hoping my logical question will diffuse his offer to help me entirely and put the decision out of my hands.

"I can walk. Keeps me slim," he feigns seriousness, seeing right through me.

My eyes trail down his body at the mention of his figure. I can tell he has no issues in that department. When my focus is on his face again, he maintains eye contact with me, forcing me to look away first.

He's so direct, so opposite from me. It's hard to believe he would be lying about wanting to help me... But, I've been lied to plenty of times.

We all make choices in our lives that end up being disastrous mistakes. I've made plenty of mistakes, one in particular being worse than the rest, and it's tainted every choice in my life since it happened.

I won't know if this particular choice is a mistake until it's too late, but I can't let my past hold me back forever. I need to live.

"Okay. Get in then," I tell him warily, reminding myself that he doesn't seem dangerous. He hasn't felt like a threat since I started interacting with him but that doesn't stop the nerves from climbing up my spine. Each muscle along my vertebrae tightens as he rounds the front of my car to get in.

Before I have a chance to second guess myself, we're confined in my vehicle only a foot apart, driving down the road. He doesn't speak at first and neither do I. The air circulating us feels supercharged. It's like every hair on my body is standing on end sensing his nearness.

Paying attention to the road in front of me is difficult when I keep trying to peek at him from the corner of my eye. He either doesn't notice or doesn't care, sitting relaxed in his seat as he observes the town from his window.

"Why are you doing this?" I can't help but ask the question that's been ringing in my mind.

"What?" His voice trickles through the space between us, once again throwing a blanket over some of the anxiety that's busting out of the seams of my brain. His tone does something to calm me, but the effect unnerves me.

"Why are you helping me? You don't know me." I glance at him before I take the turn that leads to my street. I can feel his eyes on the side of my face, but I focus on the road, refusing to look back in his direction. Maintaining eye contact with him is too extreme in this small space.

"I don't like when men bully women," he states simply, answering my question, but not quite answering it at the same time. He rests his elbow on the center console, making me subconsciously move my arm further away. I try covering it up by messing with the sleeve of my sweater.

"So, you're some sort of protector of women then?" I try to make it sound as lighthearted as possible even though I'm dying to know more about him.

His gaze is locked on where my right hand is resting in the crook of my left elbow. He definitely noticed my subtle adjustment because he moves his elbow back to his lap.

"I try to do the right thing in most situations. Try to make my mom proud I guess." My eyes flick to him at the sudden vulnerability in his voice. I barely catch his eyebrows furrow as if he didn't mean to say that last part out loud.

He shakes his head and resumes looking out the window, cutting off my silent inspection.

Chapter Eight

Thea

"Are you in for the night?" He asks as I pull up to the curb in front of my house and park. This is an old historic area, so the houses don't have driveways.

"Yeah. I don't have any plans and I don't want to run into Kyle anywhere in town." I shudder even thinking about it.

"You can always call me if you have any trouble. Put my number in your phone as soon as you can." His seriousness unsettles me. He's concerned that Kyle is going to become a bigger issue, whereas I'm desperately hoping it disappears altogether.

I jump out of my car, needing away from the suffocating air of what ifs. Kyle normally parks in the ally behind my house, so I peek through my side yard, relieved when I don't see his van. "He's not here," I say before Jay's fully out of my car, not wanting to waste any more of his time.

"Go inside and flash the porch light once you lock the door behind you. Then I'll leave and stop bothering you," he says, jokingly.

A big part of me hopes that he's not going to stop bothering me. It's nice having someone show concern for my safety.

54

It's been a long time since I've felt cared about in that way. In any way.

I give him a mock salute as I trail up my sidewalk, making him cock his head at me. "How'd you know?" He asks frankly.

"Know what?"

He follows a few steps behind me up my sidewalk but stops as I reach my porch steps. He's so much taller than me that despite my three-step advantage on the porch, I barely have the high ground. His face is below mine, but seems closer than it would be if I were standing on the ground in front of him.

"The salute," he clarifies. His inquisitiveness about that casual gesture is serious. So serious that I can't help the truth that spills from my lips while his eyes probe me.

"I read the bulletin board. I know you go to Coffee with Veterans." Once again the air around us is suffocating. He's looking at me so intensely that I'm afraid I might melt into a puddle at his feet.

"Ah." It's his only response to my nosiness while my face flames with embarrassment.

He nods his head toward my house not acknowledging my confession further, silently urging me to go inside. I take the queue, needing to get away from him before I make a fool of myself any further.

Using the spare key that I retrieved from the ground in the courtyard earlier, I attempt to unlock the door but it jams.

It's the wrong key.

I don't know how I didn't notice it before, or bother to check, but this key is not my house key. I look at the door handle for a moment, contemplating what I should do. I have my own key, but that's not the problem. The problem is that

Kyle still has my spare key.

Curiosity gets the best of me and I twist the handle... The door gives.

It creaks open slowly on its own, but I take a step backward, then another until I'm on the edge of my porch.

"What's wrong?" Again, I nearly have a heart attack when Jay speaks up from beside me.

"Good grief. Can you put a bell on your shirt or something," I exclaim while I'm trying to calm my beating heart. He ignores my comment.

"What's wrong?" He asks again, looking in through my front door.

"He gave me the wrong key. I'm an idiot. I should've checked sooner but I didn't. It was unlocked already," I explain, overburdened by this situation that I've found myself in.

"Stay here." He pulls a gun out from under his shirt, making my jaw drop.

"Have you had that the whole time?" I shout, even though I should probably whisper since Jay is currently walking through my front door into God knows what.

"Yes."

"The library is a no-gun zone." We're not in the library anymore, but I was also just in my car with a man who had a gun, and that alarms me.

"I know." That's his only response before he indicates for me to stay put while he enters my house. All I can do is stand here and pace, trying to pretend that none of this is happening.

After a few minutes, he reappears in the doorway, no gun in sight. "You can come in now."

"I'm sorry for wasting your time, but thank you for checking." I drop my purse and slip off my shoes, depositing them on the floor next to my cowboy boots. Jay stares at them for a second before looking at me.

"Why do you work at the bar?"

"Why does anyone work anywhere? I need the money," I say a little too defensively. "I'm sorry, that was rude. I'm a little tense." I rub my face again, careful not to knock my glasses off, feeling too aware of him watching me.

"The library doesn't pay you well?" He asks, not at all phased by my earlier comment.

"It does. I mean, I live comfortably on my salary, but all the renovations I needed to do to my house made things tight. Then Kyle kept up-charging me and adding costs... Working at the bar two days a week until September ends will get me caught up." Once again explaining myself to a man that I hardly know and owe nothing to.

What is it about him that makes me involuntarily spill my guts?

If he was still just a stranger at the bar, I would shut down personal questions, but I guess I have nothing to hide. It doesn't bother me that I am starting to feel a little less guarded around him. It's a nice change of pace from my norm.

"I didn't mean to pry but I've noticed a rougher crowd there. I don't want to see you mixed up in it."

"Like you?" I counter jokingly, but his face falls.

"Yeah," he laughs but it doesn't sound like a real one. "Like me."

Before I can interject, and tell him I meant no harm, he clears his throat, speaking up again. "I checked the whole house, but you know it better than anyone. Is there anywhere else you want me to look before I leave? To make sure you feel safe tonight. You'll need to change your locks as soon as you can. That way you don't need to worry about Kyle coming in uninvited anymore."

His ability to bring me back to reality and remind me of the potential danger that I'm in is unsettling, but I'm glad he's aware of risks that I might not be. Though, I still don't know why he cares. It's making my crush on him a little too real and I don't think I'll be able to handle the rejection when he realizes nothing can come of this.

Not that a relationship is even something that he's interested in... I can't fathom any other reason why a man would be showing me such kindness unless he wanted to sleep with me. Which is not going to happen.

Speaking of sleeping. "There is somewhere in my bedroom I'd like you to look if you don't mind." I'm halfway up the stairs before I realize how that might have come across.

"Oh my God. I didn't mean that to sound sexual. There's an attic in my room," I clarify. I'm too embarrassed to turn around and look at him, but I hear him stifling a laugh with a cough as he follows me up the stairs.

Despite the platonic nature of his being here, it feels incredibly personal to have a man in my room. It's been years since I've had a man in my space.

"I like your house," he says as we enter my room.

"Thank you. I wanted it to feel like home and I'm starting to get there. You know what I mean?"

He shrugs but doesn't respond.

"It's a vibe thing I guess. I want to spend all of my time here because my favorite things are here and I feel safe. Everything I buy is personal, just for me. None of my college apartments felt like this. Like home."

He's studying me closely, probably because I'm babbling so I bite my bottom lip to shut myself up and lead him over to a door that looks like a closet. When I open it, I point to the ceiling where a string hangs.

"There's a moon room up there. I don't think he'd know about it, but I'll sleep better tonight knowing that he's not lurking up there ready to kill me."

"A moon room?" He asks, staring at the door suspiciously.

"You'll just have to see what I mean." I wave him forward, giving him enough space to get past me without taking the chance that we'll touch. He pulls the string, bringing the stairs down that lead to my little hideout.

"Wow," he exclaims as he climbs the stairs to the top. I have to turn my whole body to stop from staring at his ass.

Inside is a small alcove closed off from the rest of the attic, only big enough for maybe two people. I wouldn't know since I've only ever been up there by myself.

"The previous owners were astrology buffs. They put the window in so you can look straight up into the sky. It's one of the reasons that I bought this house, even though I knew it needed a lot of work. I love it up there," I tell him as he climbs down.

"I can see why. I think I'd sleep up there if I were you."

"I'd probably fall down the ladder when I need to pee in the middle of the night." My comment makes him laugh out loud and I can't help but stare at how magnetic it is. It's so genuine and contagious, it makes me want to make him laugh again.

Instead, I distract myself by looking around at my stuff to make sure none of it's been disturbed, and so he doesn't see my heart eyes for him.

My jewelry looks untouched but when I pull open the top drawers of my dresser, I slam them shut, instantly.

"What?" He asks, his concern clear. My voice is lost for a moment, needing to come to terms with what I discovered.

"He… He went through my drawers. He messed with my underwear," I finally admit out loud.

"Are you sure?" His voice is filled with concern but his eyes are wild suddenly and burning with anger.

"Yes. I organize everything. I like things to be exactly where I need them and now they're all messed up." I turn toward my bed, feeling the need to crawl under the covers and hide, but that brings my attention to my nightstand. A drawer I will *not* be checking while Jay stands in my room.

"Is there anything you need from me? Anything I can do?"

"No. I need you to leave now because I am definitely going to cry and I don't want you to see that. Thank you for everything, Jay." I don't look at him as I say it, not trusting myself to stop the tears from falling while he's still here.

He doesn't say anything right away, both of us standing in silence for a few breaths.

"Keep a chair wedged under your front door tonight and your bedroom door locked until you get a new lock set installed. If you need anything, call me. I'm down the road at the New Hope Inn." I hadn't even thought about the fact that he might not be a resident of New Hope, that he might just be visiting, but I can't focus on that right now. "Have a good night, Sunshine."

After those words, there is a slight hesitation before he leaves, but he does, closing my bedroom door quietly behind him.

I let my tears fall.

Chapter Nine

Jesse

I'm on autopilot walking into the stale air of this bar, scanning the tables for Curtis' familiar face. I see him throwing darts and I make my way over to him.

"Hey man," I utter, lacking any enthusiasm. I'm not thrilled to be here, but what I want doesn't matter. The job is the priority.

"Hey," he says between throws. "I have a friend who needs some help with a big job. He needs a few guys to help him move a bunch of boxes to a warehouse. Said he'd pay. You interested?" Part of my cover story is that I moved here for work.

"Yeah. Definitely. Do you have the details yet?" I ask, hoping like hell this leads somewhere and it's not another dead end.

"Not yet. He's supposed to text us when he's ready. He's waiting for his truck to come in from the road." He walks down to the dart board, retrieving all the darts, and handing them to me.

I take my time throwing each one, attempting to play relatively average. I'm usually pretty good but I don't want to draw attention to myself.

"Alright, man. Thanks." I retrieve the darts, handing them back off to him. "Do you know anybody around here, maybe your age, named Kyle?"

I don't know why I ask. The last thing I want to do is get Curtis involved with my business with Sunshine. I just can't shake the disgust I have for this guy.

The nerve to snoop through her underwear drawer and violate her privacy. I want to find him and beat his ass. Not Jay, Jesse. The thought of her crying because of what Kyle did has strongly influenced my sour mood. She should feel safe in her home.

It was captivating the way she loved it. Every detail looked hand-picked and important. To think that some creep could take away her comfort in her own space aggravates me. If I had a home that I cared about, I'd cherish it like she does.

"I don't know. I went to school with a Kyle, but it's been years since I've seen him. I lost touch with a lot of people while I was in the Army." He's somber as he says it, giving me the urge to probe.

"What made you get out?" I ask as casually as I can, curious about what version of the truth he'll give me. He's always vague at our meetings, never sharing details.

"My grandma died. They wouldn't give me leave for her funeral. She raised me, but I missed her funeral." He scoffs. "After that… I don't know. Everything seemed pretty fucked up. The whole system. I couldn't be a part of it anymore, ya know?"

"Yeah. I know what you mean." I don't, not really. I never had many problems requesting leave because I never needed to. I never had a family to go back to, no family to mourn while I was serving.

I definitely don't know how it feels to want to turn to a group of people who are hell-bent on destroying the government and everyone it protects, but I sympathize with Curtis' grief. He lost his grandmother and spiraled. I'd be pretty torn up if I didn't get to attend my mother's funeral, so for that, I can relate.

"I'm sorry about your grandma," I add, suddenly seeing him as the broken kid I was once.

Luckily, after two beers it felt like a natural time to make my exit. I spent the entire time thinking about Sunshine anyway. I don't even know her real name and it's starting to bother me. The same way that she thinks my name is Jay.

There's a twisting of desperation in my gut to tell her the truth. I don't want her to think I'm some random bum that hangs out at the bar and I want to see her smile again. Dammit.

I shouldn't care. This is all temporary. I have a job to do then I'll be gone. I can't let it disrupt my life. *Not that I have much of a life.*

Halfway back to the motel, my attempt to be indifferent evaporates because I start to worry about how determined Kyle is. If he goes back to her house tonight he could force his way in. I told her to block the door, but it won't stop a grown man if he's determined.

That thought has my rusted, square-body truck parked right out front of her house in the middle of the night, but only after my pit stop to find an open hardware store. Thirty minutes out of my way.

I'll install the new lock first thing in the morning. She'll only be at risk until tomorrow. I'll keep an eye on the house and make sure there are no unwanted visitors in the meantime. Once she's safe, I won't think about her so much.

That's my last thought as I close my eyes and lean my head back to sleep.

* * *

Jesse- Seven Years Old

I don't want to be here. I don't want to see Momma like this.

"Stop crying, Jesse. Man up." Daddy elbows me from beside me in the pew, making me cry harder. Today is my momma's funeral and he doesn't want me to cry? Momma was so beautiful. She was the best momma I could ever ask for.

Why do I have to be stuck here with my daddy? I hate him. I hate him so much.

Visitors take turns walking up to the casket at the front of the church, whispering words to Momma. She still looks pretty, even though she's dead. Dead. My momma is dead and never coming back. That's what Daddy keeps telling me.

I don't know these people here. None of them ever came to our house, but some of them walked up to me and my daddy anyway, telling us that they were sorry for us. Daddy nods at them, but all I can do is look at my feet.

My brown shoes are too small. They make my feet hurt, but I keep looking at them. I wish they would pick me up and walk me out of here. I never want to come to church again. I don't want to see Momma like this anymore.

"Hi, Jesse." The familiar voice lifts my chin. It's my teacher,

Miss Carlisle. "I'm sorry about your mom, sweetheart."

I can't jump up fast enough to hug her. She's so nice and always smells like strawberries. I cry in her arms for a long time, but she just holds me. My daddy won't be mean to me in front of Miss Carlisle. I wish I could go with her instead of with my daddy.

Eventually, the preacher starts to speak and I have to sit back in my seat. Miss Carlisle stays with me the whole time, but I go back to staring at my brown shoes.

* * *

I wake with a start, hearing taps on my window. The sun is coming up and a confused, but beautiful woman is standing right outside my truck. Shit.

"Uh. Good morning," I tell her sheepishly, as I hand crank my window down.

"What are you doing?" She asks defensively, and rightfully so.

"I'm sorry. I wanted to keep an eye on you, I was afraid Kyle would come back last night." I rub my eyes, realizing I slept harder than I intended. Sad dreams will do that I guess. "I meant to be awake before you left for work," I admit.

She studies me closely and I can't help but recognize the distrust in her eyes. She is wary of me. I probably startled her by sitting out here like a creep.

"I usually run every morning and I have the late shift today. I don't go in until ten." That explains the killer legs in those jean shorts at the bar that night.

"Ah." It's the only response I can manage. I've never been tongue-tied, but I am now around her. Something about this girl is getting me turned all around in my head. She looks at me closer than anyone else does and I'm not used to being seen.

"So?" She shuffles her feet awkwardly, waiting for me to say something coherent.

"I'm sorry to ask you this, but... What's your name?" I raise the packaging of the new lock I bought, silently explaining my actual reason for being here.

Her face softens and she laughs, giving me the perfect view of the sunrise right before my eyes. Her smile lights up my soul every time, rattling me, thoroughly.

It makes me want things that I know I'll never have, that I should never hope for. It's influencing too many of my thoughts already.

"Why? Are you tired of calling me Sunshine?" She teases, readjusting her Apple watch on her wrist. My eyes are drawn there, then up her arms and across her shoulders and chest. The skin is mostly exposed since she's only wearing a strappy tank top of some sort.

"Definitely not, but it feels rude not to know your name. Especially since we're becoming such regular acquaintances." I forcefully tear my eyes from her collarbones. She laughs again, making me mentally pat myself on the back.

She's an entirely new person this morning. The fragile state she was in yesterday is long gone, or well tapped down. If she's still worried about Kyle, she doesn't show it.

"Is that what we are? Acquaintances?" She asks. Except, she's not joking around, she's serious.

"I don't know. What would you want us to be?" I can't

help the suggestive tone in my voice, nor can I pretend like I haven't thought about what her lips taste like. Or how it would feel to have her long hair wrapped around my fist...

"Friends?" She asks simply, her eyes wide and hopeful.

"What would it take to be your friend, Sunshine?" I'm not selfish, I can be friends. Being a friend is safe when this town is temporary for me.

"Well, I guess all my friends know my name." She shrugs, popping in her headphones. She takes off running down the street before I can utter another word. I have to faintly remind myself that friends shouldn't stare at their friends' asses while they run, no matter how good they look in those tight pants.

I have all of the intelligence necessary on my work computer to track down her information. I could look up her address, type in her license plate, and probably even conduct a quick Google search, but where is the fun in that?

She wants to play a game. I'll play.

Hanging around her long enough to figure out her name seems simple enough. The slight distraction from this undercover case might be the only thing that will get me through it.

Chapter Ten

Thea

Was I flirting? Was he? That felt like flirting but it's been so long since I've felt comfortable enough to openly talk to a man I'm attracted to, let alone flirt.

I crave so badly to be wanted by him, and even though I know it would never work, I selfishly want to try. It doesn't matter how many years of therapy I've gone through, somehow all of my invisible wounds won't go away.

When I first saw his truck parked outside of my house this morning, I was terrified. I panicked thinking it might be Kyle because I didn't recognize it. I was glued to my window, peering out at the faded blue truck until my eyes dried out from not blinking.

It wasn't until I was on my porch that I recognized the sleeping form in the driver's seat and ease washed over me. Despite barely knowing him, I felt comfortable enough to walk up to his window and ask him why he was in front of my house.

That's unusual for me. I'm an avoider and I don't confront people. Especially not men. I'm getting too complacent around him already. My sprouting feelings are clouding the judgment skills I've curated over the last few years.

I need to tell him the truth before things go any further. The last thing I want is for him to think I'm leading him on. I told him I wanted to be friends, that seems specific enough, but I can't deny how incredibly drawn to him I am. How I melt whenever he even looks in my direction. Or, how my neurons fire a million miles a minute when he speaks to me.

I want him so badly I could cry but it doesn't matter. I will never trick someone into pursuing me, knowing that I can never give them a normal relationship. I'll never put myself in a situation where my significant other feels misled. Never again.

I push myself to run faster. Punishing myself for daring to dream that I could have him. By the time I reach my halfway point, tears are streaming down my face. I look into the trees that sit at the edge of town a few miles from my house and scream into the depths of the forest.

"It's not fair! My life was taken from me! IT'S NOT FAIR!" I scream until my throat burns.

Luckily it's early, and there's never anyone around this area when I'm on my run. There's no one to subject my crazy to this fine morning.

By the time I complete the miles back to my house, I feel relatively put back together. My runner's high doesn't give me euphoria, it simply pulls me from the depth of my depression and lets me pretend to feel somewhat normal. Plus, the early morning sun supplies a healthy dose of vitamin D, so that helps.

Trudging up my porch steps, I admire the view since that's all I'll ever have. Jay's muscled backside is facing me as he messes with my door. It's so domestic, so normal.

"Hey," I say a little breathlessly from my run.

"I'm almost done." He spends a few more seconds tightening a screw before turning around, holding my new key, and flashing his killer smile. It makes me breathless for other reasons.

"For me? You shouldn't have." I laugh as I grab the key from him, careful to only touch the brass. "Thank you. Really."

"No worries, Sunshine." He winks. Friends don't wink. Or at least they shouldn't when they're as attractive as he is.

"Why do you keep calling me that?"

"You won't tell me your name." He shrugs.

"You called me that before you ever asked my name..." I folded my arms across my chest, aiming for a serious stance. "Tell me."

"I guess that will be my little secret until you tell me your real name," he counters. Touché.

"Guess we'll both be disappointed then." I shrug, feigning indifference.

"Yeah. I guess we will." He tilts his head, smiling at me with that lopsided grin that's driving me crazy. He makes my head spin.

"I need to shower and leave in time to run to the store before my shift so..." I shuffle from foot to foot. "I guess I'll see you around?"

"Do you want to?" He folds his arms across his chest, looking at me pointedly. It's too much, my heart is racing out of my chest.

He has no idea what he's doing to me, or how overwhelmed I am with each interaction. This is probably just another day for him and I am having a mental crisis. I want him to like me, but I don't. I can't.

I still haven't answered him and the warmth is creeping up my chest. My workout tank is not going to hide my nerves and I desperately wish I had something to hide behind. A sweatshirt, anything.

"I'm sorry. You don't need to answer that," he cuts through my racing thoughts, saving me from my inner turmoil.

"No, I'm sorry. My brain is scattered. I appreciate all you've done for me and showing up to do this." I gesture to the door. "I'm not sure if I have cash."

"Don't worry about it."

"That's not my style. I will worry." I laugh at myself but he doesn't.

"You need me to swing by the store for you? So you aren't late for work?" The question surprises me, just as much as every other thoughtful thing he's said and offered to do.

"Um no. Thank you though. I need to um... Replace all of my underwear... So..." I stammer, feeling too awkward to even look him in the eye while I explain my panty dilemma.

"Ah." That single-syllable response... It makes me want to burst.

"I felt gross even touching them to throw them away. I couldn't stomach washing them and then putting them back on and pretending like nothing happened. So, everything he touched went into the trash. Now, I'm pantyless," I blab, immediately regretting it.

Especially when he glances for a microsecond at the bottom half of my body. Oh my God. I just admitted to going commando.

"I'm sorry. That was too much information. I've gotta go." I bound past him, trying to get inside before blabbing any more dirty secrets. I slam the door without looking back and sink to the floor. What is wrong with me?

* * *

Halfway through my shift, I can't stop thinking about him. I can't believe he went out of his way to fix my door for me. He slept in front of my house because he was worried... It blows my mind.

How am I supposed to pretend that I don't like him if he keeps doing thoughtful things?

Would it be the worst thing in the world for me to keep seeing him? Selfishly, yes. I could only ever be friends with him, but being around him in any capacity would be better than nothing. Right?

The thoughts in my mind are all-consuming as I power through my tasks. I'm positive that I mixed up books when I was re-shelving returns, but I was too spaced out to recall where I put them.

Should I reach out to him? I saved his number. Maybe talking to him more will ease the other possibilities in my head. I'll keep it friendly. If he ghosts me then it will confirm that I am delusional and should never have had a crush on him in the first place.

Me: Thank you again for getting the new lock. I'll sleep better tonight knowing Kyle can't get in.

Jay: No problem, Sunshine. I want you to feel safe.

Okay, I should not have texted him. It only made the knot in my stomach worse. I know that I've read too many historical romances because every time he uses that nickname, I feel like a mid-century woman about to swoon.

I don't know what else to say so I pocket my phone and promise myself I'll ignore it until I get home. I need to focus on work.

"What happened with the dream boat?" Latisha asks me before she leaves for the day. She's been dying to all day and I've been avoiding her.

"He rode home with me and made sure Kyle wasn't there. That's all." I shrug and she huffs.

"You should have thanked him with dinner," she remarks on her way out the doors with a wink.

I purposefully didn't tell her about this morning. That would only make her harass me more. I love her, but I'm glad to be solo for the next few hours. It's too hard to explain all of my complexities with dating, even to someone like her whom I trust.

The closing shift has never bothered me. I like the quiet of the late evening hours and I tend to get a lot of work done.

Once the doors close at seven, I linger, stocking the shelves with new books we've gotten while music plays on my phone. Lit only by the random emergency lights on the ceiling that never turn off. It's peaceful and productive.

Latisha doesn't mind as long as I don't stay too late, for my safety. She doesn't want me to get mugged in the parking lot.

I'm loading a cart up with a bunch of new books when I hear a *tap, tap, tap*. My whole body pauses what I'm doing, unsure of where it came from. When I hear it again, *tap, tap, tap*, my head whips in the direction of the sound.

The doors closest to where I'm standing are darkened, but I recognize the grin staring back at me immediately.

Jay.

I jog over to the doors, unlatching them to let him inside, unable to contain my smile at seeing him unexpectedly.

"You know, you really shouldn't open these doors for strangers," he smirks, slinking past me.

"I thought we were friends?"

"Nope, only acquaintances until I know your name," he counters, making me roll my eyes.

"What are you doing here?" I re-lock the doors behind him, trying not to be blatant with my excitement to see him.

"I like libraries." He shrugs.

"It's not Tuesday or Thursday… And, we're closed," I point out.

"Ahh. Keeping tabs on me, are you?" He smirks, making my blood rush to my cheeks.

I just admitted to stalking him, again. I blink hard before I respond, needing to gather my thoughts before outing myself on any other obsessive behavior.

"So, what are you doing here? Since the library closed an hour ago," he inquires before I can come up with any type of articulate response to the last question.

"I'm getting caught up on some work while it's quiet… Your turn," I counter.

"I… Honestly, I don't have a good excuse. I drove by your house to make sure you got home safe, but you weren't there. So, I tried here," he confesses. He just admitted that he was specifically out looking for me… Do friends do that?

"Why?"

"I don't know, Sunshine. I can't seem to leave you alone," he admits, casually. He doesn't even glance up from the book that he's flipping through the pages of.

"Don't say that," I plead under my breath, but he hears it.

"Why?"

"Because I like it too much." My cheeks are warm with my confession and he studies them closely.

The silence is deafening though and I feel like he can hear my heartbeat. He sets the book down, eliminating the only buffer between us and it fills me with fearful anticipation. So much so that I thwart whatever this moment might be before it escalates.

"Jay. I need to tell you something." I take a deep breath, preparing myself to rip the band-aid off and to make sure he's clear of my intentions.

"What's wrong?" His concern for me is never wavering, it makes my heart ache, desperate to earn more of his affection.

"Nothing is wrong, per se, but I need to make sure you know the truth about something…" I'm nervous, my hands won't stop fidgeting and he notices, patiently waiting for me to tell him.

"I can't be in a relationship." There, band-aid ripped. Kind of.

"Ah." That damn syllable again. Except this time it makes me doubt if I was right about him being interested in me at all.

"I'm not saying that you wanted a relationship. With me." I indicate to myself dramatically as if I'm not the one speaking. "But, if you did then I need to make sure you know that I can't do it. I don't want to mislead you. I don't want you to think that I'm a tease if I flirt with you but don't sleep with you. I mean I like flirting with you, and I think you're incredibly good-looking, but I *cannot* be in a relationship," I ramble.

"Are you married?" He interrupts, looking toward my hand, checking for a ring. That's the last thing I expected him to ask.

"What? No."

"Why can't you do relationships, Sunshine?" He leans against the counter comfortably, as if I didn't just drop a major bomb on him. It feels like a nuclear bomb to me.

"It's complicated." *Majorly complicated.*

"Well, I'm a complicated guy. Try me."

I wring my hands together, not sure what to say or how to even begin explaining my issues. He seems so genuine, it's on the tip of my tongue to spill my guts and tell him everything, but I've been burned in the past. I've trusted the wrong people and I've been hurt because of it.

Chapter Eleven

Jesse

"I can't," she utters, unable to look me in the eye.

I wait for the familiar sting of rejection, a feeling that I came to learn incredibly early in life. A feeling that I came to expect after years of bouncing from caregiver to caregiver, from group homes to foster homes. A feeling that I've done my best to avoid in my adult life.

I never cared where the military sent me so I couldn't be disappointed. Applying for any and all special units so it never mattered if I got accepted for one over the other. I don't get my hopes up for anything.

It only hits me at this moment that I've already broken my own rule. I started looking forward to something. I've looked forward to seeing her again, every day, since noticing her in the bar.

I've gone out of my way to keep her safe and to see her smile. I've already become addicted to the way she blushes when I compliment her and the way that her cheeks redden when she says too much, or can't seem to say anything at all.

I'm personally invested in the state of her underwear drawer and have the strongest desire to kick her contractor's ass. This isn't the game I thought it was this morning. This feels like more.

I don't do relationships. I never have. Committing to someone only to be let down never seemed like a risk worth taking. I'm not meant to stay in this town and I was never meant to meet her. So, why am I disappointed by what she's telling me?

Instead of feeling the deep ache I've associated with losing out on something I've been longing for, I'm concerned. My feelings don't matter at all, not when I need to know where this conversation is coming from. I need to know because she looks so... Sad? Scared?

"You can't, or you won't?" I ask, needing a clue of what's going on inside her head.

"Please, Jay. I can't talk about it." It's hardly noticeable, but I see her bottom lip trembling and it guts me. That, plus the use of my fake name, and I feel like the biggest bastard on the planet. I have no right to keep showing up in her life like this.

I have no right to ask her about her or her personal business. I haven't even been honest about who I am. How can I expect anything from her? I can't.

"It's okay. We don't have to talk about it. Where do you need these?" I push the cart forward an inch, hoping distraction will get me out of the hole I've dug for myself.

"You're not mad at me?" Right then, with those big eyes staring at me from under her ridiculously dainty glasses, I realize she was waiting on the same sting of rejection that I was. She was fully expecting to be let down by whatever my reaction was.

"I could *never* be mad at you, Sunshine," I say with the utmost sincerity. "Besides, we're friends right?"

She smiles and I swear she releases the breath she was holding in relief. "Yeah, friends." She motions me where to go with the cart and I follow, fully aware of how much trouble I'm in.

If she needs a friend, I'll be her friend, even if it feels like torture. Being so close, but not being able to have her... I need to finish this job and get the hell out of this state. So, why does that sound even worse?

I start stacking books on the shelf automatically when we reach our destination in the back aisle of the Children's section. I'm reworking the turmoil in my head over and over trying to come up with a solution to stop all of this from blowing up in my face.

The simplest solution is to walk away from her. It's the only way to stop her from hating me when I inevitably leave, but I don't want to leave her alone. I like being around her.

"How do you know where to put those?" She asks curiously from the other side of the cart.

"Huh?" I was on autopilot and not paying attention "I was just checking the spines."

"You know the Dewey Decimal System?" The astonishment in her voice is clear as day and I'm amused by it. I guess I cracked the code to impress a librarian.

"I spent a lot of time in libraries as a kid."

"Me too. That's why I became a librarian. My local library was my safe haven after my dad died." Her confession hits closer to home than I ever would've expected.

"I'm sorry, about your dad," I tell her sincerely.

There's an aching in my chest wanting to tell her how much I relate to her, but I can't. I'm already in this too deep, trying to connect more than I already have is selfish even though

I'm desperate for it.

"It's okay, it was a long time ago. He had cancer," she explains. "My mom had a hard time dealing with it. Sometimes it felt too suffocating to be at home. My brother left and was gone for years. I was pretty lonely."

Even though she looks okay after telling me that, I have to physically fight the urge to hug her. I move farther down the aisle to use the space as a barrier. Friends can hug, but I know once I have her in my arms it won't be enough.

I should leave. I need to leave.

At the same time, I want to confess how painfully alone I've been my entire life. I want her to know that she's not alone now in how she feels.

It's like the words are climbing up my throat, dying to come out. I've never felt so inclined to share my past with anyone. I shouldn't share it with her. I can't open up to someone who doesn't even know my real name.

"I would go to the library after school to do my homework, to avoid going to my group home," I utter the words before I can stop them and my breath catches, waiting for her response. I've never told anyone that.

"Group home?" She asks, sadly.

"Yeah. I needed to use the computers for my homework and it's where I did all of my research about the Army." I add, attempting to steer the conversation away from my misfortune.

"Why the Army?" She asks subtly, picking up on my queue to change the topic.

"Eh, I don't know. Long story short, it worked out the best at the time."

She nods in understanding. She's so easy to talk to that I'm afraid to spill something that I'm not supposed to. I need to say goodbye.

"Why kids?" I ask, changing the subject to her instead of leaving. I'm an idiot but the curiosity is eating me alive about the girl I'm undoubtedly interested in. The girl I shouldn't be getting attached to.

"Kids are fun. They're innocent, ya know? They don't have the weight of the world on their shoulders yet, and if they do then I try to help them escape a little bit with the stories." She snorts. "Sorry, that was kind of cheesy."

"No, not at all," I reassure her, hiding the solemnness in my voice even though my throat suddenly feels thick. "It's great what you're doing for them."

It's so impactful to have someone like her for the kids that she's describing, the kids who were like me. I want to tell her that, but I don't.

I've already pushed the limits too far and shared too much about my real self. I'm digging my hole deeper when I need to figure a way out.

"Well, that's all of them. Thanks for helping me." She pushes the cart toward a doorway that must lead to a storage room of some sort.

Lined on the wall next to it are framed photos of all the employees of the New Hope Library. One in particular of a beautiful familiar face with blonde hair and bright blue eyes. She goes through the door, not realizing what I'm staring at.

Gotcha, Sunshine.

I stand closer to her picture, examining every little feature on her face. The way her lips curve into her signature smile and how her long dark lashes highlight her eyes. Without her glasses in this picture, there's nothing for her to hide behind.

The brightness radiates from her and my chest aches painfully. She's so pretty it physically hurts, especially because I know she's unobtainable. She's far out of my reach and it's torturous.

Below her picture is a little placard, highlighting her achievements and her schooling. At the very bottom is what I was looking for: **Thea Wolfe, Children's Librarian.**

My entire reality comes screeching to a halt. Thea Wolfe?

Thea Wolfe... There's no way.

I glance at her picture again, hoping that I'll see it in a new light and it will tell me what I'm thinking is wrong. This isn't the same Thea Wolfe who would be my best friend's sister... Right?

He lives less than an hour from here, but that could be a coincidence...

I've never seen a photo of her, aside from a childhood picture he kept in his locker for years. Neither of us ever had social media and I only ever met his mom... His mom is blonde...

My brother left and was gone for years. When she said that I assumed she meant her brother took off to sow his wild oats, not that he enlisted and ended up in the same Special Ops unit as me. Fuck.

"I'm ready." She comes walking out of that back room with her purse over her shoulder, unknowingly into the shit storm I just found myself in.

How do I ask her if she is who I think she is without revealing that I'm a total ass and lying to her about who I am?

Is Nathan going to kill me?

I need time to think. I can't solve any of my problems right now, not without making things worse. "Do you want me to follow you home? Make sure the coast is clear?"

I'm losing my mind with what I just discovered but I'm not a complete dick. It's late and it only seems logical to make sure she gets home safe after what happened with Kyle yesterday.

"Do you think that's necessary?"

I detect a small dose of fear in her voice, making me feel like an asshole. All I do is shrug, not trusting whatever bullshit might spew from my mouth.

"Okay, yeah. I guess I wouldn't mind if you don't care." I follow her out, waiting while she locks both sets of doors as we exit the library into the parking lot. She eyes me once or twice seeming confused at my shift in behavior, but I ignore her glances, trying to keep it together a little longer.

"Oh, let me pay you for the lock. I have cash, now." She starts digging in her purse as we reach our cars.

"No, don't worry about it. It's on me." *It's the least I can do.*

"What? No, here." She tries to hand me a twenty but I refuse it.

"It's for your bathroom. Keep it."

"Yeah, it's going to be a while before the demo room can be considered a bathroom." She sighs, rolling her eyes, but stuffs the bill back in her purse.

"I could fix it up for you. I'm not a professional or anything, but I've worked in construction, some," I offer without thinking.

Why the hell did I just do that?

I was forced to help a foster family build a Habitat for Humanity home one time, I'm not some handyman. I can get by, but it's not really my skill set and I should be staying away from her…

"Oh no. I couldn't ask you to do that. You've already done enough for me. You're way more generous than most people I've encountered in my life." She laughs, and it's like a punch to the gut.

Yeah. I'm going to hell.

I'll make sure she gets home safe. That's it. Then I'll fact-check her name and confirm that this is all a big coincidence and she isn't Nathan's sister.

It only takes a few minutes to get to her house since she doesn't live far from the library. I leave my truck idling on the curb but hop out.

"Did you want to come inside?" She asks me curiously once she realizes that I'm following her up her sidewalk.

Yes. Yes. Yes. "No, I was just walking you to your door. I have to go meet up with some people."

"Oh, yeah. Of course. I forget that some people aren't in bed by 9 pm every night." She laughs, shyly, avoiding my gaze.

"Did you want me to come inside, Sunshine?" The words come out and I can't stop the step that I take toward her.

Her eyes widen in surprise and it only fuels me. She's so tentative about me coming into her space that I should be ashamed of myself, but I love the way she blushes when I tease her. All of my logic spirals out of control.

"I, uh. Yes. I mean no." She stumbles over her words and backs up her porch steps slowly. I don't pursue her, only because I know that I shouldn't.

If it is true, if she is Nathan's sister, I'm screwed. Not only would I be lying to the one person I've had a genuine interest in for the first time in my life, but I'd also be lying to my best friend's sister.

She'll never trust me again and neither will he if I'm sneaking around behind his back with her. I don't deserve their trust. How did I let this happen?

"Is everything okay?" She asks from the top of her porch steps when I don't say anything.

"Yeah. Everything is great. I have to go. Have a good night, Thea." I walk away from her, mentally preparing myself for this to be a permanent goodbye.

I should have looked into her as soon as I saw her that night at the bar. If I had been more adamant about figuring out who she was then I could have avoided this regret churning my gut.

I'm not surprised that I screwed this up. I don't deserve to have good things in my life. That's been proven time and time again. Every time there is a semblance of hope, something comes along and crushes my spirit. Except this time it's all on me. I did this to myself.

Chapter Twelve

Thea

I don't know what makes me do it, desperation, loneliness, or sadness, but I text Jay before I leave my house for the bar Saturday night.

It's an impulsive bid letting him know that I'll be working in case he wants to stop by for a drink. It seems innocent enough, but I promise myself that it will be my only attempt to reach out.

I haven't heard from him since he walked me to my door after work on Wednesday night. He was gone before I had a chance to say goodbye or react to the use of my real name. The sudden loss of my nickname felt like a chapter had been closed.

The small dose of optimism I felt when he called me Sunshine made me feel normal again. Now more than ever it feels like reality has come crashing back in and I am back to my usual routine of loneliness.

I'm bitter because I selfishly wanted more time with him but if he doesn't want to be around me or be my friend, then I won't beg.

Maybe it's because I really had my hopes up that he was

different, or because I really liked him, but this feeling hurts worse than it ever has before. The broken parts of me feel amplified by a thousand.

My phone dings as I'm parking behind the bar and my heart beats rapidly for the seconds it takes to retrieve my phone. Then instantly sinks when I see that the text isn't from Jay, but from Kyle.

Kyle: $500 more and I'll finish your bathroom. I need the money.

Me: I'm sorry. Not interested.

Kyle: Thanks a lot bitch.

My jaw goes slack when I read that message. I do the only thing I know to do and block his number. I'm not going back and forth with him over text, especially when he's so disrespectful.

My shift flies by for the most part and I don't have time to think about my problems. Mostly. I do catch myself watching the door every time a guy over six feet walks in, hoping that it's Jay and praying that it's not Kyle.

By the time midnight rolls around, the band is winding down and the end is in sight, but the bar is still packed. The jukebox will kick on soon and start playing slow songs, encouraging people to make their exit. All I can do is count down the minutes until I can start closing tabs then get home and crawl into bed.

I've been spending more time than normal in bed lately. First the situation with Kyle, and now Jay, has made me feel annoyingly sorry for myself.

Feeling sorry for myself then morphed into other feelings like anger and denial. I've spent plenty of time the last few days scolding myself for believing things could be different for me. I'm angry that I let myself be vulnerable for the first time in years, only to be rejected.

"Hey, pretty lady." A drunk guy sitting on the side of the bar calls to me. I cringe internally knowing this guy is too drunk to be served and is about to ask for another beer. "Your cheapest whiskey. No ice."

Great. Even worse. He wants liquor and that is not happening. "Sorry, sir. No more drinks tonight, but I can close your tab."

He looks at me, blinking slowly like he's trying to unscramble the words I just said. "No, I want whiskey."

"Sorry, no can do," I say with my cheeriest customer service voice. Probably sounds as fake as I feel. I turn back toward the other customers, needing to break the tension that his stare is creating.

I don't expect to see Jay and his friends from that first night sitting in the vacated seats at the front of the bar. It throws me and I have to take a second to get the words out of my mouth.

"What can I get you guys? Cash up front, it's too late to open a tab." I glance at Jay, hoping I'll get to see him flash his crooked grin, but he's not even looking at me. His focus is on the TV mounted above the shelves of liquor.

His friends order, throwing their cash in a pile on the bar top. "For you?" I ask after I've handed the other drinks off and he still hasn't spoken up. He checks over his shoulder, watching his friends walk over to the dart board.

"O'Doul's, please. In a glass." His voice gives no hint of the friendliness that I'm used to. It's a slap to the face.

"O'Doul's doesn't have alcohol," I snap.

"I know." He watches me under the brim of his faded

baseball hat, not giving anything away. I nod my head stiffly and pour his beer into a glass, sliding it across the counter to him.

"$4.00." My tone gives the same amount of effort as his. None.

He throws a twenty-dollar bill on the bar and grabs his beer before walking away. "Keep it."

I'd normally feel flattered to receive such a big tip, but after being given the cold shoulder, I'm insulted. Am I some sort of charity case? Is that why he was being nice to me in the beginning?

Did he feel sorry for me?

He's acting like he doesn't even know who I am and it's humiliating.

I'm wiping down the bar aggressively, thankful that most of the other customers are leaving when I miss the hand coming my way.

"I said, I wanted a whiskey." The drunk guy grabs my wrist with what feels like all of his strength, locking his grip on me.

I only have a second to feel the biting pain before my body locks up and full-blown fear sets in. This can't happen, not here. No. No. NO!

It's too late and I realize I've screamed the word 'no' out loud. Heads turn my way as my vision starts to blur. Like a trapped animal, I tug desperately at my wrist, trying to free it. It doesn't budge. This can't happen. Not again.

My heart's pounding in my chest, feeling dangerously close to exploding. "Let me go. Let me go. Let me go," I chant over and over again between ragged breaths.

The air is heaving in and out of my lungs so violently that my throat is on fire.

My eardrums ring, drowning out the noise of the rest of the bar.

Like an out-of-body experience, I see my panic attack escalating as if I were watching from one of the bar stools.

I'm so familiar with my routine that I see it in my sleep. I've experienced it multiple times in my dreams, reliving old nightmares. Despite the familiarity, it wrecks me every time.

Strobe lights are flashing in front of my eyes and I know that I'm close to passing out when the black speckles outweigh the light. It's usually the final stage before I collapse.

My eyes will roll back in my head and I'll slump to the floor. All I can hope is that I won't hit my head on the way down.

The lights are blurring and everything around me is fading…

Right before my vision goes totally black, my wrist is freed.

On instinct, I'm stumbling away from the bar on rubber legs, trying to escape. I keep moving, hardly holding myself upright as I crash through the double doors that lead to the storage area in the back.

That's the last thing I remember before the room completely disappears.

Chapter Thirteen

Jesse

A quick Facebook search confirmed my suspicions. My Thea Wolfe is Nathan's sister, without a doubt. Only a few months ago she posted a photo with her mom for Mother's Day. His mom, whom I've met.

After my discovery, I spent hours studying every picture. Throwback photos to her childhood, quite a few of her and one other girl most likely from their early college days, and one of her standing in front of the New Hope library with her hands raised up in celebration. She's so full of light in every single one.

My head aches with the weight of my guilt. How could I get involved with my best friend's little sister?

Nathan and I have watched each other's backs for years, we've taken turns saving each other's asses. I trust him with my life. He trusts me with his.

I don't know what to do. I don't want to stay away from her, but I can't keep lying to her face about who I am, especially since I can't stop thinking about her in all of the ways that I shouldn't. I can't keep this from my friend either.

I force myself to keep my distance for a few days, only

catching glimpses of her car when I drive past her house or the library. I still attended the support group on Thursday, but I waited until just before it started to go in through the side entrance and made sure the parking lot was clear before I left. It's pathetic.

I'm pathetic.

Avoiding her isn't fair and I feel like an ass, but I'm afraid if I'm around her I'll blurt out the truth. I'll confess that I've been lying about my name and why I'm in New Hope.

When Curtis calls me Friday night to tell me the shipment we've been waiting on is in, I welcome the distraction and dive back into the job.

We end up in a run-down warehouse in the middle of the night unloading boxes from giant wooden crates with eight other guys. The crates are loaded in the back of unmarked semi trucks, looking blatantly suspicious.

This is the type of illegal activity I've been searching for. This is what I need to distract me from Thea once and for all. My life is the job. That's it.

I keep my head down and keep a low profile. By the time we've unloaded everything into the warehouse, dawn's approaching and we're all whipped. If this was above board, you'd think someone would have had a fucking forklift to use.

"Jameson should be here soon, he'll pay us," Curtis tells me as he hops onto an old rusted table that I'm standing near. It creaks underneath his weight as he sits. Hopefully, the tetanus shot he got in basic training is doing its job.

"Who is Jameson?" I ask as casually as possible.

"He's the boss. He's cool man. He's like us." Like us? What does that mean?

"He's ex-military?" I assume.

"Yeah, and you should see it. He got blown up in Afghanistan like 20 years ago. He's got an eye patch and everything. Kind of bad ass." He laughs to himself.

"How do you know him?" I push it further, trying to get some information that I can run with, but hoping Curtis doesn't think I'm being too nosy.

"Derrick and Mitch are his cousins."

Ah, being family is a good way to get someone a part of your agenda. This could be it. This could be the link to the extremist group, I just need my in.

"It's been fun hangin' out with you guys," I lie, effortlessly. "I'm thinking about staying in town longer."

Curtis thinks I'm just a drifter. I hope the prospect of me staying will get him to open up more, and bring me into the loop.

"Good. We could use more guys around here." Bingo.

"What else do you do, besides move boxes?"

"Ehh. Just some odd jobs here and there, but the real fun is hanging out at Jameson's farm. The first time I got invited out there, I swear the party was going all night. It was great, man."

I don't mention that partying all night is the least fun thing I can imagine. Those days are long behind me. "Sounds like it. Let me know next time and I'll tag along."

"Yeah. That'd be cool, but you gotta meet Jameson first. He has to kind of approve of you before you can hang." He shrugs, not explaining further.

"I see." I feign indifference, hoping like hell I can figure out what's going down at the "farm."

"Look, here he comes."

I look up as a middle-aged guy limps through the warehouse. Curtis wasn't lying about the eye patch, but it's cheap and black like a pirate costume. Despite his handicaps, there's an air of authority around him.

"Good job gettin' everything unloaded, boys. I added an extra twenty for getting the job done in one night. The next one is due sometime next week. I'll keep ya posted." Everyone had gathered in a sloppy semi-circle when he walked in, nodding their heads as he spoke.

As each person moves down the line to receive their pay, a couple of them grab Jameson's hands to shake them, looking at him with awe.

Curtis jumps in front of me so he reaches Jameson first. "Let me introduce you. Just be cool." Alright, kid. I'll be cool. Whatever that fucking means.

"Jameson, thanks for letting me in on the job. I appreciate it." Curtis stutters nervously as he speaks. "Um, this is my good buddy, Jay. He's new in town and wanted to work, so I brought him out here. He's cool. He's one of us." Again with that phrase… One of us.

"Jay, huh?' Jameson turns to eye me up and down. No pun intended. "Where are you from, boy?" It takes everything in me not to roll my eyes at his condescending tone.

"Texas, sir." I hold my hand out to shake his. "Thanks for the work."

He nods his head, taking a moment to make a decision about me. I must've passed, because he finally grabs my hand to shake it, offering my pay from his other hand.

"Just stick with Curtis here and we'll keep you workin'."

"Thank you, I appreciate it." We make our exit, allowing the few guys behind us to approach Jameson. Dawn illuminates the sky as we walk through the parking lot.

"That was good, man. Really good. He liked you." Curtis' excited chatter barely hits my ears as I make a mental note of all I learned about Jameson, how he looks, and how people treat him. This has to be our group leader.

"Let's celebrate. Drinks at Sunny's later!" He points at me as he walks away, "Maybe we'll get to see that hot bartender again."

All I do is laugh and wave, while actively dying inside thinking about Thea and everything that I've screwed up with her.

I know it's a bad idea, but I'm aching to see her again. I should be thrilled that I'm making progress on this under-cover case, but I honestly couldn't care less. For the first time in life, work only feels like… work.

The army has always been my life. Being in the Special Forces felt like my calling until it didn't. Transferring to Criminal Investigations seemed like an incredible opportu-nity. Now, it feels like any other job.

Thea draws me in on a level that I've never experienced before.

She opened up to me about her life and I let her. She's going to hate me when she finds out that I'm a fraud, all because of my fucking alter ego.

I'm going to tell her the truth. I need to. Just not yet. I'll get through this op. I'll keep my distance until the investigation is over, then I'll plead for her to understand why I did it.

I'll have to worry about Nathan killing me later.

* * *

I'm dragging my feet by the time I get to the bar. While Curtis slept all day, energizing up for a Saturday night drinking, I was on the phone with my command, doing research, and writing reports. My head is pounding, begging me to get some sleep, but I try to push through.

The moment my feet enter through the doors, I see her long blonde hair. It's straight again and her glasses are long gone.

It's so clear to me now how fake the persona she's putting on is. I prefer the authentic version, but she's breathtaking either way. Curtis waves me over to the bar, making me groan.

I don't want Curtis, Derrick, and Mitch to know how familiar I am with Thea, or how interested I am in her. I don't want them to even look in her direction. If they are involved with Jameson's extremist group, I don't want her on their radar when shit hits the fan.

The group of investigators I work with confirmed that Jameson, Thomas Jameson, was dishonorably discharged from the military. He was never in Afghanistan and never injured in combat. He fell off a tank during a training exercise and broke his femur then got addicted to Oxycontin.

They kicked him out after he got high and broke into a sergeant's house on base. He crawled into bed with his wife but was too out of his mind to realize the sergeant was also in the bed. He got the shit beat out of him.

As far as they are aware, there is no documented injury to his eye. I suspect the eye patch is all for show since playing on people's sympathy will help his cause.

I can't wait to break the news to Curtis that the badass Jameson is a phony, but not tonight. Tonight I have to pretend to be enjoying these losers' company. I have to ignore Thea even though it kills me and I have got to get some sleep at some point.

"For you?" Her sweet voice breaks into my internal struggle and I have to tear my eyes from the TV that I'm staring blankly at.

It takes every ounce of energy that I have left to maintain my neutrality towards her. I focus on the hurt I see in her eyes, letting it eat at me. Accepting that I'm a terrible person who doesn't deserve to breathe the same air as her.

It keeps me from being able to form a smile, but I'm not sure if it can erase the longing written all over my face.

She's too good for me. Too good to be lied to. The light that radiates from her shouldn't be dimmed by my dumb ass. All because I can't stay away from her when I should stay the hell away from her.

This self-loathing is putting me in a dark place. I don't know how much longer I can do this.

By the time I get back to the group playing darts, I don't have the energy to fake wanting to be here. I stand off to the side, nursing my non-alcoholic beer, and hoping that my splitting headache will subside on its own eventually.

Her voice reaches me first. Then the panic. I look over my shoulder, sighting in on some guy locked onto Thea's wrist.

My blood runs cold but it's fleeting as I'm consumed by rage.

Without hesitation, I'm barreling across the room and knocking past everyone that's in my way trying to get to her. I don't have time to care how my reaction might affect my undercover persona. Nothing changes the reality. No one gets to hurt her. To touch her. To scare her.

I register the ghostly paleness of her face before throwing a fist at the old man holding her against her will. The crack of my knuckles hitting his jaw is like a record scratch. The whole bar goes silent, staring as he falls to the ground. He's a big guy and when he hits the floor it rattles all the glasses sitting on the bar nearby.

I grab him by the collar of his shirt, forcing his face up. "Don't ever touch her again!"

Chapter Fourteen

Thea

I only need to clear this last table and then I can get back to my apartment and study. I'm exhausted but the semester is almost over and I'm close to getting a break for the summer. Working and going to school is draining but it's necessary.

I shift my catering cart around the scattered chairs, trying to get through the chaos of this ballroom. The wedding has been in full swing for hours and all the guests are inebriated. It's fine when they ignore the wait staff, but a few of the groomsmen have been eyeing me all night, making my neck prickle.

I feel like I'm being stalked by a pack of rabid hyenas. When one of them breaks from the pack, stalking toward me, my back stiffens. Please, no.

"Hey little lady, wanna dance?" He slurs in my direction.

"No thank you, I'm working." I keep stacking glasses on my cart, trying to ignore him.

"Well, work your way over here." He gives me his best 'come hither' look, but it falls flat because he's so drunk.

"Uh, no. No thanks." My voice is trembling now. Whenever my first refusal is denied, my nerves start climbing. Nothing good ever comes next.

"Don't be a waste of ass." He stomps around my cart, grabbing my forearm roughly. "Dance with me."

That's all it takes for my breath to whoosh out of me, my body reacting to the unwelcome touch. Despite my sudden tunnel vision, I watch his eyebrows scrunch up, looking at me like I've grown two heads.

My head starts swimming and the room goes black before I can attempt to care about his opinion of me.

When I blink awake and out of the darkness, my manager is standing over me, glaring with disapproval. All I can do is curl into a ball and cry.

"Call Liv. Please, just call Liv," I plead to whoever will listen.

She's the only one who knows what's wrong with me. The only one who doesn't treat me like damaged goods.

* * *

"There she is."

My conscious mind slowly starts picking up on the world around me as I blink my eyes open. Daya, the other bartender, is squatting down in front of me, brushing the hair out of my face.

"Hey, sweetie. You okay?" She asks, her blue eye shadow drawing my attention.

She's older than me, probably closer to forty, and looks like she belongs on the back of someone's Harley. Or, should be driving her own. She's sweet though and has been welcoming since my very first shift.

"Yeah. I'm okay."

She helps me stand. "It looks like you fainted. Are you going to be okay to get home?"

"Oh, I'll be fine, it's happened before. I've just had a long day and didn't eat much," I lie. "I guess I panicked when that guy grabbed me and overdid it."

"Well, I'm sorry I didn't stop him myself, that bastard is gone for life. Sunny doesn't stand for people grabbin' us like that, but I convinced him not to ban your boyfriend." She pats my arm as we walk past the empty kegs and toward the backdoor.

"My boyfriend?" Everything aside from panicking and fainting is a blur.

"Yeah, he laid it on Russ. Whooped him real good for grabbin' you. It was pretty hot actually."

I'm still confused, her words aren't quite clicking in my brain.

"Oh, there he is, he's waiting by your car."

I look up, relieved to see Jay leaning against my driver's side door. Then the earlier part of the night comes rushing back in.

"Thanks, Daya, for checking on me. I'll be okay." I hug her, glad that I've never had any trouble receiving touch from women. My problem has only ever been with men. An issue that has haunted me for more than half a decade.

She closes the back door behind me, leaving me and Jay by ourselves in the back lot. I walk toward him but stop a comfortable distance away. I still need space. My panic attack wasn't caused by him, but the wound is still fresh, and my rejection is still raw from earlier.

"Are you okay?" His hands are shoved into his pockets but his eyes are assessing every inch of me from under the brim of his hat.

"I'm fine." Says every woman ever who isn't fine.

"Did he hurt you?" He asks through gritted teeth as if it pains him to even think about it.

"No. I don't know." I examine my wrist, not paying attention to it up until this point. It's tender, but I know it's not broken. I'm sure I'll have a bruise tomorrow. I rotate it, examining my skin in the streetlight, but not being able to see if the coloring has already started to change.

"You need to ice it."

"Is that what I need? Thanks." I can't hide my annoyance at his sudden concern after ignoring me earlier.

"You need to stop working at this damn bar," he practically growls.

"I need the money."

"I need you to be safe." He rubs his hand through his hair, looking exasperated with me. Or himself? It's hard to tell.

"Why? You hardly know me." *You've been radio silent for days.* I want to add, but don't.

"I want to, Sunshine," he admits almost painfully.

"Well. We don't always get what we want," I reply harshly.

"Thea. I'm sorry."

I still don't even know when he learned my real name, but somehow it stings every time he uses it.

"For what?"

"Everything. I can't explain all of it right now, but I need you to know that I'm not intentionally trying to hurt you."

"You acted like I was a stranger in there." I throw my hand out, waving at the bar.

"I know and I'm sorry. It killed me to do it, but I can't tell you why." He folds over, bracing his hands on his knees before sinking to the gravel. He squeezes his eyes shut, pain crossing his features. I hear a grumbled "fuck," as he rubs his head.

"Are you okay?" Despite my confusion and hurt over his absence the last few days, I can't deny that I care. I can tell something isn't right. He looks like he's falling apart.

"Does your brother know that you work at this bar?"

My brother? Where the hell did that come from?

"No, he doesn't know. Why?" He doesn't respond, he just closes his eyes again and shakes his head before standing up and dusting his pants off. "Jay? What is going on?"

"Please, don't call me that." It's all he says before he walks away, not looking back or giving me a chance to register what the hell just happened.

"Call you what?" I shout at his retreating back.

* * *

Sundays are always one of my off days. The library is closed to the public, so it doesn't usually bother me to stay at the bar late on Saturday nights because I know I can sleep in. Yet, for some reason, I wake up just after seven and can't fall back asleep. My mind is racing still trying to make sense of what happened last night.

I'm so mad at Jay for how he treated me, but somehow I made it through the entire confrontation with him without shrinking away. I'm not afraid of him like I am with others.

Am I stronger than I thought? Or, is he just an outlier?

My wrist is throbbing as I pull on my favorite green athletic leggings and matching sports bra, needing the distraction that my runs normally bring. I've been running since the first attack happened. The one that changed my life forever.

My therapist suggested it as a coping mechanism to feel more in control of my physical body. It didn't fix me, but the habit became a hobby, and now I average about four miles a day if I can.

I drag myself outside and sit down on the porch steps to put my shoes on, needing the cool morning air to wake me up a little more, when I see the familiar faded blue truck and its sleeping occupant parked on the curb. The initial spark of joy is quickly replaced by confusion.

Before I can think better of it, I stomp down the sidewalk and bang on his passenger-side window. He startles, reaching to his waistband reflexively before noticing me. He takes a deep breath, wiping the sleep from his face.

It takes all my willpower to maintain my level of annoyance and not to feel guilty for scaring him. I also don't want to analyze how he almost pulled his gun on me.

He leans over, unlocking his passenger door so I can open it. And, I do, flinging it open wide. "Why are you here?"

"I couldn't sleep at the motel. I was too worried about you. I thought if I came here I could at least get a few hours of sleep knowing you were close by." He looks tired, dejected even. I don't understand the hot and cold behavior, I can't make sense of it.

"But… Why? I don't understand what's going on. Wanting to be near me one minute and then ignoring me another. Is it a game to you? Why are you doing this to me?"

"It's not a game. I promise. It's… complicated." He hangs his head, staring at his steering wheel like it will swallow him whole, and I hate how it makes me feel.

I want to comfort him, to help him through whatever is causing him so much turmoil, but I can't. For my peace of mind, I need to choose myself first.

"I want you to leave me alone. Don't come back here. Don't pretend to be my friend. I need you to leave," I say with as much strength as I can, feeling feeble on the inside. Especially when he looks at me with his sad eyes, I can't stop the moisture that gathers in my own.

I've never been a strong-willed person, I cry easily. I feel everything whether I want to or not. My therapist said I'm an empath. My best friend calls me sappy.

I hardly know Jay, but I feel like I know his emotions. Sadness, regret, helplessness. All emotions that have dictated my life. All I can do is give him a choice. Let his life be dictated by his reasons or make a new path. So, whether he deserves it or not, I give him one more chance, but on my terms.

"I'm going inside now. If you want to explain yourself, you can come in, but only if you give me the truth. If not, leave and don't come back." After closing his door, I turn, walking back up the sidewalk, up the steps, and onto the porch.

Taking a deep breath, I open my front door and walk through it before I check to see Jay's decision. He's still sitting in his truck, tapping his thumb on the top of the steering wheel.

Standing in the threshold of my home, it feels like a pivotal point in my life is taking place. Yet, I'm not the one in control of it. How did I let this happen?

How can he have so much significance in my life already?

My hand is on the door handle and about to push it closed,

shutting him out forever when I hear the heavy truck door creak open.

He moves slowly toward my house like he's dragging resistance behind him, not quite sure of his decision. Whatever the reason, I don't want him to regret this. I stand in the doorway, blocking his path, waiting for him to change his mind.

"Once you walk through this door. Only the truth," I remind him, stepping back to let him through if he chooses. I hold my breath until he does, my heart pounding against my rib cage.

Chapter Fifteen

Jesse

The first real choice I ever got to make in life was to join the Army, but from then on they made most of my choices for me. I got to throw my hat in the ring every once in a while, give preferences, and make small decisions, but for the most part, let the military control my life. It was easy, until now.

There have always been risks in my career. Judgment calls that I've needed to make. None of them amount to the risk that I'm taking now.

I have a responsibility to the United States to keep their secrets. I made an oath to obey and protect. That's why I'm here, in New Hope. So, how can I risk it? This operation, my career...

How can I risk a relationship with the only person who's ever been like a brother to me?

Walking through this door means potentially blowing up the only family I have. When Nathan finds out that I've been lying to his sister, or maybe worse, that I'm interested in his sister and lying to her at the same time, he's going to give his loyalty to his real family. Her.

So, why am I walking through this door?

I take one step then another past the threshold because I can't walk away from her. In my gut, I know it would be a mistake to walk away.

I'm risking everything to have more time with her. Even if she doesn't want to see me again and this blows up in my face, I'll know I made the right choice for me. The one that I wanted.

With the click of the front door closing, I let out the deep breath that I was holding in. My head tips back against the door and I grin. I made a choice for my own future and it feels fucking good.

"That's the first smile I've seen in days," Thea's gentle voice murmurs from across the room. She pulls a sweater on, wrapping her arms around herself, and bracing for whatever comes next.

I want so badly for it to be my arms wrapped around her, but it can wait. I need to earn her trust first.

"It's the first time that I've felt like smiling in days," I tell her truthfully. Making my way over to her sofa, I sit down on the dark green velvet. The chair she's sitting in is covered in flowers wrapped in green vines that nearly match the couch.

There's a thoughtful silence before I begin my not-well-thought-out speech. She's giving me space to start like she senses how hard this is for me. It is hard. This could change the rest of my life.

I hope it does.

"This isn't fair to ask, but I need everything that I say to stay in this room. You can't tell anyone what I'm about to tell you. No one."

"I won't," she whispers with furrowed brows, giving me her

blind faith. Something that I don't deserve.

"I'm not here passing through, I came to New Hope for a reason. I joined the support group at your library for a reason." I pause, needing to choose my words wisely. I want to give her as much of the truth as I can, but I need to keep some things close to my chest. Things that don't involve her.

"I'm not a veteran, I'm still on active duty. A Special Sergeant for the Army Criminal Investigations Unit." I stop, giving her a chance to absorb that information.

"Okay." She tucks her legs up to her chest in her seat, remaining silent. *Okay, so far, so good.*

"That first night in the bar, I panicked when I couldn't place how I knew you. I was afraid that you knew who I was and would blow up my investigation because I'm undercover." There it is, my first time outing myself during an operation. I hold my breath, waiting for her to react.

"You're undercover?" She asks like she doesn't believe me.

"That's why I can't tell you everything. It's a classified operation." This could all go bad if she thinks that I'm lying.

"A classified operation that involves you being in my library? My bar? Am I in danger? The kids? My coworkers?" She sputters with panic, clutching her sweater to her chest.

"No. No. It's just a coincidence. That's what I realized when I found you at the library," I assure her. "There are people that I've integrated myself with, where they go, I go. It's just footwork. The real target is... farther out of reach." It's hard to explain and be vague, so I shrug, hoping that she accepts my answer.

"Okay, I'll trust you."

I cringe internally at her use of that word because she's going to regret it in a minute.

"I didn't know who you were or who you are, rather. I couldn't stay away from you even though I'm on the job and I should stay the hell away from you," I admit, rubbing my hands across the scruff that I wish I could shave off. "I ignored you these past few days because I didn't know how to handle mixing my personal life with my undercover life. For that, I'm sorry. I hated every minute of it."

"Who I am?" She whispers with confusion.

"When I met up with you at the library after closing the other day, I saw your photo on the wall. Thea Wolfe."

"So?"

"Nathan Wolfe's younger sister," I explain with a small smile. One that I don't feel. I turn the small golden picture frame that's sitting on the side table between us.

I didn't notice it the other time I was here. Her, Nathan, and Callie, standing on the porch of the cabin I've been to a few times. Nathan's home. Her family.

"You know my brother," she states, finally understanding.

"Yeah. He's a friend." I watch her, waiting for her reaction. She looks confused, overwhelmed maybe, but I can't gauge what she's thinking.

"You're telling me the truth because you think Nathan will find out? And he'll be mad that you duped his sister?" When her eyes meet mine, I see the distrust and I know exactly what she's thinking. That I don't care about *her*.

"No. That's not it. I came in here because I don't want to lie to you. I know I've already screwed things up, but I don't want to hurt you." I rub my forehead for a moment, considering whether I should put my feelings out there this soon, but fuck it.

"I don't want to pretend like I don't know you and see the

hurt on your face. I don't want to leave town and pretend like I never knew you at all. I don't want to pretend like your smile isn't the only highlight of my day sometimes."

"Jay..." She tries to interrupt, but I keep going, needing to purge everything.

"I know you said you can't be in a relationship. Hell, I don't even know how to be in one, so I'm not asking for that. But, I can't keep lying to you. I want you in my real life, not my fake life... Your brother is the only family I have, but if you never want to see me again, I would understand. I'd walk away."

She sits in silent contemplation for a few minutes, not saying anything. As the seconds tick by, my stomach sinks lower. This was probably a mistake. There's no way she can accept that I've been lying to her since we met, but I'm glad it's over. Almost over.

"I don't understand. How is it that you're so close to my brother, but I've never heard of you? I didn't even realize my brother had friends..."

I snort at that comment, not surprised since Nathan can be the unfriendliest fucker alive sometimes.

"My name isn't Jay," I admit, watching her eyes widen slightly. She remains utterly silent though, so I continue.

"It's Jesse. Special Sergeant Jesse Callahan." There, it's all out there.

She startles, shaking her head like she finally realizes for the first time how deep my lies go, and how much I've been faking. "Jesse... You're Jesse," she states simply, looking at me as if for the first time.

I let her look. I give her time to connect whatever dots that she needs to and to prepare for whatever questions she has. Questions that I can try my best to answer.

The relief is undeniable. Hearing my real name on her lips feels right… Like all the decisions up until this point, led me right to this moment.

I relax into the sofa, feeling the weight of anxiety lessen and the exhaustion creep back in. I know this isn't over, she might hate me for dragging her into my lies, but for now, I can breathe easier.

"You're the Jesse that helped Nathan get Callie back," she states, already knowing the answer.

"Yeah. I am."

Nathan's fiance, Callie, was kidnapped this past year. I was able to find information on her whereabouts and pass it on to Nathan before she was sold into human trafficking. It was pretty traumatizing for both of them, but they've managed to get through it together.

"You bailed on Thanksgiving last year." She states plainly. I was invited to Nathan's cabin to meet Callie for the first time but at the last minute, I gave my leave up because someone else had a family emergency.

"I'm not accustomed to family gatherings." True.

All she does is nod her head, distractedly.

"We can't say anything to him about this. Not yet," I remind her.

She turns her head abruptly as if she can't stomach to look at me, but nods. I don't know what to say to make her feel better, nothing seems good enough to fix this. There's a few minutes of silence before she says anything.

"I'm having a hard time connecting the Jay that I know and the Jesse that I've heard Nathan talk about." She clears her throat, sounding a little hoarse. "I guess I understand why you lied about your name, but I don't like it. What else did you lie about? How can I not doubt every word you've ever said?"

"I promise that I never lied. Not about anything important. The logistics, yes, but everything else I kept as close to the truth as I could."

"But… That first night at the bar. You only flirted with me because you were trying to keep your cover story safe, not because you liked me… I thought you liked me." A tear rolls down her cheek although she tries to hide it behind the sleeve of her sweater.

"I did like you. I do. I meant what I said about wanting to be friends because if that's all you ever want from me then I'll take it, but I still think that you're the most beautiful woman that I've ever met and it's been killing me not to be near you these last few days. I don't want to miss out on this, Thea," I admit vulnerably, hoping that she can hear the truth in my voice.

She squeezes her eyes shut, wiping her face with the sleeves of her sweater and clearing her throat. "This…" She gestures between us. "This is a lie."

"It's not. Not all of it. What I feel when I'm around you is as real as it gets for me." I plead with my eyes, hoping she sees my honesty. Needing her to see the real me.

"Thank you for telling me the truth. I need some time to think about things," she chokes out, clearly dismissing me.

"Take all the time you need. I'll be around, whenever you're ready to talk. I'm not going anywhere," I promise, realizing that this doesn't have to be a stop on the road for me.

This time, walking out her front door doesn't feel like I'm walking away from anything. It feels like I'm walking into a new version of my life. A version where I'll do whatever it

takes to earn Thea's trust and forgiveness.
And, if I'm really lucky, her heart.

Chapter Sixteen

Thea

By the time Tuesday rolled around, my days off felt like a complete blur. Sunday morphed into Monday quickly, and I'm not sure if I remembered to shower or make myself a meal either day. I spent a lot of time in my moon room, staring at the sky. It helps me think.

Unfortunately, thinking meant replaying every conversation and interaction I've had with Jay -no, Jesse, since the day we met. Even before, when he was just a crush I had on one of my patrons at the library. Not someone who made me blush or smile. Before he intervened and made sure that I was safe from Kyle and the guy at the bar. Before I knew he was working undercover or that he was my brother's best friend.

Once he told me his real name, memories swept in of stories that Nathan had shared with me. Stories of missions that he had been on, trainings, and places he traveled, almost always including his teammate, Jesse. I'd never seen a photo, I'd never asked.

My brother and I haven't been entirely close since he left for the Army. He was 18, I was 14. For more than a decade, we'd shared more phone calls than in-person visits. Just this past year, he got out of the Army and built a cabin in the mountains not far from here.

I never asked if he moved here because he knew that I had gotten this job here in New Hope, or if he did it so we could be a family again, but it worked regardless. I've seen him for every holiday this year and I've watched him fall in love. Callie has become one of my best friends in the almost year that I've known her.

What they have makes me yearn for something similar. I want love, I want connection. I want...Jesse.

Jesse. Jesse. Jesse.

I've been repeating his name over and over again in my mind, and out loud since Sunday, trying to make it stick. It still feels wrong.

It feels like I'm saying a stranger's name, but Jay wasn't a stranger. He was, but he wasn't. He was so easy to talk to and to be around. I felt so safe near him that I hoped it was a sign. Now, I'm back to square one.

Jesse is a stranger and I don't know if I can accept him back into my life. I'm most afraid of all the doubt that's crept into my mind.

Did he only want to keep me safe from Kyle because he was doing his job?

Did he punch that guy in the bar because he wanted to defend me? Or because that's what my brother would have wanted?

He told me he didn't want to hurt me, but he told me a lot of things. A lot of lies. How can I believe anything?

Does he care because he sees me as his best friend's little sister? Or because he likes me? I refuse to be some taboo

116

fantasy.

I shake my head, clearing my echoing thoughts. The same questions have been racing through my mind for days.

I finish stocking the stack of books that I'm holding and return to the island where Latisha is clocking in.

"Hey, sweetie. Have a good weekend?" She asks.

Her question is innocent enough, but my tongue is stuck in my throat and I don't know how to answer without telling all of Jay's secrets. Jesse's secrets. Dang it.

"What's that look?" She questions, glaring at me from behind her bejeweled glasses. Today's are green. They're usually my favorite, but green just reminds me of Jesse's eyes.

"It's been a rough couple of days. Some guy grabbed me at the bar Saturday. I had a complete fainting spell. Wasn't one of my finer moments, but luckily I made it to the back before anyone saw me," I tell her. Avoiding the other complicated parts of my weekend.

"That's it. You need to quit. No more of that hillbilly bar. Nope, done." She wags her finger at me like a mother scolding her child. It just makes me smile because I know she cares.

"I might. I'm almost caught up on bills anyway. It was always just temporary," I assure her with a hug, needing one for myself.

"Oh, don't look now," she whispers from over my shoulder, still holding me in a hug. "Our favorite dream boat is here."

"What, why? It's too early for him to be here," I say before I have a chance to stop myself, completely giving myself away. "I mean... Who?" I busy myself checking emails while Latisha cracks up behind me.

"Good morning, honey. What can I help you with?" Latisha asks in her perfected customer service voice.

"I'm looking for a children's book that I read as a kid. I was wondering if you had it here."

I shiver hearing the heart-achingly familiar voice respond. It melts down my spine, making me realize how much I've missed hearing it in the two days since I've seen him.

"Well, since Thea is our Children's Librarian, she can help you better than I could. Thea," she says, snapping me into focus and throwing me under the bus.

"Sure. Would love to help." I plaster on the fakest smile I can muster, knowing that both of these people standing in front of me can probably see right through it.

I march towards the kid's books, not looking to see if he's following because I know he is. I can feel his nearness.

I round on him as soon as we're out of eye-shot from the rest of the library. "What are you doing?" I huff, looking past him to make sure we're alone.

"I wanted to make sure you were okay. I came by yesterday but you weren't here. I was worried." *He was worried about me...* That means he really cares right?

"It was my day off," I explain, trying to ignore my heart swelling. I'm still too confused by all my other doubts.

"Ah." He readjusts his hat, nervously.

"I've been thinking a lot the past few days but I'm still confused. The lies hurt and not being able to tell Nathan hurts. I don't even know what dating you would look like if-" I stop myself from finishing my thought out loud. *What will it even look like if you can't touch me?*

He doesn't know that part about me, yet. I've been keeping that secret from him this entire time even after he's admitted his own.

"I meant what I said the other day. I want you in my life

in whatever way you'll have me. I want to see where this goes because it feels special. *You* are special," he admits softly, tugging at my heart.

He's too nice. Despite the lies, he's been so kind to me since day one. We're only steps away from the spot we stood the other night when we both opened up about our past.

He told me he had been in a group home. That wasn't a lie, was it? No. He wouldn't lie about that.

Right?

It doesn't matter, it doesn't change the fact that I can't pursue this due to my own issues. Like a coward, I deflect my inner turmoil back onto him.

"The Army took my brother from me for years and I just got him back. How am I supposed to go through that again if this goes somewhere?" *It won't go anywhere, that's how.*

The hurt flashes in his eyes instantly as if I slapped him, and I hate myself for it. I'm putting all the blame on him. It's not fair, but I'm too afraid to admit that I'm the problem.

"I'm sorry. I'm not shutting you out, but my mind is running wild. I still need time to think."

"I'll leave you to your work then. I'll be around." He walks away, leaving me in the corner of the fiction section, yearning to run after him. I don't.

It isn't until a few hours go by that I realize his "I'll be around" wasn't a figurative statement. He never left the library, instead taking up station at his normal table, only getting up every once in a while to look at different books, then returning to his same seat.

A few times I've caught him looking at me, but just as many times he's caught me staring at him. It's all very odd to experience, but I can't deny how much I like it.

Catching his eyes on me feels secretive, but exciting. He shouldn't be entertaining me, he should be focusing on his job, but he's here for me. Knowing his secret when no one else does? It makes me feel important.

Feeling special to someone should be euphoric. I want it to be, but I also hear the clock ticking, telling me that my time is almost up. It won't be long until I'm forced to face the facts.

He can't touch me. No man can.

I have been deprived of physical intimacy because of the demon from my past. The years have gone by, and my mind has done the work and tried to heal, but my body won't listen. I need to tell him. I need to be honest.

I'm so ashamed that the very thought of admitting how broken I truly am makes me sick to my stomach. He doesn't deserve a woman who he can't touch.

I have to tell him to stay away from me. Despite the depth of my yearning for him already, it'll be easier to stay away from him than to be near him, knowing we'll never be.

I'm so confused. About him, about my life.

An hour before storytime, I'm knee-deep in the children's encyclopedias that need to be loaned to the local elementary school and I don't even notice someone hovering until Latisha clears her throat. I glance up at her, but she's on the other side of the island, raising her eyebrows at me suggestively.

I whip my head around, realizing that I'm not sitting alone in my little bubble like I thought. Jesse is leaning against my side of the counter holding a plastic bag.

"What's this?" The smell of the food hits me before I finish my question.

"Lunch. You haven't eaten today."

"I usually eat on my lunch break."

"Her break was an hour ago and she skipped it," Latisha chimes in from her side of the desk. Traitor.

"I bought a couple of things, not sure what you like." He takes out two sandwiches, a lettuce wrap, two bags of chips, and a cup of mac n cheese.

"This is really nice. Thank you." I know I've never blushed harder than at this moment. No one has ever bought me lunch or paid attention to when I ate. Besides Latisha, apparently.

I take a sandwich and chips, thanking him again. Do I invite him to eat with me? Does he want to? I'm not used to this at all. I don't know the proper protocol.

"I've got plenty," he talks over my shoulder to Latisha. "Take something for yourself." Suck up.

"Oh thank you, sweetie. You are too kind." She grabs the lettuce wrap, winking at him.

"Careful, she will out-charm you," I warn him.

"So, you think I'm charming?"

I roll my eyes but can't quite smother my smile.

"Enjoy your lunch, Sunshine." He throws me his crooked smile before walking back to his usual table. He drops the last sandwich on the tabletop before taking the final items over to one of our other regulars sitting in the corner at a computer.

He's an older man, a local around here who everyone knows or has a story about. His size and childlike demeanor can be hard to miss, but he's a gentle giant. Sometimes he likes to sit in and listen to story time with the kids, but most of the time he likes to play solitaire on the computers. Though he never wins on his own. I've helped him a few times.

I don't know how Jesse knew to approach him, but the interaction is simple and quiet. Earl shakes Jesse's hand, thanking him wholeheartedly, both of them smiling ear to ear. I can't help but stare.

How am I supposed to stop myself from falling head over heels for this man?

Chapter Seventeen

Jesse

I knew that revealing my real identity meant that she might not forgive me. She might've chosen to never see me again.

When I considered that the consequences of my lies meant never being at the receiving end of her smile again, it made me sick. I never want to go back to a life that doesn't have her a part of it. I can't. The thought of that motivated me enough to pursue her even while she was still hesitant about me.

How much I care about her hit me like a ton of bricks, but I'm not backing down. Being in her presence is more fulfilling than anything that I've ever experienced and I don't want to lose her.

So, I just keep showing up. I hang out at the library every day, bring her lunch when I know she hasn't eaten, and walk her to her car after she clocks out. I don't push anything else.

I don't ask her what she's thinking, or if she's forgiven me. I just keep showing up. I don't want to be anywhere else but with her anyway.

The second day was when I realized that she was avoiding

saying my name. She doesn't call me Jay or Jesse, instead avoiding both altogether like she isn't sure what to use.

On the third day, I considered holding her hand, maybe reaching for it in the parking lot before she got in her car, but I decided against it. She stays so wrapped up in the oversized sweaters that it's like a physical 'do not touch me' sign. She has reservations about me, I get it.

By the time Friday rolls around, I build the courage to ask about her schedule for the weekend, hoping she won't be mad if I bring up the bar.

The last time we talked about it, she was angry when I told her that she needed to quit. My head was a mess then, and even though I stand by my stance, if she wants to work there then I'll be there for her too.

"Are you going to be mad if I keep showing up while you work?" I ask, genuinely curious since she hasn't said anything about my presence at the library this week.

I've still been hanging around Curtis and the other guys at night, only managing to get a few hours of sleep before spending my day scouring the nonfiction section with heavy eyes.

Researching extremist groups, domestic terrorism, and the effects of PTSD on veterans isn't exactly exciting material. I've learned a lot firsthand and on the job these past 12 years in the military but it never hurts to double down on the literature. Any information that will help me solve this case quicker, the better.

"I haven't minded seeing you every day." She blushes, the pinkness of her cheeks making me itch to reach for her. To hold her. Kiss her.

"What nights are you at the bar?" I ask, admiring her pretty

124

pinkened face.

"I took this weekend off. I told Sunny that I needed a break after what happened last weekend. Callie and Nathan invited me over tomorrow night for a fire." It's the first time either of us has spoken of her brother since Sunday morning when I told her everything, but we didn't discuss how we would navigate this.

"Good. I'll be there too." *Liar.*

"Really?" She asks, surprised.

"Yeah, he texted me yesterday. I told him that I'm in town." *I'll just text him, it'll be fine.*

"Okay, well good, but um… Can we not tell Nathan what's going on? It's still very overwhelming for me. I'm confused enough for myself, I'm not ready to explain how and why I know you." She looks down at her car as she speaks, making me feel like she's not telling me the whole truth about something.

I'm glad she's not looking at me though because she'd see the expression on my face. She wants me to be a secret. *Ouch.*

I'm not supposed to tell anyone details while I'm under-cover, including Nathan. Which is why I told her she couldn't say anything to him before, but somehow when she suggests it, it stings. A part of me, deep down, feels the rejection. I'm not worth the complications. I'm not worth navigating through this. *I'm not worth it.*

"No problem. I won't say anything. He'd probably want to punch me anyway for flirting with his little sister," I tease, even though I don't feel at all humorous. She blushes again, soothing some of the burn that I'm feeling.

"Okay, good. And, Jesse?" She asks as she gets in her car, and I feel like punching the air when she calls me by my real name. "I like it... When you flirt with me," she clarifies, before shutting her door and starting the engine.

All I can do is grin like an idiot as she drives away. *I like it too, Sunshine.*

* * *

I'm running late. When I called Nathan and told him I had a free day on Saturday, he invited me over without a second thought. The problem was that it wasn't actually a free day.

I spent most of my day driving boxes from the warehouse to Jameson's farm. It was good because I got eyes on the farm, but bad because I am exhausted and running on only a few hours of sleep, again.

One thing is for sure, Jameson's crew jumps when he says jump. They crawl when he tells them to crawl. We've been up all night multiple nights receiving these mysterious shipments from various semi trucks, and now he's calling people back during the day to run more product.

The problem is that I'm never alone. I haven't been able to snoop inside the boxes because they're sealed shut and Curtis is attached to my hip. I'm sure it's on Jameson's orders until he trusts me. So, I'll earn his trust.

My back aches, my neck's stiff. I'm ready for a night off, so I'm glad for the excuse to come out here. Being able to be myself up here might feel like an escape. There's no one around for miles who would know me as Jay.

I pull up his driveway and park just as the sun's setting. The sky is still lit up in pinks and purples, but it won't be long before it's completely dark. The only lights out here will be the moon, the stars, and the fire that I can see burning from the backyard.

My heart kicks up in gear thinking about seeing Thea. The thought of pretending not to know her is a little unsettling, but maybe this is what we need. A fresh start. I can show her the real me from the beginning.

I make my way towards the group, Nathan and Callie are sitting together in a double Adirondack chair, while Thea sits to their right in another, leaving an empty one on the other side of them. Fuck. Do I sit next to her, or across from her?

"Jesse, you made it!" Callie calls out, her friendly personality is the complete opposite of Nathan's. I can see why she and Thea have become friends, they both light up the world around them.

"I made it." I catch her in a hug, nearly losing my hat in the process. She's a nice girl, we've gotten along quite well since she met Nathan. He hates it, but she's just too easy to like.

I look over her shoulder as Nathan comes toward me, not missing the look on Thea's face. She's looking at us, but her eyes are distant and sad, vacant almost.

"Okay. That's enough," Nathan grunts, but smiles before shaking my hand and pulling me in for a hug. A brief hug, but for him that's huge.

I step towards the fire, approaching Thea as casually as possible, hoping to play this cool, but needing to be near her.

She's traded in her usual oversized sweater for an oversized crew neck and shorts. The glow of the fire makes her tan legs look bronzed and sexy as hell, but I do my best to keep my eyes on her face. Her pretty face that I can't help but admire because her hair is pulled back in a messy bun on the top of her head, leaving me an unobstructed view of the column of her neck that I want to drag my lips across.

"Hi, I'm Jesse. You must be Thea." I extend my hand to shake hers. *Fresh start.*

She studies my hand two seconds longer than seems necessary but doesn't take it. Instead, she plops a bag of marshmallows in my outstretched palm.

"Nice to meet you, Jesse. We're making s'mores," she says in the cheery voice that I've come to know, but I can tell something is off.

She moves to the opposite side of the fire, sitting in the vacant chair farthest from me. I guess that answers the seating arrangement question, but it still leaves me wondering what the sad look from before was about.

Chapter Eighteen

Thea

A hug. That's all it took to send me spiraling. He deserves to be hugged. I watched Callie jump up and hug him so easily and I've never been more jealous of anyone in my life. It's not her fault. I know she is in love with my brother, but it made me painfully aware of what I can't offer Jesse.

How selfish do I have to be to string him along? Encouraging him to flirt with me, wanting to be around him all the time, knowing there is a wall between us that I have never been able to get around. I can't do that to him. I have to end it. Tonight.

Nathan and Jesse jump into old war stories right away, giving me too much room to condemn myself in my mind. I have to force myself to enjoy this moment because it might not ever happen again. I do my best to engage and pay attention to the conversation even though I'm sweating on the inside.

"I need to go to the bathroom." Callie stands suddenly, Nathan following right behind her. "Sorry, I'm afraid of the dark, I don't like walking back up to the cabin alone," she explains to me and Jesse, but there is no need. After everything she went through last year, she deserves an escort everywhere she goes if that's what she wishes.

"You good?" Nathan asks subtly, making sure I don't mind being left alone with Jesse. He doesn't know about my issues with men or my familiarity with his friend, it's just his normal brotherly protectiveness showing.

"I'm good," I assure him before watching them walk toward the house.

"You look pretty tonight," Jesse tells me once we're alone. I know it's his comment that makes my cheeks hot, but I try to blame it on the fire.

"I look like a slob, but thank you."

I debated all day on what to wear, but this is my usual attire when I visit my brother. I didn't want him, or rather Callie, noticing that I put extra effort in.

"You look perfect."

Yep. It's the fire, it's burning too hot.

"Jesse. I can't do this," I choke out the words before I can chicken out, needing to bite the bullet.

"You can't forgive me," he states, dully. His words aren't accusatory, or angry, they're defeated. His whole posture deflated at my admission and my heart aches because it's not his fault. It's my problem stopping this before it can even begin.

"I do forgive you. I understand why you lied about your job and your name. I didn't like being lied to, but I get it. I know how serious the military can be. Nathan was tight-lipped about almost everything he's done." I shrug.

I can't blame him for maintaining his oath. Especially since he broke it by telling me the truth about anything at all. He had every reason to keep lying to me, but he didn't.

"It took me some time to come to terms with you being Jesse not Jay, but I worked it out. That's not the problem." I feel myself teetering on the edge of falling apart.

"Then, what's the problem?" His eyes are lined with concern.

"It's complicated. I'm complicated. I wouldn't feel right letting things continue, knowing how *my* problems would affect us. It's not fair to you." I swallow back my impulsive need to cry, but it hurts. Admitting that I'm the problem hurts.

"Your problems?"

"I'm not worth it, I promise." I rest my chin on my knees, not even realizing that I curled up into my chair at some point.

"Why don't you let me make that choice?" His question is more of a statement, a demand. The way he's looking at me, I wouldn't be surprised if I caught on fire right where I'm sitting.

How can he be so sure?

We sit in silence, staring at each other while the fire crackles between us. I feel hopeless, unable to stop the train wreck that will inevitably happen. He's looking at me with such certainty, such determination. I almost believe that things might work out, but I know better.

Callie's voice startles me as they return. "Here, Thea." She hands me a seltzer, both of us have already bonded over our love of fruity drinks.

Nathan hands Jesse a beer, never asking if he wants one, both of them accustomed to their silent routine. Jesse looks at me and my drink questioningly, as if to ask *I thought you didn't drink?'*

I raise my eyebrows subtly at him as if to say, *'I told you, I'm complicated.'*

"We're celebrating," Nathan announces.

"Celebrating what?" I'm selfishly hoping that they're about to announce I might get a niece or nephew soon, but Callie is obviously drinking tonight.

Being an aunt might be my only chance to be around babies. I can't help but be eager about it, but I keep my wishes to myself.

"I'm on active duty again. I signed back up so I can finish out my career and get a full retirement," my brother explains, making my heart drop. Is he leaving again? What about Callie? Me?

"He wants to work with me, domestically." Jesse chimes in as if he read the distress on my face.

"So, no more overseas?" I ask Jesse, directly. He told me what his job was but I never asked specifics.

"Exactly," Nathan answers me, forcing my eyes from Jesse's and back to him. "I'm starting with the Criminal Investigations Unit by the end of this month. I can commute to base, still do some field work, but be home every night. I'm looking forward to it." Nathan and Callie smile at each other lovingly, making my gut twist with loneliness.

"Congratulations, man. I'm glad to have you back." Jesse and Nathan clink bottles. "I guess I'll have to stay around here after all."

"Yeah, get your shit out of Texas and build a cabin up here." Nathan's comment lights up a question in my brain.

"You're from Texas?" I never realized how far out of town Jesse came. Another barrier we would inevitably have to go around.

"Technically, I'm from Indiana, but once I enlisted I moved all over. Texas has been the longest, and most recent location I've lived in," he explains, watching me closely. The excuses are forming in my brain, giving me more reason to fight this pull between us.

"That's cool." Is the only response I can formulate with my mind whirring.

"Nathan has been trying to get me to move here since the first time I visited after he built this place. I see the appeal of putting down roots here." He looks at me pointedly.

It soothes some of my turmoil but makes my stomach tighten for different reasons. He wants to stay after his case is over.

"Roots are good, especially when you've never had any," Nathan speaks directly to Jesse, an unspoken conversation happening between them.

"Yeah." Jesse nods his head solemnly. There's a silence that follows, but it's not comfortable. More is being left unsaid and it plants seeds of worry in my head.

"Are we having s'mores or what?" I jump in, feeling the need to steer the conversation to safer topics when the sadness in Jesse's eyes lingers.

Wanting to save him like he's done for me so many times, I pass out the roasting sticks, seeing his appreciation as I hand him his.

"Thank you," he says genuinely, his green eyes lingering on me.

He doesn't seem to care that we're not alone and I catch myself being the one to tear my gaze from his each time. I attempt to fight the pull between us, but I find my eyes locking with his across the fire throughout the night anyway, whether he's the one talking or not.

The conversation among us is fueled by laughter and too many drinks, and it's the most fun that I've had in a long time. Enough that Nathan wouldn't let me drive home even if I tried, forcing me to stay for a sleepover.

"You're no fun," I accuse him after he quickly declines to sleep on the air mattress so Callie and I can have a girls-only slumber party in their bed.

"Yeah. Coming from the librarian," he scoffs.

"What do you have against librarians?" Callie teases.

"He can't read, so he knocks the whole profession," I jab, definitely feeling a buzz. It makes Callie and Jesse both cackle with laughter, and Nathan rolls his eyes.

"Wow. I thought he only bullied me, but I see why since you two grew up together." Jesse smiles at me directly, making my heart race against my chest.

His smiles feel like they've *always* been meant for me. They touch a place in my soul that I've kept buried for a long time.

"Ha. Ha. Funny." Nathan gets up, breaking up the fire, and putting it out. "You've got the couch smart ass," he says to Jesse.

"I've only had two beers. I can drive," Jesse argues.

"To where? A shitty hotel. No. It's dark, it's hard enough to drive down the mountain during the day when you're not used to it. You're staying," Nathan demands. It's his way of voicing that he cares.

"See." Jesse looks at me. "A bully."

We share a laugh, but I saw the look on his face when Nathan was talking. I think my brother's comments hit a little close to home.

Chapter Nineteen

Jesse

I stare into the ceiling above me, wood beams criss-crossing at the peak, because every time I shut my eyes I can't stop picturing Thea lying in the other room.

It feels torturous being this close, and although I am a red-blooded male, hooking up with her is the last thing on my mind. Maybe not the last... But, definitely not the priority. I just want to know what's going on in her head. Why is she fighting me so hard?

She acts like she wants me and whatever this is between us, but is being pulled away by a factor outside of her control. *It's not fair to you. I'm not worth it.*

Her words from earlier ring in my mind. If she could see herself through my eyes, she'd see how worth fighting for she is. She's the first thing in my life worth fighting for.

A faint *click* sounds from one of the doors down the hall, light footsteps slowly making their way toward where I am in the living room. Lying on my back on the couch, I'd have to crane my neck to see who's behind me from this angle, but I don't move. My gut tells me it's Thea. I hope it is but the footsteps stop at the entrance of the room, waiting.

"I'm awake," I speak into the darkness, hoping that I'm right. The tip taps of her feet make their way toward me before settling in the chair to my right, closest to my head. I still don't move, letting her get comfortable. The only light in the room is from one of the appliances in the kitchen, barely casting a soft glow.

A few moments of silence pass, and I find myself wondering if she is having the same pull to be near me as I do her. Maybe she only ventured out here because she can't sleep. Either way, I'm glad she came.

"I thought you didn't drink?" I ask the question that's been nagging me since earlier, remembering back to the first time I saw her at the bar. I downed an extra shot of jäger to get her out of it and that shit's nasty.

"I don't, normally. I only drink when I'm in a safe place. With people I trust. Here with my brother is one of those places and I usually have wine at home. Especially if my best friend, Liv, is in town, or my mom." I don't look, but I can sense the smile in her words at the mention of her mom.

"I like your mom. She's sweet."

"You know my mom?" She asks, bewildered.

"Yeah. I've been around her a few times. You look like her." I think back to the few occasions that I met Nathan's mom. She was vibrant and kind. I should've known right away that Thea was her daughter when I was still connecting the dots.

"Thank you," she whispers, followed by more comfortable silence. Silent enough that I can hear the hum of the air conditioning and the insects outside.

I want to give her space, not pepper her with a thousand questions, but my mind is racing to know every detail about her. I most importantly want to know the reason she has such strict rules on drinking and why she told me once that men make her uncomfortable. I'm afraid that I suspect why, but I need to hear it from her.

"Why do you only drink around people you trust, Thea?" I close my eyes, waiting for her response, hoping it's not close to what I'm thinking. I don't want to imagine all the possibilities that could lead a young woman to make that choice for herself.

After a heavy pause, making me think she won't answer me, she finally responds. "The same reason that I can't stand to be touched. By men."

My throat constricts with the pain of schooling my reaction. My Sunshine. No. I can't stand the thought of anyone doing anything to cause such consequences in her life. The rage I feel burning in my heart for her is frightening. It takes all of my willpower to remain silent.

I need to keep my cool. An overreaction is not what she needs. It's not what she came out here for. She chose the darkened, silent room for her confession for a reason.

"Is that the complication you were referring to earlier? Why you've been running from me this whole time?" I finally ask when I have my emotions under control, though my voice is hoarse.

"Yeah," she whispers in the smallest, most broken voice that I've ever heard. Whatever reservations I might've had in the past about being bad at relationships, or what my future holds, they vanish at that one word.

I will do anything for this girl. I want to see her so full of light and happiness that all her broken pieces disappear. I want to give her the world.

"Do you want to talk about it?" I pray she gives me a name,

so I can kill the motherfucker that dared to hurt her.

"Not really," she says softly, still sounding small, but not as broken.

I force myself to remember that she's been dealing with this on her own already. I can't jump in and try to save her in an instant when I've just entered her life.

I take a few deep breaths, needing to stop myself from launching off this couch and taking her in my arms. *I can't stand to be touched by men.*

I can't wrap my head around that statement. I haven't tried anything up until this point and I'm glad for that now, but how far does that go?

Can she touch Nathan? Did he hug her? I can't remember.

"I hope you aren't mad. I didn't mean to lead you on." Her voice is strained and undeniably sad.

How can she think I could ever be mad at her? Especially for something so obviously outside of her control.

Before I realize it, she's standing from her chair. "Goodnight, Jesse. I'm glad you came tonight."

It sounds like a goodbye, but my thoughts are moving too fast and I can't formulate an articulate response. Nothing I can come up with seems good enough or appropriate in this situation.

She walks past me and a breeze of a touch brushes against my hair. So light as if I imagined it. By the time I can react, whipping my head around to look at her, she's already disappeared down the hallway. "Goodnight, Sunshine," I whisper into the darkness.

Within minutes, I'm pulling my phone off the side table, needing to speak my peace. I don't want her to go to bed thinking that this is over. I should have said it before she left the room, but my brain needed time to process all of my thoughts.

Me: I want you to give me a chance, Thea.

My phone buzzes in the darkness not five minutes later. A text with her name on it.

Thea: I can't give you a normal relationship. I wish that I could. Please, consider that before we both get in too deep...

Me: Too late, I'm already in deep. Sleep well, baby.

* * *

I pull in through the rusted gates that normally block the driveway to Jameson's farm. You can't see it from the road, the front half of the property is thick with trees and brush. When I got the text from Curtis this morning to meet at 9 a.m., I had to kick it in gear to get here on time.

I was hoping to catch a glimpse of Thea again before I left Nathan's, but even after we sat and drank our coffee, the girls were both still asleep. It was probably best that I was pulled away. I couldn't stop thinking about what Thea told me and it was taking everything in me not to mention it to Nathan. He's my best friend, my only confidant, but I'd never betray Thea by talking about her behind her back.

I send her a quick text as I'm parking by the other vehicles around an old run-down barn. It's the only place I've been on the property since these jobs started. Curtis says the parties happen in the house but I haven't been invited to one of those yet.

Me: Had to get back on the job. I'll see you soon, Sunshine.

I turn my phone off and slip it in my back pocket as Curtis walks up to my truck. "You ready for this, man?" He asks me like I know what the hell is going on.

"Ready for what?"

"Jameson has an important job to tell us about. Says it's worth more than all the other stuff we've done so far."

It sounds ominous but I follow him into the barn anyway, nodding at the familiar faces I see. It's hard to believe so many guys are like-minded enough to follow this jack asses lead, but here we are in a room full of them.

The quiet chatter continues for a few minutes until suddenly everyone stops their conversations mid-sentence, watching Jameson enter from the far side of the building.

"Thank you boys for coming today. We needed to gather here, on the day of our lord, because we need to discuss the plague that is happening in this country and what we need to do to stop it. This is supposed to be one country under God, but we have left our morals behind to follow a tyrannical government." Everyone murmurs in agreement.

"A government that has sacrificed all of us standing here today for their own agenda. Beaten us down, watched us suffer, and offered no assistance. I gathered you all here because we need to show them what happens when they disrespect the real patriots of this nation."

The crowd around me cheers, bellowing from their lungs. I manage to raise my hands to clap, trying not to stick out like a sore thumb.

This guy is delusional. He's managed to come up with a cause generated from bullshit. He wasn't injured in combat, he is the product of all of his own mistakes. Now he's using religion as a scapegoat for his agenda.

He's grasping at straws to make these people follow him, and unfortunately, it's working. I watch everyone around me hoot and holler for this leader of theirs, all of them ready and willing to betray their government.

This group of extremists is one of the worst kinds because it's filled with uneducated, unorganized, and chaotic individuals needing any reason to cause anarchy. I look around, memorizing as many details as possible about every face I see. I don't know all of their names but I need to. This could be bad.

"We're making plans, boys. Big plans. And I need you to be ready!" He shouts to the crowd. The barn erupts in more applause.

This is insane. I glance to my right where Curtis stands, he's cheering along with the others, but there's a slight hunch to his shoulders that tells me he's not quite sure about all of this. The damn kid should never have gotten mixed up in this.

"Alright. Let's get to work." Jameson rallies everyone to follow him to another location on the property and I'm not remotely prepared for what I discover.

Chapter Twenty

Thea

The weight lifted from my chest was like a breath of fresh air when I woke up. I told him. I told Jesse my secret. I still don't know what this means for us, but the fact that I'm not hiding it anymore makes me smile ear to ear.

The anxiety that I usually feel from the moment my eyes open on any given day, is overshadowed by hope. For the first time in a long time, I dare to believe there might be light at the end of this long dark tunnel that I've been consumed by.

The cheer on my face slowly diminishes when I go into Nathan's kitchen and see that we are one person short. "Morning, sis," Nathan tells me while he stirs some pancake batter. Callie is standing next to him with sleepy eyes.

"Good morning. No, Jesse?" I ask as casually as possible.

"He had to hurry back to town. Something was going down," Nathan explains. My heart sinks. *Something is going down?* What does that mean?

He couldn't tell me any details about his undercover operation. He told me I wasn't in danger, but never said that about himself... Suddenly my problems don't seem that significant when I know he could be out there risking his life for his job.

"Is his job usually dangerous?" I wonder out loud. Callie crunches on a piece of bacon with a smile on her face, watching me. Nathan's oblivious as I mouth, "What?" To her.

"Depends on what he's investigating. I'm not technically in his unit so he can't tell me the details." Nathan continues pouring pancake batter onto a hot skillet, not at all catching onto Callie and I's silent conversation. I have to bite my bottom lip to keep from giggling while Callie makes a kissy face and winks at me.

"What?" Nathan asks when he finally catches on to us. We both burst out laughing.

"Nothing. Nothing," Callie assures him, letting me off the hook. However, after building up the courage to tell Jesse the truth about me last night, I'm feeling brave this morning.

"So, you and Jesse are best friends, right? He's a good guy?" I watch my brother, waiting for him to analyze what I said. I want a glimpse of an idea about the man who I could let break my heart.

I'm optimistic enough to see where things go with him, especially after he was so understanding last night, but pessimistic enough to assume things will end in disaster.

Regardless, the way I feel around him makes me brazen enough to take a chance. I'll just let myself enjoy it while it lasts because I think it would be more painful to miss out on it altogether.

"Yeah. He's a good guy. He's saved my life on more than one occasion," he finally answers.

"Mine, too." Callie chimes in, resting her head on Nathan's shoulder while he contemplates me. He can see the interest on my face, I wear my heart on my sleeve.

"You trust him though, right?" I ask, subtly. If my brother would go to bat for him, then that means something to me. His trust is earned and hard to come by.

He looks at me closely, hesitating before responding. I can see the wheels turning in his mind. I can only hope he isn't about to unleash his disappointment on me because I like his friend.

"I've done some stupid shit that could have ruined my career, my life, and he has always stuck beside me. He's put himself on the line for me multiple times, risking his entire career. A career that is everything to him. For him to be willing to give that up…

"Not only do I trust him with my life, I trust him with Callie's life. Mom's life. Your life. He is the person that anyone would be lucky to have in their corner. If you're telling me that you're into him…" He trails off, contemplating his next words.

"I won't stand in your way, but I won't pick sides if it doesn't work out. He's a brother to me. I owe him everything," he says, glancing at Callie. "I'm the only family he has, Thea."

It's a clear warning but it sounds like he was giving his blessing… At least that's the way I'm choosing to hear it.

Regardless, my brother's words aren't lost on me. If Jesse is a permanent fixture in my brother's life, it means he's also potentially permanent in my life.

He said he would've walked away if I had asked him to and I can see why. He is selfless. He's already stuck his neck out for me by telling me his real identity. I appreciated it before, but it feels more significant now.

He was willing to put his career on the line because he wanted me to know the truth. He could have lost everything if I took it poorly but he risked it because he wanted me to know his real name. The real him.

"Why doesn't he have a family?"

"It's not my place to tell, but he's had a rough go at life," Nathan says solemnly, feeling for his friend.

"I'm surprised you aren't being more 'protective big brother' on me," I tease, trying to lighten the topic of conversation and away from Jesse's misfortune. The thought of him living a hard life leaves a churning in my gut.

"He's the best guy I know. I would trust him to take care of you more than anyone," he says meaningfully.

"I don't need to be taken care of," I protest.

"I know, I'm sorry," Nathan raises his hands in defeat before turning back to the stove. "But, maybe he does."

I contemplate what he said as he dishes up our breakfast. If Jesse has had a hard life, then I want to be the one to make it happier. I want to be the one to put him first but I'm afraid that I'm not enough.

I might not even deserve him but the thought of not taking this chance with him, only for him to meet someone else someday... That kills me. My chest is tight, aching to be with him. To be normal...

For the rest of the day on Sunday, I replay the conversation with Nathan and all the ones with Jesse these last few weeks. All the little glimpses of his real self that he gave me before he had come clean about who he was seem more special now. He was trying to connect with me and I didn't realize how hard that was for him.

Then the truth came out and he made his intentions clear. He wants this. He wants to give this a chance despite all of the reasons we probably shouldn't.

I have tried to get over my issues in the past, but maybe I'm more ready now. I've never felt the desire to touch anyone like I do with Jesse. Never trusted anyone like him. I know he's what I want, but he might also be what I need, and the prospect excites me.

I think about sex, often. Maybe more so than the average woman because I've been deprived for so long. I want the passion, the lust, I want to be wanted.

The relationships I had in undergrad were casual, immature even. My hookups entailed drunken quickies in dorm rooms and college houses, nothing of real merit.

I've had almost six long years to think about all the ways I'd want to be touched by a man. Hypothetically at least. No one in my real life ever seemed worth fantasizing about. Until now. Now, I want to try. With Jesse.

By Monday, the doubts start creeping in. I still haven't heard from him and my hope starts to dwindle. Other than the one text telling me he'd see me soon, I haven't heard a peep. No unexpected visits and no truck parked on the curb in front of my house. I checked.

Tuesday, I'd considered that I was dumb to get my hopes up. The conversation Saturday night could have sunk in and he might've taken it as a sign to stop things between us. Thinking that he isn't willing to put up with my problems makes me sick to my stomach for most of the day.

Luckily, storytime with the kids served to be a good distraction, helping me smile and laugh for the first time since the weekend.

As I log onto my computer to wrap up a few things before I leave, I sense him before I see him. My eyes snap right to his as he approaches me at the island and to the fresh stitches spanning down his right temple, through the corner of his eyebrow.

The tiny white skin tape keeping it covered is like a beacon even under the brim of his hat. "What happened?" My concern instantly erases all of the doubts I've had the past two days. None of my problems matter. Only he does.

"It's a long story, but I'm okay. I promise." His eyes burn into mine, both of us relaying the emotions that neither of us can put into words in a room full of people.

I stare at him, the man before me that I want so desperately, realizing that I'll do whatever it takes for a chance with him. I have to.

He checks his watch quickly, blowing out a deep breath when he realizes what time it is. "Will you still be here after the meeting is done?" He asks with clear desperation in his voice.

I'm supposed to leave soon. I usually leave before it's over, but it doesn't matter.

"Yeah. I'll be here."

Chapter Twenty-One

Jesse

A cluster fuck. That's what the last few days have been. Once the ball started rolling, it didn't seem like it would ever stop. After Sunday's radical "church" service, I walked into a second barn on the property with my fellow Jameson followers, only to find tables full of what could only be bomb-making material. The amount of materials laid out would have made my jaw drop if not for my need to remain neutral.

The low-level equipment wouldn't be concerning if it weren't for the amount. There is enough product to demo the barn itself if that's what they were going for.

Household chemicals. Metal pipes. Wires. Containers of screws and other shrapnel. All from the boxes I'd been helping bring in for weeks. I had no idea and it makes my skin crawl. It's the exact reason I'm here in New Hope, but to see it was uncanny. I never would have guessed they'd be into explosives.

However, the hushed conversations throughout the day had alluded that no one actually has any bomb-making experience. All the supplies were gathered in an attempt to "figure it out." Which is incredibly stupid and dangerous.

I watched men fiddle with materials until my back was locked with stress. These guys are going to kill themselves before they can even attempt to "stick it to the man," but good riddance.

Sunday night, I heard whispers that one of Jameson's right-hand men had assembled a "test bomb" and they wanted to experiment. Unfortunately, the followers weren't invited to partake, so without the rest of the group I had to sneak back onto the property after everyone had left to see if their attempt was successful.

I hoped that they were too dumb to figure it out, that all of this material would go to waste and they'd give up their endeavors. Maybe try protesting with picket signs like normal enraged Americans have been doing for decades.

That hope was quickly squashed once the bomb went off in the field behind his farmhouse. I underestimated their determination. I also underestimated my safe cover, because the blast sent shrapnel flying in my direction and right at my face. The resulting wound was pouring blood and obscuring the vision in my right eye. I had to do everything I could to get back to my truck unnoticed.

All of Monday was spent in the hospital getting stitched up and checked for a concussion. Worse than that, reporting what happened to my command. Filling out paperwork, sending emails, and more paperwork.

By the time I left that hospital the superiors over my unit demanded my presence at the closest military hospital to get rechecked by their doctors and cleared for duty. Then more paperwork.

Thea was all that I could think about. I didn't want her to

think that I disappeared on her but my phone broke when the blast knocked me down. Which made the time waiting even more miserable because all I wanted was to hear her voice.

Hell, I was desperate enough that I almost called Nathan and asked for Thea's number, but I couldn't bring myself to do it. I've been alone my entire life and a few more days wasn't going to kill me.

By the time I got a replacement phone and drove back to New Hope on Tuesday afternoon, I was a madman. I'd barely slept in days and my head hurt. I was enraged at the slow drivers that were keeping me from getting to her faster.

Walking into the library and seeing her sweet face eased my tension instantly. I felt the first wave of relief that I've had since Sunday. The warmth that her presence radiates brings me a sense of peace that I only experience around her.

Unfortunately, all of my pent-up stress and exhaustion came back like a tsunami as soon as I walked away and into the veteran's meeting.

The pulsing in my brain is amplifying all the chatter around me and begging me to shut my eyes to tune it all out, but I can't. Not here. Here, I'm working. I'm Jay.

Another scrape of a chair being dragged across the laminate floor solidifies my decision. Fuck it. I can't do this. I'm out of my chair just as Curtis comes in through the side door, ruining my chance for a clean break.

"Damn, Jay. What happened to your face?" Curtis asks, examining me like it's the worst injury he's ever seen.

"Ah, nothing. I caught a junkie trying to break into my truck. He got a cheap shot on me. It's nothin', really, but my head's killing me. I'm going to skip this one," I explain, waving toward the room. "I need to sleep it off." I desperately need sleep.

"No worries. I'll catch you later." Curtis nods as I make my way back towards the main part of the library.

There is only one thing that I want and she sees me coming right away, tracking me worriedly as I make my way toward her. The concern is etched across her face.

"I need to get out of here. Do you want…" I start to ask if she can leave with me, but she beats me to it, grabbing her keys.

"Let's go." With a wave to Latisha across the room, we're out of the doors.

I must look worse than I thought because as soon as we get into the parking lot she's ushering me to her car. Fine by me, I don't want to drive my truck again anytime soon. There are blood stains all over the inside that need to be cleaned.

I don't know what I'm going to do. I could have lost my fucking eye when that bomb exploded and it was only one. They had enough product to make hundreds.

I'm helpless being undercover. At least during my old Special Ops missions we went and kicked doors down and got shit done. I feel pretty fucking useless standing by watching the bad guys make life-threatening devices.

They told me to keep a low profile and to collect intel, but I feel like I'm waiting around for innocent people to be seriously hurt, or killed. Even though I'm in the field, I'm not doing anything active. They aren't giving me the go-ahead to stop anything or to shut anything down.

I hate feeling helpless. Sitting by while life runs you over. I watched my dad beat my mom daily, never being big or strong enough to stop it. I sat in group homes and foster homes, never being picked to start a new life with a new family. Being kicked and beaten by kids who were older than me.

Being moved around and through so many homes that no school could keep my credits straight, forcing me to miss out on graduation. Being homeless and having nowhere to live once I turned 18.

"Thea. I need you to tell me something," I plead desperately, the weight of the memories is suffocating me.

"Like, what?" She asks as she navigates us toward her house.

"I don't know. Anything to distract me from all the shit in my head." I close my eyes, leaning my head back against the headrest, cringing as a bass drum beats against my skull.

There's a breath of silence before she blurts out. "I haven't had sex in six years."

My eyes pop open when I comprehend what she just said. Six years without sex? *She can't be touched.* Has she been deprived of all affection for that long?

At my silence, she continues. "I started telling guys that I was celibate so they would leave me alone because I couldn't stand for them to come near me. All these years I couldn't even imagine having sex with a man. Until you."

My jaw goes slack.

Until me, she imagines having sex, with me. All the blood roaring through my head suddenly heads south, causing a sudden discomfort in my jeans. "Well. I'm definitely distracted now."

She laughs, drawing my attention to her cheeks. I watch the blush creep into her coloring and it brings me so much satisfaction. The pride in my chest grows every time she gifts me with her vulnerable side and I feel like the luckiest bastard

152

on the planet.

"What do you think about?" I need more than anything to hear her deepest desires. I think I need it more than air at this very moment.

"Everything. There hasn't been a day since I met you that I haven't imagined all the ways that I wish you could touch me."

Before I register it, she's jumping out of her car while I'm absorbing what she just said. My sweet, radiant Thea has been fantasizing about all the ways she wants me. Holy fuck.

I need details. I want every thought that's gone through her mind.

With a newfound energy, I fly into the house after her, finding her in the kitchen. Without really thinking it through, I cage her in where she stands against the sink.

"Jesse," she pleads, the fear straining her voice. I don't touch her. I wouldn't dare force that on her, but I make her look at me, catching her eyes with mine and holding them hostage.

"Tell me what I need to do. Tell me what it takes and I'll do it. I want to touch you so fucking bad, baby."

She whimpers at my words and I have to grip the counter to keep from touching her, making my knuckles painfully white. All I can do is breathe in the air around her, desperately wanting to be as close to her as I can.

"I don't know what it takes. I'm broken. I've tried coping mechanisms and therapy. All my mental barriers have been worked through, but my body can't get past my trauma. I have panic attacks every time I'm touched," she whispers, only a few breaths away from my lips. Her words cool me down, my heart breaking for her.

"Do you want me?" I catch myself staring at her lips, waiting for her response.

"Yes, but…" She bites her bottom lip. That perfect, full, pink lip that I want to run my tongue across.

"No. No, buts. Nothing else matters. Tell me if you want this, if what's between us is as real for you as it is for me." *Please, please…*

"It's real."

My eyes squeeze shut at her admission. "Then that's all that matters to me. I'm not going anywhere."

Chapter Twenty-Two

Thea

C ontrary to what he just said, I watch aptly as Jesse pulls away and strides out of the kitchen, giving me room to breathe. Oh my God. What just happened? I don't know why I decided to spill my secrets about my voided sex life to him in the car, but it seemed to have made him feel better, so I don't regret it.

It set off a catalyst. The way he boxed me in against the kitchen sink was terrifying but intoxicating. He was so close that I could feel his body heat. I wanted him to touch me just as badly as I was afraid that he would.

It's all overwhelming and confusing, but what's not is my attraction to him. He's all man. Tall, broad shoulders, and thick arms. I want so badly to feel how firm every muscle is, but how soft his lips are at the same time. I want to know how well our bodies fit together.

Maybe it's all in my head and we won't be compatible, but I do know he wants me. He knows about my issues and he still wants me.

I squeeze my eyes shut, warding off the tears that are trying to escape. I can't believe this is real life. The joy oozing out of every pore right now seems like a dream. He said he'd do whatever it takes and I believe him. For the first time since that night six years ago, I feel safe enough with someone to try because I know he would never hurt me.

I'm a grown woman now. I'm in my own home. I have control here. I don't have to do anything I don't want to. This is my life and no one can take this from me.

With my newfound enthusiasm, I make my way to him in my living room, but not before pouring us both a glass of wine. In the spirit of putting myself out there, I want to show him how much I trust him.

When I sit the glass of sparkling white down in front of him on the coffee table, I see the recognition in his eyes. I only drink when I feel safe and I know I'm safe with him. Now he knows it too.

"Do you want to talk about whatever is bothering you?" I ask, wanting to be a safe place for him like he's been for me.

He sips on his wine before giving me a glimpse of his past few days, leaving out all the details that might tell me anything about his operation.

"I was laying on a shitty hospital bed for hours and all I wanted to do was call you. I even thought about searching for the library's number and leaving a message with whoever answered, but I didn't want to do that to you. I knew you'd worry about me, so I gritted my teeth and got through it.

"Then I went into that meeting today and couldn't think straight. Every sound was like a knife in my brain." He exhales slowly, blowing the air out through his mouth. "Being around you calms the noise."

"Being around you has been good for me too," I admit. "Next time, please call me. No matter what. If you want me there, I'll be there."

He leans his head back against the couch, smiling softly. "Okay, Sunshine. I will."

"Why do you call me that?" I ask, hoping this evening's open conversation will keep flowing. He stares at me for a moment, contemplating while I curl further into my favorite chair.

"At first," he begins. "I said it as a reflex when I saw your blonde hair and tan skin in that tiny Sunny's tank top, but then… I don't know, it seemed like every time I saw you, all the dark clouds parted over my head. You'd smile at me and…" He trails off, leaning his head to the side, looking at me thoughtfully. "Your smile has been the brightest light in my life," he says earnestly.

That silly black tank top with the golden suns, I swear I'll keep it as a memento for the rest of my life it means it helped set this relationship in motion. No one has ever made me feel so special, the weight of it is staggering. My heart wants to burst with all the love I have to give and I desperately want him to be the one I give it to.

"I noticed you for weeks. At the library," I clarify. "Every time you came in I couldn't stop looking at you. Latisha poked fun at me and begged me to ask you out. Obviously, I didn't have the courage, but when I saw you at the bar that first night…" I hesitate, not sure how much I want to admit.

"What?" He asks patiently.

"I was dying. You were so nice to me and so hot." I cover my face, embarrassed all over again. "I felt like a fool."

"Thea. Look at me," he says, waiting until I do. "You were the most stunning woman in the bar that night. You're the most stunning woman, period. Every man in there was

157

salivating over you, including me. You don't realize how much power you have. You could've wagged your finger at me and I would have fallen to my knees at your feet."

My jaw drops at his interpretation of that night. It's not at all how it felt to me. I felt like a black sheep in a wolf's den. The fact that he thinks I could have power over anyone is ridiculous, especially since I've spent years feeling so weak.

Knowing how affected he'd been by me causes warmth to pool in my belly, though. His words give me a new edge of confidence and way too much fuel for all my dirty fantasies. *Him on his knees in front of me...*

"I don't look like that normally though," I argue, still deeply burdened by my usual insecurities. "I prefer not to garner unwanted attention," I admit bashfully.

"Well, maybe it works for you because this is a small town and they know that they don't have a chance, but you are not any less beautiful just because you hide behind your sweaters at work." His accurate assessment of me stuns me.

Of course, he noticed my usual daily attire. He seems to notice everything. Even that first night when he pointed out my eye color so aptly. Most men don't know their pinks from purples, let alone give detailed descriptions of a woman's eye color.

"I couldn't ever see your eyes." Recalling that conversation at the bar. "I was excited that you came up to talk to me because I could see them clearly for the first time," I tell him, smiling at the memory.

"I wondered about that." He smirks at me, making me blush, then winces. "Sorry. I get migraines when I haven't slept enough," he explains, rubbing his forehead.

"I can take you back to the Inn if you need to sleep," I offer, worriedly. I don't like that he's in such obvious pain.

"Nah, I'll be fine. I don't want to go back there yet." He offers a half smile, but it doesn't reach his eyes.

"Don't move," I tell him, getting up from my chair. "I'll be right back."

"I don't think I could move if I tried." He leans back against the couch again, settling in.

He's worn out and all I want to do is take care of him, so I hurry upstairs to change out of my work clothes into something comfy. I grab my hairbrush before beelining my way back to the living room. Gingerly, I make my way towards the back of the couch, right behind where he's sitting.

"Stay still, please," I request before gently removing his hat. He stiffens slightly at my unexpected nearness, but instantly relaxes, letting me be. I have to take a few deep breaths to calm my mind, but I continue.

Slowly, I touch his sandy blonde hair with my fingertips and soak in the satisfaction of finally being able to do this. Needing a few more deep breaths here and there to ward off the anxiety threatening me, I spend a few minutes mindlessly playing with it before running my fingers through it completely.

This is fine. I'm safe. I'm touching him but he won't touch me. Not if I don't want him to. I want him too, but I'm not ready. Not yet.

I take my time, enjoying the simplicity of this interaction. Even working in a few three-strand braids in the longer pieces before brushing them back out with my fingers. It takes me a second to realize neither of us has spoken in a while and when I look, he's sound asleep.

I don't know why, but him sleeping in my home warms my

heart. I can't help but smile to myself at the innate innocence. Retrieving the brush out of my hoodie pocket, I take my time working it through his hair, adamant not to leave any tangles behind.

When I'm done, I admire his relaxed state. His arms are folded across his chest making his biceps bulge and his face is serene. The stress has melted off of him and he looks content.

More than anything, I admire him because he's here like no one else ever has been.

* * *

After a few hours, I'm deep into the second book of a fantasy series I'm reading, when he startles awake, needing a second to come to. The grogginess makes him look young and boyish. I can only imagine what he looked like as a little kid with chubby cheeks and dimples.

"I'm sorry," he groans his apology, rubbing his eyes after noticing the blanket I had draped over him.

"It's okay. You're cute when you sleep," I tell him easily.

"I've never been told that before," he smirks, running his hand over his hair like he's recalling where my fingers were. His other hand bumps into his hat where it sits on the cushion next to him. He grabs it as if he might put it back on, but instead sits it on the coffee table next to his unfinished glass of wine.

"I'm sure your mom thought so," I say before I can catch myself, immediately regretting bringing up something like that. The stupid wine made my brain fuzzy.

"Maybe…" he whispers, staring at his hands.

Chapter Twenty-Three

Jesse

When I woke up, I forgot where I was for a second, who I was. I couldn't remember if I was supposed to be Jesse or Jay. Then I looked over and saw her. Camped out in her chair with a book, her knees thrown over one of the arms, hair freshly braided and trailing down her side. All I felt was relief.

Being with Thea in her home feels like a sanctuary away from the fucked up things happening outside. Here, I'm just Jesse.

When she mentions my mom, I'm compelled to open up about my past. She's the first person that I've ever had the desire to talk to about my mom. Especially when there's an ache in my chest from memories wanting to be shared. I want her to know that part of my life. Every part.

"My mom was beautiful." I watch how her eyes soften at my use of the past tense. "She was a good mom. Loved me." I smile to myself remembering the good times with her. "But, she couldn't get away from my dad. He was a mean man and a drunk. He'd beat us, but mostly her. She died when I was seven."

"Oh, Jesse. I'm so sorry." She clutches the now-closed book to her chest.

"My dad… He killed her." She gasps, but I continue. "I was supposed to be at a neighbor's house when it happened, but I was in my room and heard everything. I was terrified.

"He tried to tell the cops that someone broke in, but they ended up coming to arrest him the night after her funeral. He shot himself before they could get the cuffs on. I heard that too." I down the rest of the wine from the glass she had given me, but it's not nearly enough to dull the ache.

"I can't even imagine…" She trails off, not needing to say anything. Words won't fix the pain I've experienced, but telling her feels cathartic nonetheless. Now that I've started, I don't want to stop.

"I think my mom saved me. I didn't know I was supposed to be at the neighbor's until I heard her tell my dad that through the wall. I think she only said it to keep him from coming after me too," I admit, not connecting the dots myself until I was much older.

"How could he be so evil?" Tears well up in her eyes and all I want to do is wipe them away before they have a chance to fall, but I clasp my hands together instead.

"I don't know. After him, and all the terrible people that I encountered in the group homes and foster homes, I got used to seeing the bad in people. No matter what happened to me though, I could never imagine hurting my wife and child. Never."

"You're a good man, Jesse. I've never doubted that. I can see it in your eyes," she assures me, calming the deep-rooted fear that I've always had. That I might turn out like my father despite my refusal.

"Sometimes I look in the mirror and I'm afraid that I'm looking at him. I don't have any photographs and the memories started fading years ago. It's hard to remember what my mom looked like, the small details."

"You're not him. You protected me, with Kyle and the guy at the bar."

"I hate men like that, Thea."

She nods in agreement, empathizing with me. "You didn't have any other family?"

"No, none that stepped in. I went into a foster home at first, but once I turned eight or nine, I was sent to a group home for boys. Then bounced around from there. The army was my way out. It was the first stable thing that I had," I admit, remembering how thrilled I was to have a permanent place to sleep and a hot meal every day. Then the paychecks came and I felt like I'd finally made it.

"But, you were all alone for so long." I can almost hear her heart breaking for me, the boy version of me.

"There was a chance at the beginning that my first-grade teacher would take me in. She wanted to, but she wasn't eligible for guardianship. I guess she was here teaching with a visa from Canada. I don't know, the details are murky at this point. You remind me of her when you're with your kids at the library."

"Were you able to keep in contact with her at all?"

"She tried for a year or two, but at some point, I'd moved so much that I figured she couldn't find me. It was easier than thinking that she might've given up on me." I shrug, trying not to relive the rejection I felt as a child.

Thea wipes away the tears from her face. My fingers flex wishing I could do it for her. "Thank you for telling me. I wish things had been different for you."

Me too, sweet girl.

"The army helped. Eventually, I had a team to depend on. It worked out."

"Now you don't have your team. Is that why Nathan wanted you to move here so badly?"

"He just misses me," I attempt to make light of my situation. How alone I've been my entire life feels pathetic, even to me.

"I might have mentioned to him that I was interested in you, by the way," she admits sheepishly. "He doesn't know how long I've known you or how we really met, but he told me all good things."

I can't hold back the smile that overtakes my face because she talked to him about me at all. A part of me was still worried that she'd want to hide this.

"I don't deserve it. He's been a good friend to me and I hate keeping the truth from him. I am going to tell him everything eventually. I owe him that. I've never lied to him before and I don't want this to be a secret."

"Okay," she agrees with a smile.

That one simple response confirms what I needed. She doesn't care that we'll have to tell her brother the truth. We're both jumping in head-first now. She's going to give this a chance.

However, I have to ask the question that's been eating at me. "Does he know about…?" I can't bring myself to finish the sentence out loud, but there is no need.

"No. I never told anyone, besides my therapist and Liv. Latisha knows foggy details because of working so closely with me these last two years, but I've never even told my mom." She shrugs as if she hasn't been carrying the heaviest weight in the world on her shoulders with hardly any support.

"Everyone thinks that I'm not interested in dating. Or maybe they think I'm gay, I don't know. I've never had any issues around my brother, I guess my brain always knew he was safe. So, they have no clue."

"Touching my hair was okay?" I wasn't expecting any type of touch from her anytime soon so I was shocked. I was more than willing to let her take all the time she needed.

The act itself seems innocent, but the connection was more than that. I felt closer to her at that moment than I've ever felt with anyone. I haven't been able to relax in weeks but it coaxed me right to sleep. I didn't mean for that to happen, but it was the most restful sleep that I've had in a long time.

"Yeah. I've never really had the chance to explore my boundaries. There's never been anyone that I've felt comfortable enough with to try," she explains, her fingers playing with her bottom lip, while I watch with envy.

"Anything you want, baby. I'm your guinea pig." I wink, making her giggle shyly. It's late, but I don't want to leave. I could sit here talking to her all night.

"Thank you for being so understanding and not pressuring me. It means a lot to me that you haven't judged me," she explains, looking at me sweetly.

"You deserve to feel safe and I would never judge you for that."

"I know, but I've not always had that experience. You're more thoughtful than all the other men I've encountered combined." She laughs, but I don't. I don't like what she's insinuating.

"Do you want to talk about it?" I'm already imagining the ways I want to eliminate every guy who's ever wronged her.

"No… No." She shakes her head, but I see her wheels turning, then she sighs. "One guy asked me out once. It was a few years back, Liv and I were at dinner. I told him that I wasn't interested. He thought forcing his way onto our table and draping himself over my chair was going to change my mind.

"I ended up flipping the table in my haste to get away from him. Liv almost got the cops called because she was screaming at him in the middle of the restaurant." She covers her face again, shaking her head but laughing. "It was a mess."

"I'm sorry that happened," I tell her truthfully. She doesn't deserve to be harassed like that. No one does. I can't stand bastards like that.

"Me too." She shrugs. Her clear dismissal worries me because I suspect it's one of the less traumatic moments of her past and that grates at my insides.

"Liv sounds like a good friend." I'm glad she had at least one person in her corner all these years.

"She's the best. She's a lawyer. Very argumentative." She laughs at her own joke, making me smile until a knock at the door startles us both.

"I'm not expecting anyone," she whispers, her eyes round with worry. I make my way to the door and look out the peephole.

For fuck's sake.

"It's Kyle. Go upstairs, stay in your room until I come to get you," I instruct, waiting for her to get up and move past me.

She halts midway up the stairs. "I should probably warn you. He's still not happy with me. He sent me a text calling me a bitch so, I blocked his number."

167

"You're only telling me this now?" I'm whispering, but my tone is exasperated. As if I haven't been showing her this whole time that her safety is important to me. She somehow still doesn't believe me.

"Sorry, I forgot. My mind's been preoccupied." She gestures between us.

"One of these days I'm going to spank your ass." I meant it as a mild threat, but the look on her face is nothing short of intrigued. Jesus Christ. "Go. Lock your door."

This woman is going to kill me.

Chapter Twenty-Four

Thea

I should be worried that Kyle is here. Frightened even. It's after 10 o'clock on a Tuesday night, he has no reason to show up at my door. If anything, I'm annoyed. Jesse and I were on a roll, making leaps in our communication, and now I'm hiding in my room all alone like a child.

I have all the faith in the world that Jesse will handle whatever the heck Kyle wants though and it's relieving. It's been so long since I could depend on anyone for anything.

The big Kyle incident was two weeks ago and I had hoped it was all behind me. Jesse hanging out at the library so much was distracting. My eyes weren't scanning the entrances for unexpected visits from Kyle, only expected visits from Jesse.

I stopped looking over my shoulder in the parking lot because he was always there to walk me to my car. The stress that I've carried for so long, even before my issues with Kyle, has fallen away in his presence.

I creep over to my bedroom window that faces out over the porch and silently open it a crack. I can't see them because the porch is covered, but if I listen closely, I can hear the interaction.

"You don't know who you're messing with, man," Kyle threatens, lamely. I can't contain my eye roll. I don't know who gave him the confidence to think he can be big and tough against someone like Jesse.

"I don't give a fuck. Don't ever come back here. If I see you around her again, I'll make sure it's the very last time." Jesse threatens and I feel the weight of it all the way up here, making me grin.

Oh my God. I shouldn't be turned on by him saying that, but I am. What is wrong with me?

First, he threatens to spank me and I get a thrill of excitement, then he threatens someone for my honor and my insides turn to jelly. Maybe, I need to go back to therapy.

The stairs creak, warning me that he's coming up to my room. I quickly shut the window and jump up before I'm caught eavesdropping.

"Thea?"

I open my door and take a step back, wondering if he'll come inside. He braces his arms on the top of the door frame, leaning against it instead, filling the space.

"Thank you, for um, handling that," I stutter out, too distracted by how imposing he looks to think straight.

"He said he forgot a tool, I told him to buy a new one and not to come back." He shrugs. "If he does, don't be nice. Call the police right away." His tone leaves no question. He's serious.

"Okay," I agree quietly. He takes a step into the room and it sends a shiver down my spine. "You're the only man that's ever been in my room." The time Kyle was in here snooping doesn't count.

"Good," he states, wandering further into my space.

I sit down on my bed, letting him look around. He was in here once before, but that was more formal. This time he takes his time, looking at the photos on my dresser, and examining some of the jewelry that I have laying out.

His being in here like this, so late at night, is wildly intimate. I'm having a hard time remembering that I can't be touched, because I want him to touch me so desperately. I want him to defile me in the bed that I've been lying in alone for years.

"Why is the drawer missing?" He asks, peering at the gaping rectangular hole in my nightstand. Crap.

"Umm. Remember when I told you that I threw away all of my panties?"

He clearly remembers. He looks at me like, *duh*. I also don't miss how his eyes flicker down my body at the mention of my underwear.

"Well, he messed around in there too. I was so creeped out that I dumped the whole drawer in the dumpster."

"Thea. What was in the drawer?" He asks after briefly squeezing his eyes shut. He knows. He definitely knows what I had in that drawer, but he's going to make me say it anyway.

"Nothing important..."

"Thea," he insists.

"My toys." There, I said it. I'm a grown woman, I can talk about vibrators.

He seems calm as he walks closer toward me, stopping just as his knees hit the edge of the bed where I'm sitting with my legs curled up, but I know better. His normally cool demeanor is suddenly rigid and wound-tight.

"What kind of toys?" He leans forward, bracing his hands on either side of me, not touching me, but close. My heart flutters at his nearness, I don't know if I'll ever get used to it.

"A vibrating wand, a dildo, and…"

"And?"

"Lube. And, a butt plug." I'm so embarrassed, I cover my face. It's so personal, I've never shared that aspect of my life with anyone. I like to pleasure myself. I experiment because it's all I can do when I've missed out on years of my twenties.

"So, what have you been doing since you threw it all away?" He asks, with a slightly pained expression on his face. All I do is raise my hand, wiggling my fingers, in response to his question.

"I want you to show me." His voice is low and gravely, scratching my insides in the best way.

"What? I can't do that," I answer, breathlessly.

We stare at each other for a beat, neither of us breaking away, sharing each other's oxygen. In and out, we breathe each other in until I'm sure that I'm getting drunk on him.

I want him to kiss me, desperately, but I'm terrified. I know it's too soon, but I've waited so long and I want him to be the one to fix me so badly.

He straightens abruptly, breaking the vortex between us as he digs into his back pocket. Pulling out his wallet, he throws a credit card on the bed next to me.

"Take that, buy whatever the hell you want. Replace all of it." He puts his wallet away, completely serious.

"I can't. I'll feel bad spending your money."

"Thea, knowing that the toys I paid for would be making you cum…" He pauses, blowing out a strained breath. He's worked up and the heat of it is burning right through me, lighting me on fire. His dark gaze sweeps across me as I suck in a breath, aware of how my body is trembling.

CHAPTER TWENTY-FOUR

"I want every orgasm to belong to me from here on out, one way or another."

My jaw drops. He's so serious and his possessiveness makes my core clench with desire.

I'm too consumed by this moment to mention that it's unnecessary. He has starred in all of my fantasies since I first saw him. My orgasms are already his, but it's so satisfying to hear him claim them. We went from giving this relationship a chance to diving head first off the diving board into the deep end.

"I'm going to leave now. I want you to get ready for bed, get under the covers and make yourself cum with your fingers. Think about me because I'll have my hand wrapped around my cock thinking about you when I get in bed tonight too." He turns to leave without another word, leaving me gaping after him. He's so outward with his desires, so bold. I wish I could be that brave.

He's just through my bedroom door when I recall something. "Wait, your truck is still at the library," I shout, reminding him.

"I'll walk. I need to cool off." He continues down the stairs without glancing back.

Chapter Twenty-Five

Jesse

I expected her to be standoffish, timid even when it came to sex, but somehow I ran out of her house feeling like the one out of my element. All I could think about was her laying naked in her bed using sex toys to fuck herself. I wanted so desperately to know what she looks like when she cums, I almost got on my knees and begged.

I suck in lungfuls of the night air as I walk the two-ish miles back to the library where my truck's parked. It's almost the end of September, but the weather is still thick with humidity this far south. The cicadas humming from the trees that line the street are helping drown out some of the absolutely depraved thoughts in my head, making room for more sane things.

For one, I need to hurry up and crack this undercover case and move on from this part of the job. I'll switch over to investigations, and tell them I'm not willing to travel anymore for extended periods. That will give me a chance to finally settle down and establish a home base. Things might be moving too fast between me and Thea, but it's too late. There's nowhere else I'd rather be than here. Life is too short to let this opportunity pass me by.

As if I conjured him out of thin air thinking about the job, Curtis appears next to me in the street, idling in his '05 Toyota Camry. I'm far enough from Thea's house now, I don't think he'd ever realize where I was or why I'm out this way.

"Hey, what are you doing?" Curtis asks through his rolled-down window.

"Taking a walk."

"Well, get in. We need to go to the farm."

Shit. The last thing I want to do is go back to that place. I was hoping I could get a few more hours of sleep tonight, but I said I wanted to solve the case and I can't do that from my motel room.

I just need their plan, then I'm done. Once the information is out there and we're able to stop them from committing a criminal act, then the group will disintegrate, Jameson will go to prison, and I'll be done.

I get in Curtis' car, hoping like hell this isn't going to be another all-nighter, but I'm not actually that naive.

* * *

Once again, the cool air that hits me as I walk through the double-door entrance to the library is like a sigh of relief after the last twelve hours.

"What happened?" Thea looks alarmed by my haggard appearance. The tape over my stitches is peeling and I can't even imagine the grime seeping in. I've been sweating for hours. I wouldn't be surprised if she smelled me before she saw me.

"I got pulled into a work thing. It's been a hell of a long night. I'm just now getting back to my truck, but I wanted to stop in and say hi before I crash." I rest my elbows on the counter in front of her and rub my face. I'm beat.

"I noticed it parked here earlier." The concern is clear in her eyes.

"You worried about me, baby?" I ask cheekily with the last bit of my energy reserves, watching her lips twitch upward at my term of endearment.

That small reaction and others like it are what makes her so irresistible. I want to witness all of them. I want to be the reason for all of them.

"Of course, I worry. I hope you can get some rest," she murmurs sweetly, her fingers twitching against the counter like she's fighting the urge to reach out to me. *Ditto, sweetheart.*

"I'll try my best. The motel bed sucks and the walls are made of paper. I can't imagine I'll get more than a few hours of sleep. I'll probably end up on your porch waiting for you to get home." My attempt at being funny falls flat, but I'm too tired to make it sound less sad. I can't even muster up a fake smile.

"Then go to my house now." She rustles around in a drawer below her, pulling out her key chain. "Here, take my key."

"What?" My brain's not computing what she's saying.

"If you think you'll end up at my house anyway, go there now. Take a shower, sleep in my bed. I have blackout curtains and thick walls." She giggles, sliding the key across the counter to me. All I do is stare at it for a moment.

"You want me to use your shower and sleep in your bed?" I

ask, confirming that I'm not making all of this up in my head.

"Yes." She grabs something else from the drawer below her. "I like knowing that you're in my space, in my bed." She slides my credit card across the counter, the one that I gave her last night to repurchase her toys.

She's using my own logic back at me. She isn't ready for me to be in her bed the traditional way but will be satisfied knowing that I'm there regardless.

"Did you use it?" I check before I stow it away in my wallet.

"Yes. Thank you." She smiles, giving me that brilliant radiance that only she can.

It's enough to spur me forward, giving me the drive to get a change of clothes from the motel and over to her house. I almost brought everything from my room, so I never have to come back, but even I realize that would be a little presumptuous.

The seal has already been broken though. Now that I know she wants me in her house and in her bed, I'll never want to leave.

* * *

12 hours ago...

"Jameson said there might have been a breach, he needs us over there securing the property," Curtis tells me excitedly like this is a high-priority mission.

All I can think is, shit, does he know I snuck onto his property the other night? I was careful, but I might have left too much blood behind after I was hit.

"Someone trespassing?" I ask hesitantly.

"Maybe. He didn't say." *Dammit.* I hope I'm not walking into a trap.

We drive in relative silence out to the farm, where there isn't much else of anything. It's near the most northern point of Rollins County. His property is the flattest lot this far into the mountains, which must be why he still calls it the farm. Aside from the barns on his land, no crops are being grown in the fields, and no animals are being raised.

We pull in through the gate and I groan. Spotlights are lighting up the property in the dead of night, illuminating the yard as we park and join the others. This can't be good.

"Now that you're all here, I can tell you what's going on. It's time to fortify the farm. We are no longer safe, our property is no longer untouched by civilization."

What the hell is this guy talking about?

"The new Sheriff paid me a visit this morning. The nerve of him." He grunts. "I am going to make him regret ever crossing me."

Is he threatening to cause harm to a law enforcement officer? I can't stand by and let anything like that happen, but I stay quiet, trying to remain unbothered.

I can't even recall who the current Sheriff is since the last one met an overdue demise in a hunting cabin outside of Whitewater last year. The name has to be on a list in the stack of information I have about the area, but my brain is fried. I'm still so tired.

"Who's the Sheriff?" I ask Curtis quietly, while the others shuffle about unloading pallets full of extension cords, barbed wire, and metal fencing.

"Uh, some young guy. McDonald, maybe? He was a state

trooper. I've heard Jameson complain about him quite a bit, some personal family beef I guess."

A trooper named McDonald... Why does that ping a transmission in my brain somewhere? *Malec.*

"Any chance that his name is Malec?" I ask, remembering the trooper who helped Nathan and Callie last year after she was attacked. He had a clean history. I didn't have any concerns that he'd turn around and backstab them like Sheriff Donahue had. Hopefully, whatever beef he has with Jameson isn't a sign that he's involved in any of this.

"Yeah, that's it," Curtis answers absently, nodding to Derrick and Mitch who are standing a few feet away.

"What happened, man?" Derrick asks Jameson. The only one seemingly brave enough to speak to him directly.

"The neighbor has been nosing in my business, sending complaints to the Sheriff and giving him a reason to snoop. So, we're locking shit down. Tonight." He walks off without another word, leaving us to work.

The rest of the night is spent securing the five-acre property. Where there was fencing, we added barbed wire. Where there were holes in the chain link, we repaired them. Spotlights and cameras were added to every corner and covered every building on the property. Last but not least, a delivery of sandbags was set up to form a makeshift barricade about twenty yards from the bomb test site that I witnessed Sunday night.

They plan to test more bombs. This place needs to be shut down now, whether they have a master plan or not.

By the time we get to leave, the sun has been up for hours. Curtis is dragging his feet more than I am but still has to take me back into town. I decide to use this opportunity to get more information out of him while he's tired, maybe his defenses will be down.

"Did you know they were planning to make bombs?" I watch his reaction out of the corner of my eye.

"No, I didn't know. Jameson was in the military ya know, maybe that stuff excites him," Curtis explains away, but even I can tell he doesn't really believe that.

"Do you think he wants to hurt people?" I take a risk with that question, hoping it doesn't make him defensive of his friend and shut down on me. He doesn't answer me for a long time, only focusing on the road, making me think I blew it.

"What do we do if he does? I don't want to hurt people, Jay. I thought these guys were just pissed off and wanted an excuse to party. I'm not so sure about it anymore." He runs his free hand through his hair aggressively. He's torn up about this and I'm fucking relieved. He's so young, the last thing he needs is to be mixed up with this.

"We'll lay low. Keep an eye on them. Maybe they're all talk. Jameson might just like the power trip." I try to ease his worry, but I don't think they're going to stop at just a few test bombs on private property. I think this is the real deal.

We pull up to the library where my truck is, but before I can get out, Curtis speaks up. "I just wanted to belong somewhere. The army was supposed to be my ticket, but then it felt like they betrayed me when they wouldn't let me come home for my grandma's funeral. I thought this was it, too. I'm sorry that I even introduced you to them, Jay."

I feel bad, knowing how much I've manipulated this kid. I'm not his friend, but I don't think he deserves it as much as I did when I first started this operation. When it's all said and done, I'll make sure he gets help. If he manages to stay out of prison, I'll hook him up with resources to get a fresh start. It's the least I can do.

Chapter Twenty-Six

Thea

U sually, I stay well past closing time when I have the late shift, but not today. I can't wait to get home knowing that Jesse's there. I'm practically skipping up the sidewalk after I get out of my car.

The house is silent when I enter, so I quietly remove my shoes before tiptoeing up the stairs. The fading light outside dims my room but it doesn't stop my eyes from focusing on the man I've been dying to get home to.

It's a surreal experience, him laying on my bed with no shirt, face buried in my pillow. I creep over, staring at him like a pervert. I can't get enough. He's here. Half naked in my bed. It makes me giddy.

Could I lay with him? There's plenty of room and I can't resist. If he starts to wake up, I'll move so he doesn't accidentally touch me. Is that weird?

Would he want to know first before sharing a bed with me? No.

He told me yesterday he would be my guinea pig. I change into comfy clothes and then slowly slide myself onto the bed above the covers.

Deep breath. I'm okay, this is good.

He shifts slightly in his sleep and my body locks up until I realize he's only grasping my pillow harder, clutching it to his face. Being a stomach sleeper wasn't something I ever wondered about him, but now I'm thrilled to know. I put one of my extra pillows between us as a buffer before getting comfortable next to him.

Feeling safe enough to do this always seemed out of reach. I never imagined that meeting Jesse would lead me here. It's comforting being able to lay in the same bed with a man that I trust. A man that I've completely fallen for.

There's no denying it. Now that I've gotten to know him, I'm a goner. I feel everything so deeply, I always have. The hopelessness and loneliness have been at the forefront these last six years, but I'm exhausted. I want to enjoy this experience while it lasts even if there is an expiration date.

If it all comes to a halt eventually, I'll still cherish what I have right now. He's everything that I've ever dreamed of and more. Kind, gentle, and understanding. He's defended me and protected me without expecting anything in return. He's capable of so much, especially after all he's gone through in his life.

My attraction to him is almost painful. I never knew the mere sight of someone could make my insides hot, but here we are.

My eyes trace across the strong muscles of his back wishing my fingers could do the same.

Why can't they?

Deep breath, I can do this.

Flexing my fingers to psyche myself up, I start at his hair where I know it's safe, slowly running them over the strands that I memorized last night. It's freshly dried and soft, I can't help imagining him in my bathroom taking a shower. Thinking of him standing under the water spray with rivulets of soap running down his body makes me lose my breath.

I squeeze my eyes shut for a minute to restore my equilibrium and before I realize what I'm doing, my fingers have trailed down to his neck. I pause, taking in the feel of his smooth skin.

Another deep breath. I can do this.

Tracing the skin across his shoulder blades and down his spine is a slow battle, my mind struggling to accept that I can do it. The pressure is light, and I'm not even applying the whole pad of my pointer finger, but I feel it. I feel him.

The blankets stop my downward trajectory, directing me over to his hip and back up his side, where I feel a scar. It's too dim in here to see it clearly, but if I look closely, I can tell there's a slight discoloration to his skin. My fingertip lingers on it, memorizing it.

"It's from shrapnel. I was too close to a car bomb," he whispers into the quiet room, surprising me. I didn't have any clue that he was awake.

I don't respond, not wanting to stop my momentum. Instead, I resume outlining his back until my finger runs across another indentation.

"Grazed by a bullet."

My heart skips a beat, but I keep going. I trace his skin until I'm certain I've touched every inch of his exposed backside. When I reach a smooth patch just to the left of his spine on his lower back, I pause again, memorizing it.

"I fell down some wooden stairs at one of my group homes," he whispers, somberly.

"How old were you?" I whisper back to him in the still-darkening room, the sun is nearly set now, only leaving a faint orange glow on the ceiling.

"12." My heart breaks. Poor, sweet Jesse.

"Were there any good homes?" I ask, hoping he had even a small piece of good in all of the bad. He turns his head to look at me and I'm struck by how handsome he is.

The sleepiness that lingers makes him look softer but it doesn't distract from the angular jawline that I can't wait to be brave enough to touch or the temptation of his lips.

"One of my foster homes wasn't horrible. I was fifteen and placed with an old woman. She made me do a shit ton of yard work, housework, you name it, but I had my own room and she fed me for every meal. I was there for almost nine months until she died. I found her cold in her bed, she passed in her sleep." I gasp, but he continues.

"After that, I was in a youth shelter until I turned 18. Then I enlisted." He speaks as if it was no big deal, but I can only imagine all the rest of the battles he fought in life before he ever even joined the military.

The pain and suffering he went through as a child is unfathomable. I still don't understand how he could turn out so put together, so unscathed.

"I wish I knew you then. I wish I was there to hold you before I was broken, so you had someone on your side," I confess, the guilt I feel inside eating me up.

I want to hug him so badly. How can I let my trauma keep us apart when he's gone through the unimaginable? His doesn't hold him back. What is wrong with me?

"I wish you were too, but it's okay. I joined the army, found some friends, found your brother. He wasn't much of a hugger, but he's definitely had my back all these years. The army saved my life." He doesn't explain what he means by that but I have a feeling that I know exactly what he's implying.

"I'm glad." My hand is splayed completely on his back now, I flex my fingers slightly, taking pride in my small accomplishment.

"It's hard to believe that I haven't met you until now. All the years I've known Nathan," he mumbles in disbelief, pulling me from my silence.

"Well, I was on the coast going to school and pretty far retreated into my shell these last few years. Nathan swears that it was a coincidence that he built his cabin so near to where I landed my job, but part of me thinks he felt guilty. We missed out on a lot of years after my dad died. He went straight into the military and I was home with a grieving mother." I think back to my high school years when I'd come home to a darkened house and my mom crying. I never knew what to do to help and I was grieving my dad, too.

"Do you resent him for leaving?"

"Umm," I hesitate, not sure if I should answer this question.

"I'm not asking as his person, Thea. I'm asking as yours," he clarifies, making my stomach flutter. He's looking at me thoughtfully, oozing with silent support and I eat it up. It's been so long since I've had someone to lean on.

"I did resent him for a while. It was really hard dealing with my mom by myself. We were both so sad all the time and it ruined most of my high school experience, but once I went to college I realized why he had left. It was freeing to get away from the memories. Undergrad was some of the best years of my life. Then..." I stop, not sure what to say.

"Then, what?"

CHAPTER TWENTY-SIX

"I came home for the summer before grad school and everything changed."

"About six years ago," he states, not needing to ask.

"Yeah."

He turns onto his back suddenly, but I hardly flinch. I'm not worried if he'll respect my boundaries. I know he won't touch me and that knowledge is freeing. I can relax in his presence and honestly, I'm so comfortable that I don't want to move.

"I want you to tell me, but only when you're ready." He looks at me so genuinely, with so much care in his eyes, it makes me want to tell him but I can't. Saying the story out loud is terrifying.

"Can I try something?" He speaks again, letting me off the hook.

"Like, what?"

"I want to brush your hair." He sits up, letting me see his entire upper half unobstructed for the first time and I think a little drool escapes me. He's perfect. Every muscle I had imagined on him is firm and sculpted. Even in the dim room, I can tell that his shoulders are broad, and his stomach is lean.

The sparse blonde hair on his chest is lighter than his other hair and almost invisible but gets slightly darker as it gets lower beneath his belly button.

"Uh, sure," I answer without thinking, too distracted by his body. It takes the entire length of time for him to get my brush off the dresser and to sit back on the bed for me to realize what he asked, and what I agreed to. "Wait."

"I won't touch you. If you aren't ready, I understand."

Of course he understands, he's the most kind and caring person in the world. He would never do anything to harm me. *I can do this. I'm safe.* I repeat that mantra over and over as I sit up and face away from him.

"Ready?" His voice is barely above a whisper right behind me.

"Yeah." I squeeze my eyes shut, picturing him behind me. The brush makes contact and I still. It's Jesse, he won't hurt me. I repeat it in my head, but it's not helping.

I try grounding myself instead. I'm in my room. I can see my dresser. I feel my bed. I can hear the whirring of my air conditioning. Jesse is behind me. Jesse is brushing my hair. He won't hurt me. He cares about me.

Except, it doesn't work. My thoughts are being carried away faster than I have a chance to control them. The image I have of him behind me starts glitching in my head. It fades in and out, replacing itself with the memory of the face I never want to see again.

I thought I could do this but the initial trickling of fear starts to escalate. Before I know it, my muscles are tensing and my anxiety is turning to panic.

"Stop." The brushing immediately ceases and I take more than a few calming breaths before I can speak again. "I'm sorry." I breathe out, burying my face in my hands, embarrassed. I'm so weak.

"No, I'm sorry. I didn't mean to push you." His regretful voice sweeps over me and with it a calmness. Hearing him speak instantly eases my fear, bringing me back to the present and out of the past.

I *can* do this. I have to.

"I think... I want to keep trying, but I need a second." I get off the bed to turn the light on, brightening all the dark shadows that have taken over. Seeing him even more clearly

188

now that the light is on, I try not to melt where I'm standing.

The distraction works to soothe the rest of my nerves and I forget for a moment why I stood up. He cocks his head at me when I don't stop staring at him.

"Sorry." *I'm not sorry.*

"You're allowed to look, Thea." He laughs and although his smile is at my expense, I soak it in.

"Right. About that… Will you come over here and sit on the floor with me?" I point to where my floor-length mirror sits.

"I'll do anything you ask, Sunshine." I can tell that he means it and my cheeks warm.

"If you sit behind me, I can see you and it might help. Also, your voice." We both sit.

"My voice?" He raises his eyebrow at me in the reflection of the mirror.

"It helps. My brain recognizes your voice and it makes me less anxious," I explain.

Chapter Twenty-Seven

Jesse

My voice helps her... I don't know why that statement stuns me, but I can't fathom that I could have such an impact on someone. All my life I have been brushed aside and forgotten, but now I can be someone's comfort. I always want to be that person for her.

"Start at the bottom and work your way up, in case it tangles," she instructs, walking me through how to brush her hair. Her tone is formal, and serious even, as if taking away the personal aspect of this act will help her get through it easier.

I've never done this before and I'm not sure why I thought I should try, aside from how much I enjoy it when she touches my hair. It's a small form of physical connection, but it'll be ours.

I ease the brush through her waves, afraid that I'll hurt her if I tug too hard. Glancing ever so often into the mirror to make sure she's okay, I catch her eyes studying me. I'm not sure that she's blinked. As if she's afraid that closing her eyes even for a second will ruin this.

"When's the last time someone brushed your hair?"

"My mom did it when I was little." Her small voice doesn't sound frightened, but she doesn't sound like her normal self either.

"Do you want me to stop?" I pause brushing, maintaining eye contact in the mirror. She blinks a few times as if she was in a trance then shakes her head.

"I'm okay, I promise." She gives a small smile, urging me on. I brush through the long strands, smoothing them down her back until I'm sure there aren't any knots. Then I keep brushing for a few more minutes since she seems content.

"The first-grade teacher I told you about, Miss Carlisle. She had dark black, curly hair. It was shorter, above her shoulders, but the ringlets would bounce when she taught and it mesmerized me. She always wore a red headband, or earrings, and red lipstick. Reminds me of you and your yellow," I tell her, thinking of all the dresses I've seen her wear at work.

"The kids like it when I wear yellow. I started buying a lot of it subconsciously until one day I realized it was my entire work wardrobe." She laughs, "I'm not even a huge fan of the color, but I do like yellow flowers."

"Your favorite color is green, then?"

"Yeah. How'd you know?" She looks bewildered.

"Your furniture for one thing and I've seen you wear green when you run." I shrug, trying to play it off like I haven't been obsessively observing every detail of her life.

"And, your eyes." She smiles sweetly as she says it.

Not only am I flattered, but her approval makes me want to jump her. I want to bury my hands in her thick blonde hair and kiss her senseless.

"What's your favorite color?" She asks before I have a chance to do something I'll regret like touching her without permission. She eyes me suspiciously in the mirror now, waiting for my response. She seems surprised that I've been paying such close attention to her.

"I like your yellow skirts." I wink, making her blush. "Or, maybe that shade of pink." I point to her cheeks in the mirror. "Or, the blue of your eyes," I add, meaning each one of my responses.

"You're too much." She giggles, shaking her head at me. "I believe every word you say so easily... I'm afraid you're going to break my heart," she whispers, surprising me.

I'm not sure what to say to make her understand how committed I am to this without making her run for the hills. I would rather die than ever hurt her.

We gaze at each other in the reflection of the mirror, her small frame dwarfed by mine. She's the most precious thing in this world to me already. Nothing else seems like it matters.

"Your heart is safe with me, I promise," I tell her as genuinely as I can, hoping it's enough for now.

"Okay," she whispers, smiling gently.

"Okay." I smile back, before setting the brush down that I've been holding. "Can I braid it?"

"You know how to braid?" She asks skeptically.

"I've braided a shit ton of paracord, can't be much different than hair." I shrug, cracking my neck like I'm preparing for a wrestling match.

"Go for it." She giggles.

I start slowly, careful not to graze the skin of her neck with my fingers when I grab each piece. I weave the strands together but quickly find that it's much harder than paracord.

Her hair is thick and my fingers are daft trying to figure out how to grab each piece while keeping hold at the same time.

I have to stop and start over multiple times, smoothing it back out. I'm concentrating so hard that I forget to check her reflection to see if she's okay until she snorts a laugh.

"What?"

"Your face. You're so serious, it's funny. But, cute, very cute," she assures me, laughing again. I don't mind that she's making fun of me, I'm just glad she's comfortable and happy. I'll make a fool of myself if it makes her smile.

"Alright, alright. One more try then I'm giving up." I take my time, braiding the three pieces together until I get a semi-decent length of braid. "Boom! Got it." I exclaim, victoriously and she claps for me.

"Now what?" She smiles, mischievously.

"What do you mean?" I look at the hair I'm holding, wondering what I'm missing.

I glance at her wrists instinctively as she raises them. "No hair tie."

"You set me up." I feign astonishment while she laughs.

"There's one in my bottom nightstand drawer." She points, and we both calculate the distance, realizing that I can't reach it from here.

"Okay, here we go. Trust-building exercise." I get to my feet, lifting her braid as she stands with me, and we shuffle over towards her bed while I try not to tug her like she's on a leash.

I have to dig through her bottom drawer until I find an elastic, then take entirely too long to figure out how to wrap it around the end of the braid while she laughs at my expense.

"I've never done this before, be nice." I plead dramatically, making her laugh harder. I mess up a few extra times, only to keep hearing her so amused and carefree. By the time I get her hair secured, she's falling on her bed in a fit of giggles. It's the sweetest sound that I've ever heard.

"Thank you, for doing my hair," she says once her laughing ceases. The way she's lying on her bed, limbs scattered and relaxed, she looks beautiful. All the little hairs I missed have fallen around her, framing her face. She's gorgeous, inside and out.

"Any time." Braiding her hair just became one of my favorite memories.

I sit on the foot of the bed, giving her plenty of space even though I want nothing more than to cover her body with mine. Especially when she can't keep her eyes from straying to my bare chest. I should've put a shirt on for decency's sake, but I like the way she looks at me. Like she can't get enough.

"When do you think you'll have to go back to Texas?" She asks suddenly.

"I don't know, but I put in transfer papers while I was doing all of the other stacks of paperwork at the hospital the other day."

Her mouth pops open in surprise and I watch her closely, afraid that I scared her off.

"You really want to stay?" she asks, bashfully, making me want to erase the space between us and kiss her as my answer. My muscles tense painfully, keeping me in place.

"Your brother practically twisted my arm about it when I left his house Sunday morning, so the timing felt right. Especially now that I can't leave his sister alone," I admit, hesitantly.

She smiles shyly but it lets me breathe easier. I'm moving

fast but I'm not trying to freak her out.

"What if they deny the transfer request?"

"I don't know," I answer honestly. "I've always been too afraid to get my hopes up for anything... Until now. I don't want to miss out on this, that's all I know." I nod my head towards her so there is no mistaking what I mean.

She sits up, leaning back on her hands, and studies me with a tilt of her head. "I don't want to miss out on it either. You mean a lot to me already, Jesse."

I squeeze my eyes shut, absorbing her admission. It's so strange to hear those words from someone when I'm not used to being cared about by anyone. I won't survive if I fuck this up. I've lost too much already.

"I'll make it work, whatever happens," I vow. Despite my fear, I don't want to regret not doing everything I can to keep her. If some higher power is offering me the chance of a life with her then I'm taking it. I'll do whatever it takes. She's all that matters now.

"What if I'm not worth it?" She asks in that small voice that I know means she's letting herself get lost in the depths of her past.

"You are. I promise."

"What if you find out everything about me and decide that I'm too damaged? What if I can't get past the touching issue?" She asks, biting her bottom lip.

"I know all about damage, Sunshine. Nothing can scare me away. Not even your fears. If I have to be handcuffed to this bed every time you want to touch me then I'd do it, because any piece of you that I get is more than I had before. My life was nothing before I met you. I was only floating through from one day to the next." I shrug, only scratching the surface with my confession.

Work was all I had. My apartment in Texas is bare bones, with no pictures on the walls, and no memories. The rare hookup with a stranger from a bar never meant anything more than a warm body in my bed. I'd wake up the next morning and strip the sheets, never thinking twice about who she was.

Holidays were regular days. On the rare occasion that I'd travel back to Indiana to visit my mom's grave, I'd barely make it 12 hours before fleeing the state. Visiting my past is like walking through hell.

"I want to tell you what happened to me, why I'm like this, but I need you to know why." She shifts closer to me, sitting on her knees beside me on the bed. "The only reason that I want to tell you everything is because *you* are worth it to me." She points to where my heart is, making me feel the weight of her words.

"I had accepted that I would never get my happily ever after in life. I was broken beyond repair. At first, when I saw you in the library, it was like seeing a life that I'd never have. All I could do was imagine what it would be like to meet a handsome stranger and have a real connection. I knew it couldn't happen for me and that was okay. I was sad, but I moved on from the idea because I couldn't live in limbo. Wanting was too painful."

"Thea..." I want to tell her how badly she deserves the world, how badly I want to give it to her, but she stops me.

"Then you came into Sunny's and I couldn't breathe. I couldn't think of anything other than you and I didn't even know you. Now, I know you, the real you, and I've never wanted anything more. I want you more than the risk of healing old wounds, more than the shame I feel when I think of what happened to me all those years ago and in the years since. I'll risk it for you because it's less than the risk of never getting a chance to be with you at all."

I grip the comforter in my hands, needing to hold something so I don't reach out to her. Not being able to touch her is painful for me. I want to so badly, and it makes it worse that I know she wants me to. She wants to be held and touched. She needs it, but she's not ready.

"I don't know if I believe in God, Thea. I gave up on him answering my prayers a long time ago, but if he is out there…" I clear my throat, warding off the emotion that's making it feel thick. "I'd thank him for leading me to this town, for leading me to you. Maybe he was trying all of these years, but instead, I've been stuck with your bonehead brother. I want to kick his ass for not bringing me around you years ago." I mean every word, but she laughs. With watery eyes, she smiles at me, once again parting every dark cloud that hangs over my head.

It takes every fiber of my being not to beg her to be mine forever right now. I never imagined that I'd get married, never thought I'd have a wife, but looking at Thea is like looking at the blueprint of a future that I never thought I deserved.

I've never wanted anything as badly as I want her. It scares the shit out of me.

"Will you stay with me tonight?" She asks shyly. No part of me could say no to her, nor do I want to.

"I'll stay as long as you want. I might have to sneak out if work comes up, but I'll always come back," I promise.

I haven't checked my phone at all, forgetting to even

pretend to care that I should be on call for Jameson's bat-shit-crazy movement.

She nods, happy with my answer.

Chapter Twenty-Eight

Thea

We lay down in my bed on our respective sides, the pillow between us keeping my anxiety at bay. With the lights off once again, the room is cloaked in darkness. The streetlights provide just enough glow to reveal the shadow of his face before me.

Our bodies are turned toward each other, our hands clutching the pillow as if it's the surrogate for where we want to touch. His hand rests so close to mine that I can't fight the allure of reaching out to barely trace his pinkie finger with my own. It's a whisper of a touch, but feels like an intimate midnight kiss.

"Are you tired?" He had just slept for hours while I was at work, yet here he is lying in the dark with me.

"I could use a nap," he says seriously, making me giggle.

"Is it okay if I tell you what happened to me now? It feels easier in the dark."

I'm trying to be brave, but I'm still afraid of my past. Reliving it is never easy. Liv was the first person that I told after it happened and I fell apart. It was the first time I had said it out loud because I had been trying to pretend it never happened.

She was concerned when the semester started and I couldn't get out of bed. She knew me better than anyone and could tell I was shattered. She begged me to go to the police but I refused. She was in law school at the time and swore she'd be by my side if I wanted to go after the man who hurt me.

I wasn't strong enough to handle the pressure of it so I lashed out and almost ruined my friendship with her. Instead of walking away from me, she helped me find a therapist. It took me weeks to build up the courage to tell my story again, but I went.

That was six years ago now, and other than snippets of confessions to Latisha, I haven't uttered the details about it to anyone else in my life.

"Only if you're ready," he assures me. He doesn't push me and it makes me want to tell him even more. There's a comfort in knowing that he takes me as me, that I'm safe no matter what. He doesn't offer conditions or stipulations, only support.

"I'm ready." *I hope.*

"Okay." He nods his head in encouragement and I take a deep breath.

"The summer after I graduated with my Bachelor's degree, I went home to live with my mom until grad school started. She was doing better by then, not grieving my dad as much. She started going to these widow's retreats for single people who were nervous about traveling after their spouses passed away.

"So, at one point she was gone for almost two weeks and I had the house to myself. I was fine until one morning I woke

200

up and the gate to our backyard was broken. I was spooked, so I called my mom and she told me she'd send someone over to take care of it." I pause, needing a second to collect myself before I start the next part.

I feel Jesse's pinkie finger flex under mine and I curl our fingers together instinctively. Compared to the story I'm about to tell, our contact doesn't seem scary at all.

"One of my dad's old friends came by to look around and make sure the other doors and windows hadn't been messed with. Fixed the gate, checked the house, and ensured everything was fine. I hadn't seen him since I was 13 at my dad's funeral." I clear the hoarseness from my throat.

"He lingered, asking about college and my future plans. At some point, I brought up that my friends and I liked to go out for Tequila Tuesdays at a local Mexican spot and that I missed it since being home. He offered to teach me how to make a homemade margarita, and being young and dumb, I said yes. I was still in that phase of life where drinking was the coolest hobby you could have." I laugh sadly, feeling no real humor towards the situation. Jesse remains silent, letting me continue.

"I thought I was a lightweight all of a sudden, but he had put something in my drink. It wasn't long after the spins started that I realized what was happening. He coaxed me into my mom's room and by then I couldn't move my body. I was awake the whole time, dizzy, but awake. I couldn't move or fight.

"He raped me. He held me down even though I was paralyzed and violated me. Over and over again." A sob escapes, remembering it so vividly. Jesse's hand trembles under mine, but I'm too far gone into the story to stop now.

"Eventually, I passed out from the pain or the drugs, I'm not sure. When I woke up in the morning, I was still in my mom's bed. The bed she shared with my dad before he died," I cry, remembering the shame I felt for letting that happen in my parent's bed.

"I couldn't move. The drugs had worn off, but I felt paralyzed still. My therapist said it was a natural reaction, but I just laid there reliving what happened, torturing myself for hours. The first thing I did was vomit, then I showered, needing to get the filth off." I sniff, reigning my tears back. I did it, the worst of the story is over. I did it.

I realize Jesse's hand is gripping the pillow violently. I'm worried it's going to burst, but I'm too afraid to look him in the eyes. I'm still so ashamed of what happened, even though I know it's not my fault. I didn't deserve any of it, but trauma has a funny way of stirring things up in your mind.

"It's okay, Jesse. I'm okay," I assure him, even though I know it's not okay.

"Thea…" He chokes out my name like he's doing all he can not to lose his mind. I'm painfully familiar with how he feels, how the anger can consume you. I take a deep breath and place the entirety of my hand over his, squeezing it tightly.

Holding hands is something that I've dreamed of doing for years and here I am doing it. I told my story and I'm holding Jesse's hand. Somehow tonight feels like the most successful night of my healing journey.

"I went to the hospital. I was so traumatized that I could barely speak to the woman at the front desk, but it didn't matter. She knew. She could tell what was wrong. She quietly bumped me to the front of the queue of people waiting.

"I was still practically mute when the nurse got me a bed.

She wanted me to take off my pants, to examine me, but the only privacy was a paper current and I already felt too exposed.

"When I managed to explain that I had already showered, she looked at me with such sad, regretful eyes... She didn't need to say the words out loud. I knew that I screwed up." I squeeze Jesse's hand again when it flexes under mine.

"I wish I could hold you, Thea," he whispers hoarsely. I would give anything to be wrapped in his arms. The security that I would feel seems like a fantasy, but one far out of reach.

"I knew something was wrong with me that day," I say, going back to my story. It seems like the easiest way to explain why we are stuck in this place and he can't hold me like we both desperately want.

"Another nurse, or doctor, I'm not sure, busted through the curtain. I didn't even know he had been standing on the other side of it. As soon as he was in my space, I was paralyzed in fear all over again. He scolded me for showering away the evidence as if I wasn't already aware. He infantilized me and I was humiliated."

Jesse doesn't say anything, but I can still feel his hand trembling beneath mine. I interlock our fingers just to prove to myself that I can. His fingers grasp mine tenderly but with powerful desperation.

"As soon as he snapped his gloves on and made a move to touch me, I screamed. It was ear-piercing. One second I was on the bed and the next I was curled up in a ball on the floor. The female nurse was nice enough to kick the asshole out of the room while I sobbed."

I close my eyes and take a deep breath, not wanting to let old emotions carry me away. "As soon as I could manage to get up, I ran out of that hospital and never went back."

"I'm so sorry, baby." His voice is full of pain for me. I feel his breath against my hand and it soothes me, bringing me back to the present. With him.

"I've had panic attacks since then and moments when my whole body freezes and I can't snap out of it. I try my best to avoid accidental touches, but I still get scared when a man comes into my space suddenly or raises his voice. It's gotten better throughout the years, I can control it sometimes when it's not something that happens on purpose. If a man actively tries to touch me though or grabs me, I panic so hard that I inevitably pass out," I admit.

"The bar." His voice is suddenly thick with anger.

"Yeah, I barely made it to the back before I blacked out. Daya helped me snap out of it. I told her I had forgotten to eat that day."

"I'll bury them," he states murderously. "All of them. Everyone who has ever hurt you. I swear, Thea. Tell me who he is. Your dad's friend." He demands, scaring me a little because he's serious.

This isn't some idle threat someone's protective boyfriend is throwing out before he goes to work as an accountant. Jesse is highly trained and capable of killing someone and I just gave him motivation.

"I'm not going to tell you that. I don't need you to kill him for me. I need you right here, with me," I plead. "I didn't tell you so that you could exact revenge for me."

His silence is eerie. It's like the calm that comes right before a tornado tears through a town, the buildup of anticipation before everyone dives for cover.

I do the only thing that feels right and place my hand on

his cheek, watching his eyes closely as they snap to mine. I see the moment that his fire-filled gaze cools and he registers my touch.

"Please, wherever you went in your head, stay with me instead. Right here," I whisper to him in the dark, trying to ignore the slight shake in my hand. I'm touching his face. Jesse's face. I have to squeeze my eyes shut for a moment to accept that I did it. I made another step toward progress.

"I'm here, Sunshine. I'm sorry," he apologizes, his eyes conveying how much he means it. "No one is ever going to hurt you again. I promise."

Whether it's because I know he means it, or because he still wants me despite the story I just told him, I let myself cry. Instead of crying for the life I thought I'd never get, I cry realizing that I might get it.

I could get the life I want with Jesse because I'm determined to. If I can make it this far, I can do the rest.

I have to, for both of our sakes.

Chapter Twenty-Nine

Jesse

The text that I was expecting came just after midnight. Thea was sleeping soundly as I grabbed my stuff, but I couldn't resist brushing a piece of hair off her forehead before I left her side. As I made my way out of her room, she rolled over to my newly vacated spot and curled into my pillow.

Understanding how badly she wants to be close to me in every way that she can, in every way that she feels safe, makes my chest tight. Her story earlier was worse than a knife to the heart.

I've never felt such anger in my life. The thought of what she went through and how someone who was supposed to be her father's friend hurt her so badly is enraging.

I was plotting my way to find the bastard and kill him when her gentle touch brought me back to earth. I still want to find him, but for now, I'll stay close to her because that's what she wants.

The last thing that I should do is to make her trauma all about me. Instead, I'll do anything necessary to make her feel safe, including hearing her when she tells me she needs me here with her. Not to go on a killing spree even though it would be so fulfilling to punish every person who has hurt her.

She's incredible and I admire her strength. She went through something horrific and still manages to put a smile on her face every day. More than that, she manages to brighten so many people's lives by being herself.

She is willing to go up against her fears because she's ready to move on with her life and away from her past. It's the most admirable thing that I could imagine.

These hillbilly extremists I'm on my way to meet have no clue what it means to persevere and overcome. They haven't fought any real battles in their life, not like Thea. The most radiant, kind-hearted woman who has experienced real evil at the hands of men would never hurt a fly.

Then you have these military rejects posing as victims to further a cause they don't give a shit about. They want destruction because they didn't get a golden ticket in life. Join the fucking club.

The drive out to the farm is a drag, but I grit my teeth and pedal down on the accelerator anyway. The sooner I get this over with the better.

Mitch and Derrick are at the gate and wave me through. The farmhouse is hopping. Cars are parked everywhere, and people are scattered across the lawn and front porch. I can only imagine what the inside looks like. This must be one of those parties that Curtis was telling me about. Great. The last fucking thing I feel like doing when I could be laying in bed next to a beautiful woman, instead.

Just as I had thought about him, he comes stumbling out of the house with a beer in one hand and a red solo cup in the other. He sees me and locks on target, making his way toward me with a shit-eating grin on his face.

"Hey, buddy! Glad you could make it!" He shouts in my ear as he forces an awkward hug on me since both of his hands are full.

"We just partying tonight, or what?" I ask, not caring to hide my annoyance since Curtis is already toasted and won't remember this tomorrow.

"Big party. Hot girls inside," he pauses to take a drink from his cup and I can smell the hard liquor. "Oh. There was someone here I wanted you to meet, but I can't remember." He chuckles, taking another drink. I fight the urge to turn around and leave.

"Oh. Oh, and Jameson wants to see you."

"About what?" My hackles rise.

"Dunno. He's in the kitchen." Curtis wanders away before I can ask him anything else, so I crack my neck and make my way inside. The house itself is old, the floorboards undoubtedly creaking if the music wasn't drowning it out.

Window panes are missing from around the door. The AC units in the living room are dripping with condensation, making the inside air sticky.

Just as Curtis said, I find Jameson sitting around an old oak table in the kitchen, surrounded on either side by people that I don't know. A few women I've never seen, nor care to, linger about.

The hot girls that Curtis was talking about must be long gone, because these girls look like they live halfway between a crack house and a whore house.

"Ah, Jay. You made it. Good. Sit down." He shoos one of the girls away, leaving the chair next to him open so I can sit.

"Get him a beer," he tells the other girl, leaving us semi-alone until she sits the silver can in front of me.

"Thanks." Luckily, she didn't pop the tab, so I feel like it's safe to drink. Thea's story is weighing heavily on my mind and the last thing I need is to be drugged in the enemy's house.

"I need to know something, Jay. You're committed to the cause, right?" He asks, eyeing me suspiciously. I fight the urge to grill him on his "cause."

"Of course, sir."

"Then there is a special job that I need you to do. All these other guys are idiots, but you have a head on your shoulders. I can tell." He leans back, resting his crossed arms on his stomach. "I think someone's been talking. I've had the Sheriff poking around more than once now and I think we have a leak."

My neck stiffens at the implication. I'm sure nothing that I've relayed to my command has made its way back here, so who else is talking? *Curtis.*

He's got cold feet. I could tell in his car earlier that he was having a hard time with this. Could he be talking to someone about all of this besides me? Fuck. I hope not.

"What do you need me to do?" I ask, keeping my other thoughts to myself.

"Keep your ear to the ground. Find out if we have a mole then take care of them. I have important goals, and people counting on me. I can't have anyone messing it up. You hear me?" He leans back toward me, too close for comfort. "Get it done."

"Yes, sir. I'll let you know what I find out." I get up, downing my beer before I even make it out of the kitchen.

Fuck, this adds another level of complications to my life.

Could someone else be leaking information?

I make a lap through everyone at the party, trying to find Curtis but he's gone. I make a second lap, this time asking if anyone has seen him. It isn't until I'm almost back to my truck that someone tells me he left with a girl.

Dawn is approaching by the time I write my reports and finish leaving messages for my unit. This time when I leave the motel, I bring the rest of my stuff with me. It's only a duffle bag and laptop, but if I never have to step foot in this rat hole again, I'll be thrilled.

Thea blinks awake as I walk into her room. "Hi," I murmur, admiring her sleepy face. Her cheeks have lines on them from sleeping so hard and her hair is wild. She's gorgeous.

"Hi." She smiles and I almost fall to my knees. This woman.

"I didn't mean to wake you up. I just got back."

She pats the bed, so I sit down next to her, stretching my arm out over her legs to brace myself without touching her.

"I need to run anyway. Thanks for coming back," she whispers, bashfully.

"You couldn't get me to stay away if you tried," I tease, but I mean it wholeheartedly. I don't want to go anywhere.

"Do you want to run with me?" She laughs immediately at what my face must look like. I'm no stranger to working out, but running sounds terrible after being up all night.

"I would but I need to shower. If you don't care," I say, watching the way she eyes me up and down.

There is an obvious interest in the way she looks at me and it makes my dick hard immediately. This girl might be fearful of touch, but she is no stranger to sexual desires. She wants me and it's making me crazy.

"Thea…"

210

"Hmm?" She locks eyes with me and realizes she's been caught. She giggles, pulling the covers over her head.

"When do your toys come?" I ask her still-covered head.

"Sometime today." Her voice is muffled through the blanket.

"Good." I get up to go shower before she says something else that will make me want to fuck her.

I spend the rest of the day while she's at work fixing her broken-down bathroom. Kyle's an idiot but he didn't destroy things too badly. He was lying about some things needing to be fixed, so all in all, the whole thing was done in a few hours. The only thing left to do is paint, but without further direction, it'll have to wait.

I'm standing back, admiring my handyman skills when her doorbell rings. It's the middle of the afternoon and I have to leave for my meeting at the library soon, so I consider ignoring it, but it rings again.

When I look through the peephole it's blocked. I open the door with caution, not sure what to expect. The surprise visitor steps back as soon as I open the door, a Rollins County Sheriff's Department patch staring at me.

"Good afternoon," the stiff voice of none other than the Sheriff himself greets me.

"What can I do for you?" I realize exactly who this is, but also know that I shouldn't.

"I want to discuss your whereabouts last night. My name is Jackson Malec, I'm the Rollins County Sheriff," he states plainly, no thrill to his voice. He doesn't seem overly proud of his position, there's no ego behind his introduction, purely professional.

"I was here, anything else?"

"I've been keeping an eye out for suspicious vehicles heading up into the foothills and your truck was up there last night. Now it's out here and you don't live here. Not in this town, not in this house. I want to know what's going on at that old farm."

Fuck, this guy is going to screw everything up. A million different scenarios run through my mind within a few seconds. Leaving this guy in the dark was high on my list, but if these bombs are going to be a big problem like I think then it might be good to clue in the local Sheriff.

It's not my call though and I could get in a shit ton of trouble, but at this point, I'd rather be safe than sorry. The local authorities would be closer than my team if shit does go down and I need to make sure I get through this unscathed. I'm not getting killed, not when I just found Thea.

I glance up and down the street, making sure we're not being watched, and take a step back. "Come in, Trooper."

His eyebrows furrow at the use of his past title. "You know who I am?" He asks, eyeing the living space around me.

"I know a lot, Sheriff. We have a mutual acquaintance from Whitewater," I explain, handing him the framed photo Thea keeps next to her couch.

"I'm working for the Army Criminal Investigations Unit. Special Sergeant Jesse Callahan. Nathan Wolfe is a friend of mine."

He doesn't give much away and he definitely doesn't trust me, but he shakes my hand anyway. That's a start.

Chapter Thirty

Thea

The day flew by, my mood was through the roof after confessing the darkest of my secrets last night. The weight of my past has been lifted from my shoulders and in its place is a newfound excitement for my life.

My joy was felt because story time was a hoot. The kids talked me into reading an extra (but very short) story. I didn't even realize how late Jesse was until he strolled in through the doors and straight to his meeting.

He threw me a wink across the library, and as if it was heard, Latisha came running at me as soon as he disappeared into the meeting room. She grilled me for information so long that I ended up confessing all the newest details. I spent the better part of an hour telling her what I could about Jesse and our relationship, though I did refer to him as Jay.

By the time I was ready to leave, I knew his meeting was almost over, so I stayed near my car. I'm not sure why, I figured he would come to my house right after, but I didn't want to go any longer than necessary without seeing him. I've got it bad.

Leaning against my car door, I watch the side door to the

meeting room open and some guys file out. Jesse is one of the last ones, holding back the younger guy I've seen him with a few times. I can't hear what they're talking about, but I can tell it's serious, so I try not to stare. It isn't until the shouting starts that I can't look away.

"Man, don't tell me what to do! I'm a fuck up, I know, but I can do something now. I can fix this!" The young guy shouts, pounding on his chest with agitation.

Jesse's response is too normal toned to hear, but I can tell from his body language that he's frustrated. The young guy tries to go around him, but Jesse blocks his path, putting his hands up as if he's trying to make peace.

Dennis, the one who runs the meeting and is also one of our part-time employees, comes out the side door to intervene. He ushers the young guy back inside with little difficulty, leaving Jesse to stare at the closing door.

He turns toward where his truck is parked right behind my car and spots me. His hands rub across his face and through his hair as he walks toward me as if he's physically switching personas. He rights his hat as he reaches me and it makes my knees weak.

He's so casually masculine. He doesn't even need to try and he's mouth-watering. I want to take the leap and kiss him so badly but I know I'm not ready. The anticipation is killing me but I ignore the butterflies in my stomach since he's obviously distressed about something.

"Sorry, you had to see that."

"Is everything okay?" I ask, fully prepared that he probably can't or won't tell me.

"No, it's not, but I hope it will be eventually." He shrugs, letting me know that's all I'm going to get.

"You ready to go home?"

He smiles and I melt under it. "Yeah, but first we need to go to the hardware store." He motions for me to follow him. "Come on, Sunshine. I'll drive."

* * *

After getting my paint samples, neither of us was ready for our errand to be over so we rode the long way around town with the windows down. For the moment, everything was okay. He wasn't thinking about his work problems and I wasn't the girl who's terrified of being close to him.

By the time we get back to the library to get my car, the sun is low in the sky.

"Should there be anyone here right now?" He asks, looking toward the other side of the parking lot. I follow his gaze, noticing only one other car.

"No, Latisha usually leaves right at seven. She's always the last one." His eyes are locked on the car. "That's not her car," I add.

"Stay here," he tells me as he makes his way over to it, but a sudden chill down my spine makes my feet move against his wishes.

I didn't want to be by myself but I should've listened to him. At the same time as I hear him whisper "fuck" under his breath, I see Dennis laying on the ground next to his car, bloody and beaten.

"Oh my God." I cover my mouth so I don't scream just as Jesse whips his head around to look at me.

215

"Call 911, ask for Sheriff Malec." When I stand there completely frozen, he says it again, harsher, making me jump. "Thea. Call 911."

I do as he says, relaying the information over to the dispatcher while he checks for signs of life. Seeing Dennis that way is breaking my heart so I keep my back turned. I know one more glance will make me fall apart. Who would do this?

"Is he breathing?" I repeat the dispatcher's question out loud to Jesse, keeping my eyes glued to the brick facade of the library.

"Barely." His voice is void of emotion, hardly sounding like himself.

The next few hours are a blur of flashing lights and emergency vehicles, repeating the story three times to three different deputies. All while Jesse stands off to the side speaking to the Sheriff.

I know who he is, I voted for him after Nathan told me he was one of the good guys. He's young like Jesse and Nathan, but taller and more rigid. His light brown hair is cropped on the sides, making him look serious and authoritative.

By the time it's all over, I'm a bundle of nerves. Poor Dennis was transported to the hospital, but no one could tell me his condition. I'm worried about him, I'm concerned about why it happened, and I'm terrified that it happened here at the library. This is supposed to be a safe place. My safe place.

"Time to go." I nearly jump out of my skin when Jesse speaks up from behind me.

"Dammit, Jesse," I screech, clutching my heart.

"Shh, Thea. It's Jay here."

His reminder wasn't malicious, but my nerves are frayed

216

and I snap. "Don't sneak up on me. I've been scared to death standing out here and talking to all these strange men. Whoever you are right now, I don't care."

I jump in my car, peeling out of the parking lot before I let him have a word in. By the time I pull up to the curb in front of my house, I'm crumbling.

My forehead falls against my steering wheel and the tears that have been threatening to fall for hours flow free.

I cry for Dennis and I cry because I'm rattled. I cry because I still don't have control of my emotions when anything upsetting happens. I cry because I bit Jesse's head off and I shouldn't have.

Minutes tick by before the tears slow down enough that I can catch my breath. I should go back and apologize to him, but I can't stomach the thought of being back there just yet. The last thing he needs is to walk on eggshells around me because I can't handle myself.

A sob breaks free just thinking about going back to the scene of the crime. I know there are evil people in the world, but how could someone hurt Dennis so badly and just leave him? It's inhumane.

After wiping the moisture from my face with the sleeves of my sweater, I gather my things with shaky limbs to go inside. As soon as I round my car, I see him. Sitting on my porch steps, waiting for me. I never even heard his truck pull up behind mine.

He's here even after I snapped at him. I should have known he'd follow me home anyway. It makes me want to weep again.

"I'm sorry," I apologize, my tears coming back in a fresh wave. He squeezes his eyes shut, grasping his hair in his hands.

"Don't. You have nothing to be sorry for. I'm sorry for not staying with you when the cops talked to you, I wasn't thinking. I'm sorry." He raises his hands slightly, reaching for me, but pulls back once he realizes. He pats the spot next to him instead with a pleading look.

"All of this is my fault. Making you play along with this stupid character that I have to be, not protecting Dennis. It's all my fault." He hangs his head in his hands in defeat.

I sit next to him, gently resting my head on his shoulder. It's not easy at first, but after a minute I'm able to relax and lean into it. Providing comfort in this small way feels huge, so I focus on it. My minor accomplishment can't drown out the bad that happened this evening, but at least I can show him that I'm here for him.

"It's not your fault. You can't control what happened, we weren't even there," I whisper against his shoulder, feeling him shake his head. His whole body is radiating with tension.

"I want to stay here with you more than anything, but I need to go take care of some work stuff. I'm not sure when I'll be back. Stay inside the rest of the night, okay?" He asks with desperation.

"I will. Be safe, please," I beg, not having the heart to tell him that I wish he would stay. It isn't his choice. Duty calls.

"I'll try." He waits as I reluctantly move my head off his shoulder before standing to leave.

I don't want him to go. I want him here where it's safe. He's halfway down the sidewalk when he turns back towards me like he could read my mind.

"I'll come back. I promise." It's not enough to let me not worry, but it's nice to hear regardless.

Chapter Thirty-One

Jesse

I spent all night looking for Curtis after convincing Malec to let me bring him in on my own. After our heart-to-heart earlier, he was willing to work beside me while I worked to take down Jameson's operation.

He admitted that the county doesn't have the manpower to deal with something like this on their own yet, he plans to expand their resources now that he's in office but it will take time.

I tried all of the spots I could think of, even tracking down Curtis' last known address, but no luck. He was the last person Dennis was seen with and as of now, the only suspect. There are no other witnesses and no cameras aimed at that part of the parking lot.

My gut tells me that Jameson and his crew are involved somehow, I just don't know why Dennis got caught in the crosshairs.

Before dawn arrives, I head to the farm hoping to get an idea of who might be involved. Since Jameson's paranoia started earlier this week, there's usually someone patrolling the entrance so I park down the road, hiding my truck in a pull-out that's hidden by brush.

After helping install the security measures, I know where the holes are and sneak my way onto the property. It's quiet in the early morning hours, forcing me to move slowly and silently through the thick trees that surround the outer perimeter. I approach the back side of one of the barns and hear music playing from inside.

Peering through a small gap in the wooden slats, I can see four men inside standing around a table with various types of metal debris. They're filing down the pieces, most likely sharpening the edges to be used as shrapnel. Still no sign of Curtis. *Where the hell could he be?*

I watch them for a few minutes, making sure there aren't any other surprises, before making my way toward the house. Sitting at his kitchen table wearing only a pair of boxers, is Jameson.

He peels back his eye patch and scratches his perfectly healthy eye before standing and grabbing a beer from the fridge. Mitch walks into the kitchen from the living room so I stay out of sight, listening to their conversation.

"Still no sign, boss."

"I want him found and brought to me. I want to know what he told that old man." Jameson grunts, the chair creaking as he sits back down. "Someone needs to check the hospital. Find out if the bastard made it through the night. If he did, finish the job this time."

"Yes, sir."

I knew Curtis didn't do it. He is a lost kid, he's made bad choices, but my gut told me he wasn't the real culprit. Now I know that Jameson is willing to kill for his agenda.

I call Malec once I'm back in my truck. "Curtis didn't do it.

Jameson thinks Dennis found out about their group and they beat him to keep him quiet," I explain, blowing out a long breath.

"They got their wish. He's in a coma. It's not likely that he'll wake up," Malec tells me. My gut churns thinking of the poor man who selflessly leads a group of veterans twice a week. A man who just wanted to help people.

"Any way you can keep security outside his room just in case? They might be stupid enough to finish the job."

"I'll ask the hospital what they can provide. There's no way I can keep one of my guys there. I don't have anyone to spare," he admits. I thanked him after he agreed to keep me updated.

The sun is rising when I pull up to Thea's and I hate that I've been gone all night. The hour that I might get with her before she leaves for work is not enough when I'm happy to spend every waking minute with her.

When I enter a silent house, my heart picks up speed. She should be getting ready for her run. I left her here alone last night even after what happened at the library. Was that a mistake?

What if someone followed us here? What if I blew my cover and didn't realize it? Avoiding the spots that usually creak under my weight, I ascend the stairs with stealth.

My heart is pounding in my chest now, my blood rushing anxiously. I'll never be able to live with myself if I get her hurt. I hold my breath as I reach for her door. Please be okay, Sunshine.

All my breath rushes out, leaving me lightheaded when I see her curled up in bed. Thank God.

I don't hesitate, stripping down and climbing in next to her. The tension in my spine unwinds in an instant, and my heartbeat returns to normal.

The heaviness of what's happening all around me starts to fall away when I focus on her deep, slow breathing, and let sleep pull me under.

* * *

I wake too soon, feeling eyes on me. "Good morning," I mumble against the pillow when I see her sweet face next to mine. My head whips up once I realize that hours must have passed and she's still here.

"What's wrong? Why are you home?" I ask, fearing the worst again like something else bad happened since last night. "Are you okay?" My mind is disoriented and reaping with negative thoughts.

"Nothing's wrong, everything is fine." She laughs at my half-awake distressed state. "I called Latisha last night after you left and she insisted that I take the day off. So, I slept in, but I did just get back from my run. I needed to clear my head. I couldn't stop thinking about Dennis."

I notice then that she's freshly showered, her hair piled on top of her head. The small wispy pieces are still damp. I let my head fall back in relief that there isn't any more bad news for the moment.

"Sorry, I'm a little amped up. Malec said Dennis is in a coma," I tell her honestly, not wanting to keep her in the dark about her coworker.

She nods her head, frowning at my words. "Latisha told me. She talked to his wife this morning. We're going to start a meal train and send flowers." She shrugs and we sit in thoughtful silence. Nothing will fix what's happened but it's a nice gesture regardless.

Thea isn't used to this type of violence like I am and I don't want to upset her further when there isn't anything more we can do. She starts playing with the ends of my hair right below my ear after a few minutes and I take it as a sign that she needs a distraction.

"What time is it?" I squint at the bright light coming in the windows, too tired to gauge what time it might be. I never remember to take advantage of her curtains before I climb into bed.

"It's eleven. I was going to make some lunch, but then I couldn't resist getting back into bed with you for a few minutes." She smiles softly, tracing my jaw with her fingertip. It's those light touches she offers me that make me willing to do anything for her. Those small expressions of conquering her fears keep getting bolder every day.

Her finger moves along my chin and across the scruff that I can't stand but keep long for appearance's sake. The hair on my head hasn't been this long in my life. Jay keeps it messy because he's a messy guy.

"I usually keep it shorter," I tell her when she reaches for the ends of my hair again.

"I like it. I don't know what you look like without it, but I can imagine you're pretty hot no matter what." She smiles, shyly.

"I can't wait to shave," I admit. Her eyes ping to my facial hair longingly; I assume it's because she likes it. "I usually just clean it up and make it shorter. I won't get rid of it."

"Good." She giggles when she realizes she's been read like

a book. "I like how you look." She blushes and it sends a signal straight to my cock. My morning wood was already stiff beneath me, but now I'm hard as a rock, and she's not helping.

"Thea. If you keep blushing like that I'm going to want to see how hard you blush when you cum." I watch her cheeks redden even more at my words, but she doesn't shy away, instead, her eyes blaze with curiosity.

"Okay," she whispers, making my dick strain painfully against my underwear.

"Where are those toys?" My blood is pulsing in my ears. She reaches over to her nightstand, where I'm just noticing the drawer has also been replaced, and pulls out a vibrating wand.

"Would you like to review your investment?" She teases, but I have a feeling she's stalling, so I play along for a minute.

I sit up, grabbing it from the pillow between us where she placed it. I click through the buttons, feeling the settings. I'm not overly experienced with women using vibrators, but I get the gist. As much as I want to feel Thea myself and drive her to orgasm with my touch, this will do for now.

I leave the toy with her and move to the chair sitting across from the foot of her bed. I want to be near her, but I need space to stay in control of myself.

Only in my underwear, I don't bother hiding away my erection and she notices, eyeing it with intrigue. Exactly why I needed some distance between us, I'm trying to be strong but I'm no saint.

I get comfortable, leaning back and spreading my legs so she can see the tent in my lap. So she can see exactly how much she turns me on. "Take your sweatshirt off, baby."

She hesitates at first, not wanting to tear her eyes from me, but eventually moves to do as I said. She slides her oversized crew neck over her head, exposing her toned belly and light pink bra. Though, it's not much of a bra, it's held together with a few strings and lace, and practically see-through. It's the sexiest thing I've ever seen.

"My God. Do you wear that under your clothes every day?" I'm going to be imagining it each day for the rest of my life.

"Sometimes. Bralettes are more comfortable than regular bras," she answers shyly as if she has to explain herself.

"It's perfect, Thea. You're so sexy it hurts." I suck in lungfuls of air, trying to stay in my right mind. Fuck, I want her.

Chapter Thirty-Two

Thea

I'm slightly concerned that the arms of my chair might crack with the grip that Jesse has on them, but then again I can't find much thought to care. The way he's looking at me is all-consuming.

I've always been a little self-conscious with how small my chest got after I took up running, going from a full C to barely a B cup, but seeing Jesse so obviously attracted to me makes me feel divine.

I've been hiding myself away for so long, and having someone admire me is liberating. Not just someone, Jesse. It gives me the courage to slide out of my shorts, showing him my new matching panties.

A benefit of Kyle going through my drawers was a freshly updated lingerie collection. I'm glad Jesse gets to reap the benefits.

"Now what?" I ask as he fights for his life ten feet away from me when he sees my lacy pink thong.

"Fuck, Thea." His jaw ticks. "Get on your knees. In the middle of the bed," he grits out. I do as he says, pushing aside my shyness and soaking in the feeling of being desirable to him. I haven't wanted to be sexy for anyone the majority of my adult life, but I am sexy and I deserve to show it off.

My feelings are validated just by looking into Jesse's eyes. He wants me with a fire so hot that I hope it can never be extinguished. I know my desire for him won't.

I pull the hair tie out of my hair, letting the loose curls fall down my shoulders. Feeling like my authentic self for the first time in my life.

"You're so beautiful," he says with wonder in his voice. It makes my heart skip a beat and I know without a doubt that I am falling in love with this man.

"So are you," I tell him, meaning every word. With his powerful legs stretched out in front of him, someone could carve his likeness into stone. Even better, a marble statue in a Greek museum. A beautiful picture of strength.

"Touch yourself. Everywhere you want me to touch you." His eyes are wild, waiting for me to comply, so I start slowly, tracing my collarbones with my fingers, up my neck, and to my lips. When I start moving towards my cleavage, we both hold our breath until I pass between my breasts.

I trace a line down my sternum, past my belly button, only veering off path once I hit my panty line. My fingers drag down my thighs and back up, stopping once I reach my chest. I cup myself, squeezing lightly, imagining it's him instead.

My skin is hot, tingling with need. My nipples are tight, poking through the lace of my bralette, and painfully sensitive. I shy away from them before he stops me.

"Don't stop," he grunts. "Pinch your nipples. Play with them, because I would. I want to lick them. God, I want to suck on them." His voice makes me quiver. The dirtiness of his words goes straight to my core, making me even wetter than I already was.

"Jesse, please," I beg, needing direction, dragging my fingers across my nipples again. I wish it was his fingers, I wish his mouth was on me. The way I'm feeling right now makes me believe that it's possible, but for now, this is amazing.

"Take it off, let me see you." I do as he says, pulling the lacy material over my head, and boldly throwing it in his direction. He catches it with a quick snap of his arm, his eyes never leaving my exposed chest. "Fuck."

I love how obvious it is that he likes what he sees. He makes me feel so wanted. He looks like he wants to devour me.

"Lay back, spread your legs." He clutches my bra to his chest as I obey his instruction, clinging to the fabric as if he can feel me through it. "Touch your pussy, baby."

I run my fingers over my panties, feeling the heat through the lace, my body jumping slightly when I brush across my clit. I keep my body angled so he has a perfect view between my legs, but I can still see him. Seeing his reaction to me is just as electrifying as the sensations from my fingers.

When I pull the fabric aside, exposing myself to him, he grabs the arms of the chair again, holding on for dear life. When I slide my finger through my folds he nearly buckles, throwing his head back for a moment and taking a deep breath.

His gaze doesn't stray long though, whipping back to where I'm teasing my tight opening. I do it like I have all the nights that I've laid awake thinking about him. All the times I've been desperate to know what he would feel like here.

"Please," he begs this time, so I give him exactly what we both want. I slide my middle finger inside, all the way to my last knuckle. We both groan.

Pushing in and out, my eyes watch him lazily. It feels good, but I have no urgency to chase my orgasm yet. I know I'll get there, but I'm enjoying the ride too much.

"I want to see you, too." I breathe out, seeing how he's gripping his hardness through his underwear. He hardly hesitates, tugging down his briefs without breaking eye contact. His hand finds his erection immediately, loosely rubbing the long hard shaft. It's thick and juts up past his belly button, making me clench at the thought of having it inside of me.

"Get your vibrator, baby. I'm already hanging on by a thread." His pained expression is proof of his words even though he's only slowly working his length. The sight of me is doing that to him.

I pick the first setting, and place the vibrating head on my clit, flinching when I feel how sensitive the swollen bead is. This is it. I want to cum so badly next to the man who has brought me this far. I want more, but I've waited so long that this feels like I've already won.

"Grab your tits, Thea. Yes, just like that. You're so fucking beautiful, baby." He peppers me with praise, picking up speed with his hand. I watch him fuck his fist, wishing desperately that it was me. My hand, my mouth, and my pussy. The buildup of my orgasm is climbing and I know I'm within seconds of exploding when my belly starts tightening.

"Jesse, please," I beg, though I'm not quite sure why until I say it. "Come closer, please."

He stands up to the foot of the bed right between where my legs are spread, still pumping his hand, watching me intensely. "I'm going to cum, Thea. Tell me you're close, baby," he pleads.

"On me," I stutter out. "I want you to cum on me," I beg.

At my words, he explodes. The hot stream of cum stripes across my pussy and inner thighs.

Seeing him finish, feeling his cum on me, tips me over the edge. My whole body contracts with my orgasm, the waves crashing down on me over and over until it's too much and I all but throw the vibrator across the room.

When I look at Jesse's face, I'm expecting a serene look of pleasure, but what I find is the deepest depth of affection in his eyes.

He's looking at me like I'm the most important thing in his world. I imagine it's a reflection of my gaze looking at him.

Chapter Thirty-Three

Jesse

My heart will only ever beat for this woman. I am going to be right beside her as she overcomes every dark memory from her past, guiding her through each obstacle, and taking all of the pain away. I'll carry the trauma for her even if it makes me bleed. I'd rip my heart out if she thought hers was beyond repair.

It's taking all of my willpower not to utter the three words hanging on the tip of my tongue because she doesn't deserve a post-orgasm confession. She deserves the grand gesture. She deserves a romantic, soul-binding exclamation of what's actually in my heart. But, damn, I want to say it now.

Seeing her come apart in front of me was a life-altering experience. I'll never want another woman the way I want Thea. I want to be here for every orgasm she has for the rest of her life.

I didn't even touch her but my body was a live wire, needing her more than I needed to breathe. Then she begged me to cum on her and I almost blacked out. Seeing her reach her orgasm while I stood above her, coating her with my own was a spiritual experience, and I'll never stop chasing that high.

I've never been a possessive person, never caring enough about the girls I was with to notice if someone else was holding their attention. Now though, I understand the need to claim someone. I want to own, possess, and mark every inch of her body for my own, never letting anyone within a hundred feet of her again.

"Jesse," she whispers my name, snapping me out of my animalistic haze.

"Yeah, baby?" I ask, looking at her pretty pink cheeks. The perfect shade of blush, everything I ever hoped for.

"You've got me trapped." My arms are pinned on either side of her, boxing her in so she can't get off the bed. Even my body is subconsciously trying to possess her.

"Sorry," I utter, but don't move. I'm not ready to add any space between us.

"You're just staring at me now." She giggles, seemingly aware of my inability to move.

"You're really nice to stare at," I counter, making her smile harder.

"We should shower," she suggests. I get the hint, pulling my limbs away from her and out of her bubble.

I can imagine she might be experiencing some discomfort now that the sex cloud has dissipated and she's left with stickiness coating her body.

I didn't touch her, but I'm on her, in her most intimate area. God, I fucking love it.

"I'll turn the water on, take your time," I offer, letting her have some space. She might need room to breathe, to process what we just did, and I'll let her. I'm obsessed with her, but I'm not an asshole.

When I glance back as I leave the room, I watch as she gazes at her reflection in the mirror, oblivious to my presence. A sense of wonder crosses her features when she notices the sheen of cum on her skin. Instead of fear or disgust, she looks proud. Her fingers trail through the wetness, smearing it into her skin, marking herself further.

Two things are confirmed at once in my head. I'm definitely in love with her and she's even freakier than I thought.

My dick hardens, ready for her again, but I don't want to push her. Instead, I back down the hallway and out of sight.

Once the water is hot, I usher her into the freestanding claw foot tub while I lean against the bathroom sink, letting her have her privacy behind the curtain.

She hums quietly to herself as soap bottles are clicked open and closed, while I'm imagining all the ways I can show her how much she means to me. For as long as I breathe I am going to give her the princess treatment she deserves.

"Why are you smiling?" She asks, peeling the curtain to the side, completely exposing her wet naked body to me. Whatever distraction I might've had two seconds ago is long gone and my boner is back and raging.

"I honestly can't remember now," I admit, not even wanting to blink. She's stunning. Everything I've ever wanted and never thought I deserved, and she's right in front of me. I'm the luckiest man on the planet.

"Go ahead." She nods towards the still-running shower, but her eyes are aimed below my waist. We both have to move on autopilot to navigate around each other.

I'm trying to give her space and not rush things, but she clearly has sex on the brain like I do. It takes a considerable amount of mental strength to get in the shower and not to follow her back to her room.

I'm rinsing soap out of my hair when I hear the metal rungs of the shower curtain scrape against the rounded rod holding it up. I crack an eye open against the wetness to see her watching me.

"Everything okay?" I ask, wiping the water from my face.

"Yeah. I just wanted to see what you looked like in here. It was kind of on my bucket list." She shrugs. "I'm not at all disappointed." She smiles before closing the curtain and leaving me slack-jawed and wildly amused.

My ray of sunshine strikes again.

* * *

The lazy morning turned into a lazy afternoon, only getting out of bed to get food from the kitchen. She asked me four times if she could see my progress in the bathroom and I realized it would probably be the only time I ever tell her no to anything.

She'll get the grand reveal once I paint. Even without seeing it, she keeps thanking me immensely. She also keeps promising to pay me, which I adamantly keep denying.

"I don't want your money, Thea," I insist, leading her back up the stairs and to her bed, right where I want her.

"You have so much going on, the last thing you should be worried about is my bathroom. You should be compensated." She plants her hands on her hips, fighting a losing battle.

"You can compensate me," I digress. "But, I don't want money."

CHAPTER THIRTY-THREE

"What do you want?" She eyes me suspiciously, making me grin.

"Touch me. I like it when you do." I fold my hands behind my head and lean back against the pillows, my bare chest still on display since I only put shorts on after the shower.

"Where?" She asks, a little breathless.

"Anywhere you want. My hair, my face, my arms. It doesn't matter. I'm yours to do what you please." I wink.

She studies me intently for a moment, going somewhere deep in her head. I'm worried that I said something wrong but she snaps out of it and climbs onto the bed next to me. "You're mine?" She lets her gaze drift up and down my body. "You'll let me do whatever I want because you belong to me," she whispers to herself.

"I'm yours, Thea," I confirm, letting her process through her inner thoughts. I realize that whatever is going on in her head is solely for her. As quickly as everything has happened between us, I know that she's still healing and will still need to take things at her own pace.

I never expected to reach where we are now, I was content waiting for her as long as she needed. I'm no stranger to it, I spent years waiting to be adopted. Years waiting to be aged out of the system, waiting until I was old enough to enlist, waiting for financial stability. Waiting to start my life. *Waiting for her.*

If I have to wait for years to see all her wounds healed, then so be it. It doesn't matter, because, in the end, it will all be worth it. I know how good things are with her now, and how good they'll continue to be and better. She's worth the long game.

If she's telling me that she wants me now though then I'm

here. I'm not one to play hard to get, I'm hers and she'll never have to ask twice.

She doesn't realize how life-altering being with her is for me. Every touch is a gift and way more valuable than money. I'll figure out how to fix her entire house if it means being compensated in this way.

I expect her to run her fingers through my hair or touch my jaw like she was this morning, but instead, she goes straight for my chest. Her fingers move slowly across my skin, leaving an electric current in their wake. I don't move, I hardly breathe, letting her take what she wants.

She moves across my ribs, tracing down my sides until she reaches my hip bone. "What's this?" She asks, pointing out another old scar.

"Your brother shot me." I laugh at her startled face. "We were in training, using sim rounds, bullets filled with paint. I was being a smart ass. I'm not even sure what I said at this point, but he shot me, point-blank, without an ounce of hesitation. It hurt like hell, I couldn't put on pants or sit down without wincing for weeks, but it was also the hardest I ever laughed. We pretty much became best friends after that."

"Men…" She mumbles, rolling her eyes, but smiling. "His wedding is in November. Are we… Are you and I…" She trails off.

"Thea. Are you asking me to be your date?" I ask, making her blush.

"Well, yeah, but more than that…" She bites her lip, and it makes blood rush to my cock. I can't control it.

"You're it for me, Sunshine. Other than being on the low while I'm undercover, I'm not hiding this. I want everyone to know how I feel about you. The world, your friends, your family. I especially don't plan to keep it from Nathan. I know you talked to him, but I still want him to know how serious I am about this. If he's pissed at me… We'll cross that road when we get there." I shrug.

"He has no right to be pissed one way or another. I'm a grown woman and I've been taking care of myself for a long time. If he was really concerned about me, he wouldn't have been gone almost the entirety of the last decade." She snaps her mouth shut, covering it with her hand like she wasn't expecting the intensity of the words that flowed from her mouth.

"I'm sorry if you felt alone. He should have come home more, I should have made him. What we did for so many years was dark, it was hard to come back to the real world like nothing happened. I'm not saying that it's right, but he loves you. He had a picture in his locker of you and him as kids. Hanging on a jungle gym I think." Her bottom lip trembles at my words and I desperately want to soothe it.

"I wasn't completely alone. I had Liv through my hardest years. So I guess if I had to share my brother with anyone, I'm glad it was you." She laughs, wiping away the moisture under her eyes. "I wish he would have brought you home to meet me. We wouldn't have wasted so many years being strangers."

"You're right. I'm shooting him with a sim round next time I see him," I say seriously, making her laugh again.

"Can I try something?" She asks, biting her lip.

"Anything you want." *Literally anything.*

She moves down the bed, lying down next to me. "Stay still, please."

I don't move a single muscle while she scoots up close to me and ever so slowly, lays her head on my chest. Her arm rests across my stomach, making my abdominals tense reflexively.

The anxiety is radiating through her, but I don't speak on it. I let her work through this on her own, knowing she's strong enough to handle it. I focus on slowing my breathing, hoping my calmness will affect her in a positive way.

After a few minutes, she relaxes into me, her head becoming heavier as she finally releases the tension in her limbs. Her breathing begins to match mine, slow and steady, while her hand embraces my side.

Her grip is strong but tender, not fearful. She's holding onto me, but she's not panicking. She did it.

Chapter Thirty Four

Thea

Apart of me is healed. Being able to partake in such a normal act of intimacy after all of these years makes the demon from my nightmares seem less scary. All of the hatred and self-loathing I experienced as the result of being torn from the chance of having a normal relationship isn't erased, but it isn't controlling me anymore. I'm conquering it one step at a time.

My cheeks hurt from smiling as I listen to his heartbeat rhythmically in my ear. The steady rise and fall of his chest is a comfort that I hadn't realized I needed so desperately until right now. I only wish that he could hold me back. The thought of being trapped in his arms is still terrifying, but kind of exciting at the same time.

Deep down, I know I'll love it when he holds me, but I'm so afraid that I'll freak out and scare him away. Or, he'll witness a panic attack and finally understand that I am too much to handle.

I would be mortified if I fainted as a result of him touching me for the first time. I would never want him to feel like he did something to hurt me or that it was his fault.

He's been hurt by so many people in his life, I never want to be the reason for more pain. Thinking about him as a little boy all alone in those unfit homes makes me sick to my stomach.

I want to be his home. I know he cares about me, I feel it in the way he treats me but we're both scared. We're two broken people learning to trust each other and to love together.

As I'm snuggling closer to his body, I hear his sleepy sigh and peek up at his face to see that he's snoozing soundly. Both of his hands are still firmly gripping the bars of my metal bed frame. Even in his sleep, he's refraining from touching me by accident.

I let him rest, occupying my mind with affirmations and pep talk. I want to go further, I want to push myself even farther out of my comfort zone. I just need a little groundwork laid so that I'm prepared.

* * *

After a few hours he's still napping and I'm busy straightening my hair in the bathroom when I get a phone call. "Hey, Liv." I put my phone on speakerphone so I can multitask.

"Hi, stranger. I haven't heard from you in a few days. Everything okay?"

"Um. Yeah, actually. More than okay." I have to bite my lip to keep from squealing.

"Really? What's going on?" She asks excitedly. Liv has been the bearer of a lot of my negative thoughts and experiences, so it's nice when I have something positive to fill her in on.

"You'll never guess what I did."

"Finally drop a book on a kid's head? I told you it would happen eventually." She laughs at herself.

"No. Still haven't done that." I roll my eyes. "I have been seeing a guy. He slept over and we… Well. We were able to do stuff," I admit, feeling like a little kid. It's like I'm telling my mom that I lost my virginity or something. I'm embarrassed.

"What?" Her breath catches. *"Thea, did you have sex?"*

"No, not yet."

"Not yet?!" She shrieks, making me laugh.

"He still hasn't touched me, but we, I don't know. Masturbated together?"

"Shut the fuck up. I am freaking out. Are you saying this is it? Is he someone that you want to touch you?" She understands how huge this is. *"Is he safe?"*

"Yeah. He's special. I trust him, a lot." I smile to myself as she talks my ear off. Eventually, I'm able to turn the conversation to her and I'm glad not to be the center of attention.

"I think I'm going to open my own firm, I don't know. It will be a lot of work, especially getting good clients, but I think I can do it."

"You're a great lawyer, Liv. I believe in you. If you need anything, let me know. I can help."

She thanked me and we finally ended our phone call as I was finishing up my makeup. The only thing I have left to do is lipstick.

"You have to go to the bar?" Jesse asks, startling me. He's dressed and standing in the doorway, watching me.

"Yeah, my shift starts at seven." I eye him cautiously in the mirror, seeing how his eyes are downcast and sad.

"How many more shifts are you working?" Maybe it's because he just woke up, but his tone is grumpy and it puts me on edge.

"I don't know. My original plan was to finish out the summer, so a few more weeks maybe." I unplug my straightener, preparing to defend myself.

"I need to do work stuff and I won't be able to come see you. I'm worried about you after what happened last time." He rubs the back of his neck, referring back to the night I was grabbed by the drunk guy.

It startled me too, that's why it's almost been two weeks since I've been back, but I can't let that control my life. I've been controlled by fear for too long.

"That was an isolated incident. I'm usually fine. Daya will be there, and Sunny. I'll be okay," I promise him, hoping it's not a lie. He nods his head to himself and then I see it. The scared boy afraid to see someone he cares about get hurt.

"Will you call me? Even if everything is fine, let me know you're okay. I'm going to have a hard time focusing on what I need to do tonight as is." He gives me a half smile that doesn't reach his eyes.

"I'll call you, text you, and send smoke signals. I'll be thinking about you all night anyway," I add, hoping to cheer him up. The smile this time does reach his eyes.

"Alright, I'll be home as soon as I can." He turns to leave, butterflies erupting in my belly when he says 'home'. I wish I could bottle that feeling. The pure joy radiating through me at his simple use of one word and the way I can't stop smiling around him. Everyone should get the chance in life to experience this unbridled happiness.

It gives me the strength to do what I've been wanting to do

for a long time, so I chase after him. "Wait!" I yell as I reach the steps, seeing that he's almost out the front door.

I bound down the steps, planting my feet on the last step right in front of him. "I wanted one more experiment before you left," I state breathlessly.

He watches me inquisitively, understanding reaching his eyes when he sees mine glance at his mouth. "Stay very still, please," I whisper, only a breath away as my heart races.

He doesn't move, but his eyes darken when my hands gently cup his cheeks. He sucks in a small intake of breath but otherwise doesn't budge. I lean in and ever so softly press my lips to his.

It's only a brush of a kiss, the contact is minimal, but my heart thumps in my ears. Not with impending doom or panic, but excitement. I did it.

I smile, pulling back to look at him, but he's practically trembling. "Jesse?" His eyes are still closed.

"Just need a second," he utters, shoving his hands in his pockets. "You should probably step back. I'm having a hard time keeping my hands to myself," he chokes out. "There are so many things I want to do to you right now, Thea. Letting me taste your lips opened Pandora's box."

His words stir up some anxiety in the pit of my stomach, but it's far overshadowed by the lust that I feel. I want him far more than the fear I have about having a panic attack. At this point, I'm weighing the risks of having one if it means I can experience him touching me back.

"Do you really have to go to work right now?" I ask, still only a step away, deciding to take my chances by not moving away from him. He groans, deep from his chest, it almost sounds like he's in pain.

"I do. I really do. But, I am close to throwing away my entire career just so I can stay," he grits out, his face full of anguish. I know I'm not being fair and I can't let him neglect his duties, so I relent.

"Be safe, tonight. I want you all in one piece for what I have planned later," I tease, turning back up the stairs and out of reach. I don't look back until I reach the top, seeing his mouth agape and hazy-eyed in the same spot I left him.

The ability I have to affect him like that is empowering and I'm going to reclaim every ounce of power that has ever been stolen from me.

Chapter Thirty-Five

Jesse

When I walk through the doors of the Rollins County Sheriff's Department, I'm surprised to find the space in disarray. It's late, the only person here seems to be the Sheriff himself.

"Malec," I say in greeting.

"Callahan." He nods, setting a box down that he was holding.

"You don't strike me as the hoarding type." I catalog all of the various boxes and stacks of paperwork littering every surface, and how the desks and chairs have all been moved and shifted in a way that is less than ideal.

"I'm not. We're moving the station back up to Lawson, next to the courthouse. It makes no sense for it to be out in these parts when the most populated city in this county is 15 minutes up the road. Maybe it worked here at one time, but I think Donahue just liked flying under the radar out here," he explains. It's the most words he's spoken to me at one time. "There is junk everywhere, paperwork dating back a decade..."

He rubs his hands across his face, and despite his stoic

exterior, I realize he's stressed. "I'm sorry, what can I do for you?" He asks, back to his default persona.

"No worries man. I'm impressed with what you're doing for the county. They're lucky to have you." And, I mean it. After Nathan and Callie were almost killed last year because of Sheriff Donahue and his brothers-in-law, it's relieving to know that Malec won't stand for corruption. Of the few conversations I've had with him, it's clear that he's straight-laced and by the book.

He doesn't respond to my compliment, he almost seems discomforted to receive a verbal pat on the back. It doesn't bother me, most guys have the emotional intelligence of a brick wall, mine has just been torn down, stomped on, and broken to pieces for the majority of my life.

"I still can't find Curtis," I admit. "What I overheard at Jameson's hasn't helped me figure out where he is."

"I know you believe the kid is innocent, but I'm going to need evidence or a confession from someone else. Those boys have pretty much gotten away with it unless we can get them on something else," he states ominously.

"Yeah. I'm working on it. All of the time I've been spending at the farm and I still haven't heard them talk about their endgame. Right now, there are a bunch of pieces of things that could potentially assemble bombs, but other than the one test they did, I haven't seen any more made. It just looks like he's collecting household products or starting a scrap yard." I blow out a breath in frustration.

"Next time, if you think something might go down, record it on your phone. If I see a video of something illegal, even if it's done anonymously, I'll have the power to get a warrant for the property. This is a small county, but I don't want anyone getting hurt."

"Me neither," I agree, thinking of Thea. How can all of this be going on so close to where she lives?

It feels like bad luck. All I can worry about is how unsafe she could be walking into the grocery store, or stopping by the post office. Malec's right, it's a small county with seemingly no targets. What's the agenda?

If Jameson wants to stick it to the government, he would be better off going somewhere else. I can only hope that's his plan. If he tries bombing a military base he'll leave in a body bag. Exactly what he deserves.

"I'll ask around, subtly talk to my guys, and see if there is anywhere around here that could be used as a political target. I also want to keep checking in with the neighbor who made the complaint on Jameson. His property is the biggest on that side of the county. Even from miles away, he heard the bomb that night. It scared his bears."

"Bears?"

"Yeah. It's some sort of black bear sanctuary. He runs a tight ship and he wasn't happy about an explosion going off so close to his property," he explains as his phone rings. He sighs deeply when he reads the caller ID so I excuse myself to continue my search for Curtis.

If the neighbor is what spooked Jameson into thinking someone was onto him then maybe Curtis isn't whistle-blowing at all. So, why is he hiding?

I end up driving around for a few hours, checking hotel parking lots for his truck, campsites, and neighborhoods. It's a waste of time, but I have nothing else to go on until I get a text from Jameson. **Get to the farm, asap.**

The uneasy feeling in my gut sits with me until I climb out

of my truck in front of the farmhouse. Derrick and Mitch are sitting on the porch steps, watching me.

"Fellas," I say as casually as I can. They nod.

Jameson walks out of his house, closely followed by someone else. My fists clench when I see an unmistakable face and I do my best not to react.

The fucking prick contractor.

Why the hell is he here?

"Jay, we've got problems." Jameson motions to Derrick and Mitch. "They found out Curtis blabbed to someone about us and now he's MIA."

My heart is beating against my ribs, trying to keep my cool. I am well aware of how slippery the kid can be, that's why I'm dealing with this shit in the first place.

"He knows you're looking for him?"

"Oh, he knows." Derrick scoffs, bumping shoulders with Mitch. "He weaseled away from us before we could teach him his lesson."

Jameson looks at Derrick pointedly. "Shut it."

That look on his face is loud and clear. Jameson doesn't want me to know about Dennis. He's keeping that incident in his trusted circle, which I'm not a part of. They only want me so they can get to Curtis.

"We saw him poking around town and we followed him to Sunny's," Mitch says.

My heart stops at his mention of the bar, but I play dumb. "So, where is he now?" I ask, avoiding Kyle's shit-eating gaze from over Jameson's shoulder.

Should I have suspected a kid like that would be mixed up in all of this? How could I though?

This area is too small, there are too many connections

among the locals. I'm an outsider but I should have antici-pated it.

"He slipped them after they saw him talking to the blonde bartender. We need to find out what she knows, that's why he's here." Jameson turns back to look at Kyle, but he's gone. "Where the hell did he go?"

The blood in my ears is roaring. Why would Curtis be talking to Thea?

My worst nightmare is coming true. Despite my efforts to keep her at a distance, she's somehow gotten involved with these fuckers. I'm going to kill Curtis myself when I see him.

I whip my neck around when we all hear a car start up and drive down the lane towards the road. *That's why he's here.* Those words ring in my ears.

Kyle is going after her.

"Whatever," Jameson utters, oblivious to my distress. "Find out where Curtis is and the first one to bring him to me gets to detonate the next bomb." He laughs, endlessly amused with this cat-and-mouse game he has created. "My nephew already has a head start, so you better get moving." *Nephew.*

I'm already running to my truck while I process that information. Gunning it down the driveway, I pull my phone out and see two missed calls from Thea. When I call her back it goes straight to voicemail and I bang my hand on the steering wheel. DAMMIT!

If he's going straight to her then he could do anything before I make it there. I can't let this happen, I can't let anything happen to her.

I'm taking curves like a maniac, pushing my old truck to its limits while getting her voicemail again and again. Cursing to myself, I listen to the two she left me earlier.

Hi, it's me. Just calling to check in and tell you that I miss you. Can't wait to see you later. The bar's been pretty slow so they're going to let me leave at eleven.

I glance at the clock, it's almost midnight, so she's definitely home by now. Dammit, if she was still at the bar she'd probably be safer. I listen to the next voicemail that came in just after eleven.

Hey, I don't want you to worry, but I just got done talking to that guy you know from your veteran's meeting. He was asking about you, wanting to meet up. He said he knew that I was your girlfriend and asked me to pass on the message. Am I your girlfriend? I'm sorry, that's silly, ignore that. See you at home.

Despite my pain-stricken terror, I laugh. My sweet Sunshine. I'm going to ruin this before I even have a chance to make it clear that she's my girlfriend. She's already so much more than that, but for now, it's a safe title.

I'm such an idiot. I don't deserve her. I don't know why I thought I could handle this case and be involved with her at the same time. If I lose her because of it... Fuck, I can't think like that.

Home. I just want to go home to her. Please, don't let anything happen to her. I'll start praying, I'll sacrifice myself. I'll do anything to ensure that she doesn't get hurt. I push the accelerator as hard I can, racing towards town.

Maybe, Malec can help.

I dial his number, relaying what's happening as soon as he answers. He promises to get to Thea's as soon as he can and we disconnect. Right as the call ends, another one comes in. Thea's name stares at me in all-white letters. Thank God.

"Thea!" I shout into the phone.

"What's wrong? I was in the shower."

"Get out of the house. Get in your car and go," I try telling her calmly, but I can hear the panic in my voice.

"What? Why?" She asks fearfully, but I can hear her moving around like she's doing as I said.

"Kyle's coming. He's involved with the people I'm investigating. Fuck. I'm so sorry, baby. I never thought this would get to you." I feel the licks of fury climbing up my neck at the thought of Kyle being anywhere near her, it's unbearable. Knowing that I'm not with her and can't do anything is making me lose my mind.

"He's here," she says suddenly.

"What? Where are you?"

"The kitchen, my keys," she mumbles, distractedly. "His van is in the alley out back. What do I do?" The terror in her voice guts me. Knowing that it's partly my fault is like a knife twisting in my abdomen.

"Run. Thea, run! I'm a few minutes away." She doesn't respond, the call just disconnects, making me slam my phone down on the seat. "FUCK!" I roar into the confines of my truck.

Minutes later I'm slamming my truck into park in her front yard after ramping the curb. Her car is still parked on the street but her front door is wide open. I run full speed into the living room, gun out, looking for any sign of her.

"Thea?" I yell, clearing the kitchen and the rest of the downstairs. His van isn't out back anymore.

As I go to run upstairs, I almost step on her phone lying face down on the landing. Did she drop it when she ran out of the house? Or is she here somewhere? Did he take her?

I pocket it, trying to focus enough to clear the two smaller bedrooms upstairs and the bathroom, before finally going into her room. There's no sign of her, she's gone. "FUCK!!" I roar, again.

"What happened?"

I'm startled, instinctively pointing my gun toward the voice before realizing that it's Malec. I drop it like it's on fire, the gun thumping onto the bed as he stands in the hallway watching me warily.

"I can't find her. I told her to run, but I don't know where she is." My hands claw at my hair, pulling painfully at my roots. I deserve the hurt, I deserve to be punished for not keeping her safe.

"Are you sure? It's only been a few minutes. Did you check everywhere?" He asks, glancing up and down the hall at all the doors I've left open in my flurry to find her.

"I cleared the house. I found her phone on the stairs," I say, tossing it onto the mattress. My knees buckle and sink to the edge of the bed. *I lost her.*

"Is there any reason she would go willingly?"

"No. No way. I told her who was coming. She's terrified of-" I start to say men, but change my mind. Not wanting to air out Thea's business. "This guy. She's had problems with him for weeks. She wouldn't go willingly." I stare at my hands, resting on my knees.

I've never felt fear like this before. Soul-crushing terror.

Chapter Thirty-Six

Thea

I can't move. I can't speak. I can hardly breathe.

My body is barely holding onto survival while I listen to Jesse calling my name from below me. I'm lying on the hard wooden floor of my attic, under the light of my moon window, in a paralyzing state of fear.

The only movement that I can register is the intense shaking that is racking my body. So intense that my teeth are chattering, despite the stuffy heat up here.

Usually, I'd keep the door open, or crack the window to allow ventilation, but still break out in a sweat if I was up here too long. Now, I'm faintly worried that I'll die of heat exhaustion or lack of oxygen before I can will my body to move.

Despite knowing how unhelpful I'm being in this situation, my body can't reconcile it. I'm stuck.

"Are you sure she isn't here somewhere?" I hear a male voice say, though it's quite muffled, I can tell he's in my room. I assume it's the Sheriff.

"I don't know, I looked in every room." Jesse's voice touches a place in my soul, my mind begging my body to obey. Please, he's right there. He's worried about me.

"You're distracted. You need to think," Malec states sternly.

"What?" Jesse asks incredulously.

"Could she have gone to a neighbor's? Or be hiding? I don't know, we need to check everywhere before I can declare her missing. I can drive the block," his voice suggests cooly.

There's a long silence. Neither of them speaks, but I can only hope they aren't leaving. I mentally beg Jesse to find me and not to leave.

I'm here. I'm right here.

"You're right. Fuck, you're right."

Jesse's voice gets closer. "She showed me this a while ago." I hear the closet door creak open below me and I breathe a sigh of relief. He found me. It's okay. I'm safe.

The ladder is pulled out, letting a gush of cool air in through the square cut out of an opening beside me. I sob in relief when Jesse's head comes into view, my body still trembling.

"I got her, she's here. Thea, baby. I'm so sorry." He reaches for me and stops, remembering the frail girl that I am. "What can I do?"

I shake my head, my first signs of movement. "I don't know. I don't know," I repeat over and over, my mind not able to process how to handle this. I want out, I want out of this attic but I can't move. My body still won't cooperate.

"She just needs a minute. Thanks for coming out here so quickly," Jesse speaks to his counterpart, giving me the privacy that I'm going to need to deal with this.

A normal person would be elated to be rescued, to crawl down from here and thank the people who came to save them, but I'm not normal. I'm broken and it's been a long time since I've felt it this much.

"Call me when things settle," his voice utters and I hear his steps leaving the room. I know I wasn't in danger since Jesse was here, but I still feel better knowing there isn't someone else down there.

My body relaxes a little more. My breathing settles slightly but I'm sweating. My body's overheating and I know I need to get down from here.

"Get me out. Jesse, please. Get me out," I beg. I know what the consequences will be once he grabs me, but I beg anyway. "Please, please," I ramble, the impending panic attack setting in. If I'm going to lose it one way or the other, I'd rather do it in my room and not up here.

"Okay, okay, I got you." He looks at me with regret in his eyes, realizing how badly I'm struggling if I'm begging for this. He gently grabs my legs, pulling them towards him and the opening to the ladder. I squeeze my eyes shut, trying to ignore what's happening, but it doesn't matter. My body starts trembling even more violently, my breath becoming ragged once more.

He manages to wrap my legs around his waist, draping my arms over his shoulders while I focus on not fainting. The splotches in my eyes warn me of its desire to take me.

"You're doing so good, baby. I know it's hard, but cling to me if you can, hold on to me so I can get us down," he speaks gently, urging me to hug him like a koala. His voice once again soothes something in my soul, lessening some of the splotches taking over my vision.

"T-talk, ttt-to, m-me," I stutter through my jitters, hoping he can understand me because I can hardly hear myself over the pounding of my heart.

"I'm right here, sweetheart. You're safe. I've got you," he

continues whispering to me as slowly descends the ladder. It's old and rickety, and not meant to bear the weight of two people at once. He's trying to be safe, but it feels like an eternity. "Almost there. Keep holding on. You're doing so well, sweet girl."

Whether on purpose or not, my face ends up buried in his neck, where it stays for the entirety of this trek. Even after I feel the softness of my bed beneath me, my face stays pressed against his skin.

"Thea, you did it. You're safe," he whispers to me and I realize the rest of his body is no longer plastered to mine. It's my arms and my legs that are clinging to him. It's the only thing keeping us together.

Instead of letting go completely, I unwrap my legs from his waist, letting my bottom half drop to the mattress.

"I'm sorry, I'm so sorry," I sob, still grasping his shoulders. My body is flaming with embarrassment because he had to experience this reaction from me. I'm too ashamed to look him in the face.

"No, don't. This is my fault. It's all my fault. You have nothing to be sorry for," he chokes out. "I don't want you to be scared like this ever again. It's all my fault."

I don't want him to blame himself, but all I can do is cry and focus on calming down. It takes several minutes for my anxiety to cool and for my body to start functioning somewhat normally. I still haven't removed my face from his neck or unlocked my arms from his shoulders though.

"Lay with me, please?" I ask, realizing he's still standing, hunched over me so he doesn't accidentally touch me any-where else while I cling to him.

"Are you sure?" He pulls back far enough to look into my

face. His eyes are full of devastation and concern, studying me closely.

"I need you."

He's the only thing that has brought me positive change in my life. Even though some changes are still scary for me, I know that I wouldn't have made it to this point without him. I'm not ashamed to admit how much I need him because he's given me so many pieces of my life back.

"Okay," he whispers, moving to lay on his back beside me. He grabs the bed frame above his head immediately like he's terrified to send me into another fit of panic. The initial fear is gone though, the terror I felt in the moon room, waiting for him to arrive, desperately hoping Kyle wasn't going to find me, is gone.

I know I'm safe with Jesse, I was just blind with terror. I'm bitter that my first time being held by him was because of this situation. Another experience that should have been a happy one was taken from me. I should be used to it by now.

My head rests on his shoulder and I bury my face against his neck once again. The way I fit here feels almost like a hug. I focus on breathing, making sure I've really calmed down and I'm not jumping the gun. It takes several minutes, but I finally feel like I'm back to my normal equilibrium. Despite the weight of my exhaustion taking over, the questions start racing through my mind.

"What happened? How did you know he was coming?" I ask, sniffing back the last of my tears. He takes a deep breath, hesitating to answer.

"He's involved with the case I'm working on. I only found out tonight. It all happened fast. One minute he was there and the next minute he was gone. I knew he was heading here." He shutters, needing to take another deep breath. "All I could think about was you being scared or hurt. I failed you." His voice cracks and he clears his throat like he's fighting back tears, "I'm so sorry, baby."

"He tried the front lock and I heard it so I ran upstairs. The door banged open by the time I was climbing the ladder. If you wouldn't have changed my locks he would have gotten to me. I barely had enough time to pull the ladder up," I explain breathlessly, trying to keep it together.

"I want to kill him for coming after you." The murderous tone leaves no question of his sincerity, but I don't have the energy to refute it. I don't condone violence, but I really hate Kyle right now.

"What would have happened if he found me?" I ask in a small voice, afraid to know the answer.

"I don't know," he utters, shamefully. "Nothing good."

Chapter Thirty-Seven

Thea

I'm not entirely sure when sleep came, but as I blink awake, I can tell that I hardly moved an inch. My entire body hurts from lying in the same position for so long. My neck is stiff as a board.

I peel myself off of Jesse's hard body, noting the near-perfect imprint of my ear on his skin. His arms are still locked around the bars of my bed frame.

"Jesse," I whisper, wanting his attention but not wanting to startle him. It only partially works, because he jolts awake, flinching when he tries to pull his arms back. "It's morning, we haven't moved all night." I relay my obvious findings.

"My arms... I don't think there's any blood left." He shakes his limbs, trying to regain some circulation. This silly bit of distress makes me laugh, so less severe than our problems from last night.

"I need to get ready for work," I mumble, but don't move. The last thing I want to do is go to work right now. I can only imagine how puffy my face looks from crying last night.

"Can you take another day off?" He asks, reading my mind.

"Technically, yes. I have plenty of time to use but hate

259

calling off at the last minute."

"I'm sure Latisha would understand, but do what you think is best. I'd rather stay in bed with you all day, but I can manage hanging out at the library if you want." He closes his eyes and leans back into the pillows as if that were a completely normal statement.

"Why would you be hanging out at the library?" He doesn't even open his eyes at my question.

"I'm not leaving your side today. Not even out of my sight."

"That's probably not necessary." Though I can't lie... I'm not looking forward to being out of his sight either.

"I'm not changing my mind. You're way too important to me to leave it up to chance. I thought I might lose you last night, Thea. I never want to feel that way again." He squeezes his eyes shut tighter, frowning slightly as if to stop replaying what happened yesterday in his head.

"Do you know where my phone is?" My decision to call off has been made. Life is too short and unpredictable to spend the day pretending we're okay. Last night affected us both in different ways but solidified the fact that we're both terrified to lose each other.

"Somewhere on the bed, I think." He watches me closely as I climb off and search through the blankets until I find it.

As I make my call his shoulders relax, especially when he hears Latisha through the phone insisting that I stay home. Once I told her what happened, her voice raised a few octaves with concern. I had to tell her over and over that I was fine before she accepted it.

"Is he there? Cutie from the library?" She asks, whispering into the phone finally.

"Yes. He's here." I blush, glancing at where Jesse is sitting on my bed.

"Wooo goood!" She yells, making me pull the phone farther from my ear.

"Okay, he can hear you. Goodbye Latisha, love you." I attempt to end the call before she can embarrass me.

"Love you too sweetie! AND, YOU TOO CUTIE!" She yells again, making me and Jesse both laugh. Latisha's silliness helps lighten both of our moods.

I sit my phone down and crawl back into bed. "I won't have to be back in until Tuesday."

"What about the bar?" He asks, making me cringe. Ugh, the bar.

"I'll call Sunny later, tell him that I'm done." I decide at that moment.

"Are you sure? I'd be there no matter what. Fuck anything else, I'll sit there and make sure you're safe the whole time if you want to keep working there," he tells me earnestly.

There's no guilt-mongering or manipulation in his voice. He's being honest. He would sit there every night for hours if I was determined to keep working.

"After last night, I'm ready to be done. I don't want either of us to be worried about a job that I don't even like. I'll burn the uniform." I laugh, realizing how happy I am to never parade around in it again.

"Keep it." There's a twinkle in his eye that I've missed since everything happened last night. His worry is finally dissipating enough to regain some of his normal charm. "You can wear it for me."

"Okay," I whisper against his shoulder, kissing him lightly through his shirt. I don't know why I did it, but now that I did, it makes me want to keep kissing him. I want to kiss every inch of him. "Will you take your shirt off?"

He pulls it off over his head without saying a word, keeping his eyes trained on me. I lick my lips at the sight of his bare chest. He's so sexy, I can't believe that he's mine to touch. To experiment with.

"Thea, you look like you want to eat me," he states, leaning back on his hands.

"I do," I say distractedly, still deciding where I want to start. He mumbles incoherent curses under his breath while I crawl behind him.

Sitting on my knees behind his back, I lean forward to trail kisses along his shoulder, across his neck, and down his other shoulder. Each kiss is a thank you and a promise that I can't find the strength to say out loud without crying and ruining our morning.

Thank you for saving me. Kiss.

Thank you for being here. Kiss.

Thank you for being you. Kiss.

His breathing intensifies as he's affected by what I'm doing. I keep kissing him, crawling around him to drag my mouth up and down his biceps, his chest. Listening to his breathy sounds fuels me to keep going, dying to hear more.

I promise to give you everything. Kiss.

I promise I will fight all of my demons. Kiss.

Thank you for being mine. Kiss.

I move down to my knees on the floor in front of him, right between his legs, continuing to kiss him down the center of his chest towards his belly button. "Thea..." He warns, grumbling out more curse words.

I don't know if his reactions are giving me all the strength to keep going or if last night scared me enough that I don't want to miss out on any opportunities with him. All I know is that I'm not prepared to stop my downward trajectory.

"You're mine to do what I please, right?" I ask, hoping he doesn't want me to stop. I want this too bad to stop.

"All yours, baby," he groans out, tossing his head back when my nails trace his waistband. I tug on it, and he lifts his hips, allowing me to pull his jeans down and with it his briefs. His cock springs free, almost hitting me in the face. It's even bigger than I realized now that I'm this close. The first nerves about what I'm doing flit in. What if I can't do this?

I look up at him, doubts filling my mind, but when I see how he's looking at me, they disappear. He's looking at me with such lust and adoration as if he's in awe of me. His obvious affection gives me the confidence to keep going and to enjoy it. This is for him, but it's also for me.

My hands wrap tentatively around his hard shaft, feeling him twitch slightly at the contact. His thighs are shaking, faintly brushing against my arms. Being trapped between his legs should scare me, but I feel perfectly safe. After everything that happened last night, I know I'm safe with him.

Being here on my knees in front of him is turning me on. Warmth is pooling low in my belly making me even more eager to do this.

Moving slowly up and down, my palms feel every inch of thickness from base to tip. A drop of precum spills out the top, drawing me in. I kiss it away, licking my lips to taste it.

"Fuck, baby," he moans, still gazing at me lovingly, but with fire in his eyes.

Not allowing the chance to second guess myself, I take the head of his cock in my mouth and suck lightly before popping off. His hands fist my bed sheets, desperate to hold on to something.

With each bob of my head, I go farther and farther, taking him deeper into my mouth. He tastes so good and his skin is like velvet. My hands wander, grabbing at his thick thighs and clawing down his taut stomach. It's primal like I can't get enough. Taking him as deep as I can, I hum in pleasure, feeling his crown hit the back of my throat.

"Oh my God," he mumbles breathlessly. I pull back just long enough to whip my shirt off, getting a look at his jaw clenching when he sees that I'm not wearing a bra.

Taking him as deep as I can again, I gag slightly, pulling back enough to catch my breath before diving back in. My saliva drips down his length, lubing the base, my hand working where my mouth can't reach. When I choke myself again, eager to take more than I'm able to, he moans, throwing his head back.

"Thea, you're going to kill me. I can't take it, I'm close." I process his words, knowing what I want from him.

"I want it. All over me." I take him back into my mouth, licking and sucking until I'm breathless. It only takes a minute before his legs start twitching and his abs tighten under my fingertips.

"Now, baby," he grunts, giving me a chance to back up a few inches. He pumps his hand up and down his shaft, once, then again, before painting me with his cum. It covers my chest, dripping down my breasts, and coating me.

He stands there, mouth agape, staring at me for several seconds before he seems to blink out of it. "I've never cum that hard in my life," he admits. There's no dramatic flair in his voice, he almost seems taken aback. "If that's how it is after a blow job, I can't imagine what being inside of you will feel like."

I'm even more turned on after hearing his thoughts voiced out loud. My core clenches, dying to have him inside of me. My whole body is hot, tingly, and desperate.

I want to cum so bad I think I might cry. I'm silently begging him to help me. I don't know how to do it, but I need him.

Chapter Thirty-Eight

Jesse

"Jesse…" She whimpers with ragged breath, making the softening of my dick reverse in an instant. Her fluttering eyelids and pink cheeks tell me that she's turned on and needy.

Maybe it's sadistic, but it's a beautiful thing to witness. I want her to want me as badly as I want her. She doesn't need to beg because I'll give her anything she wants, but I want her to want to beg.

"You ready to cum, sweet girl?" I pull open her nightstand drawer, inspecting the rest of the new toys she bought for the first time. "Take your shorts off, lay on the bed."

She all but leaps off the floor, climbing onto the bed like an eager little sex fiend. My girl is wound tight and in need of release.

I pull out the wand we used yesterday, along with a purple dildo. It's not huge, smaller than my hardware, inflating my ego a little. When she is ready for my cock, I want it to be the biggest thing she's had.

"Do you trust me?" I ask, leaning on the bed next to her. I watch her eyes closely, making sure I see the consent that I need. Not because she thinks that I want her to say yes, but because she means yes. I want to see the trust when she looks at me.

"I do." Her eyes are full of nothing but eager anticipation as she drags her shorts down her legs.

I admire her perfect body, wanting to memorize every inch. My cum still glistens on her chest and for the first time, I notice just how smooth and bare her mound is. "When did you do this?" I ask, looking at her soft skin.

It's so clean that I wouldn't even begin to guess what color her pubic hair might be. Not knowing that detail urks me for some reason. I want to know everything about her.

"A week ago. I go every six weeks to get waxed. It's an exposure technique that my therapist recommended," she admits, shyly, and a flair of jealousy passes through me. When I look at her with concern, worried about what she's being exposed to, she clarifies.

"It exposes me to touch. The only people who have seen my vagina in the past six years are my OBGYN and my esthetician. Both are female." She giggles at my sigh of relief.

This newfound possessiveness I'm feeling is intense and uncalled for. She has made it clear she wants me and only me, but the thought of any other man being near her makes me see red.

"Good. The only man who gets to see you is me," I demand, staking my claim like an asshole.

"You're the only one I want," she assures me, smiling sweetly. It's music to my ears. I sink to my knees on the floor, so I can rest my arms on the bed beside her, making our heads only a few inches apart.

"I get one, you get one. Take your pick." I hold out the two toys I selected, watching her eyes widen when she processes what I'm saying. They flick back and forth between the two, an internal debate happening in her head before she makes her decision. She tentatively takes the vibrator from me, leaving me with the phallic purple dildo.

"Turn it on, baby. Put it on your clit." I watch as she does it. The initial spark of sensation when she makes contact with the vibrator puts the sexiest look on her face, a mixture of arousal and eagerness.

"How does that feel?" I ask, admiring her pretty face starting to flush.

"Good," she answers in a breathy, raspy voice.

"You're so beautiful, Thea. I love seeing you like this. You're the sexiest woman I've ever met." My words seem to affect her, making her eyelids flutter more while her cheeks get even pinker.

"Open your mouth," I instruct. She does immediately, making my dick pulse.

"Take this, suck on it like you sucked on my cock, baby." I push the purple toy between her lips, sliding it along her tongue. Her lips go round trying to take it in deeper. "So good, you're doing so good, pretty girl." She moans at my praise, her fluttering eyelids closing completely.

I slide the dildo out of her mouth slowly, only wanting it to get prepped for what I want to do next. She resists slightly, making a popping noise when it's released from her lips. So greedy.

"I'm going to put this inside your pussy now, Sunshine. Is that what you want?" I ask, needing to make sure she's okay with this. She nods her head, but I need more.

"I need your words, sweet girl." Her eyes peek open, gazing

at me lustfully.

"I want it," she breathes. Thank God.

I position it right at her entrance, having to snake my arm under her arched knee. It's risky hoping I don't accidentally touch her and ruin this, but I'm too into it to stop.

"I want you to imagine that it's me, that my cock is about to slide into your sweet cunt. Can you do that?" I ask, loving the way she whimpers at my dirty words.

"Yes," she breathes out. I push in slightly, teasingly slow. Her vibrator is still buzzing on her clit, already putting her close to the edge from what I can tell. Her breathing has picked up, and her muscles twitch slightly.

"You want it, baby. You want my cock inside you?" I ask, selfishly wanting to hear her beg for it. She whimpers again, biting her plump bottom lip.

"Please, Jesse. I want your cock, please." Her pleading is like music to my ears, the words lighting a fire in my soul. I push the purple toy into her tight opening, giving her what she wants. She gasps at the intrusion.

"Just like that, baby. Take it." I thrust it in and out, absorbing all of her little cries of pleasure. My dick is desperately flexing against the side of her bed, embarrassingly eager. It's too much, she's too damn sexy.

"Oh my God. Oh God. Jesse. Jesse." She moans, mumbling my name over and over. It's the sexiest thing I've ever heard. I pump the dildo in and out faster, harder, rocking my hips in succession. I can't stop. I wish it was me inside of her. I use my free hand to fist myself, needing relief.

"You're so sexy, Thea. You take this cock so well, I can't wait to fill your pussy with mine. I'm going to sink so deep into you that you'll never get me out." Our breathing is in sync, fast and heavy. Both of us are lost in this moment.

"I want it," she murmurs, making my jaw clench. Fuck, I want to give it to her.

"Soon, baby. Soon," I promise, knowing that we'll get there eventually. She's already made so much progress in our small amount of time together. She's determined, so I know we'll get there together.

"Jesse, I need..." She trails off, making me look away from her lower half and to her face. It's turned toward mine, only inches away.

"What, baby? What do you nee-" Before I can finish my question, she uses her free hand to grab my jaw, dragging my lips to hers. She kisses me hard and desperately, so much differently than the first time. I try to stay still, but my lips mold around hers on instinct, fusing us together.

It's amazing, it's soul-binding. Having her mouth on mine is the greatest gift. It almost puts me off the deep end. I'm so wildly turned on by her and everything she gives me. I'm only faintly aware of my hand still fucking her with the dildo and I'm surprised when she cries out with her release.

Her breathy moans of pleasure fill my mouth, drowning me in ecstasy. I feel high absorbing all of her sounds, tasting her on my lips. Before I can think better of it, I follow her, finishing for the second time this morning. Except this time it's all over my hand and the side of her bed. Fuck.

I ignore my pubescent reaction for now, instead focusing on her. She turns off her vibrator, and I pull the dildo out slowly, gently. Her face is still so near mine and she rubs her nose along mine sweetly. "Thank you," she whispers.

"Don't thank me, that was the greatest moment of my life," I admit, making her smile. "You're perfect, Thea."

"I think we might've been made for each other," she says, still a breath away from me. Her fingers still hold my jaw, keeping me in place even though I have no plan to move yet. Neither of us has any desire to widen the gap.

"I think so, too." There can be nothing better than this. She's what I've needed my whole life.

"Kiss me," she whispers against my lips. I hesitate slightly, knowing this will be different than the other times. She leaves just enough space to allow me to initiate it, giving me the consent to make the connection for the first time. It's so simple, but it means everything.

I press my lips to hers, feeling her response immediately. She doesn't freeze, or spook, she reciprocates. Offering me the world with that gigantic step of trust. I'm so in love with her it feels like it's bursting out of my chest.

"You are everything to me, Thea," I whisper against her lips.

For two people who were not supposed to cross paths the way we did, we're moving fast. I have no objections though, especially when she smiles that radiant smile that has changed my life, righting every wrong that has even been done to me. Opening my world to endless possibilities and a happy future. Owning me entirely.

"You are everything to me, Jesse." She kisses me again and I savor it.

With that, all was temporarily right with the world.

Chapter Thirty-Nine

Thea

"I can do that," I insist again, but Jesse ignores me. He shoves the bed sheets into the washer, letting me admire his flexing back muscles and how his jeans hang low on his hips.

"I'm going to make a mess of these sheets a lot more often, so I should get used to doing laundry here," he winks, making me laugh. I never imagined I could be so happy.

I feel so fulfilled now that Jesse and I have become intimate together. I know the physical stuff shouldn't mean everything, but to me it's huge. He's given me my life back.

"You fix bathrooms, you do laundry, you give orgasms, what can't you do?" I tease, going back into the kitchen to make us lunch.

"I can't take you to any family reunions," he counters as he comes into the kitchen himself.

"Jesse." My jaw drops at what he just said.

"Sorry, just a little orphan humor." He laughs to himself, pulling a chair out from the table. He smiles, finding himself amusing, so I roll my eyes and turn back to my task at the counter.

"Do you have to do anything today?" I ask, bringing our plates over to the table.

"I need to get in touch with Malec," he explains, taking a huge bite out of his sandwich. Men.

"He was here last night, right?"

"Yeah, I called him when I was afraid that I wouldn't get here in time. He raced straight here. I owe him one." He doesn't look at me as he speaks like he's having a hard time even thinking about it. I don't blame him.

"Tell him I said thank you when you talk to him," I insist.

"I will." He finally gives me a small reassuring smile. It makes me want to kiss him, so I do.

"I'm never going to get tired of that," he murmurs once I pull away.

"Well, good." I smile, thoughtfully enjoying my happiness for a moment before I bring up the next topic. "What about your friend from the bar last night?"

"Right. Curtis," he informs me with an exasperated look on his face.

"He startled me a bit when he came to talk to me. Asked if I was Jay's girlfriend. I didn't know what to say, so I just said yes. He told me he was in trouble and needed your help. He said he'd text you." I shrug.

"He shouldn't have come up to you, but it's my fault. I should have kept you further away while I was investigating all of this. I got too comfortable." He shakes his head at himself.

"I'm glad you didn't keep me far away." Hopefully, he feels that way too despite everything. We wouldn't be where we are now if he waited to talk to me after his investigation ended.

"I'll never be able to live with myself if something happens to you, Thea. If I do something that gets you hurt…" He closes his eyes briefly as if he's willing away the thoughts.

"You won't. I'll be fine." I try to make him feel better, but I can tell he doesn't quite believe me. There is still a sadness in his eyes.

"Do you think you'd be able to stay with Nathan tonight? I'm going to need to deal with some stuff and I don't want you here alone with Kyle still out there."

"I'm sure he wouldn't mind. Do you think it's necessary?"

"It's necessary." His definitive tone sends a chill down my spine. "And, Thea. You're not Jay's girlfriend. You're my girlfriend."

He's looking at me seriously, leaning in enough to indicate that he wants a kiss. I oblige happily. "Jesse's girlfriend. Got it," I answer against his lips.

* * *

He's fixing the minor damage to my front door from Kyle kicking it in when his phone dings. The hard look on his face clues me into who it is but I don't ask, giving him space. I can only imagine how stressful all of this is for him.

He's essentially out here on his own trying to break this case, with no backup, no support. Aside from what he's told me about Sheriff Malec, it doesn't seem like he has anyone to rely on.

"Go pack, I'll take you to Nathan's in a bit," he instructs, cleaning up his mess.

CHAPTER THIRTY-NINE

"I can drive."

"No, I want to make sure you get there safe and sound. Plus, if your car is here and Kyle tries anything else thinking you're home, Malec will have more fuel to arrest him with."

"Okay," I concede, understanding where he's coming from. I try not to focus on the fact that Kyle is still out there and might want to hurt me.

I make my way upstairs to pack my overnight bag, startling slightly when Jesse sneaks up behind me as I'm almost finished.

"You really know how to sneak around," I say once catch my breath.

"Sorry. I didn't mean to scare you." He laughs, gazing at me lovingly. Some of his obvious stress from earlier seems to have dissipated. I lean against my dresser, looking into his handsome face, still in awe of this relationship.

"What?"

"I'm really happy. It's been a long time since I've loved my life but with you... It's so easy," I admit.

"Yeah, I feel the same way, Sunshine." He steps closer into my space, but without touching me.

"Promise?" I whisper against his lips, letting him close the distance. He kisses me gently, not daring to push me any farther, but I want more. I stand on my tiptoes, wrapping my arms around his neck, deepening our kiss.

It feels safe and comforting to kiss him this way, but at the same time I feel hot and on the edge of losing control. Knowing that I can lose control if I want, that I'm safe to do so, turns me on beyond belief.

"I want to give you the world," he confesses against my lips between kisses. I slide my tongue across his, making him groan.

"I have it, I have you." I suck on his bottom lip and my body leans deeper into his, feeling his hardness against my belly. He groans again at the contact.

"Thea," he warns, making me want to torture him more. His arms are braced on either side of me, holding onto the top of my dresser with a vice grip. He's so patient with me, he never pushes me to do anything I don't want to, and it makes me want to give him *everything.*

"When do we have to leave?" I kiss his jaw, then run my tongue down his neck.

"Later," he grits out through clenched teeth. "I owe you another orgasm."

"Should we take our clothes off, now?" I ask, scraping my teeth across his collarbone, just above his shirt. He doesn't respond, but quickly steps back and whips his shirt off like he can't wait another second.

"Let me see you, baby." He undoes the button of his jeans, letting them hang on his hips until I snap out of gawking at him and take my shirt off. I'm wearing another lacey bralette and I'm glad because I can tell how much he likes it. He has to fight to get his jeans off past his hardness.

"God, you're perfect." He lights me on fire with his eyes as I toss my shorts aside. Leaving me in my teal bra and matching thong.

"I want you to touch me," I tell him, but my voice wavers slightly and he notices.

"I know, baby. I want to touch you, too, but I can wait. I don't want to push you if you aren't ready." He steps closer, bracing me against the dresser again, being as close as possible without making contact.

My mind is reeling, trying to come up with a solution to my problems because I am desperate for him. It's like my brain needs to be mentally prepared for every touch and I can't get passed it.

Anticipating his movements might ease some of my anxiety, so I take one of his hands in mine, guiding him to my floor-length mirror with ease. He doesn't ask questions and he doesn't resist, giving me full control.

Facing our reflection, he stands behind me, watching me closely. I soak in the way he looks at me, letting it ease my worry. His eyes are nothing but kind and curious. His faith in my ability to overcome my inner turmoil is more than enough to keep me going.

I undo my bra, letting it fall to the floor at my feet while his eyes gaze heavily at my bare breasts. My nipples are already tight with arousal, desperate for his touch. It's exactly where I want to start.

Placing his palm atop the back of my hand and interlocking our fingers, I guide our conjoined hands to my chest. With my palm flat against my skin, his larger one dwarfs mine, giving the illusion that he's the one touching me.

I stare at it, imagining that my hand is gone and that he is touching me. The shaky rise and fall of my chest is the only indication that I'm struggling a little. It's just a hand, I don't know why it scares me so much, but the anxiety is prickling at my skull.

"I've got you, Thea. I will never hurt you. I'm going to keep you safe for the rest of my life, baby. No one can hurt you again," he whispers closely to my ear, soothing me.

His words encourage me, fighting off the anxiety creeping in on me and letting me breathe a little easier. I can do this.

Chapter Forty

Jesse

I want to remember this moment forever. Thea standing before me, clutching our joined hands above her heart, fighting off the demons that plague her. The pure determination in her eyes is breathtaking. There is something so beautiful about her strength and I feel privileged to see it.

She takes a deep breath and lets it out slowly, making our hands rise and fall before she steadily moves us down to her breast. She cups the right side in her hand, curling our fingers around it and giving me the briefest contact with my fingertips. That tiny amount of soft skin against mine makes my nostrils flare.

"You're doing so good, baby. You're so beautiful," I whisper, making her sigh longingly. She's turned on, but she's still fighting against her nerves, so I let her. There's no rush. If nothing happens past this moment, I'd still praise her for progress.

Her other hand fumbles slightly against the top of my left before locking onto it and lifting *my* palm to cover her other breast, curling her fingers over mine to cup the weight. The sound I choke out is nothing short of surprise.

I'm touching her perfect body, no barrier between us.

"Fuck, baby. You feel so good," I say breathlessly. Holding a girl's boob shouldn't make me feel so triumphant at this stage in my life, but I can feel my cock pulsing with excitement.

This is a huge step and I'm so proud of her, but I'm also doing mental fist pumps in the air because I'm touching her. I've been dreaming of having her like this, feeling her.

Her breathing is elevated, but she seems in control, her eyes are locked onto our hands in the mirror's reflection. She gently swaps our hands on the right, letting me cup that breast as well, and if possible my dick swells even more.

Her eyelids close and she leans back into my chest, inhaling deeply. It's the closest thing to a trust fall I've seen in real life. She takes a few minutes somewhere in her head before opening her eyes again.

She blinks at our reflection, her gaze pinging to our hands and then to my face. I offer her a small smile and feel like a champion when she smiles back.

"I'm so proud of you." There's a tightness in my chest, so many emotions that I'm feeling instantaneously. All of which I recognize as love and pride for this beautiful woman in front of me.

"I'm ready for more," she admits into the mirror and I watch my eyes bulge. Fuck, I was not expecting that either. I'm the one who is supposed to be calm and in control, but her eagerness always surprises me. I feel simultaneously unprepared and turned on.

Before I can respond, she's tentatively dragging my hands across her body. Up and down her flat stomach, along her panty line, and up her sides. She takes her time letting me feel the heaviness of her breasts again before dragging my fingers across her nipples making herself gasp. I'm hypnotized watching her, absorbing every reaction.

She's using me, using my hands as a tool, seeking sensation. There's a fire in her gaze now, no more unsureness. She's in control and taking what she wants. I love her for it.

When she dips my hands back down to her hips, she hooks the sides of her thong making me drag it down her thighs until it falls to the floor. I can see her pussy glistening in the reflection of the mirror, she's so wet and we haven't even gone below her hips yet. My mouth waters just thinking about dipping into her warmth. I want to touch it, taste it. Fill it. Fuck it.

She presses my fingers onto her bare mound, the tip of my middle finger barely touching the top of her clit, at the same time as she pushes her ass into my groin.

"Fuck," I groan, overwhelmed by the sensations she's gifting me. It's too much, I'm practically seeing stars and I'm still in my underwear.

It takes me a few deep breaths before I realize Thea is trembling slightly. My eyes snap to hers in the mirror and in them, I see the slightest bit of fear.

My whole body lurches, attempting to pull back, but she keeps me locked where I am. I could move out of her grasp, overpower her if I needed to, but with the fear there's determination.

I stay deathly still, not wanting to give her any reason to panic, but dying to comfort her in some way. I do the only thing I can think of and speak.

"The first time I ever saw you, I was drawn to you. I loved your tan skin and your blonde hair. I loved the stain of blush on your cheeks when I spoke to you. I thought you were beautiful then, but then I saw you in the library. You were smiling, laughing with the kids, and you fucking ruined me, Sunshine. I loved your bright yellow skirts and your grandma sweaters. I loved your skinny round glasses that would break if the wind blows too hard. I loved your smile. God, I love your smile. Without all the makeup, without the tiny tank top, I stood there and fell for you. Natural, beautiful, you. Getting to see you like this, touch you like this, is a dream come true. You are my dream come true," I tell her earnestly, seeing the affirmation register in her eyes.

"You're my dream too, Jesse." She leans her head back, kissing the underside of my jaw, making me clench my eyes in relief. She's okay.

I want to scream from the fucking rooftops how much I love her, but for now, I'm hoping she sees the promise in my eyes. I've never said the words to anyone and I don't want to screw it up. She's perfect and when I tell her it has to be perfect.

We gaze at each other for a moment, not in the mirror, but with our heads turned inches apart. She stands on her tiptoes to kiss me, so I close the gap, kissing her first. At the same time, I feel her slide my finger further into her warm crease. My knees threaten to buckle.

"I'm okay, I'm ready," she whispers into my mouth as she continues to kiss me. She slides her tongue into my mouth and it's over, I couldn't stop my fingers from moving if I tried. I circle her small nub, rubbing it gently with the pads of my fingers, making her moan into my mouth. It's the sexiest sound and my hips thrust involuntarily into her backside.

The accidental movement halts me, not wanting to step over the line. My fingers are touching her most intimate area, but she's in control. I don't want to do anything she isn't ready for.

Within a moment, her hands are dragging my underwear down my hips, freeing my cock. It makes a home right against her ass as she grinds back against me and utters, "More." I let out the breath I was holding.

My hips thrust against her, my precum giving me more than enough lubrication to keep rubbing my cock between her cheeks as I work her clit. She flinches and whimpers, not in fear, but in full ecstasy, making me wild.

"So good, you feel so good, baby." I praise her incoherently, lost in my pleasure. Touching her pussy and grinding against her is enough to make me a ticking time bomb, so when she bites my bottom lip and begs me to put a finger inside of her, I know I'm not going to last. I've been imagining touching her like this for too long.

I guide my middle finger to her opening, pushing in slowly, making her cry out at the entry. It's hot and tight, and I'm dying to get my cock in her. Just thinking about it is making me feral.

I work my finger inside her instead, using the heel of my hand to rub against her clit, while I thrust against her ass. I'm not even inside her but I'm so close, my balls are tight against my body about to explode.

She spreads her feet minutely, mumbling "more," and the desperation in her voice nearly does me in. I push my ring finger in with the other, and her walls clamp around me immediately.

She cries out, her orgasm racking through her, and the pulses of pleasure making her body twitch against mine. It's more than enough for me to bury my cock in between her ass cheeks and cum, hard. My whole body tenses with my release.

I'm bent over her, holding her up from collapsing at the knees before I even realize what I'm doing. I blink to clear my post-orgasm haze, confirming that I am holding her up around the waist. Her body is a limp noodle in my arms.

"Thea?" I try to get her attention, hoping she's not struggling with how I'm holding her. She slowly lifts her head, letting the hair fall off her face, and gives me the happiest brightest smile I've ever seen.

I exhale roughly, relieved that she's fine, my heart still beating out of my chest. This woman is going to give me a heart condition. When I finally get my cock inside of her I might have a heart attack.

* * *

"Are you sure this doesn't bother you?" I ask Nathan as he leans against his kitchen counter. Thea and Callie are on the living room couch chatting.

"It's a little weird, but if you care about her then why would I have a problem? I trust you." He shrugs.

"That's it?" I ask surprised, expecting he'd give me a harder time about it.

"Yeah."

If that is the extent of his ability to express his feelings then I won't push him. I'm also not mad that I avoided being punched in the face or something more barbaric.

"I do really care about her," I clarify, making sure we are

283

on the same page. "I won't hurt her, I promise." He looks at me for a moment, scrutinizing what I just said. He can intimidate a lot of people with that look, but not me. I know him too well.

"Okay." He nods, leaving it at that. Internally, I roll my eyes. *Real deep, buddy.* All this time I was worried about what he would think and he barely blinked.

"I have to go, I need to coordinate with my team in Texas before it gets too late," I say to the room, though my words are directed to Thea.

"She'll be safe here, man," Nathan says sarcastically, slapping me on the shoulder a little harder than necessary. There's the brotherly shove I was waiting for.

It doesn't bother me though because it means that he loves her. He's as invested in keeping her safe as I am, but it doesn't mean he won't rag on me a little now that he knows I care about her too.

"Bye, Jess." Callie gives me a brief side hug, but my eyes stay on Thea as she approaches me. All I can focus on is the adoration that looks back at me. Maybe mixed with a little fear since I'm leaving to get back on the job.

"Be safe." She plants her palms on my chest before stretching up to kiss me. That simple gesture, getting a kiss goodbye, makes me want to pick her up and spin her around in circles. She's come so far and I'm so fucking proud of her.

"Always." I wink.

Nathan snorts from the kitchen and I throw him an evil eye. In the past I haven't always been the most level-headed, some might've referred to me as a risk-taker, but not now. Now that I have Thea, I actually have someone to come home to.

I gaze at her, soaking in her sweet smile for another couple of seconds before I leave, secretly dying for another kiss.

"Ugh. Gross. You're already in love aren't you?" Nathan protests from the kitchen, making Thea roll her eyes, but she blushes. She tries to hide it, but I register the pinkening of her skin as if it were my own. I love it too much.

"You have no room to talk," Callie corrects him, staring at him pointedly. "Leave them alone."

From what they've told me, he told her he loved her only a couple of days after they met. Thea and I are behind by at least a few weeks per their standards. I have no plan to let the time keep passing. When I get Thea back home tomorrow, I'll tell her how I feel.

"Bye, guys. See you in the morning." I direct that last sentence directly to Thea. I intend on being back here bright and early to retrieve her because by then Kyle should be behind bars and Curtis will be back on my radar.

Chapter Forty-One

Thea

"Thea... Thea... Wake up." I groan awake. My brain knows it's too early to be woken on the weekend. It takes me a moment to clear away the fog and realize that it's my brother trying to wake me.

"What? What do you want?" I grumble grumpily.

"I need you to check your phone," he demands, instantly rousing my brain. Even in a half-sleepy state, I know that's not a normal thing to ask someone. Sirens are wailing in my mind.

"Why?" I really look at him, sitting on the floor at the edge of the air mattress I've laid claim to in the spare room of his cabin. His face is serious, more so than normal, and I feel a chill skate over my skin. Something is wrong.

"I need to know if you've heard from Jesse. Anything, a missed call, a text." He nods towards my phone, urging me to hurry. I do, but there's nothing. Not a single notification from Jesse.

"What's going on, Nathan? You're scaring me," I barely manage to get those last words out above a whisper. He hangs his head in his hands, rubbing his forehead before looking at me.

"Jesse's MIA, missing in action. His command said he missed two check-ins and his phone was disconnected. They called me to make sure I haven't heard from him since I'm his emergency contact."

I feel the blood draining from my face...Jesse's missing?

"What do we do? We need to find him?" I jump off the bed, ungracefully since a quarter of the air has leaked.

"We can't Thea. You especially. We don't know how dangerous all of this is. I'm not clued in on the mission. Even then, I wouldn't let you go running around looking for him." He blocks me from leaving the room, making me shove against his chest.

"Move." I shove again, but he's like pushing a brick wall.

"No, calm down."

"Calm down? Really? I finally found the love of my life, now he's missing, and you want me to calm down?" I nearly scream at him, making him flinch. He might be big and tough, ex-special forces, but he's not ever been one to fight with me.

"I'm sorry. That's not what I meant. I need to talk to you with a clear head. I need all the information I can get about what he's been doing the last few weeks." He sees the understanding cross my features, and the defeat, so he ushers me into the kitchen.

Callie's already waiting with a cup of coffee. She doesn't say anything, she doesn't need to. She can tell how devastating this is for me.

"I don't know much. He never talked about it because he wanted to keep me out of it," I explain, holding my head in my hands on the counter.

"Think. Any details might help." Nathan sits next to me,

knocking his shoulder into mine.

"He was going to the Veterans Support Group, on Tuesday and Thursday at the library. There was a guy there, Curtis. He got into some trouble and tracked me down one night at the bar when I was working."

"What? Why are you working at a bar?" Nathan interrupts.

"Not important right now." I wave him off. "Somehow that led to this other guy, Kyle, who is the asshole that broke into my house. Jesse said he was involved with his undercover job but didn't realize it until that night. It was two nights ago, which is why I'm here. He and Sheriff Malec are working together I guess." I shrug, not remembering anything else important.

"Malec?" Nathan questions, glancing at Callie.

"Yeah, he's been around a few times. He and Jesse have some sort of working agreement, I don't know." My brain is mush at this point but at the same time reeling.

"Okay, I'll see what I can find out. Stay here, inside with Callie." He kisses the top of my head, and it's the last thing I remember before I start to cry. Violent, sobbing crying that makes my head hurt and my eyes burn. Callie comforts me through it all, somehow moving me to the couch and holding me until I finally cried myself to exhaustion and back to sleep.

* * *

A door slams, jerking me awake. "Jesse?" I ask before my brain catches up.

"No, sorry, Thea. Just me," Callie says from beside me on

the couch. I rub the sleep from my eyes, wincing at how sensitive and swollen the skin is from how hard I was crying.

"You haven't heard anything?" I ask her, even though I know she would have told me already if she had. The knots of worry in my stomach are making me nauseous.

"No. Nathan just stopped home for a minute to grab a few things. He just left again." She looks away as she speaks like she's keeping herself from saying everything.

"What? What aren't you telling me?"

"He took his rifle and another handgun. He didn't say where he was going, but that he was with Malec and he promised to be safe." She shrugs, not knowing what else to say, but concern is evident in her features.

"Do you think they're going to find him?" I can't help but wonder out loud. It's only been a few hours since I found out he's missing, but he's probably been missing for way longer already.

"I know they will because Jesse wouldn't stop if the roles were reversed. Nathan won't either." She grabs my arm, squeezing reassuringly. I'm glad she is here with me and I'm not dealing with this alone. Out of anyone, Callie knows how skilled Nathan and Jesse are. Her confidence that they'll come home safe gives me a little hope.

Unfortunately, I still can't help but think the worst. How dare the universe set me up like this?

I was finally given a chance, and I was happy. Jesse was my dream come true and now he's missing. I know what missing means… It means he could be dead. The man I want a future with might be dead and there is nothing that I can do about it.

We wait around all day, hoping to hear something, anything,

from anyone. After a few failed attempts to get me to eat, Callie finally relents, sitting with me while I stare at the TV. My mind only wanders…

No one knows where he is because everything he was doing was classified. There are no witnesses. No search parties are looking for him. I'm so mad at his team back in Texas for letting him go missing. They should haven't left him out here to fend for himself. They should have protected him and had his back, exactly like Nathan would have if they were still working together.

"He changed my life," I say aloud, startling her. "He is so gentle and understanding." I laugh, despite not feeling very humorous at the moment. "He's the one, Callie."

"I could tell you guys had a connection last time you were here. I'm glad it worked out. You've always seemed happy, but I can tell he's really made you happy."

"We met almost a month ago. He came into my library just by chance. He didn't even know who I was until a few weeks went by. When he realized I was Nathan's sister, it freaked him out, but it was too late. We were already falling for each other," I admit. Saying all of this out loud feels therapeutic so I keep going.

"I had something terrible happen to me in college. It ruined my life for a lot of years… I couldn't stand to be around men. I couldn't even be touched because of how much that incident broke me." I look into Callie's sorrowful eyes, seeing her understanding of what I'm telling her. She doesn't need me to say it, she knows exactly what type of trauma I'm referring to. Women always know.

"I tried once, about three or four years ago. There was a guy in my master's program who asked me out. I had been around him at our work-study placement, and in class, so I thought I'd give it a shot. I lied though, I told him I was celibate. He thought I was religious, but it worked, he didn't try anything physical at first. A few weeks went by, we had gone on several dates, and he tried to make a move. I blurted out bits of the truth to get him to stop." I laugh hollowly again, shaking my head, still in disbelief about what happened.

"He looked at me with disgust. He scoffed and complained that I wasn't even a virgin." I roll my eyes even thinking of that night. "I left obviously, avoided him the rest of the semester. He probably told people, but oh well. I don't see them anymore anyway."

"Thea, I am so sorry. That is horrible." Callie looks at me in shock after hearing all of this. "You should have never been treated that way."

"After that, I never attempted to date. I never even cared to try. Until, Jesse." I smile to myself. "He never pushed me, never expected anything of me, or made me feel like I owed him. We have been able to make progress with my physical issues though."

"I saw you kiss him yesterday. It looked natural." She smiles, fueling my need to talk about him. Girl talk is a good distraction from real life at the moment.

"Yeah. He's been amazing. We've even... Ya know." I giggle, feeling a little embarrassed. Callie squeals, begging me for details. So I give in, sparing her a few bits of information, but keeping some things for myself. I hold onto our most intimate moments with all my might, hoping they aren't the last.

"I'm in love with him," I tell her, watching as she nods her head in understanding. "But, now he's gone. He might be gone." I sob, the dam breaking before I can control it. "I might not ever get the chance to tell him."

Callie wraps me in her arms, offering all the comfort she can while the crying racks my body. I'm heaving for breath when she wipes the dampened hair off my forehead, getting my attention. "Come on, let's go get some fresh air. It might help," she says, her own eyes filled with tears as well.

"Nathan said to stay inside."

She shrugs at my comment. "What he doesn't know, won't hurt him." With a smile, she drags me outside.

We stand on the porch for a few minutes, watching the sun start to sink into the sky. It's a few hours until dark, but I can't help the fear ravaging my body because Jesse is out there somewhere alone or hurt. He can't be gone. I need him to come back to me.

"I need a minute." I squeeze Callie's hand before letting it go, grateful that I have her as a sister-in-law. Nathan really couldn't have found anyone better.

I walk across the lawn that circles the cabin, stopping when I make it to the tree line. The forest goes on for miles out here, the dense trees too thick in some places to even see through.

Just as I do on my runs some mornings, I stare into the woods and scream. I pour my emotions out, making my throat raw and my eyes water. I scream and scream, and scream until my legs give out, dropping me to my knees.

"Where are you, Jesse?" I rasp into the expanse of nothingness before me, hoping my voice is heard by whatever great power can help me.

Chapter Forty-Two

Jesse

Thea's here. Her wavy blonde hair is flowing down her shoulders, her bright yellow skirt is shifting in the breeze. It has flowers on it but I can't tell what kind.

My eyelids are drooping heavily, blurring my vision. I'm so tired.

When I blink through it, fighting off the exhaustion, she's strutting toward me in her tight jean shorts and cowboy boots. Her top is stretched tight across her perky tits and it makes me salivate knowing how they look underneath.

"I'm ready, Jesse," she says but it's faint. I have to strain to hear her even though she's right in front of me.

"Ready for what, baby?" I'm mesmerized by her tan thighs as she starts to straddle me. I hold my breath, anticipating her sweet hips meeting mine, but before she makes contact with my lap she disappears.

A sob tears free from my throat. She was right there. She was so close.

Sometime after hour twelve, I started to see her. The hallucinations are on a loop and my brain can't rectify it.

I know she isn't real but the loss feels real every time.

I'm too afraid to close my eyes and sleep, and not see what's coming for me. When I do close my eyes, I see Curtis. His body slumped over the steering wheel of his ratty car.

The plan was to meet him at midnight in the parking lot of a bowling alley, but when I arrived, I found him unconscious. I thought he was dead, and it took me off guard.

My distraction was used against me, and within a second, at least three guys jumped me from behind. They used an inhalant, chloroform probably. I was knocked out cold before I even saw their faces.

It left me with a split lip and a swollen eye. My old stitches have reopened and at least one rib is broken. The pain has helped keep me alert though, so I'll take any advantage I can get.

I'm probably past the twenty-four-hour mark now. It feels as if I've been stuck in this chair for days, but a long day turned to night only once. So, I know it hasn't been more than that.

The barn that I'm in looks like one of Jameson's. I don't know what they know, or why they took me, but I've been sitting here sweating in this stuffy building for too damn long.

Thea must realize something is wrong by now. She's probably worried to death. I never meant to be in this situation. This work was supposed to be less dangerous than the special ops shit. It's supposed to be information gathering, not life or death.

I can't leave her this way. I don't ever want her to be alone, my sweet Sunshine. This will devastate her, and I won't be there to fix it. She doesn't deserve this. She doesn't deserve anything bad that's happened to her and I'm going to traumatize her even more if I can't get out of here.

"She'll forgive you." A woman's voice sings from somewhere.

"What?" I sputter out, stretching my neck as far as I can to look around me, but I don't see anyone. My hands strain against the ropes behind my back. I've tried for hours already to free myself, but it's no use. It's too tight and there's a chain around my ankles.

"She knows you wouldn't leave her on purpose. Just like I didn't," the soft voice whispers.

My eyes squeeze painfully shut. My mind is trying to recall the voice, but at the same time, it knows. I shake my head trying to erase the delusion rattling me.

"I'm glad you found happiness, my sweet boy." The voice fades right past my ear and the implication makes me choke back another sob. My mom. I miss my mom.

I lost her and my life was empty from that day on. Until I met Thea.

I can't lose her, too. I finally have the life I always wanted.

My head hangs heavily in front of me. It's too late. I can't make it much longer. My body aches and my limbs have lost their circulation. I can't get out of this. I'm going to lose everything.

"Hold on, sweetie. Keep holding on." A mere whisper in the wind is all I hear.

A door squeaks open from the opposite side of the barn, snapping my head to attention. The motherfucker walks toward me with the cockiest grin on his face. I want to kill him. I've never needed to kill anyone like I need to kill him.

"Well, well, well. Look who we have here." Kyle stops

walking, folding his arms over his chest. "How nice to see you, Jay."

Okay, he doesn't know my real name. That's a good sign. If he knew I was undercover, I'd probably be dead already.

"Where's Curtis? Is he dead?"

"Curtis? You need to worry about yourself." He smirks, making me grit my teeth. I can't wait to get my hands on him.

"What do you want?"

"I want you dead," he shouts. I don't even flinch. "But, Uncle Tommy says I need to make you sweat so I can get information," he scoffs, referring to Jameson.

"Information about what? I don't know anything." I hang my head, acting defeated for his sake.

"We know you've been hanging out around Curtis. We know he's a snitch. We already had to show the old guy a lesson when he wouldn't talk, so be careful," he warns.

"You beat Dennis?"

"No, Derrick and Mitch took care of that. I went after Curtis, but I lost him. He was my ticket. I tried to make money. Uncle Tommy said I needed to show commitment and pay my dues before I could be one of his main guys, but your slut of a girlfriend fired me," he yells. My blood boils at his insult against Thea, but I try desperately to keep my cool. Reacting will only give him fuel.

"Then he said if I brought Curtis to him, he'd make me VP, but he lied. He still wants to know who else Curtis snitched to before he makes me official." He pulls a switchblade out of his pocket, flipping the blade out. "So, you're going to tell me."

He points the knife at me but stays at a measurable distance. He's still afraid to get within arms reach of me even though I am tied up. I shrug, "I don't know what you mean."

Kyle steps towards me, slapping me across the face, then quickly stepping back. *Pussy.*

"You do know! Tell me!" He yells so hard that spit flies out of his mouth. It still doesn't faze me.

"I don't know anything." My calm demeanor is pissing him off more and my statement is true. I don't know if Curtis snitched to anyone. He might've confided in Dennis, but I wasn't a part of that. I think the leak is all in Jameson's head. He's paranoid and mentally unstable.

"That's alright." Kyle shrugs. "I guess I'll just go visit Miss Wolfe. See if I can get some information from her. I always thought she was hot. Maybe, I'll fuck the information out of her. I've always wanted to shoot a load right onto her little glasses."

My blood ignites. Before I can control my reaction, I'm pushing my body through the air and colliding with Kyle while I'm still chained to the chair. "Mother Fucker!" I yell, not caring that I just fucked myself. If my hands were free, I'd beat him until he bled to death.

Kyle manages to push me off of him so he can stand, leaving me lying on the dirt floor. He shoots me another cocky smile before he starts kicking me, repeatedly. He kicks me in the stomach, in the ribs, my shins, and lastly, my head. The world around me spins, making me lose all sense of up and down and what's happening in front of me.

"If you don't know anything, I'll just kill you," he spits, coming at me with his blade. My mind is still in and out of focus. I have to keep blinking to see his form in front of me, but I feel the steel on my neck. Swallowing tightly, I realize he's done talking.

Except, one second the blade is there, then the next it isn't. Kyle starts pacing the room, mumbling to himself. He's talking himself up to kill me. He can't do it.

"Never kill anyone before, Kyle?" I ask, not able to keep my dumb mouth shut.

"SHUT UP!" He yells, pacing some more. He walks toward me, blade out, but quickly turns back to pacing.

I close my eyes, preparing for death. He'll gain the courage, it's just a matter of when. All I hope is that Thea can grieve for me and move on with her life. I hope she doesn't let this break her when she's come so far in her healing. I never should have gotten twisted up in her life. It's all my fault.

Wanting to see her face in my last moments, I focus on her. Even in death, I never want to forget her beauty, her smile. I never want to forget the love I have for her or the love I hope she has for me. I imagine her looking down at me now, running her fingers through my hair. Lying in bed, covered in the early morning light. The only sound around us is a mourning dove outside her window.

A mourning dove…

A mourning dove?

In my confusion, my daydream quickly fades into reality. Kyle is grabbing at his hair, struggling with his morality while I lay aching in the dirt. All the shit I've done in my career and this is how I go? Unreal.

Seconds pass agonizingly slow while watching my fate unfold until I hear the mourning dove again. What the hell? Am I losing my mind?

I can't see anything aside from the inside of the barn, the gaps in the boards in the ceiling are my only clue that it's still nighttime. Birds like that don't call at night.

Sometimes during our special forces operations, we'd signal each other using bird calls, but I'd know about it beforehand. This could just be a coincidence. I'm out of it, it's probably a barn owl.

I'm too far gone to think that I'll get out of this myself, but if there is a chance for help, I'll hold onto hope. I don't know if I am doing the right thing but I do know I'm desperate. So after the dove calls again, I start whistling. It's a slow, sad tune, signaling to whoever is out there that I know they're here, but I'm not doing well.

It's probably another hallucination. I don't know how else to explain the chance that someone found me. No one knows I'm here and my phone is long gone. Nathan is with Thea, and Malec wouldn't even be aware that I'm missing until it's too late.

"Shut the fuck up!" Kyle yells at me then takes a deep breath, shaking his head. "Any last words?"

There's a coolness over him now that tells me he's come to terms with the murder he is about to commit. This is it.

"Fuck you." I spit blood in his direction, solidifying my statement. This time he comes at me with determination, the blade glistening in the light of the swinging bulb above us.

I love you, Thea.

Squeezing my eyes shut, I tense for the strike. Instead, my whole body flinches as firepower comes flying over my head. *Pow, pow, pow, pow, pow, pow!*

Silence descends.

All I can hear is the sound of my ragged breathing.

When I open my eyes, Kyle's prone body lies bleeding on the floor in front of me. His cold lifeless eyes stare back at me.

Chapter Forty-Three

Thea

As the sun rises, my head rests on my knees, watching the rays stretch across the bedroom ceiling. Callie insisted I sleep in bed with her. She's snoozing restlessly beside me. Blinking awake ever so often to check on me. It's like her body is aware of my turmoil.

Despite an emotionally draining last twenty-four hours, I've hardly slept a wink. All I've been able to do is think about Jesse and all the horrible things he might be going through. Wondering if he's scared or in pain. My mind continuously thought of worse and worse scenarios as the night went on. I'm grateful that morning is here but devastated that I still haven't heard anything.

I know that the more time that passes, the worse the outcome. The likelihood that he might not come back to me becomes greater and greater with every passing hour. The knot of dread in my stomach grows with every passing minute.

When a chime sounds from somewhere in the living room, I shake Callie awake. "I think someone's here, I heard your alarm."

She shoots up to a sitting position, rubbing her eyes. "Did it sound like a doorbell or a beep beep?" She asks, making me look at her in confusion.

"Uhh. A doorbell I think." I shrug.

"That means someone came up the driveway, let's go." She jumps out of bed, grabbing the gun that was sitting on the nightstand. I look at her incredulously when she sees me staring. "You never know. Don't worry, Nathan taught me how to use it."

I can't argue with that logic, so I follow her as she jogs to the front door, peeking out the peephole. "It's Nathan's truck." She sets the gun down on the table by the door, looking back through the peephole. "Wait. Jesse's with him!"

At the sound of his name, my body goes into autopilot, moving past her and throwing the door open. "Jesse," I cry out, as he steps out of the truck.

"Thea, don't…" Nathan's words die in the air before they have a chance to get to me, I'm already flying towards Jesse at full speed. I collide with him, throwing my arms around his neck, and breathing in his scent.

"Ooof… Ouch," he moans. My body goes still. Oh no. "Hi, baby," he grunts out.

"What happened?" I pull back enough to take in some of his injuries. He's bloody and bruised everywhere. My hands flutter over his upper half, not touching anything but wanting to touch everywhere.

"Come on, inside." Nathan grabs me around the arm, hauling me back toward the cabin. I let him guide me, not able to unglue my eyes from Jesse's hurt body.

"We'll give you guys a minute," Callie says, pulling Nathan back to their room once we're all inside.

Jesse moves to the couch, wincing as he sits down. He takes a few short breaths, cringing as he does. "What happened?" I ask again.

"I got ambushed. It's a long story. Come here, please." He raises his arm, pain registering on his face, but I slide in next to him anyway. I can't *not* touch him.

"I was so scared," I whisper against his chest.

"I know, baby. Me too." He groans again when he takes a deep breath, needing a couple of seconds to regroup.

"Are you going to be okay? You seem really hurt."

"I'll be fine. It'll heal up in a few days." He tries to smile, but it falls short. We sit in silence for several minutes.

Never again do I want to see him like this. I can't stand the thought of him enduring any more pain in his life. Why is it that the toughest battles go to the ones the least deserving of them? Jesse didn't deserve this and he surely didn't deserve the childhood he had. I'm so mad at the universe for doing this to him.

"All I could think about was you, Thea. I spent every minute worrying about what would happen to you if I died. I never want to do that to you," he confesses. "I'm sorry for even putting us in this situation. It was selfish of me to bring you into this life. I shouldn't have."

I don't know if it's from the stress or the lack of sleep, but my brain is registering that negatively. "What do you mean?"

"I couldn't focus on my job. I didn't care about anything but getting home to you. Maybe it's what almost got me killed. I don't know."

I almost got him killed.

He stares blankly towards the wall, sending my heart plummeting. He's breaking up with me. He doesn't want this anymore. My stomach fills with lead as if I swallowed it. I can hardly breathe.

I stand up suddenly, needing space after I just begged to be by his side again the last twenty-four hours. On wobbly legs, I back away from the couch, needing to bolt. He looks at me blankly, blinking slowly, but doesn't speak.

"I'm ready to go home. If you're telling me that you need time to think about things, about us, then you can do it here. I won't smother you." I turn toward the spare room where my stuff is, but pause before I go down the hall. "I'm glad you're okay," I admit on trembling lips.

There's a weight on my chest, slowly suffocating me while I gather my things. After everything that happened, I'm going to lose him regardless.

The walls that were around my heart for so long had crumbled, finally feeling safe enough to love, now it seems to be all for nothing. My eyes burn with unshed tears. I refuse to cry until I get home. He doesn't get to see me fall apart anymore.

I rap on Nathan's door. "I'm ready to go home. I'll be in the truck." Then I turn and walk back down the hallway, past the living room where Jesse is standing by the couch staring at me, and out the front door. *Don't look back. Don't.* If he's done with me then I won't let him see how broken that leaves me.

I throw my bag into the bed of the truck, not a care in my mind if it blows out on the way home. Yanking the backdoor of the truck open, I climb inside intending to slam it shut behind me to let off some steam. Only it stops short, jerking my arm from the handle as it opens back the opposite way.

"Scoot over," Jesse grumbles at me.

Thrown off guard, I move over to the other seat without a fight but I don't turn my body in his direction. I can't. I'm afraid I'll cry when I look at his face and see what I'm about to lose.

"Thea. Look at me," he demands sternly, forcing my eyes to his. He looks tired and pissed. "I don't know what the hell just happened. I don't know what I said to make you run from me, but dammit, everything hurts and I don't want to chase you." He lets out a breath, wincing slightly.

"I will chase you if that's what it takes, but please don't make me." He leans his head back against the headrest, catching his breath. We both glance over toward the cabin when Nathan and Callie make their way towards the truck.

Jesse rests his hand on the center seat between us, palm up, as an invitation. "I'm with you, no matter what. We'll talk when we get home." *Home.*

I squeeze my eyes shut, hardly containing the sob threatening to break loose. He still wants me. He wants to go home, to my home, with me.

I'm so tired and my emotions are fried. I just want to go home with him too, so I take his hand, interlocking our fingers. Soaking up the little squeeze of reassurance that he gives me.

"Ready?" Nathan asks from the front seat.

"Yeah, take us home." I lean my head back against the seat, rolling it to the side to look at Jesse.

Home.

* * *

304

After reanalyzing our conversation during the ride home, I accepted that I might have misconstrued what Jesse was saying earlier. We're both exhausted and he's in pain. I insist he goes straight to bed after Nathan and Callie leave. He needs rest. I need rest.

I get him settled, making sure he has water and Tylenol, before climbing into bed next to him. I'm afraid to touch him, only because I know he's hurt. I don't want to add to it, so I keep to my side. "I'm sorry if I freaked out earlier," I admit softly.

"I'm sorry if I said something to make you freak out. I honestly don't even remember what words came out of my mouth, everything's a little foggy." He reaches out, offering his hand again like he did in the truck. I take it immediately, needing to be connected in some way.

"It sounded like you were breaking up with me. You said that all you could think about was me, but it couldn't work that way. You said it almost got you killed," I whisper the last part, hating to even say the words.

"Shit, Thea." He squeezes my hand. "I didn't mean it that way. I'm not second-guessing you. I'm second-guessing the job. I don't ever want to put you in this position again. It's not fair to you. I told you once that your heart was safe with me and I meant it. I'm not going to break it, not even by dying."

I laugh, but it's mixed with a sob. How could I have doubted him?

"My brain is so fucked up. I can't fathom that someone could truly care for me," I admit.

"We're all a little fucked up, baby," he responds quietly. "I'm so attached to you, you'd run away if you could read my

305

thoughts."

"I'm never running again," I promise, kissing his hand.

"Just my hand?" He pouts, making me giggle. So, I kiss his shoulder, then his jaw, and ever so lightly kiss his lips, careful to avoid the busted part.

"I love you, Thea." He utters the words and my breath catches. Before I can truly react, his head lulls to the side and he's out like a light.

I squeeze my eyes shut, relishing those words. He loves me. The man who has become my entire world and gave me my life back loves me.

I try with all my might to contain the hysteric squeal that is threatening to let loose. I thought I had lost him, but now he's here, safe, and at home. With me. He loves me.

"I love you too, Jesse," I whisper against his shoulder, watching him sleep until my own eyes are too heavy.

Chapter Forty-Four

Jesse

The knife is coming at me. Move. Move, dammit. Kyle is walking straight towards me, his switchblade aimed right at my throat. I fight and jerk my limbs, but nothing happens. My body is full of sand. I can't budge an inch. Fuck, why is this happening?

I look back toward Kyle, but instead, my father is walking towards me, knife raised. It's him, my dad, but it looks like me. "Time's up, little man."

I startle awake, sucking in lungfuls of air, trying to catch my breath. The immediate pain spreads through me like wildfire. Ugh, my ribs. I groan and wince until the pain subsides, leaving a dull ache as long as I don't breathe.

I pull myself up to a sitting position and regret it immediately. My whole body hurts, my brain feels like it's bleeding.

"What do you need?" Thea stumbles out of bed, disoriented with sleep lines across her cheeks. Despite my pain, it makes me smile.

"Water, Tylenol," I grit out uselessly because the items are sitting right next to me. "I'll get it."

"No, no, no. I got it," she insists. "Let me take care of you."

Those words have never been said to me by anyone other than her, and I appreciate it so much more because of that. Deciding instantly to lean into it and let her take care of me because I'm needy as hell right now, I don't object as she feeds me the pills. As soon as they're in my mouth she's ready with the water.

I admire her sweet face of concentration as I swallow them back, hoping they'll work fast. "Come on, get back in bed. I didn't mean to wake you."

"It's okay, it's the middle of the day, I should probably stay awake," she explains but climbs back on the bed anyway. "You can sleep though, you need it."

Sighing, "I don't think I could fall asleep now. My dream fucked me up. My blood's pumping a little too hard."

"We can talk about it," she offers, grabbing my hand again.

There's so much that I want to tell her, but I can't. So, I take a minute to gather my thoughts, wanting to explain the things I can.

"Curtis is still missing. I thought maybe he was dead, that's how they ambushed me, but Malec said he never found a body. So, I don't know what happened to him.

"Nathan said it's all thanks to you that they found me. If you wouldn't have told him about me working with Malec, he wouldn't have known where to start to look for me. So, thank you." I squeeze her hand, pulling it toward me, wanting her closer.

"I felt bad that I couldn't help more. I tried going out myself to look for you, but Nathan wouldn't let me." She pouts, making me smile.

"Good. That's why he's my best friend. No matter what, I'd rather you be safe." She grumbles and rolls her eyes, I laugh softly.

"Kyle almost killed me," I utter the words that I've been avoiding, but needing to rip the band-aid.

"What?" She gasps, covering her mouth. "Because of me?" She asks, her face paling.

"No. No. It was because of the group I was looking into. It was just a bad coincidence. Supposedly that's why he needed money from you so badly." I shrug, deciding not to mention all of the spewed threats he directed towards her. It's better if she never knows that part.

"What happened to him?"

"He's dead. Malec killed him, or Nathan did. I don't know, they both claim it was their shot that did it. I'm just pissed they didn't let me do it." Malec insisted on claiming the kill shot for paperwork's sake. He said it was going to be a nightmare regardless, so Nathan let him have it after a brief chest puffing match.

"He's dead?" She was scared of the kid, he stole her money and vandalized her home, but she still has the biggest heart. Someone's death will never be simple to her, and that's okay. I like that part of her.

"Yeah. He won't ever try to hurt you, or me, ever again." That helps clear her conscience, I see it in the way she relaxes slightly.

"Now, what?" She asks, making me think about what parts I can tell her.

"The operation has been shut down. I'm done working on it. The commanders in my unit don't want to be involved anymore, since it got too messy," I explain, rolling my eyes internally. I begged them to take the threat seriously for weeks, and all they wanted me to do was collect intel. It got

309

serious then they wanted to bolt.

Jameson is in the wind, and so are Derrick and Mitch. Malec plans on making sure the farm stays shut down, but there is no sure way of knowing what will happen next. Jameson could regroup, try to carry out his mission, or he could flee across the country.

I wish I could have stopped him, and made sure he was locked up, and I wish I knew where Curtis was. Those are problems I have to keep to myself though, the details of the operation are still classified.

"I can't believe it's over." She shakes her head in disbelief. I can only imagine all of the gaps she has in her head that will never be filled, questions left unanswered. Kyle is dead, but that was only a small factor in a much larger scheme.

"At least your panties will be safe," I tease. Laughing when I see how her jaw drops at my lame attempt at a joke. The karma is instant though, the shooting pain in my ribs leaves me breathless for more than a few seconds.

Once the pain dies down, there is a different signal pinging in my brain. Something incredibly important that I am having trouble recalling as a memory or my imagination.

"Thea... Did I..?" I cringe, remembering a sense of urgency to admit my feelings just as I was falling asleep. "Did I tell you that I love you?"

She bites her lip, trying to hide her amusement. "You might've let it slip."

Instead of being embarrassed or upset that it didn't happen how I wanted it to, I'm relieved. No more time is wasted without her knowing.

"Good, because I do. I love you with every part of me." I look into her eyes, hoping she sees my sincerity. She scoots closer, placing her palms on my cheeks, and touching our foreheads together. "I'm sorry I didn't say it sooner. I was waiting for the perfect time and then I almost died. I couldn't stand the thought of you not knowing."

"I love you, too." She kisses me lightly and smiles softly. "So much."

"Say it, again," I beg.

"I love you, Jesse." She giggles and my whole world lights up.

"I knew you were special right when I met you. I fell in love with you when I finally opened my eyes at the library. I watched you read to the kids and you looked like an angel sent from Heaven. Every day since then I've wanted to witness every smile, every laugh. I wanted you so desperately, more than I've ever let myself want anything. It was terrifying," I admit.

"I felt the same way about you. I didn't think anyone would ever care for me, let alone love me the way you do. You became my safe haven. And after everything that you told me about your childhood…" she pauses, seeming unsure. "I want you to know that you are my family now, too. You'll always have me, Nathan, and Callie. I want to be your home, as much as you are mine."

Hearing her voice her commitment to me, to us. She is my home, my world, and the center of my universe. The literal sun that shines down on me and lets me get through another day.

I nod my head, only to acknowledge her, the lump in my throat too thick to respond verbally. I can't begin to explain how deeply her words mean to me. The young boy in me is drowning in the joy and love that he never got to receive.

She nudges my shoulder, urging me back down to the pillows where she lies next to me as closely as she can without touching me. When I notice her furrowed brow as she adjusts again, I realize her concern is about me, not herself.

"You can touch me. I won't break."

She looks at me worriedly before shifting her body closer and resting her head on my shoulder, gently placing her hand on my chest. I hurt. My whole body aches, but the thought of her not being able to touch me is a far greater pain. Whenever she wants to touch me, I'm hers. Forever.

We lay quietly for a while, neither of us saying much, but rather absorbing everything that happened and everything said. Until another thought pops into my head that dampens my mood entirely.

"I have to take a red eye tonight to Texas." I'll have to leave in a few short hours. "It was an order, not a request after my commander found out what happened."

"Oh."

"I have to debrief about everything. Probably drown in paperwork, but then it will officially be over. I'll make sure my transfer is a done deal and then pack up my apartment," I tell her, hoping it eases some of the sting of my leaving.

"Pack up to move here, right?"

"Yeah, I should be stationed close by."

"I mean, should I make room for your clothes?" She asks, shyly.

"Is that what you want?" I watch the pink stain her cheeks.

"Yes."

"Thank God. I don't want to be anywhere but here."

She laughs at my relief and I wince when I try to laugh along with her. Broken ribs are no joke.

* * *

The first week gone was spent debriefing with my unit. We didn't find any more information about where Jameson could be hiding or what he was planning.

Curtis is still a missing person. I checked the Rollins County and surrounding areas coroner's reports every day, hoping I didn't come across a body matching his description.

I advocated for him, still hoping he would turn up. My commanders agreed to dismiss his pending charges and only punish him for going AWOL. He was a lost kid, but as soon as he realized Jameson was up to bad shit, he wanted no part of it. I insisted they know that.

The second week, I wrapped up all of the paperwork I needed to and made sure my transfer was officially approved.

The rest of my days in Texas were filled with packing and selling stuff I no longer needed. It was like purging my old life away in the most freeing sense and getting to start fresh.

It was the longest three weeks of my life, but at least I knew at the end of it I was finally coming home. It doesn't matter what city I'm in, it doesn't matter what house I live in, it matters that I'm with her.

"Hey, Sunshine, what are you doing?" I tuck my phone between my ear and shoulder as I grab my carry-on.

"I'm picking out what I want to wear tomorrow," she responds, distractedly.

"For what?" I rack my brain, trying to think if she's told me of any plans.

"I have a 5k tomorrow. I kind of forgot about it until Latisha mentioned it at work today," she explains.

"Something for charity or something?"

"It's for veterans, kind of like a wounded warrior vibe. I try to do one every year. I even made Nathan run with me once." She snorts, both of us know how much he probably hated that.

"Huh… I'm surprised I didn't hear about it while I was there." I go through my mental log of all the things I heard in the news while I was in New Hope, but nothing stands out. A run for veterans… It sets off alarm bells in my head, but I don't let Thea in on it.

The Army's case against Jameson's group is still pending, but I'm done investigating him now that my chapter is closed in Texas. Yet, I can't help but see an opportunity here. Would he come out of hiding? Expose himself for his cause?

"It's actually in Lawson. They probably advertise it over there more. It's great for local business though, the library usually sponsors a few teens who want to run. I'm going to give my ribbon to Dennis when I'm done." She goes on, talking about some of the past 5ks, but my mind is still distracted, my thoughts unsettled by her mention of Dennis.

From what she'd told me, he woke from his coma but was still recovering in the hospital. Malec relayed that there haven't been any sightings of Derrick, Mitch, or Jameson there either.

"Hey, I'm sorry, I have to call someone from work. I'll call you in a little bit."

"Sure, talk to you later. I love you." I'll never get tired of hearing that.

"I love you, too." I end the call, immediately dialing the next.

"Hey, what do you know about this 5k in Lawson tomorrow?" I ask Malec as soon as he answers.

Chapter Forty-Five

Thea

I pull my hair out of the top knot on my head now that I'm freshly showered and shaved. One less thing I need to worry about in the morning before the race. I didn't train for this one, I don't usually have to for 5ks since I run so much anyway, but my ritual remains the same.

Somehow I know that I'll run faster if my legs are shaved, or if I'm wearing neon socks, but especially when I do double French braids in my hair. That's something that I swear by, and I'll do it first thing in the morning before I leave home.

I walk through the doorway into my room and shriek like a little girl, almost dropping my towel. "Oh my God!"

Jesse's sitting on my bed with a sly grin, his hair is slightly shorter and his facial hair is all cleaned up and trimmed. He's as handsome as ever.

"Surprise." He laughs, making me smile. It spurs me into action and I run at him, launching onto his lap. My momentum knocks him back, taking me with him.

I end up straddling him with the towel pooled around my waist, his hands firmly planted on my ass from trying to catch me when I jumped.

316

"I missed you," I whisper, kissing his lips. His fingers flex against my backside when I deepen the kiss, not letting him up for air. The hardness in his jeans is pressed right where I want it.

I've been dreaming about this since he left three weeks ago. With so much time alone to think, I concluded that I'm done holding back. I don't want to wait any longer to be with Jesse. Even if it takes us all night, I plan on being thoroughly fucked by the love of my life.

"This is a warm welcome," he says breathlessly when I finally give his mouth reprieve and we sit back up. His eyes are hooded and he does not look at all bothered that I practically tackled him.

He glances down at my naked breasts, their proximity even closer since I'm on his lap. My nipples are hard and eager to be touched.

My hands thread into his hair, keeping his face level with my chest. "Kiss me," I request desperately. He tries to pull back to look in my face, but I keep his head where it is, pushing even closer to his face. "Kiss me, here." My voice is breathy and full of need.

He lets out a breath of relief, and the air skates across my skin making me inhale sharply. His mouth descends on me and my heart beats faster. When the warmth meets my pebbled flesh, I whimper in satisfaction. It's everything that I ever could have expected.

His tongue flicks out across my nipple and my whole body lights up. I never believed it when I read about women in my books having orgasms from nipple stimulation, but now I very much believe it to be possible.

I pull his head closer, my bare pussy grinding in his lap.

"More, please," I beg. He takes my invitation and runs with it, ravaging my breasts. Kissing, biting, sucking.

I know there will be hickeys tomorrow, and I hope there are. I want to be thoroughly owned and marked by him. Each time he suctions his mouth to me, I feel it as if it's being directly applied to my clit. That needy part of my body is throbbing in anticipation for him.

His hands have stayed steady on my ass, not straying an inch. I know it's solely for my benefit. He's still determined not to cross any boundaries, and I love him for it.

"Touch me, Jesse." His head whips up to look at me when he processes my words.

"What? Where?" He asks desperately, always willing to give me anything I want.

"Anywhere. Everywhere. No more limits. I want all of it. Touch all the places you've wanted to, please." He searches my eyes, looking for any sign that I'm in distress or not serious about my request, but I'm deadly serious.

"You being taken and hurt scared the hell out of me. I knew after that moment that I wasn't willing to deprive you of any part of me. I didn't want to. I'm yours, wholeheartedly, to do what you please. I've come to peace with that these last three weeks apart. I've actually been really fucking excited," I admit to him, adamantly.

"You're sure?"

I nod my head rapidly.

"You can still say no, or tell me to stop at any time, baby. Promise?"

"I promise," I reply eagerly. I love this man, I love him so much.

Instead of exploring below my waist further, or my breasts,

he surprises me by using his hands freely for the very first time to kiss me. It's not a sweet or gentle kiss, it's fingers threaded in my hair, hands pulling me in. A hard and brutal kiss.

He takes over my senses, claiming my mouth so passionately that I lose track of time and space. It's the most consuming kiss I've ever had with clashing tongues and teeth. I've never felt more loved and cherished.

Finally, his hands start their trail down my body, making my core throb harder before he's even near it. His fingertips traced down my spine and up my sides before cupping my breasts firmly making me moan. He pinches both of my nipples at the same time and I can't help but throw my head back in surprise at the sensation it elicits. I've never experienced that before.

"You're so beautiful, Thea. I'm so glad you're mine." He applies more open-mouthed kisses to my chest, lapping at my nipples thoroughly with his tongue before sucking them into his mouth like he can't get enough. It's a shame that I didn't let him do this weeks ago, I've been missing out.

His hands have moved back down towards my hips, rocking me against his erection. The friction is torturous, making me needy for his cock. Before I can beg for what I want, I feel his fingers skim up the backs of my thighs and brush against my sensitive sex, making me twitch. I'm wet, I have been for a while, and now he feels it.

He spreads the lubrication up and down my slit, teasing my clit and my entrance over and over. The back and forth is incredible, but torturous. I want him to give me something, rub my clit, finger fuck me, anything.

"Please." I try to grind my hips in a way that'll force his

hand. He doesn't relent, continuing to tease me.

"You can beg better than that sweet girl," he murmurs, biting my neck.

"Please, Jesse. I want your fingers inside me," I plead, but it opens up the floodgates. "I want to rub my clit against your cock, but I want it inside me too. I want you to fuck me. I want your cock in me."

His two fingers slide into my tight hole at my last request, going in easily since I'm so wet. He pumps in and out, crooking them slightly to rub against my inner wall. My eyelids flutter at the sensation.

"What else do you want?" He asks, breathlessly.

"I want you to fuck my mouth and eat me out. I want your tongue everywhere," I admit, riding his fingers. "I want you to fuck all of my holes… Choke me while you take my ass."

He makes a coughing noise, but I'm too far gone to really hear it. "Fuck, Thea." The fingers inside me leave suddenly, making me whine in protest, but I'm quickly distracted when he picks me up and lays me on the bed. The towel that was draped around my waist falls to the floor.

He eyes me hungrily, sticking his fingers in his mouth to suck my juices off, making my eyes go wide. "Spread your legs," he demands. I do it immediately.

"Who's pussy is this, Thea?"

"Yours."

"Who do you belong to?"

"You," I answer without hesitation, loving being owned by him. He rewards my responses by firmly licking me from my entrance to my clit and my whole body gasps.

"Who do I belong to?" He asks before nibbling on my inner thigh making me squirm.

"M-me," I stutter out, too distracted by where his face is. I want him to devour me so badly, but he's teasing me. Only offering small, scattering bites and licks until he finally grabs my thighs securely, keeping me from moving.

"Grab my hair, baby, pull me back if it's too much," he demands but doesn't wait for me to agree. I thread my fingers into his newly trimmed locks and hold on for my life as he dives in.

It's ecstasy, it's everything. I can't even think straight as his tongue tastes me everywhere, licking and flicking every sensitive part of me. The noises coming out of me are incoherent until I'm almost making no noise at all. I can hardly even breathe.

He doesn't just eat me out, he ruins me for the rest of my life. All I'll be able to think about forever is how amazing this is.

His fingers push inside me, making me see stars. "Fuck, oh my God!" I'm so close to an orgasm I can taste it, but I don't want this to end. The build-up of electricity from teasing me and everything he's giving me now is too good, making me toss and turn my head on the sheets.

He reaches up, grabbing my tit and squeezing roughly, making me cry out. I cover his hand with mine, needing to hold onto something. Despite my tailspin, my heart skips a beat when he interlocks our fingers.

I'm on the cusp now, grasping his fingers painfully in mine as he terrorizes my clit. It's too much. It's incredible.

The wave of my climax crashes down on me, making my whole body clench forcefully. My pussy clamps down on his fingers, elongating the soul-altering orgasm he's giving me. I can't breathe or see straight, but I'm in utter bliss.

Only once my breathing calms down does he pull his fingers out of me, cleaning them with his mouth once again. It's dirty and wildly erotic, and I love it.

"That was the sexiest thing I've ever seen," he utters, applying kisses to my knees and the soft flesh of my inner thighs.

"I think I'm dead," I confess, making him laugh.

Chapter Forty-Six

Jesse

Everyday. I'm going to give her orgasms every day for the rest of her life. She comes alive when she's about to climax and it's better than anything I've ever witnessed.

I strip my clothes, watching as she eyes me greedily. "If you're too tired I can stop. We can lay in bed and go to sleep," I offer her. The way she's looking at me tells me she is nowhere near done. My needy girl.

"Please," she begs so sweetly, spreading her legs wider. If I was planning on holding back, that little move would have done me in for sure. Luckily for both of us, I have all the plans in the world to fuck her, here and now.

I crawl onto the bed, kneeling right between her thighs. My cock juts out over her pussy, eager to be inside of her. I'm painfully hard, but if she showed an ounce of hesitation, I'd stop. "Is this okay?" I ask, leaning down to kiss her. She kisses me back hungrily.

"I'm ready," she says against my mouth. I line up in front of her tight opening, needing to take a deep breath because the anticipation is killing me and I don't want to cum in two seconds.

My face level with hers, I watch her eyes as I finally push inside. The warmth, the tightness, it makes me want to melt. Seeing her eyes widen at the fullness is invigorating.

She gasps as I settle fully inside of her, squeezing her eyes shut. It's a snug fit, and I give her a second to adjust. I also need a second to pretend like it's not the most incredible feeling ever, or I'm bound to make a fool of myself.

"Are you okay?" I ask, needing to make sure before I go further. No matter what, her comfort comes first. So, I panic when I see tears building in the corners of her eyes. "Baby?"

She doesn't respond. Her eyes are still glued shut and it feels like a brick wall between us. A brick wall that I am not letting her hide quietly behind.

"Thea. Open your eyes. Let me see those gorgeous blue eyes." I try my best to keep my voice gentle, without the urgency that I feel. This is too much, we went too fast. "Sunshine, look at me. It's okay, I'm going to stop."

"No! No." Her eyes ping open, finally, blinking away the moisture that has gathered. "I don't want you to stop," she pleads, but I can tell that she's struggling.

My mind is traveling at lightning speed trying to figure out how to fix this, how to keep her from spiraling. She wants this too badly and she's being stubborn. Brave but stubborn.

"I'm not going anywhere, we don't have to rush this. We can go slower," I assure her, resting my forehead on hers.

"I don't want slower. I want you," she whispers sadly, breaking my heart.

I stare into her eyes, trying to read her mind. Trying to give her what she needs, but doesn't know what to ask for.

The only thing I can come up with has me hooking my

arms behind her back, hauling her body off the mattress and back onto my lap like we were at the beginning. She was fine then, in control.

My cock is still buried in her and as her weight settles in my lap, her core clenches around me, making my blood pulse. Her tits are in front of me again and they steal my focus momentarily. I want to bury my face in them, but I restrain myself for the time being.

"Eyes, Sunshine," I demand again, waiting for them to focus on my face. She blinks rapidly, her chest rising and falling with her attempt to control her anxiety. I see it the moment she regains her thoughts. She lets her head fall against mine, wrapping her arms around my neck.

"I'm okay. Thank you," she whispers sweetly, kissing me. Within seconds it goes from gentle to hungry. Her lips are demanding against mine, telling me exactly what she wants. My strong, badass woman, kicking her demons out the door.

My hips flex subtly to their own accord as she caresses my tongue with hers, my body is reacting when I'm trying to keep my mind in control. I want this, I want her, but I need it to be on her terms.

"Jesse. Fuck me, please. I'm ready, please," she begs and it's like the sweetest song.

"You're okay?"

"I'm more than okay," she responds, raising her hips and dropping them, impaling herself on me slowly, over and over.

Thank, fuck. There is no chance I can stop now that she is moving. It's too addicting, my conscious mind is a goner.

"I love you, Sunshine." I brush the hair from her face, kissing her lightly. I'm eternally grateful to be the one she chose to do this with. I'll never take this gift she's given me for granted.

"I love you." She kisses me harder, rocking her hips slightly. I take her queue, lifting her hips and pulling almost all the way out of her before dropping her back down, making her moan. I do that again and again, agonizingly slow, soaking up all the little sounds she makes as I move inside her.

I don't want to fuck her, I want this. I want to show her every bit of love that I have for her this way. She's my life, my future, and I want this first time together to feel as special as it is. I hold her tight, lazily kissing her sweet lips, telling her how much I love her. She returns the favor, licking and nipping at my jaw and neck.

Neither of us rush it, but it still doesn't take long before her breathing gets heavy, and her moans turn to whimpers. With each thrust, I guide her hips up and down, rocking them against me in a way that stimulates her clit. Every time her most sensitive area rubs against me, her nails claw deeper into my back, marking me.

I know I'm close, but I try to enjoy this moment while it lasts. I want a permanent memory of her like this, of us together. I push inside her to the hilt repeatedly, hitting her back wall, watching her face writhe in blissful torture.

Her mouth drops open, letting out small gasps of breath before she clutches my shoulders in her hands, pulling me against her snugly as she crests the wave of pleasure.

She cries out, her walls clamping so hard around me that my heart stutters. I can't react quickly enough. I'm tucked so deeply inside of her that I explode before I can think straight. My cum fills her, my cock thrusting gently, drawing out both of our orgasms.

I hold her lax body tightly, feeling my cum drip out between us. Fuck. That might not be good but I don't want to ruin the moment while she's still catching her breath.

"I'm so happy," she whispers against my hair. I can hear her smiling as she draws circles on my back.

"Me too." Her nails scrape across my skin, and despite just finishing, it turns me on again. "Thea, unless you want a big mess, you better stop touching me so sweetly." She laughs, but it just makes my dick swell more. She gasps when she feels it.

"Come on, let's get in the shower." I pull out of her reluctantly, knowing I could stay buried in her forever, and gently set her feet on the floor.

Dragging her with me to the bathroom, I let both of us get sudsed up and clean before I bring up my worries. "I didn't use a condom." I clear my throat, feeling like a complete asshole. "I should have been more careful. I'm sorry."

"It's okay." She shrugs.

"It's okay? You aren't mad?" I ask incredulously.

"Why would I be mad?" She goes back to rinsing off like we're just talking about the weather.

"I should have never put you at risk like that. I fucked up," I explain, hoping she gets where I'm coming from. "I promised to keep you safe and that includes an accidental pregnancy."

She laughs, a lighthearted, goofy laugh. I'm dumbstruck. Why isn't she mad at me?

"Jesse, I have an IUD. I have had it for years. I was never going to have an unwanted pregnancy forced on me by anyone. After what happened to me, I knew I'd never risk it." My jaw locks, knowing exactly what she means, and hating to think about it.

"I didn't know, I'm sorry." She wraps her arms around my

waist, letting the water trail down both our bodies.

"I trust you. I knew you'd never put me in jeopardy by giving me an STI, and obviously, I haven't been with anyone since college. It's fine. I wouldn't put all that pressure on you anyway. I'm a grown woman." She kisses my chest, reassuringly. "Besides, if you got me pregnant, I would not be mad."

"What?" My jaw drops. "You want a baby with me?"

"Of course. I would love having your baby," she giggles sweetly against my sternum. I almost can't comprehend her words.

She wants a baby with me…

I knew that being with her meant that I finally found the person I wanted to spend my life with, but I never imagined that I'd ever actually have a family of my own. It's too hard to imagine getting that after years of being utterly alone. I don't even know how it feels to have one… I could have a family with Thea, a real family…

"I want a family with you," I choke out, my eyes burning. Never in my life did I think I'd be this lucky. After years of wanting a family, I gave up. After so many letdowns and heartbreaks, I was too afraid to hope for anything.

"Then let's have one," she tells me, cupping my cheeks in her hands. "Whenever you're ready. I want so many babies that people think I keep you chained to the bed." She looks at me pointedly, making sure I believe it.

"Okay." I hold her tightly, pouring all of my love into it. All the love that belongs to her.

"Okay," she agrees, holding me back just as tightly.

"But, we're getting married first," I assure her, making my intentions known.

CHAPTER FORTY-SIX

She laughs sweetly. "Good. Can't wait."

* * *

"I told them I was done doing undercover work. I'll work in the field or assist on undercover cases, but nothing that will keep me away from you."

Thea is braiding her hair in the mirror. I meant to tell her this news last night, but after our shower, I ended up buried inside of her again, and then we promptly fell asleep.

"Are you sure? Won't you get bored?" She asks, looking at me behind her in the reflection.

"No, I think I'll be plenty busy with you and all of our future babies." I wink, making her grin. Now that the idea of having a little family with Thea has sprouted, I haven't been able to stop thinking about it. I'd get her pregnant today if I wasn't adamant about making her my wife first.

"I'm glad you're home for good then." She gazes lovingly at me in the mirror, making it hard to resist her. I wrap my arms around her waist, careful not to disturb her hair progress, kissing her exposed shoulder.

True to what she said last night, she hasn't been put off at all by my touch. She hasn't even flinched, accepting all of my physical affection with a warm embrace and eager reciprocation. It's hard to believe she's the meek girl I met all those weeks ago. Luckily, I still have no problem making her blush.

"There's going to be a heavy police presence this morning. I want you to be aware, but I don't want to scare you..." I trail off, watching for a reaction in the mirror.

"Why?"

"The case I was working on went cold because it wasn't resolved, the main suspect was in the wind with no leads. When you told me what this 5k was for, I had some worries. I asked Malec to bring his 'A' game." She furrows her brow, clearly worried about what I'm telling her.

"It could be nothing. Better safe than sorry, though." I give her a reassuring smile, but it falls flat in my eyes. My gut is telling me this might be a shit show of a morning, but I have no proof and no jurisdiction, so all I can do is be there for Thea.

"Well, I'll try to run fast then," she says seriously, making me burst out laughing. I guess that's one solution.

Chapter Forty-Seven

Jesse

The pit in my stomach grows as we arrive at the pre-race area set up in downtown Lawson. It's even bigger than I originally thought. The main road that's been blocked off is packed with people participating, volunteering, and spectating the 5k. It's the worst-case scenario for a mass casualty incident.

I grip Thea's hand in mine as we file through the crowd looking for the check-in booth, when I see a familiar face towering above the crowd.

"Malec!" I shout, watching as his attention zeroes in on where he heard his name. He waves and motions for me to stay where I am.

"I need to talk to the Sheriff for a minute, do you want to stay with me? Or, do you need to check in?" I ask Thea. Her eyes widen slightly at Malec's large frame coming towards us. Although she's gotten over her aversion to men with me, she hasn't applied the same principles to everyone else. Selfishly, I'm glad to be the exception.

"I'll go check in and meet you back here." She kisses my cheek before diving back into the thicket of people around us.

It's probably better that she doesn't hear this conversation anyway.

"All has been quiet so far," Malec says, shaking my hand. "I've got the full force out," he says sarcastically, rolling his eyes. "I'm so low-staffed that I asked my old lieutenant to spare some troopers. Lawson PD is busy enough with how many people are here."

"Good, thanks for humoring me. I hope my gut is wrong, but I'd never be able to live with myself if I hadn't shared my suspicions with someone," I tell him honestly.

"I wish we had more manpower. Donahue left this county a mess. I'm still working out the budget." He shrugs, casually observing the crowd around us. I am too, consciously becoming aware of all the alleyways, the large vehicles, and anybody who doesn't look like they belong. Even without a potential threat looming over our heads, it's a hard habit to break when in a large crowd.

"Anything I need to know before the race starts?" I ask, seeing that people are starting to line up by the start.

"I've got guys camped out every half mile along the course, and more right here where it starts and finishes. A few more watching the parking lots. If I had someone qualified, I'd get a sniper in one of these buildings just to keep watch from above, but…" He sighs, clearly feeling the weight of all of this. It's his responsibility to keep the people of this town, and this county, safe. It's a lot of pressure for one person.

"I'm sorry this fell in your lap. I'm here to help in any way I can, whatever you need."

"When the hell did you get back?" I hear a familiar voice behind me ask.

"Last night." I hug Nathan, slapping him on the back. "What

are you guys doing here?"

"We came to support Thea, she texted Callie yesterday but we didn't know you'd be back." Nathan shakes Malec's hand.

"We didn't want her to be alone," Callie explains.

"Thanks, I appreciate you looking out for her." I bump her shoulder making her laugh.

"That's what families do." She shrugs, not realizing the weight of that statement. Of course, that's what families do, I just wouldn't know. I'm glad I'm being looped in.

"Guys, guys!" Thea jogs up to us, embracing Callie when she sees her. "I've gotta go, hopefully, I see you lickity split." She's hopped up from some pre-run powder she took, making her smile from ear to ear. "Bye, love you." She kisses me, giving my ass a pat.

"Love you too, I'll be here when you're done," I assure her, even though I know she knows. I love seeing her excited, but I hate watching her walk away from me. A time like this is not when I want to be separated from the one person who means the world to me.

"Any chance you guys want to watch the race with a view?" Malec asks Nathan and Callie, clearly scheming.

"Would that offer be for the same reason that there are at least double the amount of police patrolling than usual?" Nathan asks, his senses already picking up what's going on without being told.

"Yep." Malec and I say in unison.

"Then, point me to the roof you want me on." Malec and Nathan walk off, his hand on Callie's lower back as she happily trails beside them, glad to be included. I'm relieved they'll be up and out of the action. I only want to focus on Thea, especially if shit goes down.

I find a spot next to a street lamp to stand that will give me a good view of the crowd, as well as the racers taking off. Thea stands with the front of the pack along with the other seasoned runners. She waves when she spots me and I wink just before the announcer starts their countdown.

Then I watch as the most precious thing in my life gets farther and farther away. The pain in my chest is purely anxiety. I'm not used to it. I've never been an anxious person, not until I met Thea.

Worrying about her and her safety is way more important than my own safety ever was. I'm still convinced I might need to start seeing a cardiologist because of all the heart palpitations I've had since she's been in my life.

"If this race is like any of the other notorious ones, the finish line is where we need to focus," Malec says, coming up beside me.

"Agreed." I'll give him credit, he's taking this very seriously and he seems to know what he's doing.

"I'll make my rounds, and check in with my guys. I gave one to Nathan, I want you to keep one too." He hands me a handheld radio. "Don't steal it. I can't afford to buy new ones yet." He says it so seriously it makes me laugh, helping ease some of my tension.

"No worries, man." I shake my head as he walks away through the crowd, thinner than a few moments ago now that the race is underway.

The majority of the spectators are taking their places along the barriers on either side of the finish line, waiting to cheer for their runners as they return. The volunteer crews are readying their places, preparing to receive the racers as they finish.

The rest of Main Street to my right is mostly empty, but I scan it anyway. I scour continuously left to right until my neck aches, accounting for every person who walks by. Looking for any more familiar faces.

I hope Jameson isn't rash enough to show up, but then again, I never thought he was very smart. His ideologies, and his speeches, were always full of lies and random propaganda. He couldn't keep his agenda straight, but I know he wanted destruction and that's what worries me.

The majority of the hardware he had was confiscated at the farm after Kyle was killed, but it's not hard to get your hands on similar stuff. The average person can make bombs out of items in their house, they're just not dumb enough to do so.

The radio in my hand picks up chatter and I have to hold it to my ear to focus on it. *"We've got a commotion down here at the barricade at the end of Main St. Appears to be a domestic situation."*

My neck prickles... This can't be a coincidence. A disturbance that could potentially distract part of the police force? This doesn't feel right.

"Get them out of here, but don't leave the post unmanned. Stay alert." Malec's voice filters through, voicing my thoughts exactly.

I keep my guard up, scanning the area even more intensely. That could be part of a bigger scheme, but I hold on to the hope it's simply bad timing. I need this event to end smoothly, I need my girl home safe.

"I've got movement, out of the northeast alley. One man, shirtless, appears to be carrying a backpack." Nathan's voice cackles out over the radio and every neuron in my body reacts. This is it.

335

Before I even know what I'm doing, I'm halfway across the street heading straight toward the alley that was mentioned. I hit the sidewalk as a person stumbles out, struggling to right themselves. A person I know distinctly. Who I've been checking coroner's reports on for weeks.

Curtis.

His eyes are glazed and a sheen of sweat coats his skin. Nathan was right, he is wearing a black backpack, but it's heavily duct taped around the straps and his hands, holding it snugly onto his shoulders. He couldn't have done this himself, he doesn't even look like he knows what's happening. He's a zombie, glancing past me like I'm invisible.

He steps off the curb, stumbling again, making the blood pound in my ears. If what is in his bag is what I think, this could be deadly for both of us. It could be deadly for a lot of people.

"Jesse, stand down. Wait for backup." I hear Malec's voice shout through my radio, but I ignore it. This is my mess to fix. Curtis was my responsibility and I failed him.

"Curtis. It's me. Jay. Look at me, man!" I shout, trying to get his attention. It isn't until I wave my hands in front of him that he finally blinks, noticing me for the first time. His eyes are bloodshot, barely a thought behind them.

"What's in the bag, Curtis?" I ask, hoping he'll snap out of whatever drug-induced state he is in. His pupils are mere pinpoints as he stares at me, his head lulling from side to side. It looks like he's lost twenty pounds since I last saw him and he didn't have the extra weight to lose.

"Dunno," he mumbles. He tugs his straps like he's trying to remove the bag, but with the thick tape, there's no use.

"I need you to stop walking. Don't go any closer to

336

those people." I can hear the chaos behind me, the deputies evacuating the crowd. There's a lot of people and not a lot of safe ways out of here.

He takes another step, not processing what I'm saying. "Curtis!" I yell again, making him startle. "I need to know what you have in the bag!"

He blinks rapidly, trying to clear some of the fog in his head, but he stays silent.

"We've got two more in custody. They were hiding in an unregistered vehicle down the block." The radio sounds from my back pocket.

"Is there a trigger? Check the vehicle. A timer, a phone, anything?" I shout into the mouthpiece.

"Stand by." Fuck, this is taking too long, a bomb could blow at any second. My skin is crawling with dread. Being this close to a bomb is idiotic.

"Jesse, you've got to move. You can't stay there!" Nathan yells from across the street, but I don't look, keeping my eyes trained on Curtis.

"Jesse..." Curtis mumbles to himself.

"Yeah, buddy. My name is Jesse, not Jay. I'm sorry I lied, but I was doing my job. Right now, I'm trying to keep people from getting hurt. Remember when you told me you didn't want anyone to get hurt?" I keep talking, trying to get through to him, hoping my words will puncture through his haze.

"I don't want to hurt anyone," he says, a little clearer than before, but still slurred.

"I know. Can I look in the bag?" I ask, moving closer. He doesn't move, so I step past him, looking intently at the bag. No exposed wires, and no timer, but all that could be inside. If I pull the zippers though, it could trigger it. FUCK!

"We've got a timer in the van. Unsophisticated. The countdown is active. Four minutes, 58 seconds." The words reach my ears and I swear the world around me slows.

I have less than five minutes to figure out how to save this poor kid and myself. In less than five minutes, I could be dead. Thea will be left alone, and our life together will be over. Less than five minutes until I lose the chance to have a family with her.

I suck in a deep breath, throwing myself into action. If the timer is unsophisticated, then the bomb probably is too. I could be wrong, but the way Curtis was stumbling already tells me it won't explode if it's tilted off-kilter. It's an assumption, but one I'm going with.

"Curtis, I have to get the bag off." I point my attention to where the straps are tightly taped to his arms and cringe. This is going to be brutal.

"JESSE! NO!" My head whips up when I hear her voice. Thea's running towards me quickly, ducking under the arms of the deputies clearing the crowd, straight toward the danger. No, no, no.

"THEA, GO!" I thunder desperately. Please, don't do this, baby.

Before I can even make the split-second decision of staying here with Curtis or getting Thea away, an arm reaches out, latching around her waist and hauling her off the ground.

"NO!!" She screams, kicking and fighting Nathan as he pulls her away from me and farther away. Thank God. I can't do this if I know she's not safe.

I can hardly do this at all knowing she's out there needing me to come home to her. Fuck, I don't want that to be the last time I got to hear her voice or see her face, but I need to stop Jameson from hurting anyone.

There are still people too close for comfort and families probably occupy the buildings surrounding us, so I turn back to the bag. I pull my pocket knife out and start sawing away at the layers of tape around his left shoulder and hand. It's thick and annoyingly sticky. It's taking me forever. Too long.

I'm only halfway through the left side when I hear, *"Two minutes."* The warning sets my nerves wild. Fuck, I can't do this in time. I keep slicing and ripping at the tape, ignoring Curtis' cries of pain.

"What's your plan?"

I look up as Malec jogs toward me. I should tell him to leave, warn him away, but I can't deny the relief that he's here offering help. The look on his face tells me he wouldn't leave anyway.

"I'm trying to cut the bag off. If I can get it in a dumpster before it blows, it'll stop a lot of the damage," I explain, sweat dripping down my face as I concentrate on my task. Malec doesn't hesitate, pulling his own knife out to cut the right side.

"Bomb squad is going to take too long. When we get to a ten-second warning, we're out of here, with or without your friend," he whispers to me. All I can do is nod. I don't want to leave Curtis if it comes to it, I don't know if I can, but for now, I agree.

The tape finally gives and I'm able to get it sliced cleanly through one side of the strap, but it's still wrapped around his shoulder and hands, stuck to his skin. Malec has the realization at the same time as me. There is no time to keep cutting.

"I'm sorry, buddy." That's all I can utter before we both

start ripping the tape from his body, pulling the bag from his back. His blood-curdling screams burst our eardrums, but we keep going. We can't stop, we're too close. We rip and rip, taking skin with us as we go. It's nasty and I know it's unbelievably painful, but if we get through this at least he'll be alive.

"*Twenty seconds,*" the voice from the radio warns.

"Finally," Malec utters, ripping the last of the tape free. "I got it. Go, Jesse."

"No." I pull my side free and Curtis falls to his knees in front of us, on the verge of passing out. "Take him, I've got the bag." I snatch the backpack before he can argue, racing towards the closest dumpster just inside the alley. My responsibility.

"*Ten seconds.*"

I open the top hatch, placing the bag gently inside, not wanting to risk an early detonation but bracing for it regardless. When it doesn't immediately explode, I slam the lid shut and take off back towards the street.

"*Five... Four... Three...*" The countdown drowns out as I reach Malec dragging Curtis' dead weight across the double yellow lines. I loop my arm under him too, only making it a few steps before we're knocked off our feet. We collide hard with the pavement as the blast detonates, my head bouncing off the curb and making my ears ring.

One minute the world around me was moving at warp speed, then the next, everything was black.

Chapter Forty-Eight

Thea

No matter how often I run public races, I forget the electricity that surrounds me. The runners who are flying past everyone else, booking it to the finish line. The runners who are participating in their first event and filled with an air of accomplishment. The runners who aren't really into it, but are glad to spend the morning with their friends regardless. It's a community like no other.

So, I'm confused as I approach the final stretch and don't hear the roar of the onlookers cheering and cowbells jingling. Instead of seeing the winners being praised with applause and ribbons being passed around, I see scared faces and utter chaos. Deputies are directing the mass of people right across the race line, pushing them towards the other side and down the side street.

My heart picks up speed, even worse than from the miles I just ran. Something is very wrong and I don't see Jesse. I push my way through throngs of people, trying to get closer to the spot I last saw him before the race. He wouldn't leave without me, he's here somewhere.

When I see him, or the top of his head rather, my heart

eases a little. He's separated from the crowd, standing in the middle of Main Street, but he's not alone. I recognize his "friend" from the library and bar.

I'm trying to find a way through when my heart stops altogether. They aren't just standing alone, they're being steered away from. Everyone running around me is being evacuated *from* them.

I work my way diagonally across the fleeing sea of people, needing to get to Jesse and get him out of there. I don't pay attention to the bodies colliding with mine, I ignore the annoyed remarks until a few murmured words reach my ears. *Bomb... Backpack... Bomb...*

A bomb?

That's what he was worried about. This is why he mentioned there would be a strong police presence. No wonder he was stressed about his undercover operation, he was dealing with crazy-ass bomb makers!

He promised me that he was done with the risks, he was ready to be done. For me. Why is he doing this?

I know the answer. It's who he is. He protects people. He proves time and time again that he's not like his father. It's unnecessary and it doesn't stop me from being mad as hell right now because I just got him back.

He reaches for the backpack just as I'm to the deputies at the barricade. "JESSE! NO!" I scream, begging him to see me and come with me instead. His eyes find mine and they're blown wide with panic.

"THEA, GO!" He yells back, but it doesn't even begin to falter my steps. If he's staying here then I am too. If he dies today then I die too.

Before my foot can make contact with the ground again,

I'm lurched out of thin air, colliding with a hard body. The steel band around my waist feels like a death sentence. I can't get to him.

"NO!!" I scream in agony.

"Thea, stop fighting me. STOP!" Nathan yells, sucking all the fight from my body. If he's given up on Jesse, then why won't he give me up too? I can't go back to my life before, I can't.

"Thea, please. Jesse knows what he's doing. Malec has the bomb squad coming," Callie assures me, holding both sides of my face, and forcing me to look at her.

"I can't lose him," I cry, feeling the enormous weight of helplessness pressing down on me. "Please," I utter to no one in particular.

"I'm going in." I hear the words spoken from somewhere behind me, but I don't look to see who said it. The only thing keeping me from collapsing where I stand is Nathan's arm around me.

"Bomb squad?" Nathan asks without finishing his sentence. The silence that answers him tells me all I need to know. They aren't coming. It's really the end.

This is all my fault. If I didn't sign up for this race then Jesse wouldn't be here. He wouldn't be standing with a maniac about to be blown up.

"We've gotta move back, get behind this building," Nathan says to Callie, dragging me along. I hear the dullness of his voice, I know it's not a good sign.

Jesse is Nathan's best friend, if there was anything he could be doing to save him, he'd be doing it, but he's not. He's standing here, making sure Callie and I stay safe as if I even care to make it through this without Jesse.

"Deep breaths, Thea. In and out, slowly," Callie chants softly, making me realize that I'm hyperventilating. It's the same feeling I get before a panic attack, except this time it isn't because of my past trauma, but because of the trauma that I'm about to experience in real time. Only this is something I'll never get past. Ever.

I focus on Callie's voice and the worried screams of people around us still looking for their loved ones, but my head lulls back, staring into the sky. Deep breaths... In and out... I can't do this right now... Don't panic... Don't pass out...

I know the blast happens, but somehow my brain blocks it out. In its place is a high-pitched ringing in my ears. My eyes stay glued to the birds above my head, flying scatteredly, anywhere but here. I feel their pain.

"Take her," Nathan shouts to Callie, our hearing all affected by the blast. He plops my body against Callie, giving her my weight. I watch him run back toward Main Street, but it still takes my brain a second to come to.

Jesse. He's checking on Jesse.

All the strength that had evaporated from my body comes back in a landslide, I pull out of Callie's arms and take off toward the blast zone. "Thea, no!" She shouts but chases behind me anyway.

I need to see him. I need him. I run harder, skidding to a stop when I get to the corner where the finish line *was*. The street in front of me is in shambles. The barricades are knocked down, and the race tents and banners have collapsed into tatters from the mass of people they had to evacuate. The dumpster across the street is on fire and a store's awning is catching flames, but the firetrucks are still firmly parked down the street behind another barricade.

What I'm looking for is about twenty feet in front of me. It's him. Jesse, Curtis, and Malec all lay hunched over the curb. Their bodies are utterly still. Please, no.

My eyes ping to Nathan. People are shouting at him not to, but he breaches the perimeter anyway, running toward his friend before collapsing to his knees. The sight of it paralyzes me.

What if he's dead?

The sob tears from my throat at the thought of him being gone. "Please, Nathan!" I shout, needing to know one way or another. Not knowing is agonizing, the slight hope in my heart is torturing me slowly.

He bends down, checking his pulse while seconds tick by. When he squeezes his eyes shut, embracing Jesse's limp body, it guts me and I fall to my knees.

Callie embraces me as the bomb squad finally comes rolling through the barricades, but all I can see is Jesse's prone body as Nathan raises his head and looks at me with tears in his eyes.

* * *

"With a head injury like this, all we can do is wait. He'll wake up when he's ready, then we'll run tests. Try to rest, maybe get a bite to eat. It could be awhile," the doctor tells me and Nathan reassuringly. Or, as reassuring as he can since we're in a hospital.

I slump back into the chair next to Jesse's bed, not daring to leave him even for a minute. The wires and bandages scattered across his body are foreign and hard to look at. He doesn't look like our Jesse. Holding his hand is the only way this even seems real.

Nathan's torn up, pacing the room while Callie's down the hall. She offered to call our mom before she sees the events on the news.

"He's going to be fine," my brother mumbles, but it sounds like he is saying it to himself.

Seeing his best friend injured has shown a different side to him that I've never seen. He's never been a worrier. He barely cried at my dad's funeral. I've only ever seen him fuss over Callie.

He already expressed his immense guilt for not being with Jesse when the blast went off, but he knew his priority needed to be me and Callie. He even said Jesse would do the same thing in his shoes and that's the only reason he could stomach not being right beside him.

"Why didn't you bring him around sooner?" I ask, feeling that despite what the doctor said, my time with Jesse could be ticking away. He might not wake up.

This feels too similar to the day we spent in the hospital watching our dad die slowly. The cancer ate away at him until there was nothing left. This cannot happen like that, I won't let it.

"I don't know. He met mom a few times when she visited. You never came with her, and when I came home a few times... I don't know. I wanted to pretend like things were how they used to be before I joined the military."

He doesn't talk about it much still, even though Callie told me he had a hard time the last few years. He never told me. I always thought he was a workaholic. It never occurred to me that my brother could be struggling in life like I was.

"You should have come home more," I whisper, barely keeping a lid on my emotions. The day has been too much already.

"I know," he admits. "Callie won't tell me what you two talked about at the cabin that day he was MIA, but she scolded me for being a shitty brother." He laughs, but there is no humor in it.

"No, she didn't," I argue, knowing Callie would never tell him that.

"No, she didn't, but she said I should have been there for you more. That I should try to make up for lost time." He shrugs. "That's what I thought I was doing when I moved here," he finally admits.

"So, buying land the town over from where I happened to find a job wasn't a coincidence?" I ask, giving him a hard time. He always denied it, but I knew. I think I always knew.

"I thought being closer would let you rub off on me a little more. You were always so happy. You seemed like you loved life and I needed that. It wasn't until I was here and I was seeing you more that I realized maybe I didn't know you at all."

"I am happy. I do love life," I reassure him, but I know what he's saying. He saw that there was a broken part of me hidden under everything else.

"I really like you and Jesse together," he smiles, one of his famous half-smiles that you usually have to pry out of him. "You're two of the best people I know. I think you guys are going to be happy."

His continued openness shocks me. Something about a hospital room makes people want to expose their emotions I guess. It just reminds me that if Jesse doesn't wake up, there will be no more happiness. No more future.

"He saved my life, Nathan," I confess, watching the confusion sweep across his face. "I had given up. I didn't think I was ever going to have a normal, happy life. I was content only because my job fulfilled me. My kids at the library made me get out of bed some mornings. I love you and Callie, and Mom, but I was missing having someone to share my life with. Not because I didn't want it, but because I couldn't."

Nathan's brow furrows deeply, clearly concerned about the things I'm telling him. In the spirit of hospital confessionals, I might as well keep with it. I run my hands over my arms, taking a deep breath.

"I was raped, the summer after college. It ruined my life. I didn't take two extra semesters in grad school to continue studying, I failed my first year and had to start over because I couldn't get out of bed to go to class. I never told you and Mom because I was ashamed. I was ashamed that it happened and that I let it…" I pause, gathering myself. I don't look at Nathan, fearing what I'll see there.

"It took me years to even begin to get past it. Years of therapy. Years living with Liv because I was scared to be alone. It's been six years and Jesse is the first man that I can touch without panicking. The first man I truly felt safe with. Before him, every time a man tried to touch me, I'd freak out. If they grabbed me, I'd pass out. Six years." I blink away my tears, trying my best to tell this story again without crying.

I gain the bravery to look up at Nathan and my heart breaks. His face is full of so much anguish it physically hurts to see. "My baby sister," he utters in such saddened disbelief, I can't help but jump up to hug him.

348

We stand for a long time, holding each other while we cry. It's the first time I've ever really seen my stronger-than-life brother break.

He holds me tightly, apologizing over and over even though I promise him there was nothing he could have done. It wasn't his fault.

For the first time, despite everything, I truly believe that it wasn't my fault either.

Chapter Forty-Nine

Jesse

"Open your eyes, baby. I want you to watch as I fuck you." I thrust into Thea's tightness, pumping my hips from behind her while she faces the mirror on her knees. It's been a month since the 5k, and my road rash is mostly healed, only leaving faint scars behind.

I was lucky that my only lasting injuries were superficial scrapes from hitting the pavement. Though I was slightly concussed, I felt right in the head within a few days.

Malec suffered about the same but woke up before ever being transported to the hospital that day. He visited me when I woke up, only bragging slightly that he wasn't knocked unconscious for hours. I countered that it was because he had a thicker skull. As with Nathan, male friendships seem to take off when ridiculing each other.

Unfortunately, Curtis didn't get so lucky. His ripped skin from the tape required skin grafts and the drugs that were thick in his system took weeks to detox. The last I heard, he was in a treatment center ensuring he could avoid a lasting addiction to the fentanyl Jameson had pumped him with.

Jameson, Derrick, and Mitch were arrested and are all

awaiting trial for their crimes. The other members of the group are still being hunted down and questioned about their involvement.

Thea was pretty pissed at me for putting myself at risk, but she understood why. She gave me the cold shoulder for a few days, letting me heal up before angry-fucking me so hard that I almost passed out.

"Jesse, please," she begs prettily, making me eager to give her what she wants. I move my right hand from where it was molded to her breast, dragging it down her stomach and to her swollen clit. "Yes," she cries when I start rubbing it in circular motions.

I tighten my hand around her neck, plastering her back to my chest, using the extra leverage to pick up my momentum. I pound into her pussy rapidly, never easing up on her clit, and making her squirm. She bucks her hips back, meeting me thrust for thrust, using me like her own fuck toy.

"I'm gonna…" She doesn't finish her sentence, her orgasm ripping through her making her gasp in pleasure. The shock waves pulse through her so hard I can feel them clenching my cock.

I slow my thrusts, cupping her mound firmly, letting her soak up the entirety of her climax without adding more sensation to her already over-sensitive flesh. "You look so pretty like this, with my hand around your throat, and my cock inside you," I whisper in her ear, making her sigh with contentment.

She loves when I talk to her and when I say dirty things. Sometimes I think she has a dirtier mind than me. It was repressed for so long, she's able to finally let loose, and damn am I glad that it's with me.

"Hands on the floor, sweet girl," I tell her, watching as she complies. I thrust hard and slow, pulling my dick all the way out until just the crown remains, then pushing back into the hilt.

I watch her body being impaled from our reflection in the mirror, seeing her ass bounce back and forth against my abdomen. My hands grip her hips, increasing the power behind my thrusts.

"So fucking sexy, baby." Her eyes flutter at my praise, her whole body flushed with her arousal. I pick up the toy that's been sitting beside me, waiting to be utilized, and stick it in her mouth, making her suck on the dark blue silicone. She holds it in her mouth, only leaving the rhinestone base visible, warming it up.

Pulling it from her lips, I tap it on her tongue a few times for my own twisted pleasure and place it where it belongs. Pushing past her tightened hole and slowly settling it to the base. She whimpers at the fullness and I'm mesmerized by it. I can't tear my eyes from where my dick is still pumping inside her pussy and the plug is sitting pretty in her ass.

She's eager to experiment. She has yet to tell me no to anything. It's all fair game aside from missionary. I realized after our first time that my body on top of hers like that brings back bad memories.

However, a few times she insisted on it, determined to conquer her anxiety. Those instances are slow and gentle. I make love to her, reclaiming the position as our own.

"I'm not going to last much longer, Sunshine. Touch your clit, and make yourself cum again. I know you want to," I goad her, knowing how greedy she is for orgasms and how her second one usually comes quickly after the first.

She does as I said, reaching her hand underneath her to work her clit, moaning while I continue fucking her hard from behind. I pump into her fiercely, feeling my balls tighten as I chase my release.

"Yes, Jesse. Yes!" She cries, gasping for breath as another climax hits her. The way her walls tighten around me is too consuming, sending me over the edge. I fill her with my cum, pushing it deeper and deeper inside with lazy thrusts until the last drop is spent. I stay seated deep inside her until we both catch our breath.

She has an OB appointment in a month and I can't wait until she loses the birth control. Neither of us were quite ready for a baby before, but now I'm getting impatient. It doesn't mean I haven't loved all the practice though.

"We need to shower, we're running late," she says, still a little out of breath. I pull the plug from her gently, making sure not to hurt her, helping her up from the floor.

"I'm sure they won't start without us," I tease, winking at her reflection still in the mirror.

"Yeah, I'm sure they'd be thrilled to know that we're late to their wedding because we were horny." She laughs at herself, making me smile. This newfound sex fiend in her has been a pleasure to see and experience, not only for myself but for the confidence and joy it's brought her.

No matter where or when she's in the mood, she loves jumping me, knowing I'll never turn her down. It's given her a sense of power that I'd never think of taking from her. Except the time when we were on her front porch steps and almost gave the neighborhood a show. I made sure to move behind closed doors before she got my pants off.

"Go jump in, I'm right behind you." I try to locate the clothes

I'll need because she's right, we are running late.

"It's okay, I changed my mind." I turn to her as she pulls on a lace thong, trapping all the cum I just shot into her from escaping. "I like feeling you drip out of me."

My jaw drops to the floor every time she hits me with some statement like that. She loves being marked by me, owned. She never wants my cum to go to waste. Such a greedy little thing… And, she's all mine.

* * *

After the officiant recites his words, Nathan and Callie exchange vows while I can't tear my eyes from Thea in her velvet bridesmaid dress. It fits like a second skin.

She's standing on the other side of the aisle, acting as the maid of honor, while I stand as the best man. Under a big tent in Nathan's backyard, we get to enjoy this momentous occasion together. It's a small affair, only a few friends and family, half of whom traveled from Tennessee to be here for Callie.

It's all about love, happiness, and family. There haven't been many instances like this where I truly feel like I'm surrounded by family, but with Thea, Nathan, and Callie, I feel like I am. I've finally found my place in the world.

I'm also about two seconds away from making the officiant stay where he is so I can marry Thea next. I'm not that crazy, but I am more than ready to marry her. I fucked up my big gesture when I told her I loved her, so I want the next one to count. No spur-of-the-moment words flying out of my mouth. I want to make it special for her. Which includes not sharing her brother's wedding day. I sigh, inwardly. It just means I have to wait longer.

"You may now kiss the bride." The officiant declares, making everyone clap and cheer. I smile as Thea wipes away tears. I can't wait to see her cry happy tears at our wedding.

We make our way up the aisle behind the happy couple, arms linked together while everyone stands and continues clapping. This is what life should be, nothing but joy. It's a shame it took me this long to get here, but now that I have it, I'll fight even harder not to lose it.

The cool fall evening carries on, we eat and dance and give speeches. Mine draws laughs, and Thea's speech requires a tissue box to be passed around to her and the audience. When she hands the microphone off to Nathan, he quickly hands it to Callie, making us all laugh.

"Thank you all for coming and sharing this day with us..." Callie carries on, vaguely reciting the story of how she and Nathan met a year ago, and how she believes it was fate.

You can tell by her words how much she loves him, and you can tell by the way he looks at her that the feelings are reciprocated. I'm happy for them.

I wrap my arm around Thea's shoulders, hugging her to me, happy that fate has worked out for all of us.

"Since we wanted such a small wedding, I won't be doing a big bouquet toss, but... I think I already know who is next to be married." Callie rounds the small table reserved for her and Nathan, coming towards me and Thea. Making Thea gasp quietly.

"I love you, thank you for being the sister I always wanted." Callie hugs Thea tightly, handing me the bouquet instead to free up their arms. I wave it in the air cheekily, making people laugh, and letting these two have their moment.

Once they're done giggling and wiping the wetness from their cheeks, Thea comes back to me, reaching for the white flowers, but I hold them out of her reach. Instead, I draw her in by the back of her neck, kissing her hungrily. She's mine, and I do intend to marry her. I want everyone to know it.

"Jesse, please don't get on a knee at my brother's wedding," she says breathlessly, smiling, still only a whisper away from my face.

I grin back, loving that I know her so well, and glad we're on the same page about the matter. "Don't worry, Sunshine. I left the ring at home." I wink, making her laugh. She turns around, leaning back into my chest with her glass of champagne to watch some of the little kids in attendance dance.

"Wait." She turns suddenly after a moment, eyeing me critically. "Are you joking?"

I shrug, hiding my smile behind my drink. "Guess we'll find out."

Chapter Fifty

Thea

"I have an old friend in town, do you mind if he stops by? I ended up with some of his souvenirs after our last cruise, I wanted to get them back to him," my mom tells us from her spot at the table.

We're just finishing dessert after our Thanksgiving meal. Jesse and I hosted this year since Nathan and Callie just got home from their honeymoon a few days ago.

"Sure, mom. No problem." I clear away some of the dishes, feeling stuffed and ready for a nap. Jesse bumps my hip, shooing me from the sink. "I can do it," I tell him.

"You cooked, I can handle dishes," he insists, but I still lean against the counter wanting to be near him. Even after being together a couple of months now, I feel like we're glued to the hip and I love it.

"Malec's going to come to watch the game," Jesse says eventually as we all make our way into the living room.

"Okay, sounds good." I yawn. I'll probably be out like a light before halftime.

"I'll get it," Nathan offers after the doorbell rings since he's closest. I don't pay attention to it, claiming my seat on the couch. "Chris?" I hear Nathan say, surprised.

"Look, Thea, it's your dad's old friend, Christopher. He's in my widow group now."

My mom's words are lost on me as I process what I'm hearing in slow motion... People are moving around me, the TV is on, but I can't focus on any one thing. My world is suddenly spinning upside down.

"Thea, are you okay?" I hear Jesse's voice but my head is swimming. I turn to him, but my eyes make contact with the man standing in the doorway over his shoulder. *Christopher.*

I had forgotten his name, or chosen not to remember it after all of these years, but hearing it sends me right back to that day. The tequila, the drugs, the violation, the agony that I suffered.

"My dad's friend..." I mumble almost incoherently, feeling the blood drain from my body and go who knows where. Jesse looks at me then over his shoulder, and his face morphs to fury. He moves quickly, but it looks like stop-motion flashing in front of me.

He's on him, tackling him to the ground and punching him before anyone can even react. Nathan's quickest, trying to pull him off, and letting the now gray-haired man stumble down the porch steps. Once he's out of sight, I suck in a strangled breath of relief.

"What the hell, man?" Nathan shouts, struggling to hold Jesse back.

"He's the one who hurt Thea. That bastard raped her," Jesse yells, making everyone balk.

I don't react, my fluttering eyelashes are the one thing keeping me from being completely paralyzed. I'm just lively enough to see the accusation register on Nathan's face. He lets Jesse go and they both disappear from the entryway while my ears ring. My head hits the back of the couch and my vision goes white before I can see what happens next.

I don't know how long I'm out for, but I have to blink away the blurriness in my eyes before I can see Jesse pacing in front of me. "Jesse?" I mumble, seeing his instant relief.

"Hey, baby. Are you okay?" He grabs my hands and kisses them before sweeping the hair out of my face.

"I'm okay, what happened?" I ask, noting the bloodiness of his hands, but choosing to ignore it. "Is he gone?"

"Yeah. He's never coming back." His voice is so hard, so void of emotion it startles me.

"What did you do?" I ask, panicked. If he killed him then he could be taken from me forever. I never want that to happen. Christopher isn't worth losing Jesse.

"We chased him down and beat his ass," Nathan says from somewhere in the room. "*Someone* wouldn't let us finish the job…" He grumbles.

"You invited me over to watch football, not so I could witness a murder," Malec interjects.

"Yeah, yeah. Whatever," Nathan mumbles, making Callie scold him quietly.

I don't know why, the situation isn't funny in the slightest, but I laugh. A full, deep belly laugh that makes my eyes water. It's so ridiculous, the whole situation. What are the chances that he would show up here? How could he have the nerve?

I don't care, he got what he deserved. I hope he's disfigured the rest of his life from the beating he received.

"I think she's cracked," someone murmurs, but I'm laughing too hard to know who it is.

"Thea, sweetie, I'm so sorry," my mom says from beside me.

I hadn't even realized she was sitting there. "Why didn't you tell me? We could have had him arrested!"

"It's okay, Mom, I never wanted you to know. I never tried pressing charges because I was too traumatized already. A trial would have been torture, especially with no evidence. It would always be his word against mine." I hold her hand, only being able to imagine how she feels right now, discovering her daughter had this dirty secret. I've had six years to process it, she's only had a few minutes. "I'm ready to move on," I assure her, trying to sound serious. The giggles are still bubbling out of me like a loon.

"There's your answer," Jesse speaks quietly to Malec, making him nod his head.

"If she changes her mind, there's no statute of limitations," he responds quietly back to Jesse. He clears his throat when he notices me watching their exchange. "If you change your mind..." He starts, but I nod cutting him off.

"I'll think about it. Thank you." I meant it, I'm ready to move on, but I would be lying if I didn't admit that a part of me wants him to rot in prison for his crime. I've worried for years that I'm not his only victim, but I don't know if I'm strong enough to learn the truth.

"I just wanted to make sure you were okay, which might still be up for debate," he says, noting the tears still on my face from my laughing fit. "He knows he messed up by coming here, but I'll make sure he leaves town." He turns to Jesse and my brother. "Please, stop breaking laws and making me witness it. I don't want to arrest you lunatics," Malec states sternly, moving toward the door. "Jesus Christ..." He mumbles after taking one last glance at their bloodied appearances.

360

It makes the laughter burst out of me again, even harder, making me double over to catch my breath. Jesse rubs my back reassuringly, letting me ride it out. "Happy Thanksgiving," he utters, sending me orbiting again.

* * *

"It wasn't that bad... Just the ending was bad," Jesse says after I suggested that his first official family Thanksgiving was ruined. We've been going back and forth about it all weekend. I wanted everything to be perfect.

"I'm sorry you had to take care of me. I thought I was over my past. I don't like how affected I was by seeing *him* again," I explain, not even wanting to speak my rapist's name.

"I will always take care of you. Always. I'm only sorry he's still breathing." Jesse draws a finger down my bare back, tracing my spine. We spent most of the day today in bed.

"I have an early Christmas present for you," I whisper, curling into his chest.

"Christmas is a month away." He laughs, holding me tight.

"I know, but I want this to be your best one yet," I tell him, nervously. I'm worried what he'll think of my surprise. I've been working hard to set it up perfectly, but he might not have the reaction I'm hoping for.

"It will be, no matter what. I have you, Sunshine." He kisses my forehead, making me sigh happily. "I don't think I'd ever decorated a tree before. I don't even remember doing it as a kid before my mom died."

The only thing we did this weekend after the disastrous

Thanksgiving day, was put up my artificial tree, lights, and ornaments. Having him here to celebrate the holidays has healed even more parts of me that I didn't realize were broken. Not only was I missing the physical intimacy for years, but I had missed out on all the simple traditions that you share with your person. Now I can't even fathom spending a holiday without him.

"This surprise will require you to take a few days off of work. I know you just started at the new base, but do you think they'd give you vacation time?" I ask, biting my lip, the nerves getting to me.

"I'll make it work," he says, suspicious of what I'm telling him. Or rather not saying.

I climb off the bed and go to my closet to pull a box out from the back, returning to the bed before opening it. My heart is beating fast, making my fingers unsteady on the lid.

"Okay." Deep breath. "When you were in Texas, I spent my extra time doing some research." I remove the lid, exposing the contents of the box. It's full of newspaper clippings, documents, and more.

He eyes the papers, his eyebrows furrowing in confusion. "What is all of this?"

"It's you. Stuff from your past. I used the Indiana libraries database to look up newspapers and census information from when you were a kid." My voice is almost a whisper, anxious to see his reaction.

"What?" He asks, unbelievably. He goes to touch the top piece but pulls his hand away like he's afraid.

"Here," I encourage him, handing him a newspaper clipping of his hometown. "Your birth was announced in the local paper. It has your parents' names, and yours." I point to show him, seeing his eyes trail across the words.

I rifle through more of what I have, showing him small tidbits that might be about him or his hometown. I wasn't sure how accurate it all was. My research was more of a guessing game, following names and leads, and trying to connect the dots.

"This." I show him a faded photo from a newspaper. "It's your first-grade class. The paper ran a story about your spelling bee. It has everyone's names listed at the bottom.

I look again at the little chubby, gap-toothed face of Jesse as a six-year-old before I hand it to him. My sweet boy before all of the tragedy. Even without the names, I could tell which one was him. His shaggy blonde hair hangs over his forehead, but it's him, I'd never mistake it.

Right next to him, is his teacher, Miss Carlisle. Her dark curly ringlets are held back by a dark headband, that I can tell even from this faded black and white photo, matches her lipstick.

He looks at the photo in awe for a long time and I give him all the time he needs. For him, this is only a small piece of the childhood that was torn from him. While I hope it brings good memories to his mind, I'm afraid of the bad memories that could take root.

"I can't believe you found this," he chokes out. I lean in close to him, leaving the box and papers strewn on the mattress in front of us, and rest my head on his shoulder.

"I have more, but only if you're ready. I don't want to make this hard on you," I assure him, feeling him rest his cheek against the top of my head.

"Thank you, Thea. For all of this." I lean back to look at him, only intending to offer him a warm smile, but he takes the opportunity to kiss me deeply. He holds my face tenderly, fusing our lips like it's his source of life. I know the feeling well.

After readjusting my brain after that kiss, I push through the pile of papers, looking for the one I want. "This is an article about a teacher exchange program, apparently Miss Carlisle was part of it. They interviewed her before she went home to Canada."

He grabs the paper gently like it might crumble to pieces before looking at it.

—

Having the opportunity to teach in the United States has been extraordinary. I came into this expecting to explore a new way of teaching, and maybe a new culture, but I never expected the way it would change my life. Teaching the bright young students of New Liberton Elementary is something I'll never forget.

It was so much more than what took place during school time hours. You learn who they are as people, and what they've gone through in their short lives. You hold them so dear to your heart that it seems unfair to leave them behind.

One child will forever have a piece of me, wherever he goes, and wherever he ends up. I will always be thinking of him and worrying about him. I never had the desire to be an American citizen or a mother. I loved my home in Canada and my life, but I still fought fiercely to gain permanent residence in the United States as my time in the program ended. Solely for the chance to give that boy a loving home.

It didn't work out for me in that way, and soon, I lost touch with that little boy altogether, but I'll always be grateful for the chance I had to teach him. To love him. Thank you to all of my students, and my advisors, for allowing me to participate in this life-changing program.

-All my love, Miss Catherine Carlisle

—

His silence begins to worry me. I know he's finished reading the words by now, but he continues to stare at the page until small rivulets of tears escape his eyes. The wet paths descend his cheeks, landing with a delicate drop onto the old paper. I tug it softly from his hands, wanting to preserve it.

"She didn't give up on me," he whispers, though it seems to be to himself. He squeezes his eyes shut and I wipe his cheeks, drying up the moisture, and letting him rest his face in my palm.

"She loved you. She still does."

"It's been two decades, she probably barely remembers me now." He shakes his head, blowing out a deep breath.

"She remembers," I say, nervous once again. He looks at me peculiarly, trying to figure out what I'm saying. "I spoke to her."

"What?" His eyes go wide in disbelief.

"I found out where she teaches. She's about to retire, but I found her email through the school's website. She never married, her name is the same. I sent her a message and asked if I could talk to her on the phone one day, and I was hoping to reconnect her with an old student. She called me as soon as I sent her your name and my phone number. We talked for a few hours."

"What?" He says again, as if not processing everything that I'm saying.

Chapter Fifty-One

Jesse

"Jesse, she more than remembers you. She loves you. She cried when I told her about the man you are today. She said the biggest regret of her life was going back to Ontario. She tried to fight immigration, tried to extend her visa, everything, but she was stuck. I didn't tell her everything else you went through, it's your story to tell, but I know she didn't choose to abandon you."

Thea's words run through my mind. Miss Carlisle. She found her. She remembers me. She loves me. I can't believe after all of these years I'm gaining insight on my past. It feels like closure, but at the same time opens an entirely new realm of questions.

"She wants to talk to me?" I ask, still a little dumbfounded. Thea laughs, snapping me out of my haze.

"She wants to see you. She asked me, no begged me, to bring you to see her. She told me she doesn't have a current passport or she'd be on the next flight out." She laughs again, charmed by my old teacher. I still can't believe it.

"That's my surprise. I want us to fly to Ontario before Christmas for a visit. If you want to of course," she explains, looking unsure. I realize my lack of communication is making her anxious by the way she's nibbling on her lip.

"Okay," I utter, but that's all I can muster.

"Okay?" She asks, looking nervous, but hopeful. I nod my head, pulling her into my chest. This wonderful woman has changed my life in so many ways, I'll never understand what I did to deserve her.

"I love you so much, Thea. This is incredible," I tell her honestly, feeling the love I have for her bursting out of my chest. It feels like how I felt the day I told her I loved her for the first time, but exponentially greater. It's like I'll explode if I don't express how much I love her.

"I love you, too, but I have one more thing to show you. Then I'll be done." She laughs, holding me tightly. Her excitement is the only thing keeping my lips sealed, so I nod, urging her to continue.

"This is a yearbook that I found archived in the New Liberton Public Library database. I called them and they shipped the physical copy along with the newspaper clippings. We'll have to get photocopies and send it back, but for now, I wanted to show you what's inside." She flips through the pages, finding what she's looking for. She lays the book open in front of me, the page is filled with Senior portraits of the graduating class.

I study the dated photographs, not understanding what she's showing me because all I see are bad mustaches and permed hair. Until one smile catches my eye and my breath stills in my chest. "Mom," I hardly whisper.

"It's her senior photo. I found it when I got her maiden name from your birth announcement. I didn't know if she'd look how you remembered or not." Thea squeezes my bicep, letting me gaze at the only picture I've seen of my mom.

She looks the same as I remember, yet entirely different. The years have made so many of the details fuzzy. I spent many years mourning her death all over again when I realized I couldn't remember what her laugh sounded like or what the details of her face looked like.

"It's perfect." A drop of moisture hits the paper and Thea quickly wipes it away. "I miss her," I utter, wiping my face with the back of my hand.

"She's beautiful. When I saw the smile, I knew without a doubt it was your mom. You look a lot like her," Thea says, gently running her fingers through my hair.

Knowing that I have my mom's smile brings me a comfort that is beyond words. Knowing that Thea loves the smile that belongs to my mom makes me feel even more connected to her. It feels like a sign.

"I wish you could have known her," I admit. "She would love you."

"Maybe your mom and my dad are up above smiling down on us. Maybe they orchestrated the whole thing." She laughs, nudging me playfully with her elbow.

"Yeah, maybe they did. Maybe my mom is asking your dad for his blessing so that I can marry you," I tell her, making her smile.

"I hope so."

"Thea," I say seriously, making her cock her head at me.

"What?"

"Marry me," I demand, blowing my chance at another grand gesture.

"What?" She asks incredulously, trying to figure out if I'm joking or not. I'm not.

"I don't want to wait any longer." I hold her head gently in my hands, bringing her lips to mine. "Be my wife," I demand again, kissing her lightly.

Her eyes search mine like she's still not sure she should take me seriously. It's my fault, I screwed this up by springing it on her. I jump off the bed, only wearing my underwear, not a great proposal look but it doesn't matter.

What matters is that she knows how serious I am. I grab the velvet box that I've had hidden in my old duffle bag in the closet, returning to the bed.

I pull her towards me, making her sit with her with her feet on the ground in front of me. I drop to one knee before her, resting the open box on her lap. "Thea. I didn't want to rush things, and I meant to make this special, but I can't wait.

"We fell in love quickly, but I've never been more sure about anything in my life. I want a family with you. I want all of my new memories to be made with you. I only want a future with you in it. Please, will you marry me?" I finally ask, changing tactics and trying not to be a completely demanding lunatic. "It would be the greatest gift of my life."

She stares at me, her tears flowing freely down her face before a sob breaks free. Her arms shoot out, pulling me towards her as she wraps them around my neck. "Yes. I want to marry you. I've never wanted anything more."

The breath I was holding whooshes out of me, relieved that I didn't screw this up completely, but even more relieved that she actually wants to marry me. No matter how incredible our relationship has been, there's still a lost boy inside me that's been rejected over and over again in life. A part of me will probably always expect the worst, but I'm learning that I don't have to with Thea. My Sunshine.

We hold each other tight for a long time, laughing and crying in utter joy. It's only when I hear the lid to the ring box snap shut between our bodies that I realize I'd forgotten about it.

I pull back to open the box again, presenting it to her. It's a small golden band, woven around the teardrop diamond to look like ivy with smaller stones encrusted as leaves. It's nontraditional, it's dainty, it's beautiful, and it reminded me of Thea as soon as I saw it.

I slide it on her finger as soon as she gives me her hand. It's a perfect fit, only because I stealthily took one of her rings from her jewelry box before I went to Texas last month. All of my training in Special Ops paid off for that moment alone.

"Do you like it?" I ask, even though I can tell she does by the way she's smiling.

"I love it. It's perfect."

Just like her.

Epilogue

Thea

Two months later...

"Slow down, we don't need to run." I giggle as Jesse pulls me up the steps toward the Rollins County Courthouse. He slows to a stop, only to turn on me and kiss me hard in the middle of the landing before we reach the doors. "What was that for?" I ask breathlessly.

"Because I can." He winks, making me smile. He's been on cloud nine since we finally set a wedding date. I made him wait until after the holidays even though he was ready to elope the day he proposed. I insisted that he give me time to buy a proper dress and to plan a wedding since I never thought I'd get one. He understood, but he was still wildly impatient. I loved it.

"We're only here for our marriage license. Do not trick me into a courthouse wedding," I accuse him, eyeing him playfully. He holds his hands up in defense.

"I won't. I thought about it, but I won't." He shrugs, taking my hand again to pull me inside. We only have a few weeks until the wedding now. I insisted on Valentine's Day since neither of us has special memories of that date yet. We want

371

all of our future holidays to belong to each other.

Latisha cried when I suggested getting married in the library and has helped me plan every detail. My idea board is filled with string lights hanging from the ceiling, book stacks as centerpieces, and floral arrangements everywhere. Most importantly, our friends and loved ones will be there, including Miss Carlisle who gleefully accepted our invitation when we visited back in December.

She and Jesse have continued to keep in contact, giving him a chance to heal a part of his inner child. There will always be wounds, but I will be there with love and a first aid kit every step of the way.

"Hey, man." I look up when I hear Jesse greet someone, greatly unaware of my surroundings when I'm with him.

"What are you two up to?" Malec asks. He's dressed in his Sheriff's uniform, green tactical pants, matching shirt, and black vest with all the bells and whistles. It makes him look even more imposing and intimidating. Before, I would have run in the other direction, not because of who he is, but because he is a large man and I would be terrified. Now, I simply lean into Jesse's side, seeking a small amount of comfort, but otherwise doing fine.

"We're getting our marriage license, finally. You're coming to the wedding right?" He asks him, Malec now being one of his good friends here.

"Wouldn't miss it." Malec smiles, it's nearly emotionless, but it's pretty much the most heartwarming reaction I've seen from him. He's mostly tight-lipped and unperturbed in all scenarios and someone who keeps his feelings to himself.

So when I see his eyes wander, tracking a dark-haired woman walking across the lobby of the courthouse, my interest is piqued. He watches her until she disappears down a hallway. "Do you know her?" I ask, amused as his eyes dart back to mine, surprised that they'd wandered in the first place.

"Huh? Who? No." He deadpans, almost making me laugh. Jesse snorts, not easily put off by Malec's stoicism.

"Yeah, that was convincing," Jesse says, making me cough to hide my giggle.

"What?" Malec asks, genuinely confused about our insinuation. He checks his watch. "Sorry, I need to get to court. I'll see you guys later."

He shakes Jesse's hand and holds his hand out to me almost on instinct. He doesn't know about my aversion to touch per se, but he's never initiated contact either. I think whoever the woman was that walked through here has sent his head for a loop.

I stare at it only a moment before I reach out and shake his hand, gripping Jesse's side in my other hand for support. Malec turns to leave completely unaware of the mental and physical hurdle I just jumped. Jesse knows, though. Once we're completely alone, he pulls me in for a hug.

"I'm proud of you," he whispers, kissing my temple.

"Thank you. Me too." I smile, genuinely proud of how far I've come.

"But, let's cool it. No need to go around hugging people next," he teases, making me elbow him in the ribs. We walk onto the elevator hand in hand, ready to start the next chapter of our journey.

"Why not? Everyone loves hugging a pregnant woman." I shrug. The elevator doors close and we just start to move when he slams the emergency stop button.

"What? What did you just say?" He asks, bewildered.

"I was going to wait to tell you, but I can't stand it any longer. I took a test this morning," I tell him, watching his eyes get even bigger. I guess both of us are bad at planning grand gestures. "I'm pregnant."

He rushes me, guiding me gently to the wall but kissing me madly. "You're pregnant?" He asks hopefully against my lips.

"Yes. We're having a baby," I tell him with tears in my eyes. Just like that, both of our lives are changed forever and for the better.

"Are you sure you don't want to get married today?" He asks, kissing my neck, making me giggle. "Please," he begs, dragging my skirt up my thighs with his hands.

I gasp when he picks me up, pushing the hardness behind his zipper in between my legs. He grinds into me, making me whimper when he rubs against my sensitive clit. I'm already wet and now I'm afraid I'll leave a spot on his jeans. "Jesse," I try to protest, but part of me wants to tell him to keep going.

"What, baby? What do you want?" He asks, teasing me mercilessly.

"Marry me, then take me home and fuck me. Please," I beg.

"As you wish, wife." He kisses me again, hard and passionately, and full of promise. I didn't even realize the elevator started moving again until the doors opened. Luckily, there is no one waiting and I'm somewhat decently covered. I can't believe I almost begged for an orgasm in a courthouse.

Jesse takes my hand and pulls me down the hall towards the probate court. "We'd like to get married, please," he says, smiling at the older woman behind the counter. I can tell that she is not at all phased by the request, but I stare at him awestruck and filled with love, more than ready to be his wife.

The End

Stay tuned for Book 3, First Surrender, as the stoic Sheriff Malec attempts to dismantle the epidemic of dangerous crimes in Rollins County while navigating a turbulent relationship with a woman who insists on making his life hell.

About the Author

Amber Cassidy is a new indie author whose current focus is the small-town romantic suspense genre. This author has a Bachelor of Science in Psychology and a Minor in Sociology. Previous work as a Mental Health Specialist has enabled her to observe the intricacies of the human mind and how it is affected by significant events in one's life.

You can connect with me on:
- https://www.tiktok.com/@ambercassidy_author
- https://www.instagram.com/@ambercassidy_author

Also by Amber Cassidy

Check out the Chance Encounters Series on Amazon!

First Sight
Find out how Nathan and Callie's paths crossed in the most unexpected of ways!

First Surrender
The third installment of the series and Sheriff Malec's story!